CONFESSION OF THE HEART

"You are very free with my name, sir," Arabella responded coolly. "I noted that when we last met at the footbridge."

"That's because I call you Bella when I talk to you in my daydreams," he responded, smiling down at her.

"Indeed? And do you talk to me often, sir?" she inquired, still not smiling.

"All the time."

"And what do I say?" she asked.

"Well, first of all, I say 'Bella, I have loved you since I first met you all those years ago at the Christmas ball and picnicked with you on the stairs of Boxwood Hall. In view of this long-standing attachment, will you do me the honor of becoming my bride?' "

Arabella still did not smile. "And what do I say to that, sir?"

"You reply, 'I know that I could find men who are more handsome, more clever, more wealthy, Mr. Russell—but I know too that I couldn't find one who loved me better.' "

Arabella did not reply, but appeared to be studying the toes of her sandals carefully. Once more he lifted her chin so that she would look into his eyes. "Can you say that to me, Bella?" he asked softly.

She smiled up at him. "I might find a wealthier man, Mr. Russell, but I could never find one more handsome or clever or one whom I could love more . . ."

from *Arabella To The Rescue*, by Mona Gedney

WATCH FOR THESE REGENCY ROMANCES

A BRIDE'S BOUQUET

Cathleen Clare
Carola Dunn
Mona Gedney
Jenna Jones

Zebra Books
Kensington Publishing Corp.

http://www.zebrabooks.com

CONTENTS

AN UNSUSPECTING BRIDE

Cathleen Clare

Prologue

Dower House
Bradbury Manor

"Oh, Mama, it will be so glorious!" Patricia trilled, whirling about the room in artless abandon. "A Season in London! It was my fondest hope!"

Sarah, Lady Bradbury, smiled somewhat poignantly as she watched her daughter's mirthful gyrations. Patricia was so guileless, so unaffectedly beautiful. It was her heart's desire that the girl should have the very best chance to find a perfect husband, even though it meant the closing of a most important chapter in their lives. For if Patricia was successful in the quest, as she surely must be, she would no longer need her mother. Indeed, she soon might be a parent herself. And Sarah would be alone.

"I can scarcely believe it!" Patricia danced on, curling her arms as if she were waltzing with a gentleman. "It is like a dream!"

"How can you ever have doubted that we would do this?" Sarah asked quietly.

The girl twirled to a halt in front of her and gracefully sank to the carpet, taking her mother's hands in hers. "I thought you would wish me to stay with you . . . or at least nearby."

"Stay with me? My goodness, no!" She lifted a perfectly sculpted eyebrow and faked a happy smile. "I wouldn't want you to squander your youth with a rotting old widow. And insofar as the neighborhood is concerned, you haven't found a local gentleman who's interested you in the least. Certainly, you shall have a Season."

Patricia's blue eyes sparkled merrily. "Rotting old widow indeed! Mama, you are only six-and-thirty. Perhaps you should seek a husband as well."

Sarah's laugh was genuine. "Not I! I am much too fond of my way of life. I'm set in my routines. No, I shall never wed again."

Her daughter clicked her tongue. "Such a waste."

"Fustian!" She flushed slightly, then unsuccessfully attempted to inject a quelling seriousness into her voice. "Do not be impertinent, young lady. It is *your* Season and *your* marriage, and *only* that, that we shall contemplate."

"But it is such a waste," her outspoken daughter persisted. "I know I should not be disrespectful of Father's memory, but he was too old and sickly for you. You deserve better."

Sarah lovingly squeezed the girl's hands, then withdrew her own from the clasp and patted the cushion beside her. "Get up off the floor and sit like a lady. We shall talk of your future. Mine will be sufficiently pleasant."

Patricia obediently rose and sat down beside her, but Sarah could tell by the stubborn set of her daughter's lips that she wasn't finished with the subject.

"Mama," she continued, "if I am fortunate enough to find a husband to love, what will you do without me?"

The elder woman amusedly shook her head. "I shall find hundreds of things to do!"

"Such as?"

"Really, Patricia, how can you ask such a question? You know how busy I am. I shall continue tending my garden, of course, and participating in the good works of the church. I'll embroider and attend the neighborhood gatherings."

The girl groaned. "It sounds deadly dull."

"Perhaps I'll redecorate the house," Sarah suggested.

"Oh, Mama!" she wailed. "It could not be lovelier than it already is!"

"Well, I'll definitely enjoy dandling my grandchildren on my knee!" she proclaimed.

"Hm! There are women your age who are still having their own babes."

Rolling her eyes, Sarah tucked a stray lock of golden hair behind her ear. "That will be enough, young lady," she said with a slight edge to her tone. "Suffice it to say that I shall be well entertained. Now I must insist that we speak of you."

To Sarah's relief, her daughter deserted the topic and bounced excitedly on the sofa. "Very well! I know just the kind of man I want. He shall be tall, dark, and handsome as Adonis!"

"And wealthy, titled, poised, and of suitable age," her mother dryly added.

Patricia giggled. "We have just conjured up a veritable paragon. Do such men exist?"

Unbidden, the memory of just such a gentleman sprang to Sarah's mind. "Oh yes, I remember one," she murmured.

Her daughter curiously eyed her. "Tell me about him."

"Well . . ." Flushing, she sharply snapped her thoughts from visions of the past. "Fiddlesticks! Why the bother? He is probably long wed by now. My example merely proves that there are such men in this world. They may be few and far between, but if such a one is available, we shall find him!"

"Would that we could." Patricia sighed. "Perhaps your paragon has an eligible son."

"Perhaps, but he would not be suitable for you. He would be too young."

"He could be my age."

"That, my dear, wouldn't do," Sarah stated. "He would still be too young. Don't you understand? Young ladies need husbands who are older and settled."

"Papa was older and settled," her daughter said grimly.

"Patricia, you know I would not see you wed to an elderly gentleman!" she gasped.

"I merely wanted to make sure."

"Then you may rest easy."

Sarah had made no attempt to trick her daughter into believing that her marriage had been an ideal one, but neither had she complained about it. Patricia had only a vague memory of her father and had asked questions about him. These, Sarah had answered truthfully. The girl, with her adeptness at seeing straight into another's soul, had drawn her own conclusions. That was probably why she had been so surprised when Sarah had informed her of the upcoming Season. Patricia had gleaned that London brought back unhappy memories.

Determinedly, she batted those gloomy cobwebs from her mind. "Let us ring for refreshments and make our plans. I thought we would leave on Monday."

"So soon?" Joyfully, Patricia leapt off the sofa and hastened to tug the bell rope in the corner. "What arrangements have you made for our accommodation? Mama, let us celebrate and have Blake bring us champagne. Please? And what of our wardrobes?"

"Goodness! Which question shall I address first?" Sarah protested. "You may have ratafia. Champagne would go to your head."

"Oh, I want something to go to my head!" She twirled her way back to her seat.

"Prospects of a Season have already done so."

"*Mama, please!* Just this once! We are seldom festive . . . just the two of us. Let us be daring!"

Sarah smiled. "Very well, but we shan't make a practice of it."

The butler remained stony-faced when she gave him the order, but his eyes twinkled.

"He's been listening at doors," Patricia snickered when he had left.

"Loyal retainers have a habit of knowing what's about," Sarah said. "Remember that when you are the mistress of your own home."

Patricia sighed again, dreamily. "A husband . . . a home of my own . . . It is almost unimaginable." Quickly, she broke from the pensive mood. "Now about our housing and wardrobes!"

"This morning, I received confirmation of our renting a small house in an excellent part of town."

"You didn't even tell me what was afoot," the young lady marveled, "and I did not discern it."

"I wished to make certain that all was in order before raising your spirits," Sarah explained. "As to our wardrobes, we shall have new ones made by a London modiste. But while we wait, we have a number of dresses that will suffice."

Patricia nodded. Her mother might prefer to remain buried in the country, but she did it in style and comfort. With Sarah's innate sense of taste and the assistance of the fashion journals, the Bradbury ladies' clothing was the best that the local mantua maker could produce.

"I know we are well dressed, but it will be wonderful to have *real* London fashions," the girl mused. "Will we be invited to a great many parties? You have been away from Society for so long. Will any of your sisters provide *entre?*"

Sarah barely controlled a wince. "Frankly, I do not wish to involve my family if it is at all possible."

"Why?" her daughter asked softly. "I never did know why you avoid them."

"We parted on less than friendly terms."

"Because of my father?" she pried.

Thankfully, Blake arrived with the refreshments, giving Sarah a chance to organize her response.

"I have always suspected that you were in love with someone else, and your parents forced you to marry my father. Isn't that true?" Patricia prodded when he had left.

She tightly shook her head and lifted her glass to sip the bubbly drink. "It was only a fancy. Nothing would have come of it, but I was young enough to believe in dreams."

"Tell me."

"There is little to relate. My Season had scarcely started when your father made his offer. He was quickly accepted, of course. Though elderly, he was wealthy and titled. My family needed the money to bring out the rest of the girls." She lightly shrugged. "I was obedient."

Her daughter stared at her in awe. "Mama, dearly though I love you and wish to please you, I could never be so humbly dutiful."

Sarah laughingly hugged her. "Nor would I wish you to be. I have brought you up to be independent in your preferences, though I hope you will always consider my advice."

"You know I will! But don't you ever cry for what might have been?"

"How could I do that?" She kissed the girl's soft cheek. "I have you as a result, and you, my love, are the world to me."

Brow wrinkled, Patricia settled back to taste her champagne. "We must find you a husband, too. I do not wish you to be alone."

"Do not start that up again, or we shall stay home! I am quite serious about that, Patricia," she warned. "I will not indulge in such nonsense. When we are in London, I intend to sit unseen among the chaperons and watch you fly!"

"But if the right gentleman came along . . ."

"Believe me, he won't! Have I not said that I enjoy my way of life?" Sarah glanced with satisfaction around the pretty salon of the dower house. "I am perfectly happy right here where I am! I don't want another husband. One was quite sufficient. Now, please! Let us speak of you and of the details of our adventure. Then I shall spend the afternoon writing to old friends. We can depend on them to provide us with more than ample social engagements."

"And vouchers to Almack's?" Patricia asked hopefully.

Of this august honor, Sarah was unsure. Because of her family's flagrantly obvious husband hunting, she hadn't received one herself. "We shall see," she promised, "but if we do not, all will not be lost. You will be quite busy."

"But—"

Sarah lifted a hand. "I shall do my best. That is all that I can say."

Her daughter questioningly tilted her chin. "Didn't you go to Almack's?"

"No, and it made no difference to my future."

"Are you certain?"

"*Patricia!* Your success will not depend upon whether or not you attend Almack's," Sarah proclaimed. "Many young ladies who do not receive vouchers end up with fine husbands."

"I was thinking of the gentleman-paragon you mentioned," the girl went on inexhaustibly. "If you had participated in all that Society had to offer, he might have cut Father out of the chase."

"I wish you would cease speculating about my past!" cried Sarah at wit's end. "What's done is done. Besides, Lord Spenwick was too young to commit himself, so nothing would have changed."

"One still can't help wondering."

"I can." Standing, Sarah crossed the room and sat down at

her desk, withdrawing paper and pen. "Direct your mind to what we must pack for our journey. I shall begin a list."

"Lord Spenwick," Patricia deliberated, following her. "Was he the object of your dreams?"

Sarah bit her lip. "Our departure is fast approaching," she succinctly reminded her and began to write.

"Would you have married him had you the chance?"

"I didn't, so how could I know?" She forced a laugh. "It all occurred so long ago that I'd quite forgotten the man until we began to speak of Seasons."

It was a lie, the first she had ever told to Patricia. Scarcely a day went by that she didn't think of Ashby Spenwick. He was the one significant reason she dreaded going to London. He would be wed by now, and seeing another lady on his arm would be devastating. But only she would know, and so it would be easier to combat her desolation. Her daughter might be curious now, but when they reached London and plunged into the Season, Patricia would be too excited to think of her mother's long-ago dream. None of her friends had known of her feelings. Neither had Lord Spenwick, who probably wouldn't remember her, anyway. Sarah could sit among the chaperons and hide her broken heart. If a tear escaped, she could always blame it on Bradbury's death.

"I believe," she stated, "that your blue ensemble would be a good choice for traveling. And your white muslin with the little rosebuds might come in handy, and what of your pale pink morning dress?"

Patricia drew up a chair beside her and feigned interest in the list, but Sarah sensed that the girl's thoughts were far away. She hoped that they centered on London and the excitement that awaited her, and not on Sarah's long-lost, would-be beau.

Chapter One

London

Sarah was pleased with the town house she had rented, sight unseen, on the advice of her man-of-business. It was a tall, narrow, three story brick with black shutters and door. A short stone path connected it with the pavement and street. Although it and the neighboring houses were built close together, it possessed a garden in the rear, a feature most welcome to a lady who had lived in the country for so long that she dreaded the absence of trees, flowers, and shrubbery. London's parks were fine, but they didn't make up for one's own private space.

Inside, the house was attractive enough. The rooms were not large, and the colors were darker than Sarah herself would have chosen. But with the draperies flung wide, there was sufficient light to prevent dreariness. Indeed, the place was rather cozy at night. At least, nothing gave cause for embarrassment.

Sarah stood in the salon, slipping on her gloves. Tonight, she and Patricia would attend their first social engagement, a ball given by her old friend, Eloise, Lady Chardon. If Patricia was as successful as Sarah hoped she'd be, there would be gentlemen callers filling this room on the morrow. Absently, she straightened a tulip in the bouquet she'd arranged earlier. If all went well, there would be more flowers, too.

Her daughter, dressed prettily in a simple white gown trimmed with rosebuds, entered the room in a flurry. "Oh, Mama, I am so nervous I can scarcely breathe!"

"Are you certain it's nerves?" She smiled, noting the girl's maturing bosom. Patricia was definitely becoming a woman. The dress, one of those brought from the country, had become slightly snug, exhibiting her to advantage.

"It's too tight, isn't it?" The young lady tugged at the bodice.

"A bit, but not so much to make it improper, especially with that delicate lace tuck."

Sarah couldn't help sighing. This night, she would begin to let go of her daughter. What would life be like with out that merry laughter, that cheery chatter? Her smile quivered and began to fade. Quickly, she turned back to the posies to hide the sudden stab of pain.

"Are you nervous, too?" Patricia asked urgently. "I saw your lips trembling."

Sarah took a deep breath and faced her. "I can disguise nothing from you! Yes, I am slightly on edge, but the feeling will soon vanish. It will for you, too. I promise!"

"I suppose that becoming a wallflower would be the worst thing that could happen to me," she remarked with abrupt practicality.

"Not particularly," Sarah said dryly, "but no matter, nothing bad will occur, especially if you remember to hold your outspoken tongue. So let us be on our way, and soon you will be enjoying yourself immensely!"

Her daughter gritted her teeth. "I hope so."

They departed the house and entered Sarah's comfortable carriage. Proceeding at a smart trot, they reached the street of their destination in speedy time. There, they joined a long queue of coaches, slowly approaching Chardon House to deposit their fashionable occupants at the ball.

"So many people!" Patricia gasped. "Lady Chardon's home must be huge to accommodate such a crowd. How will we ever entertain? Our house isn't big enough!"

"It will be sufficient for our needs," Sarah assured her, laughing. "After all, in Society, a party is not considered a success unless the guests are so crushed together that they can scarcely move!"

"Really? That doesn't seem very comfortable."

"Much that one must suffer in order to please Society is uncomfortable."

Patricia shrugged. "Well, there is one thing good about this type of situation."

"What is that?"

The young lady giggled. "If no one dances with me, few will notice."

Sarah opened her mouth to inform her that the *ton* seemed to observe every move one made, but she abandoned the warning. Patricia was well-schooled. She had no reason to fear her daughter's behavior. If thoughts of obscurity eased the girl's anxiety, so much the better. Instead, she occupied the wait with discussion of guests she recognized, until they were leaving the carriage and entering the house.

"Wish me luck, Mama," Patricia whispered as they gave their cloaks to the footmen and started up the stairs to the ballroom floor.

"You truly have no need of it," Sarah vowed. "You are absolutely lovely and will have no lack of partners. Now bite the color into your lips and smile! The evening will be yours."

Through a broad archway, they glimpsed the scene of the night's entertainment. Hundreds of candles twinkled from the sparkling crystal chandeliers and wall sconces in the ballroom, their light enhancing the guests' shimmering gowns and glittering jewels. From the sheer number of people milling within, Sarah knew that Eloise Chardon would be deemed a distinguished hostess. The very cream of the *ton* seemed to be in attendance, and they were displaying their best. The ladies' fashions were obviously products of the city's most talented modistes, and their superb jewelry represented fortunes, new and old. The gentlemen's clothing, though limited in style and color to the conventional black evening attire, was none the less impressive for its fine fabrics and tailoring. The Chardon ball was an exquisite assembly, one which would surely be remembered for some time to come.

Waiting their turn to pass through the long receiving line, Sarah noted that Patricia's blue eyes were wide with awe, making her appear terribly gauche and naive. No matter how much Sarah had warned her to expect lavish arrays, her daughter was simply overwhelmed by the spectacle. Ah, well, perhaps there were gentlemen present who would appreciate such a total lack of town bronze. After all, young ladies new to society should be fresh and innocent. Still, Sarah surreptitiously nudged her.

"Darling, you must behave as if such a sight is a normal day's occurrence."

"That is difficult," the girl whispered. "It is all so grand."

"You will become accustomed," she murmured encouragingly.

"But our gowns . . . everyone else's are so much finer."

"That isn't true. No one can fault our good taste."

Patricia tensely clenched her teeth. "Perhaps not, but I would feel more confident if we had waited for the modiste's creations, before going out."

The receiving line was upon them. Sarah took a final, critical survey of her daughter's attire. Patricia looked absolutely charming in the simple white dress, and Sarah's own sophisticated, deep blue gown was the perfect foil for the girl's seeming fragility. Together, she hoped they made a becoming pair.

"Do not worry. You are perfectly lovely," she hurriedly encouraged. "All will be well."

"Sarah Bradbury!" Eloise Chardon cut her husband's greeting short and warmly clasped Sarah's hands. "How grand it is to see you again, and how magnificent you do look! We have been too long without your company, my *dearest* of friends. Shame upon you for ignoring us these many years."

Sarah smiled. "I've been quite busy in the country."

"Fustian!" the countess scoffed.

"But I have. I've been rearing my daughter." She drew Patricia forward and made the introductions. Lady Chardon surveyed the girl up and down. "A lovely child! No doubt she shall be quite as much an Incomparable as her mama."

"How you do run on, Eloise!" Sarah laughed, happy that her friend was as cheery and informal as she had been in their girlhood.

The lady trilled. "I could chat for hours; however, I must regretfully allow you to pass. I am holding up my own receiving line! My dear, are you sufficiently settled in to receive callers?"

Sarah nodded. "More or less."

"Then tomorrow I shall come for a comfortable coze. Now, do allow me to introduce my daughter, Eliza."

The Chardon offspring was not as agreeable as her mother. With chilly disdain, she greeted Sarah and inspected Patricia, quickly dismissing them as if they were not worth her while. Apparently, she did not intend to continue the mothers' affectionate companionship to the next generation. Sarah was disappointed. She'd hoped that her daughter and Eloise's would become good friends.

"Lady Eliza perused me as if I were nothing," Patricia breathed as they descended the few steps to the ballroom. "Are you certain I look all right?"

"You are stunning," Sarah said confidently. "The girl is probably jealous."

"I'm not so sure. Did you note her dress, with all those diamond chips? In comparison, we look countrified."

"We are attired in good taste."

"I hope you are right, but we are gowned so simply. Just look at all of the ruffles and flounces!" She shuddered. "Oh, Mama, if I were not wearing these gloves, I am certain I'd bite my nails."

"Oh, for Heaven's sake! You are making more of this occasion than it deserves! Lift your chin and smile."

Glancing leisurely around the room, Sarah noted and pleasantly nodded to several people she'd known in the past. Surely there would be more old acquaintances. The crowd was just so immense that . . . Breath catching audibly, she ceased her observations with a jerk. *No, it couldn't be.*

Gray eyes stared back at her with dawning recognition.

Unable to look away, Sarah stood helplessly transfixed. It *was* he. Of course, he was older, but time hadn't ruined that brutally handsome face. If anything, it had improved it. The boyish charm had been replaced by mature, masculine virility. She wasn't surprised. She could have guessed that he would age marvelously.

He half started toward her, then hesitated.

She quizzically tilted her chin. Could he remember her from those dozens of debutantes long ago? Yet, there had been that one wonderful ball the night before Bradbury had asked for her hand. Could it possibly have held as many wondrous memories for him as it had for her?

"Mama, what is wrong?" Patricia cried softly. "You are as white as a sheet!"

Unable to unlock her gaze from him, she watched a beautiful woman come up beside him and possessively link her arm through his. Of course he would have a wife. Still, her heart seemed to sink to her toes, and her stomach churned.

"Mama!" Patricia exhorted. "What is the matter?"

"Nothing." Breaking from her trance, Sarah grasped her

daughter's arm and hastened her toward the balcony door. "I feel faint. Let us seek some fresh air."

"But . . ."

"Patricia, I must have a moment's respite!" Propelling her daughter outside, she advanced to the edge of the gallery and leaned weakly on the stone railing.

"Mama, are you all right?"

Sarah took a great, unladylike gulp of the gentle breeze. "In a moment. My goodness, it suddenly seemed so close in there. All of those mingled scents of perfume were just awful!"

Patricia sternly cleared her throat. "Who is he?"

She drew another deep breath. "Who?"

"Do not play the innocent," her daughter chided, as if she were the elder and Sarah, the younger.

"I do not know what you are talking about." She tried to laugh lightly, but the tone was so false that she grimaced.

Patricia giggled. "I am referring, of course, to the gentleman with whom you were bartering gazes . . . the gloriously handsome one."

Sarah cast off all subterfuge. "I think he recognized me," she murmured in wonderment. "But how could he? After all these years? Although we danced and played our roles, I didn't think that he would ever, really remember me."

"Obviously, you thought wrong. I do believe he was going to come forward." She made a moue of disgust. "But that woman spoiled it."

"That woman was probably his wife."

"Maybe, but I doubt it. He seemed vastly attracted to you."

"Men about town often have a roving eye. You must remember that," Sarah lectured. "Frequently, a wife's value is judged by her ability to look the other way when her lord strays."

"That may be, but I did not sense an air of marital familiarity. Even though the woman tried to gain his attention, that gentleman gaped at you as if he were seeing his lost love."

"Such a fairy tale! You cannot be so ridiculous," Sarah said breathlessly.

"I do not think I am." Patricia grinned. "Moreover, why shouldn't he remember you? You are a very attractive lady."

"I am a mother!" she exclaimed, gripping the stone until her fingers hurt.

"Does that preclude you from being beautiful?"

Sarah merely shook her head.

"You still haven't told me who he is," her daughter prompted.

"My dear, you have just beheld the Earl of Spenwick, the handsomest man in the world," Sarah announced. "Isn't he the finest specimen of male pulchritude you have ever laid eyes upon?"

"He is fine looking . . . for his age."

"Age!" Sarah cried. "He isn't old!"

Patricia mirthfully shrugged. "He is of your generation. Since you always claim to be so ancient, Mama, I naturally must count him elderly."

"*Elderly!*" she shrieked, then turned to catch the girl's merriment. "You naughty thing! You are bamming me!"

"Yes, Mama, I am. I admit that he is extraordinarily handsome. Is he not the gentleman you dreamed of, during your Season?"

"No!" Sarah denied it.

Patricia tittered mischievously. "You cannot fool me! I remember your mentioning Lord Spenwick. Do not try to hide your passion for him."

"This is absurd!" She turned away from the railing. Now we must return to the ball before our absence is remarked upon."

Patricia followed her, still laughing. "You may end up with a beau before I do!"

"Total foolishness!" In her agitation, Sarah crossed the balcony with the long, free stride of a country woman. At the door, she caught herself. Merciful heavens! If anyone had seen her, they'd think her a bumpkin! Taking a deep breath, she slowed to a glide. Ah well, she wasn't out to attract. Patricia was the shining jewel. Before long, there would be a throng of lovesick suitors dancing attendance on her daughter.

I shall be so proud when she claims a prize catch, she thought, and slipping her arm through Patricia's, she entered the ball room.

Shaken, Ashby, Lord Spenwick, removed a flute of champagne from the tray of a passing waiter and quaffed its contents in a rather undignified manner. It *was* she. It had to be. No lady had such golden hair or brilliant blue eyes. None possessed such a classical facial bone structure. But Sarah had changed. The girlish sylph had become a woman, with loin-stirring curves replacing her previous slenderness. Before, she had seemed delicate. Now, she was eminently touchable. And who reaped that reward? Ashby set his jaw. That damned old relic, Bradbury!

"You must be quite thirsty, my lord." The beauteous widow, Lady Corcoran, lifted a languid hand to the footman, demanding the servant's instant return.

Wordlessly, Ashby exchanged his empty glass for a full one. Viscount Bradbury! That ivory skinned, age-smelly antique had stolen a march on him! He ground his teeth. It was absolutely mortifying, even though no one had known of his love for Sarah.

Beautiful, vivacious Sarah. If Ashby had been foxed, he would have wept right then and there, no matter who would see. Why had he let her slip through his fingers? The answer was simple and yet so complicated. He had been young, afraid of his feelings, and damnably, damnably *dumb*. Besides, who would have expected someone to offer for her so early in the

Season? Later, he might have gotten up his nerve. But he hadn't had the chance, and so he had lost her.

"Is something wrong, Lord Spenwick?" Lady Corcoran smoothed his sleeve, drawing his attention.

"No," he said shortly, aggravated by her presence. If this predatory female hadn't claimed him, he could have approached Sarah. Now, she had disappeared within the huge crowd.

"I feel as if your attention is hundreds of miles away," Lady Corcoran complained. "What a lowering thought, when I dressed with so much care this evening! I am greatly cast down."

Hideous woman! He should inform her that Sarah was the only real Beauty in the room. But he heaved a sigh and submitted to social expectations.

"My lady, your appearance is lovely beyond mere words. Do pardon my seeming distraction. I am struggling with a rather knotty problem concerning one of my estates," he fibbed.

"Oh. Well, I am certain that you will rise above any challenge." She smiled coyly up at him. "Perhaps I can assist in taking your mind from your troubles. For tonight, at least."

Through the throng, he glimpsed Sarah and the young lady who so greatly resembled her that she must be her daughter. They were exiting rapidly through the balcony door. With any luck, he could pawn off his unwelcome companion onto another gentleman and intercept them. Hurriedly, he glanced around for a victim.

"Desmond!" he called, espying one of his best friends. Slipping Lady Corcoran's arm through his elbow, he drew her forward.

"Hallo, Ash." The baronet separated himself from a group of conversationalists and greeted him.

"You are acquainted with Lady Corcoran?"

"Indeed, I am, and greater comeliness I have not beheld at this gathering." Sir Richard Desmond bent over her hand. "Madam, your radiance illuminates the room."

The widow preened. "Oh, sir, how you do run on."

Ashby felt like casting up his accounts. "If the two of you will excuse me, I have a matter of business to attend."

Lady Corcoran's smile changed to a pout. "At a *ball?*"

Sir Richard grinned knowingly. "Allow me to amuse you, my lady. Don't you know that affairs of great importance often occur in just such a place? I fear our friend will be of no great company if we thwart his endeavor. Off with you, Spenwick!"

Ashby gratefully bowed and departed. Later, he'd have to explain to Richard, but for now his friend had freed him from the vixen's clutches. Determinedly, he dodged his way toward the door.

"Lord Spenwick! You seem intent on flight." Lady Chardon stopped him as he almost gained his objective.

Oh, Lord! Must he be foiled at every juncture?

"You are fleeing to my balcony," she teased, fluttering her fan. "Haven't I provided enough lovely young ladies to be of interest to you?"

"Actually, I spied an old friend with whom I wish to make re-acquaintance," he admitted.

"Indeed? And who might that be? Perhaps I might be of assistance in locating this person."

Nosy wench, he thought, realizing that she would hold him at bay until she received some sort of answer. "I saw Lady Bradbury and thought her husband might be nearby."

"Alas, I must disappoint you," she proclaimed with a sparkle that belied the gravity of her declaration. "Viscount Bradbury has been dead these many years."

"Dead!" Ashby cried, hoping that his happiness was not terribly obvious.

"Dead," his hostess repeated, eyes twinkling. "My dearest friend, Sarah, is a widow."

"Then I must offer her my condolences."

"Of course. That is exactly what you must do." Simpering

mischievously, she tapped him on the shoulder with her fan and moved on to mingle with her guests.

Ashby smiled, barely able to keep from shouting with joy. Sarah was free! Would she prove to be as desirable now as she had in the past? He certainly intended to find out. He fairly dashed out onto the balcony, only to find her gone. No matter, he had all evening to hunt her down. Sarah would not escape him this time. With any luck, she wouldn't wish to! Turning on his heel, he strode into the house to begin his search.

In the ballroom, her knees still rather weak, Sarah led Patricia to the nearest vacant pair of little gilded chairs and sank down.

"What happens next?" her daughter asked.

"You will meet gentlemen who will ask you to dance."

"How?"

She passed a trembling hand across her forehead. "Friends will introduce them."

"Are you certain?" Patricia nervously fingered her dance card. "Oh, Mama, I *know* I shall be a wallflower!"

"You will not! You are perfectly lovely."

"I agree. I think you are most attractive," intoned a nearby voice.

Sarah whirled to face Lord Spenwick.

"Together, the two of you are enough to cause any man's heart to beat in triple time," he expounded, bowing over her hand, his lips lightly brushing the delicate bones. "Lady Bradbury, I pray that you remember me. I am—"

"I know." Her words came out in a gasp. "Lord Spenwick! How kind of you to greet us."

"I fear it is not kindness, my lady, for the pleasure is certainly mine." He smiled his earth-shattering smile, then sobered. "I must, however, tender my sympathies for the death of your husband."

She began the proper response, but Patricia unexpectedly piped up, overriding her.

"Oh, my father's death is so long in the past that we never think of it anymore." She shrugged. "I can scarcely remember how he looked, and I imagine my mother echoes my sentiments."

Lord Spenwick blinked.

Sarah blushed, heart leaping to her throat. Her daughter's flagrant disregard of social nicety could cast her beyond the pale if the earl repeated it to others. She surreptitiously kicked the girl's ankle.

"Ow!" she cried, wincing.

Lord Spenwick bit his lip, but was unsuccessful in hiding his grin.

Sarah flushed more deeply. "Do overlook my daughter's outspokenness, my lord. This is her first ball, and she is extremely nervous."

"I fear no one will dance with me." Patricia said frankly. "And our dresses . . . well, we brought them from home, my lord. They are not the first stare of fashion, are they?"

Sarah wished that a great hole would open in the floor and that she and her daughter would fall through it. What had gotten into the child? Why was she speaking with the elegant earl in such a familiar manner? She knew better!

"The modiste has not finished our new fashions," Patricia rambled on. "I thought, perhaps, we should avoid entertainments until—"

"My dear," Sarah apprehensively interrupted, "Lord Spenwick is not concerned with ladies' gowns."

He smiled. "Suffice it to say that you and your mama appear just as lovely and fashionable as any lady in the room, Miss Bradbury."

"Are you certain, my lord?" Patricia prodded. "In *country* fashions?"

"*Patricia!*" her mother hissed.

Lord Spenwick's smile broadened. "I cannot discern the difference."

The young lady straightened her shoulders. "I suppose I should not have worried, since Mama designed and supervised the construction. Her sense of style is quite marvelous, you know."

Sarah hastened to end the horror. "Goodness, my dear. I did no more than point out the picture in *La Belle Assemblee*. Mrs. Hollis did the rest. Now there is an end to it!"

"You made dashing adjustments."

She opened her mouth to discount the acclaim, but Lord Spenwick interposed.

"Do not denigrate your considerable talent, my lady." His gray eyes wandered to her low cut bodice. "From what I observe, you are quite remarkable."

"She is, indeed," Patricia agreed with a quick, satisfied nod. "Mama is accomplished at . . . just everything! Wait until you attend one of our parties. In comparison, this affair will seem—"

"Hush, my dear," Sarah said firmly, wishing she could again escape to the balcony to cool her flaming cheeks. Merciful Heavens! Was she going to have to remove her suddenly blunt-speaking daughter from the premises?

Once again, Lord Spenwick smiled directly at her, and there was understanding in his eyes. He turned back to Patricia and bowed. "I may not be an authority on ladies' fashion, Miss Bradbury, but I can definitely remedy one of your torments. Will you allow me this dance?"

The girl stared wide-eyed at him. "Your wife will not object?"

"I have no wife. I have never married."

The blood raced through Sarah's veins. Unwed? It was beyond belief!

Patricia beamed. "Splendid! I mean . . ."

He extended his hand. "Shall we?"

"Oh, yes! Thank you! Mama, may I?"

Slightly breathless, Sarah smiled and nodded. "Enjoy your-self."

She watched the two stroll onto the dance floor. What a handsome couple they made! Patricia's fair, dewy beauty was the perfect foil for the gentleman's dark, handsome sophistication. And he was a bachelor! Sarah's heart pounded. As she looked from the exquisite earl to her pretty daughter, an idea quickly germinated in her mind. Patricia and Spenwick! How ideal a match! The young lady would make him an admirable countess who could give him all the heirs a man of his station would wish for. She was well-schooled in household management and entertaining. She was knowledgeable in the feminine arts of embroidery, piano playing, and watercolors. As she gained in confidence, she would be able to acquit herself just as well as Sarah in these accomplishments. The earl was old enough and experienced enough to provide the settling influence she needed. Nothing could be better, except . . .

A sinking feeling assailed her stomach. *I will forget all I ever felt for him,* she vowed. *I am not eligible to be his wife, even if he actually wished it. In a nut shell, I couldn't give him the sons he must have.*

Her throat constricted painfully as she accepted the awful truth. It was too late for her, but not for Patricia. For herself, she must forget Lord Spenwick, in favor of her daughter. Sarah gritted her teeth and determined to do so. She would assist the girl in landing this prize catch. There was nothing to lose. Even if they failed, the earl's interest, which he had already displayed, would boost Patricia's popularity. She would never lack suitors if she would hold her outspoken tongue! Sarah must severely warn her as soon as possible.

Equilibrium restored, she reveled in her daughter's grace and Lord Spenwick's polished skill. She marveled again at how splendid they were for each other. Hopefully, they would realize it soon.

When the dance ended, Patricia returned, her face pink with delight. "Oh, Mama, Lord Spenwick is so very talented! My dancing master was like a cow compared to him!"

Sarah could scarcely answer the girl, let alone quietly remind her about her forthright speech, before she was besieged by young men and their sponsors begging introduction to her daughter. Soon the girl's card was filled, and she was elated. Because of Lord Spenwick, Patricia's first ball promised to be a complete success. She glanced around to speak with him further about Patricia's virtues and saw him in conversation with a group of men. Ah well, she would seek him out later and sing Patricia's praises.

Proudly, she watched her daughter stand up for set after set. She hoped that Lord Spenwick was eyeing her, too. The girl made a most becoming picture.

"Lady Bradbury?" The earl suddenly materialized at her side. "May I sign your dance card?"

Sarah startled. "Merciful Heavens, I haven't one! I am a chaperon."

"Can't chaperons dance?"

"No." To underline the fact, she laughingly shook her head. "I shall receive my enjoyment by watching Patricia. She is such a pleasure to behold!"

"Indeed she is, but I would greatly relish a waltz with you," he cajoled.

"No, my daughter will do the dancing for both of us." She demurely folded her hands and sighed. "I am very proud of her."

"She is a great credit to you." He nodded to the chair beside her. "May I?"

"Certainly, my lord." She took a deep breath as he seated himself. Her senses reeled from the spicy, masculine scent of the cologne he wore. Goodness, she must keep her mind on her business!

"Lord Spenwick, I hope you will forgive Patricia for her

nonsensical speech. I fear her nervousness got the better of her. I assure you that she is extremely well-schooled in the proper social graces . . . and so comely.''

"She is almost as beautiful as her mother," he remarked.

Sarah eyed him with surprise. "What a charitable thing to say!''

"Charitable?" He laughed. "Madam, what I said was simply the truth.''

"My, Lord Spenwick," she teased, heart thumping. "Perhaps you need spectacles. I left all pretense of beauty, long ago.''

"What a whisker!" he snorted. "You are more glorious now than ever.''

"And you, sir, no matter what you claim, are a flatterer!''

"Never! And furthermore, I do insist on that waltz," he asserted.

Patricia, returning from the set, overheard. "The orchestra is tuning up for a waltz right now.''

"Please don't disappoint me, Lady Bradbury," Lord Spenwick begged.

"Mama, you should dance," her daughter admonished, sitting beside her, unmindful of the swooping down of her own admirers.

"I am a mother, a chaperon," she protested. "I am an old woman!''

Lord Spenwick, Patricia, and Patricia's train of young men laughed.

"Come, Mama, show us how it's done," her daughter urged.

Without further ado, Lord Spenwick rose, took her hand, and drew her to her feet. "Please, my lady, let us not disappoint your daughter.''

Sarah felt as if every eye in the ballroom was fixed on her. "Oh, very well," she agreed, to avoid a scene, "but I warn you, it will be a disaster!''

"I'll willingly take my chances." The earl escorted her to the floor.

"I am not accomplished at waltzing," she warned him once more. "In my time, it wasn't done."

"Yes, madam, I constantly forget how very ancient you are." He abruptly swept her into his arms and began the dance.

Sarah had learned the steps from Patricia's dancing master, but his version of the waltz was far different from that of the earl. Momentarily, she thought Lord Spenwick would swing her off of her feet, but, an excellent dancer, she quickly accustomed herself to the rhythm and movement. Soon, she was following him as effortlessly as if she'd been dancing with him all of her life.

"Strange," he marveled, "you don't dance like an old lady."

She smiled.

"Also being of your generation, however," he continued, "I suppose that I am such an old man that I don't realize the difference."

Before she had time to answer, he expertly spun her in a graceful circle. "My lord!" she cried breathlessly. "Do you think to sling me down?"

"Of course not." He grinned wickedly. "But I do enjoy taking your breath away."

He could always do that, but he could do it even more so when he held her in his arms. Sarah helplessly looked up into his wonderful face. How could she ever accept him as a son-in-law? Tears sprang to her eyes.

He noticed immediately. "Is something wrong?"

"No." She shook her head and smiled through the blur.

"Are you certain?"

"Let us not talk at the moment," she murmured. "I must concentrate on the steps."

"As you wish, my lady."

He tried to draw her closer, and Sarah gently pulled back, keeping her distance. Her heart seemed to do a flip-flop. This, she realized, was the danger of the dance. The very intimacy of the waltz ignited certain unmentionable, primitive desires. She might be a mother and a widow, but she was not immune to them, especially where this particular gentleman was concerned. She must refuse to waltz with him ever again.

Determined though she was to escape her feelings, she was sorry when the dance ended. Curtsying, she forced a smile. "Thank you, Lord Spenwick. It was most exhilarating."

"Thank *you,* Lady Bradbury. It was been a very long time since I have enjoyed a dance quite so thoroughly. You are an admirable partner, and . . ." His smile faded as he gazed back at her. "You are the most beautiful woman I've ever laid eyes on. *Ever.*"

Pulse racing, she could only stare at him.

He took her hand and tucked it in his elbow to lead her from the floor. "Did you hear what I said?"

"Yes," she whispered, then quickly retreated to the safety of acceptable social banter. "Goodness, my lord, you do have the knack of making a lady feel very special!"

He set his jaw. "I meant it."

Panic filled Sarah's breast. A horrible thought assailed her. Lord Spenwick could not have honorable intentions toward a woman her age. He could only mean to make him his mistress! Now what would she do? She still wished to have him for Patricia, so she couldn't bluntly dismiss him. Somehow, she must make him understand that she was ineligible.

She regarded him seriously. "My lord, I suppose I should be appreciative of your compliment. However, I am no longer interested in a gentleman's esteem. My life now revolves around my daughter, my home, and my church work."

Disappointment flickered in his gray eyes. "I must apologize. I did not intend to cause you distress. I hope that my remark will not wreck our friendship."

"No, I am happy to be counted your friend, Lord Spenwick."

Her apprehension abated. He knew now where she stood, and he seemed to accept it.

"If you will escort me back to my chair?" she asked pleasantly.

Ashby mentally cursed himself. He'd moved too quickly and frightened her. He'd behaved like a bumbling young buck in love for the very first time, and damn it, that's how he felt! He looked down at the golden-haired goddess gliding at his side, who was still so desirable she made his heart ache. Somehow, he must win her.

Leaving the dance floor, they found Patricia in the midst of a group of young people. In spite of his troubles with her mother, Ashby couldn't help smiling at the girl's animated face as she prettily flirted with young Lord Darlington. She was clearly enjoying her first ball, and she seemed to have gained a good measure of popularity.

"Mama, you were magnificent! And so were you, Lord Spenwick!" she gushed as soon as she saw them, then hastened into her next topic. "You don't mind if Lord Darlington and I dine with my new friends, do you?"

"Dine?" Sarah asked.

"That was the supper dance," the girl explained.

"Oh, I didn't realize ..." Hesitantly, she glanced up at Ashby.

"Enjoy yourself, Miss Bradbury," he put in. "I shall take good care of your mother."

"We should ..." Sarah began, but her daughter had taken his reply as permission and scampered away with her newfound companions. "Well I never! She obeyed you instead of waiting for my reply!"

"I said what she wanted to hear," he chuckled.

"She is behaving like a juvenile."

"My lady, she *is* a juvenile."

"But she isn't!" she disagreed. "When I was her age, I was mere weeks away from being married, and nothing has changed. Most of these young ladies will be engaged or wed by Season's end."

"More's the pity," he muttered.

"I'm sorry, my lord. I didn't hear you."

"It was nothing." He lifted two glasses of champagne from the tray of a passing waiter and handed her one. "Look at the crush at the dining room doors. Let us wait until it has dispersed."

She frowned worriedly. "We should catch up with Patricia."

"Madam, I have no intention of dining with those children."

"But Lord Spenwick, I must keep an eye on her!" she dithered. "This is her first ball. She might need me."

"Did you need your mother?" he queried.

"No, but . . . Oh, if it were someone other than Darlington!" she wailed.

"The young man is a member of my club. I can vouch for the fact that he is honorable," Ashby assured her. "Furthermore, he is the elder son of the Earl of Sissonby. He is highly eligible."

"But he is so young!"

He shrugged. "Does that greatly matter?"

"Yes." She nodded adamantly. "A young lady should fix her interest on an older gentleman."

"Like you did?"

Sarah favored him with such a stern stare that Ashby wondered if he hadn't gotten himself into the suds again. Before he could smooth over the remark, however, her gaze faltered. "Lord Spenwick, I did not mean *elderly*."

"And I did not mean to be impertinent. Please forgive me, Lady Bradbury."

She smiled with absolution. "Of course. Now shall we proceed to the dining room? The crowd has thinned."

"Very well." He presented his arm.

Luckily, there were no vacant seats at Patricia's table so

Ashby was spared the predicament of separating Sarah from the girl. Unfortunately, the only seats remaining were at the table of the most talkative and boring lord and lady in the realm. For the duration of the meal, he was scarcely able to complete one full sentence to Sarah. Afterwards, the mother and daughter reunited.

Patricia's eyes sparkled as her escort took his leave. "Lord Darlington is fascinating, Mama. I am positively thrilled that he requested two dances."

"Two?" Sarah cried. "You should not have agreed to that!"

The girl simply smiled. "He is so handsome and amusing. You will like him when you are better acquainted. He'll be calling tomorrow." She directed her attention to Ashby. "I hope you will call, too, Lord Spenwick."

"It will be my pleasure."

"Mama and I will look forward to it." As the music commenced, she departed with her next partner.

"Miss Bradbury is having a wonderful time," he observed.

Sarah fondly watched her daughter. "Yes, I wish I possessed her liveliness. She has always been so energetic. She has never been ill a day in her life. Furthermore, she spreads affection and happiness to others. She is quite adept at managing staff. They all esteem her and, as a result, work harder to please her. Her own future household will run smoothly and efficiently."

"I am sure you have trained her well."

"Certain things go beyond mere training, my lord. Patricia was born with the ability to excel." She flushed. "I know it sounds as if I am shamelessly praising my daughter, but I would envy her, even if she were not my own."

Ashby smiled inwardly. It was easy to see that the way to Sarah's heart lay through her daughter. "From what I have seen, Miss Bradbury is most commendable," he told her and spent the rest of the evening extolling the young lady's virtues.

* * *

Homeward bound, the carriage moved through the dark streets of London. Sarah was glad that the evening was ended. Chaperoning a daughter was not an easy task, especially when one was amorously tempted by the very gentleman one wished to have for a son-in-law. Nor had Patricia made it smoother when she had allowed her tongue to run away with her, and as the evening progressed, when she had seemed to show such a preference for Lord Darlington. But her daughter was not the only one who'd been in error this evening. Sarah herself had irritably deemed the girl a juvenile. Horror of horrors, Lord Spenwick had agreed with her, hopefully from politeness. Later, however, she seemed to have countered the adverse statement with her praise of the young lady's qualities, for the earl was quick to listen and to concur. But her own *faux pas* made her reticent about admonishing Patricia. She would remind her before their next engagement and let the matter slide for now.

"Did you have a good time?" she asked, interrupting Patricia's reverie.

"Oh, yes." The girl sighed dreamily. "It was everything I hoped it would be."

"And you were a success! You had any number of eligible gentlemen bowing over your hand."

"I only care about one." She giggled. "Remember when we discussed the very *paragon* of manly character? I didn't truly believe that such a gentleman could exist, but he does!"

Sarah smiled sadly, glad that the shadows obscured the dampness in her eyes. "Lord Spenwick is wonderful."

"Yes, he's a very pleasant gentleman, but—"

"He will make you a fine husband, Patricia, just the sort I had hoped you would find."

"Lord Spenwick?" she asked incredibly.

"Yes. *The paragon.*" She laughed. "Isn't that whom we are discussing?"

"Actually, I was thinking of Lord Darlington. He is all that is perfect!"

"Darlington!" Sarah cried. "That is impossible!"

"No, it is not." Patricia clasped her hand. "Mama, he was most attentive. I am certain that he is as daft for me, as I am for him. I can scarcely believe my good fortune!"

"But my dear, he will not do. He is too young."

Her daughter tensed. "I like him."

"As time goes on, you will understand," Sarah worriedly explained. "Just now, you are experiencing puppy love. It passes quickly."

"Like your crush on Lord Spenwick?"

Sarah inwardly cringed. No, she would never entirely get over her feelings for the earl, but she would definitely set them aside for what was practical. "I thought you considered Lord Spenwick to be marvelous."

"I do," Patricia said readily. "For you."

"I am not seeking a husband."

"I believe you should think on it, Mama." Her daughter laughed. "Lord Spenwick was very particular in his attentions to you . . . not to me. You are the object of his desires."

"Fustian!" Sarah removed her hand from her daughter's and busily straightened her skirts. "He was interested in hearing of you, that's all. Any regard he showed me was due to politeness. There are many reasons he must select a younger woman to be his bride."

"We shall see," Patricia maintained, "but Mama, you really should be reflecting upon that fulfilling life you claim to lead. You may wish to change it."

The coach drew to a halt in front of the rented house. Sarah's footman assisted the ladies to the pavement and escorted them to the door, which Blake had opened wide.

"We were a success," Patricia informed the old retainer. "Especially Mama."

"Balderdash," Sarah muttered, ascending the stairs.

The girl repeated her statement to Hastings as Sarah's abigail welcomed them home. "Mama will end up being the bride. Lord Spenwick hovered over her like a bee to honey," she stated.

The maid beamed.

"This is all nonsense." Sarah stripped off her gloves. "Any popularity I enjoyed was due to my being your mother, my dear. The earl's entire conversation was centered on you."

"Ha! That was probably because you directed it so." Patricia spun around the room in a make-believe waltz. "You should have seen Mama dancing, Hastings. She was marvelous!"

Sarah snorted. "It was *marvelous* that I didn't step on his toe. Hastings, if you will unfasten my gown, I shall tend to my own undressing while you assist Miss Patricia. I am weary of the evening's clamor. If I hear any more of this frivolity, I'm sure my head will ache."

Her abigail hastened to assist, but she refused to depart until she helped her mistress into her night gown.

"Poor Hastings," Sarah sympathized. "Aiding two ladies during a Season is too much work for you. I shall hire a lady's maid for Miss Patricia as soon as possible."

The servant grinned. "I like the excitement, my lady. I can do it, truly I can."

"Well, at least you need an assistant. We shall see about it tomorrow." She shooed her daughter and the maid from her chamber. "Go along now. It's late."

When they had departed, she sat down at the dressing table to braid her long, blond hair. Such a chaotic evening it had been! And the morrow promised little respite. They would have callers. She must see to obtaining aid for Hastings. Most important of all, she had to guide Patricia's affections away from Lord Darlington and toward Lord Spenwick. At the moment, none of it seemed easy.

Yawning, she leaned forward to peer closely into the mirror. There were two tiny lines at the corners of her eyes and faint smile marks at the edges of her lips. The image was shocking.

"I look *old*," she whispered aloud, and knew, right then and there, that Patricia was totally wrong. Lord Spenwick could not have a *tendre* for her. He might have had it in mind to play fast and loose with her, but her harsh rebuff had not sent him away. Therefore, he must be interested in her daughter. At supper, he'd avoided Patricia's company simply because he hadn't wanted to be a part of a large group of young people. When the time was right, he'd make known his regard.

With a sigh, Sarah rose and sought her bed. Those thoughts made it somewhat easier to accept him as a son-in-law. The wrinkles, however, didn't help her self-esteem. Old! No matter what she claimed, she hadn't truly consider herself as aged. But she was.

Chapter Two

The small house was filled with flowers. All of them were for Patricia, except one beautiful bouquet of red roses which Lord Spenwick had sent to Sarah. These, she gave a special place of honor on the hall table. Arranging the last stem, she stepped back and smiled. How kind he was to remember her!

"You see?" Patricia smirked, coming from the salon to join her. "He cares about you."

"He also sent posies to you," she reminded.

"They were common old flowers. He sent you roses." She laughed. "Mama, you have made a conquest."

"No, he merely wishes to be in my good graces." She hadn't revealed the contents of the card, in which the earl begged her to forgive any distress he may have caused her.

The girl shook her head. "You are blind."

"Hm! We shall see. Nevertheless, I do not intend to bicker today. I have too much else to do."

They startled at the sudden rap on the door.

"Callers!" Patricia cried. "Hurry! Let us take our place in the salon."

The two ladies scurried into the drawing room and sat down, picking up their embroidery.

"Mama, do I look all right?"

"You are lovely," Sarah said proudly, as Blake escorted the first of Patricia's many male callers into the room.

As the afternoon progressed, she grew more and more weary of the young gentlemen. A chaperon was like a spare wheel, in the way, but necessary in case of adversity. She was ever so glad when her friend, Eloise Chardon, was ushered in.

"Goodness, Sarah!" the countess exclaimed, embracing her. "Your house looks like a flower shop! My ball must have been most outstanding for your gel."

"It certainly was." Asking Blake for a tea tray, Sarah led her to a grouping of chairs across the room from Patricia and her admirers. "I could not have wished for a better way to introduce her to Society."

"I am happy to be a part of it." Eloise seated herself, busily arranging her skirts. "La, I am even more ecstatic to escape from my house. Eliza has so many callers. I forced Chardie's mother to act as chaperon, so that I could come for this visit. It is certainly good to be with my old friend again."

"It has been a long time."

"Much too long. Shame on you, Sarah, for hiding yourself in the country!"

Sarah smiled. "I've been busy rearing my daughter."

"That's what nursemaids and governesses are for." Eloise laughed. "But you are not the type to leave matters to others. What are you going to do, pray tell me, when Patricia leaves the nest?"

She sobered. Lately, she had been so occupied that she had pushed all that from her mind. A sudden loneliness swept over her. This was a topic she wished to avoid. Fortunately, Blake arrived with the tray, alleviating the need for a reply.

Eloise sipped the steaming tea. "My, what an excellent brew!"

"Thank you," Sarah said gratefully. "Patricia and I spent the past winter blending varieties to come up with the recipe."

"The entire winter, playing with tea? Oh, for God's sake!" chortled the countess. "You should have been husband hunting!"

She relaxed. "There was no need. My daughter had exhausted all neighborhood possibilities."

"I was not speaking of Patricia. She'll land a prize catch. It's you I am thinking of."

"I am not seeking a husband!" she gasped.

"But you must!" her friend proclaimed. "You are too young to go through this life alone."

Sarah firmly shook her head. I do not intend to remarry."

Eloise cackled. "Perhaps Lord Spenwick will have something to say of that. His attention to you, last night, was quite marked."

She continued to wag her head. "You have it wrong, Eloise. The earl is interested in Patricia."

"Is that why he waltzed with you and took you in to supper?"

"He first danced with my daughter," she pointed out. "Unfortunately, her card filled so quickly that he didn't have the opportunity for another. You will see. Patricia is his quarry. Merciful Heavens! The man must have an heir! He will select a younger lady."

The countess negligently lifted a shoulder. "Mrs. Montague recently presented her husband with a fine son, and she is all of forty."

"This is fustian," Sarah muttered, sipping her tea.

"He hovered over you like a knight protector, glaring at any gentleman who came near."

"Eloise!"

Further discussion was cut short by the announcement of a caller. "Lord Spenwick," said Blake in his most dignified tone.

Sarah glanced at Patricia who barely looked away from her coterie. "Oh, dear, why does she ignore him?"

"Because the gel is wise enough to see that he is interested in her mother," her friend murmured.

"Excuse me, Eloise." She rose, crossing the room to greet the earl. "I fear that my daughter's admirers have gone to her head," she told him, elated when Patricia cast him a smile and a little wave.

He bowed over Sarah's hand. "I am pleased with her speedy success."

"All thanks to you, my lord. Your interest spurred the enthusiasm of others."

"I am delighted to be of service."

Turning a fond gaze on her daughter, Sarah saw a young man reluctantly rise from the circling chairs to take his leave. "Ah, Lord Spenwick, a choice seat for you."

The earl briefly closed his eyes, grinning. "Please, madam, do not relegate me to that passel of puppies. I would much rather converse with you and Lady Chardon."

Sarah swallowed, nerves tingling in her stomach. Could Patricia and Eloise be right? Had he developed a *tendre* for her? No, of course not! Lord Spenwick was merely too lofty to wish to join the crowd of youngsters surrounding the girl. He would know that she'd never consider one of them as a serious contender for Patricia's hand. Therefore, he'd sit back and wait for the right moments to show his favor.

She nodded understandingly. "How foolish of me. Please join us. We are taking tea, but perhaps you would prefer something stronger."

"Tea will be fine." He proffered his arm to escort her back to her chair. "Good afternoon, Lady Chardon."

"Lord Spenwick." Eloise drained her cup and rose. "I am sorry to miss your company, but I really must be on my way. I've left Eliza with Chardie's mother, a tenuous situation at best."

"Must you go so soon?" Sarah cried.

"I shall come again at a better time, my dearest of friends. Sit down and drink your tea. I can show myself out."

"I shan't allow it." She excused herself from Lord Spenwick and walked with her friend to the door. "I wish you wouldn't leave."

"Make the best of your time with him," Eloise ordered. "The man is serious about you."

"He can't be!" she wailed.

"Sarah, I shall never forgive you if you allow that prize catch to swim away."

"But it's Patricia he wants!"

"Heed me." Laughing to herself, Lady Chardon quickly exited.

Others immediately followed. When she again seated herself, only Lord Darlington remained with her daughter. Noting Patricia's outright radiance as she hung on the young man's every word, Sarah frowned slightly.

"Is something wrong?" Lord Spenwick peered closely at her as she poured his tea.

Her scowl deepened as Darlington bent over the girl's hand and kissed it lingeringly.

The earl glanced over his shoulder. "Darlington?"

"He is behaving with all too much familiarity." She loudly cleared her throat as a warning and was rewarded to see the young man straighten and leap to his feet.

Lord Spenwick chuckled. "He reminds me of myself at his age."

Sarah wondered how much the earl had changed. During last night's waltz, he had certainly conducted himself too familiarly. She flushed.

His mirth waned. "No. Truthfully, he is dissimilar. I was afraid of young ladies. I was afraid of you."

"Me?" The remark took her so by surprise that she burst out laughing. "I cannot believe it!"

He grinned, grey eyes glowing. "I was terribly in love with you. Did you know?"

She shook her head, her laughter dying.

"But you did remember me."

"Of course. We shared several dances." Heart aching, she swallowed against the lump in her throat. "I remember . . ."

"Go on," he prompted, leaning forward.

Sarah precisely remembered the moment when she had last seen him. It had been at the Eversham ball. She had danced twice with Lord Spenwick, one of the sets being the supper dance, thus providing them with a lengthy span of time together. Though they had dined with others, the earl had given her his absolute, undivided attention. She had blossomed under his regard and spent the happiest evening of her life. She'd wondered if there might be hope for a future with him, but the next morning Lord Bradbury came to call on her father, made his offer, and was accepted. After that, the young lord and his favor became a bittersweet memory. If she had known then that he had a *tendre* for her, what would she have done? But those times were gone. Now it was too late, even for speculation.

She clenched her jaw. "It was all such a long time ago. So much has happened since then."

"I recall the Eversham ball," Lord Spenwick reminisced.

"You recollect it?" she blurted.

"Yes." He thoughtfully sipped his tea. "After that, you disappeared."

Sarah lowered her gaze. "The following morning, Lord Bradbury made his offer. He wished for a speedy wedding, so we immediately returned home to prepare."

"And you have remained in the country ever since," he finished.

"Yes, this is the first time I've been away."

"A pity," he mused.

"Not really." She squared her shoulders, unwilling for him

to feel sorry for her. "I have been quite busy with the estate, and parish activities, and with rearing my daughter."

"You have done a magnificent job." He looked across the room at Patricia. "Miss Bradbury is lovely."

"I thank you, my lord." She eyed her progeny.

The girl, sensing their attention, stood to send the delaying Lord Darlington on his way.

Sarah nodded her approval.

When Patricia had seen the young man to the door, she joined her elders, nimbly pouring herself a cup of tea. "Lord Spenwick, I have a knotty problem." She smiled shyly at him. "Would you help me?"

"If it is within my means," he responded.

"Vouchers for Almack's." She sighed. "All of my new friends will be attending."

"Patricia!" Sarah gasped. "You should not brazenly ask Lord Spenwick for such a favor!"

"But Mama, I thought he would be happy to help."

Shoulders slumping, Sarah deflated. "My lord, I can scarcely believe my ears. Do forgive my daughter's forwardness."

"I shall do more than that." He grinned. "I will try to assist."

"Oh, thank you!" Patricia gushed. "You are so kind."

Sarah stared speechlessly at her.

"I'm glad to be of use," the earl assured them.

"I knew you would." Finishing her drink, Patricia rose. "Now, if you will excuse me?"

"I cannot believe my ears. Oh, but I am mortified," Sarah groaned as her daughter departed. "I cannot believe that she would treat you in such a fashion."

"I don't mind." he soothed.

"These outbursts are so unlike her," she moaned.

"She is high-spirited, and perhaps she feels the need of male guidance. Do not be distressed, Lady Bradbury. I am only too glad to fill the role she has invented."

"It's not what I had in mind," she whispered.

"If you would prefer to enlist the support of your father . . ."

"No!" she cried. "Oh, bother! Why are things going the way that they are?"

"Are matters awry?"

She turned appealing blue eyes toward him. "Oh, Lord Spenwick, if anyone should know of Patricia's outspoken tongue . . ."

"You can trust me." He took her hands in his. "I shan't tell a soul. And I *will* obtain those vouchers. Sally Jersey owes me a thing or two."

"I wish you wouldn't." She grimaced at the very thought of the formidable patroness of Almack's. "Whatever will she think of us?"

"I will be discreet." He got to his feet. "I'm sorry to say that I've overstayed my welcome. Your butler has been giving me hard glares for the past few minutes."

"Blake?" Sarah glanced toward the hall and saw the old retainer standing protectively at the door.

"Loyal servants have a way of looking after one." He bowed over her hand. "You will go out this evening, Lady Bradbury?"

"Yes." Her fingers tingled. "Patricia and I shall be attending several routs."

"Excellent. I shall see you then."

Sarah gazed after him, emotions awhirl. Sometimes, she thought he was interested in Patricia, but at others . . . *In love with her?* How exciting! He had returned her regard in that time of dreams. It was nice to know . . . but what good would old memories be when he was her son-in-law?

"Blake?" she called as she heard the butler return from the front door. "I would dearly love a glass of sherry."

When Ashby left Sarah's house, he found a dejected Lord Darlington waiting for him on the pavement.

"My lord, might I beg a favor?"

It must be the day for such things. Seeing that Darlington had come calling on foot, Ashby motioned him to his carriage. "I'm going to White's. Will you accompany me? You can explain matters on the way."

"Thank you, sir," he said miserably.

Inside, he smiled at the young man's lovesick expression and hoped he hadn't appeared so pitiful when he first felt that stab of devotion for Sarah.

"Well, Darlington, what can I do for you?"

The young man sighed. "Isn't she wonderful? I've never met a young lady like Miss Bradbury. So beautiful, so kind, so amusing."

"She is quite attractive."

"She's more than that! She's everything that is marvelous! I've been searching for years for a lady like that."

Ashby bit his lip to keep from laughing, until he recalled, once again, how he'd felt about Sarah when he was Darlington's age. Many youthful romances were fleeting, but his feelings had remained constant, even when she'd married another. Was poor Darlington destined to be the same as he?

He patted the young man's shoulder. "Cheer up. You will see Miss Bradbury tonight, if you go to that host of routs."

"I wonder which ones they will attend."

"I don't know. I should have asked." Ashby felt a sense of panic. In the swarm of guests at routs, it was entirely possible to spend the evening missing the very person one wanted to see.

Darlington determinedly lifted his chin. "I'll find her. If I have to go to the ends of the earth!"

"I doubt that will be necessary," the earl replied. "Is that what you wished of me? To see if I knew where the Bradburys are going tonight?"

"No, not really. I want to take Miss Bradbury for a carriage ride!" he erupted. "Do you think her mama will allow it?"

Ashby had his doubts, but he kept them to himself. "I cannot answer that."

"I don't think Lady Bradbury likes me, and I can't understand why! I've never stepped over the boundaries . . . well, excepting today, when I stayed a bit too long. What a hard look she gave me!"

He smiled faintly. "The lady is very protective of her daughter."

"Doesn't she realize that I would never harm her? Ah well . . ." Darlington squared his shoulders. "I suppose I can only do my best, but, my lord, the favor I ask is this. Miss Bradbury told me that you are an old friend of her mother. Could you put in a good word for me?"

Ashby gazed at the youthful lord and, as was becoming usual, seemed to see himself at that age. But there was one great difference. *Darlington had the nerve to admit to his feelings and push his suit.*

"I'll do all I can," he vowed.

"Thank you, Lord Spenwick. I'll never forget it."

They arrived at White's, but Ashby was suddenly not in the mood for male camaraderie. He left as soon as he could and went directly home. His brief conversation with Darlington bothered him more than he liked to admit. The young man was not afraid of his heart. Nor was he embarrassed to ask for assistance. Ashby wished he had someone to help him with Sarah. But, as in the past, he refused to bare his innermost feelings to others. He was on his own, and Sarah seemed awfully resistant. It wasn't an easy challenge. Could he achieve his goal, or would she break his heart again?

Soon after they began the evening's circuit of parties, Patricia decided that she did not like routs, especially when she saw that the receiving line was as long at the second house as it had been at the first.

"This is totally ridiculous, Mama. How can these events be called parties? At a party one is supposed to enjoy oneself. How can anyone be amused by waiting in long queues, both in the carriage and on foot, and then pressing through such crowds that it is impossible to speak with anyone but those nearby?"

Sarah smiled. "Such is the way of Society."

"I would rather go to balls," Patricia pouted.

"There are none, tonight." She eyed her daughter's scowling face. "Do cheer up, my dear, and remember that there are certain things in life that one must do."

"I thought I would see Lord Darlington," she muttered.

Sarah's smile faded. The girl was concentrating all too much on that young man. What could she do to divert her attention from Darlington to Spenwick? Hopefully, time would take care of her child's youthful crush. First love had a way of igniting furiously and then burning out. Perhaps that would be true for Patricia and Darlington. But Sarah had a niggling doubt. Deep inside, no matter how she tried to ignore it, her own first passion still flamed brightly. Could it be the same for her daughter? She didn't want to think about it.

"Mama, this room is positively steaming." Patricia waved her fan.

"Would you like to go home?"

"No, I am determined. Oh, how I would like to knock all these people down!"

Sarah couldn't help laughing softly. "Such a fine and proper young lady!"

Patricia was forced to abandon her frown and giggle. "I would certainly be remembered!"

"There is no doubt of that." She curtailed her laughter and put on a pleasant expression for her host and hostess. Exchanging a few words with them, she drew Patricia into the throng. "Let us seek refreshment. My throat is veritably parched."

"So is mine. I am roasting alive. Lead the way, Mama. I'll follow."

Chatting with those around them, Sarah began to work her way through the assemblage toward what she hoped was the dining room. It was a slow trek. Everyone seemed to wish to visit with her and congratulate her on her lovely daughter.

Halfway through the mob, Patricia caught her arm. "Mama, there is Lord Darlington."

Glancing past several bobbing plumes, she saw the tall, dark young man. "Come along, my dear. He is clear across the room. You haven't a hope of speaking with him."

"But Mama, he is standing by what appears to be a balcony door. We could go out into the fresh air."

"Patricia, I must have something to quench my thirst!" Ignoring her protests, Sarah doubled her efforts at making her way toward their destination. At last, after receiving several sharp elbows to her ribs, she reached the buffet table. Selecting a glass of champagne for herself, she retrieved a cup of punch for the young lady.

"Finally!" she gasped, turning to present the drink to her daughter, but Patricia was not behind her.

Worriedly, she surveyed the crowd. The girl was not to be seen. Heart sinking, Sarah immediately knew that Patricia had gone off on her own to meet Darlington, probably on the balcony. What a scandal! She hoped that it was just as congested as the interior rooms. If so, she might have a chance of reaching the young lady before anyone noticed that she lacked a chaperon. Grimly, she set out in that direction, just as someone turned and bumped her, splashing the contents of the punch cup onto her dress.

"Merciful Heavens!" Sarah stared helplessly as the raspberry liquid flowed down her bodice.

"Lady Bradbury!"

She spun around to face Lord Spenwick. "Oh, look what has happened," she wailed.

"Allow me." He pulled out his handkerchief and reached out to dab at the stain, realized its location, and sheepishly grinned. "Perhaps you'd best do it."

"Yes." She handed him the empty cup, which he disposed of by tossing it across the buffet to a servant.

"Luckily, the punch matches your gown, my lady."

"Indeed." She wiped up the worst of the mess. "However, I do believe that it is time to leave as soon as I find Patricia. We have become separated."

From his height, he was easily able to scrutinize the gathering. "I do not see her."

"She may have gone to the balcony for fresh air. She mentioned seeing friends near the door." Sarah bit her lip. "My lord, I must urgently seek her. She has no chaperon."

"There is a solid throng, but maybe I can help." He took her arm and sliced the mass of people in a way that Sarah never could have done.

"Thank you, my lord," she breathed, eventually stepping outside on the stone floor.

The balcony was thinly populated. Most guests apparently preferred to mingle inside, so it was easy to see that Patricia was absent. Sarah groaned. "Now what?"

"We shall locate her," he said confidently. "Refresh yourself for a moment first."

"But she has no chaperon!" she cried.

"No one will notice in this crush."

Soothed by his confidence and relishing the relative silence, she strolled to the railing. He was right. Anyone noticing her daughter would probably assume that a responsible adult was nearby.

"It must be difficult to parent a child," Lord Spenwick mused, joining her. "I'm sure I would be most ill-suited to the role."

"Certainly not, my lord!" she smiled. It was on the tip of her tongue to tell him how instinctive much of it was, but she bit back the remark. Such words might make him think of Patricia as a juvenile, who needed parenting, and not as a possible wife.

"Perhaps I am overprotective," she added. "Patricia truly has no need for my constant vigilance. She is a grown woman and quite knowledgeable of what is proper."

The earl raised an eyebrow. "Indeed?"

"Oh, yes! She knows all that is virtuous. She merely wants experience."

He shook his head. "These young ladies placed on the market each year . . . They seem like children to me. I much prefer an older woman."

"But that is impossible!" Sarah burst forth, thinking of his need for heirs.

"Indeed?" He eyed her keenly. "Why?"

"Well . . . uh . . . My lord, I cannot address such an intimate subject. Do excuse me. I must seek my daughter."

"Wait, Lady Bradbury." He took her hand.

Sarah hesitated. Her gaze locked with his, rendering her as immobile as she had been when she had first seen him at the Chardons' ball. She did not know how long she stood transfixed, but from what seemed like a great distance away, she heard the babble of conversation within.

Lord Spenwick exhaled slowly. "I will assist you momentarily. Won't you spare me a few more breaths of fresh air?"

She blinked and forced herself to stare into the garden. "I shouldn't have come out here. People will say I escaped. They will accuse me of being an unsuitable mother and chaperon."

He laughed. "I doubt it. There is so great a crush that no one will have noticed."

"Someone will," she predicted direly.

"Oh, for God's sake, Sarah!" He flushed. "I do apologize for the informality. I must admit that I think of you as *Sarah. Lady Bradbury* doesn't seem to suit you."

Hearing her first name on his lips nearly turned her knees

to water. "Nevertheless," she managed, "it is the proper appellation."

He pursed his lips. "Yes, I suppose it is. For the moment, at least. But someday, I shall call you *Sarah.*"

I'll consider it when I am your mother-in-law, she thought, but said aloud, "Perhaps you will. But now, Lord Spenwick, I positively must go inside."

"Very well." He sighed and presented his arm. "Let us go."

Biting the inner flesh of her mouth, she reluctantly shook her head. "I must return alone. Otherwise, people might gossip."

"Oh, for . . ."

"My lord," she admonished.

"Do as you wish, but you'll never get through that crowd alone."

Sarah glanced at the horde inside and then back at him. "I fear you are right."

With a grin, he tucked her arm through his elbow and started in.

With Lord Spenwick's guidance, she soon located the errant girl, standing with Lord Darlington and partially hidden by a large potted palm.

"Mama, where have you been?" Patricia exclaimed. "I have searched everywhere."

"On the balcony, looking for you," she said sternly.

"And seeking a breath of fresh air?" Her daughter smiled mischievously. "With Lord Spenwick?"

"Certainly not!" Sarah bristled. "Well . . . we did pause for a moment, since we were already there."

Patricia smugly raised an eyebrow. "I see."

Lord Spenwick chuckled.

Sarah fought back a flush of anger. Just who was the parent and who was the child? She felt as if she were being reproached by her own daughter. Worst of all, she possessed a sense of guilt! Lips tightened with irritation, she belatedly greeted Lord Darlington.

"My lady." He bowed as well as he could in the compact circumstances. "Perhaps we should return to the balcony. It is so stuffy and hot in here."

"An excellent idea." Without waiting for her assent, Lord Spenwick tugged her back toward the door.

"I must go home. My dress . . ." Sarah sputtered, but no one paid heed to her.

"This is much better," Patricia enthused as they reached the far corner of the gallery. "These routs are much more palatable when one can find a quiet place. Mama, you are very lucky to have obtained that glass of champagne."

Sarah gazed at the forgotten drink she held in her hand. "I do not even want it. My dress is drenched, and I am becoming chilly. I must go home."

"Be sporting," her daughter urged.

"Your mother is uncomfortable," chided Lord Spenwick in fatherly tones. Slipping off his coat, he settled it over Sarah's shoulders.

"There, Mama! Isn't that better?" Patricia asked.

No, it was not. Sarah's head spun as she inhaled the masculine scent of the garment. Oh, why was she so tempted at every turn? The earl was to be her son-in-law. Breathing deeply of the mingles aromas of cologne and *gentleman,* she wondered how she could bear it.

"Would you care for my flute of champagne, my lord?" she murmured.

"If you do not want it."

"I don't." She pushed it into his hand.

"Now I am the lucky one." He sipped the pale fluid. "Of course, I'd already deemed myself fortunate, by being in the company of two such lovely ladies."

"If I had a glass, I would toast that!" agreed Lord Darlington.

"We appreciate your compliments, my lords. Indeed, this is

shameful. Everyone should have a drink, whether or not one wished to offer a toast," Patricia expounded. She gazed at the crowd inside and shook her head. "I cannot help believing that few people experience pleasure at such a party as this. The hostess, no doubt, accounts herself as successful. I rate the thing as a failure."

"The *ton* evaluates parties by the number present," Lord Darlington said.

"I score by a hostess's skill at serving her guests. Mama, how would you give an enjoyable rout?"

Sarah smiled. "I fear I would cut down on the number of invitations. I would be very unfashionable."

"There you have it," Patricia said proudly. "As simple as that!"

"But I would gain no fame as a hostess," she claimed.

Lord Spenwick reflectively studied her. "Would you like to be a great hostess, Lady Bradbury?"

"Oh, goodness me, no!" she laughed. "My only desire is to live quietly in the country, continuing my charitable works."

Patricia groaned.

Excitedly, Sarah saw the chance to bestow praise on the young lady. "My daughter, on the other hand, would excel at it," she proclaimed. "With only a small amount of experience, Patricia would be a fine hostess. I have greatly depended upon her to help with our own little gatherings."

"Mama, you know that your expertise alone has made our invitations coveted," the girl said flatly, turning the tables against her compliments. "I can scarcely write legibly enough to address the cards. I couldn't arrange flowers if my life depended upon it. And as to preparing menus, I am lost! You, however, could be the finest hostess the *ton* has ever seen."

"Fustian," Sarah muttered, her elation dimming. How could she aid in making her daughter's achievements shine when Patricia kept shifting the plaudits in her direction?

"Furthermore, her talent for blending people is reknowned,"

the girl pounded on. "Mama can cause the most diverse guests to intermingle with ease. It has been said that one would be on one's deathbed before turning down an invitation to the dower house!"

"I hope you will entertain us sometime, my lady," Lord Darlington told her. "I know I would certainly covet an invitation."

"Yes, Mama," Patricia urged. "Do show the *ton* how it's done. Your parties would be all the rage!"

"Well, I must do some entertaining, but not just yet."

"Please do it soon! I will help with the guest list," her daughter offered. "You, my lords, will be the first names upon it."

"I can scarcely wait!" Darlington declared. "Please, my lady, set the date as soon as possible."

They eyed her expectantly. Sarah felt as if she were caught in a trap. "I shall set about making the plans," she told them, "and now we must go home. My damp dress is very uncomfortable."

"We have been thoughtless of you," Lord Spenwick apologized.

She almost agreed. The earl had set her head spinning again. Patricia had escaped her and then ruined her compliments with more of her own. Lord Darlington was disturbing by his mere presence. Nothing had gone well. She seemed even farther from matching her daughter with Lord Spenwick. Why did things have to be so difficult?

She returned the coat to him. "Actually, sir, you have been very considerate," she said politely, instead.

The two lords efficiently escorted them through the crowd and out to their carriage.

Lord Darlington paused as he closed the door. "My lady, may I have your permission to take Miss Bradbury for a drive in the park, tomorrow?"

Sarah's ragged temper flared. "I'm sorry. It is impossible. We have a whole day's shopping to do."

"But . . ."

"*No*, Lord Darlington!" She waved her coachman to proceed.

"Mama, please," Patricia begged.

"We shall be busy."

"Can we not divide the errands . . ."

"No, Patricia! You will not go with Lord Darlington!" she snapped. "I have had enough, this evening. You had best not persist in this."

The girl wisely fell silent.

"Damn!" Darlington kicked out at an imaginary object.

"You caught her at the wrong time," Ashby observed. "Couldn't you recognize that?"

"When is the right time?" he spat.

"Not when she is obviously distressed. Not when you've just finished spiriting away her daughter."

"I didn't do that! Patricia came to me."

"You should have immediately taken her to her mother," he lectured. "You know what is proper."

Darlington refused to accept criticism. He rounded on Ashby. "I thought you were going to help me!"

"I didn't have the chance," he soothed. "In time . . ."

"I know!" He stuck out his jaw. "You want her yourself. *You* want Patricia! You're probably doing everything in your power to convince her mother to avoid me."

It was all Ashby could do to keep from striking the young lord's inviting chin. "That's not true."

"It is! It really is! I've finally discerned the fact!"

"Shut up, Darlington," he said tightly. "People are looking our way."

"I don't give a damn." He lowered his voice only slightly. "You intend to possess Patricia!"

"Brainless idiot." He turned away to look for his own carriage.

Darlington caught his sleeve. "You're trying to keep her away from me. You're conspiring with that old witch!"

Stars exploded in Ashby's head. He glared at the hand on his arm and then to the face of its owner. "Name your seconds, Darlington."

The young man blanched, dropping his hand to his side. An expression of horror crossed his face. "What?"

"I said 'name your seconds,'" he hissed. "I will not have the woman I love so insulted."

"The . . . the w-woman you love?"

"Yes, dammit!" he rushed on. "I'm in love with Lady Bradbury!"

Darlington's mouth dropped open. "Lady Bradbury? Good God!"

Astonished by his outright admission, Ashby ground his teeth. "Is something wrong with that?"

"No." He shook his head, gaping. "I just didn't think . . . a woman her age . . ."

"What is wrong with her age?" he demanded.

"N-nothing! I merely thought you were friends. Sir, I admire Lady Bradbury. She is a handsome woman. In the heat of her rejection, I allowed my tongue to run away." He grimaced. "My lord, I don't want to meet you at dawn."

Ashby relaxed somewhat.

Darlington took it as a promising sign. "We can work together to obtain our heart's desire. Not that you need the help, of course! You are a belted earl. Anyone would leap at the chance to marry you."

"Not Sarah." He sighed. "I fear that she wishes to have me for her daughter."

"No," the young lord mourned.

"Of course, I would never wed her. I am determined to have her mama." He smiled wryly, relieved to have shared his feelings with another. "Patricia will make a fine daughter."

Darlington brightened. "When you succeed, sir, would you like to have me for a son-in-law?"

Ashby studied him. "I believe I might, especially if you'll hold your tongue on all I've said. I've never admitted how I felt about Sarah to anyone else."

"I won't reveal it. I swear!"

"See that you don't." Self-conscious, he turned to enter his coach, then hesitated. "Let's go to White's, Darlington. I feel the need of brandy and male companionship."

"So do I!" The young man eagerly followed him. "We can plot our attack on the ladies."

Ashby settled himself against the luxurious squabs. Outright attack was not a good plan. He had pushed Sarah too far again tonight, when he'd called her by her first name. He would patiently remain at her side, and at the present, wait for further developments. Maybe she truly didn't care for him. Only time would tell.

Patricia was ecstatic when the vouchers for Almack's arrived. Sarah hoped that the precious documents would cause her daughter to look more kindly upon Lord Spenwick and to consider him as a serious suitor, but the girl continued to treat him as a friend and often spoke to him as if he were her father. It was frustrating. Nothing Sarah could do seemed to have an effect on Patricia's affections. The young lady obviously preferred Lord Darlington.

Personally, Sarah had nothing against the youthful gentleman. He was very polite and pleasant. He was the heir to a wealthy earldom. Even in his youth, he appeared to be well-respected by the *ton*. He was simply too young to wed. For that reason, and truly that alone, she could not give her blessing to the would-be match. Her daughter needed a stable, established husband . . . a gentleman like Lord Spenwick.

In spite of Patricia's casual conduct toward him, the earl remained in attendance. He still avoided the gaggle of young people, but Sarah was certain that he was merely waiting for Patricia to gain some town bronze before he asked for her hand. Why else would he take such an interest in them? He had not repeated his earlier attempts at familiarity with Sarah and seemed satisfied to be merely her friend. So he knew he would not gain her as a mistress. He must realize that she was too old to be his wife. Therefore, he had to be waiting for Patricia to sow her innocent oats.

As the Season progressed, however, Sarah began to wonder if Patricia would be returning unwed to Bradbury Manor. Though a part of her rejoiced in the fact that the girl would remain a while longer with her, she could not embrace such selfishness. Patricia was ready for marriage. She wanted a new home and a family. Sarah would not stand in her way, unless she knew the match to be wrong. And Lord Darlington was definitely not the man for her daughter.

Finally, the girl's preference for the young lord became so publicly marked that Sarah was forced to sit her down for a serious conversation.

"My dear, people are beginning to talk about you and Lord Darlington," she said gently. "I have noticed that the crowd of gentlemen you previously attracted has thinned."

Patricia lifted a shoulder. "I do not particularly care."

"But you must," Sarah counseled. "Do you not wish to wed, this Season?"

"I wish to wed Lisle."

"*Lisle!*" she cried. "You call him by his first name?"

The young lady smiled dreamily. "Only in private."

"To his face?" she gasped.

Patricia nodded. "And he calls me by mine."

"That is most improper!" She colored, remembering how

Lord Spenwick had attempted to address her with such familiarity. Her name had been sweet on his lips, but of course, she could not allow it.

"No one knows, Mama, but he and I. And now you." Eyes cast down, she nervously tucked a stray lock of golden hair behind her ear. "I love him with all my heart. I wish you did not hate him so."

"I do not *hate* him."

"That's how it seems." A tear slid down the girl's cheek and wobbled precariously on her chin. "I want you to love him, too. I want us all to be close. Mama, I want to marry Lisle."

Sadness wrenched Sarah's vitals. "My darling, I wish all the world for you, but you cannot wed Lord Darlington. He is too immature."

Patricia sniffed mightily. "He is older than I."

"It is different for men than for women." She removed her handkerchief and dabbed at her daughter's face. "The female of our species matures much more quickly."

"I don't care."

"But you must! Do not permit this fancy to get in the way of your good sense."

Patricia lifted her head, batting away Sarah's hand. "It is not a crush!"

Sarah sighed, wadding up the lacy cloth in her fist. "You have not given others a chance. Lord Spenwick—"

"Lord Spenwick is in love with you!"

"No." She firmly shook her head. "For the sake of his future heirs, he knows he must choose a younger lady. He is waiting for you. If you would only spend more time with him, you would see how marvelous he is."

"Mama, I do think he's wonderful. *For you.*" Patricia set her jaw. "Why will you not see? You once had a crush on him. Did it pass? I don't think it did! I believe that you love him still!"

"I do not," Sarah valiantly claimed. "As soon as I saw him, I knew he would be perfect for you."

"Well, I do not agree!" she cried. "I am going to marry Lisle!"

Sarah had hoped that it would not come to this, but the conversation had not gone her way. Patricia had flown from wanting to marry Lord Darlington to determining to do so. She must call a halt to the mismatch, and in so doing, risk her daughter's love and a possibility of attempted elopement.

"Patricia, I will not permit you to marry Lord Darlington."

"You promised I could have my choice of husbands!" the girl loudly accused. "You are a liar!"

Sarah blanched. "When I said that, I expected you to use your good sense. You have not done so."

"You are just like your father! You would make me marry an old man, just because *you* deem it to be a good match!" Patricia leapt to her feet and began to pace back and forth. "You would wed me to Spenwick!"

"Lord Spenwick is not an old man!"

"He is of your generation! And you always claim to be so damned ancient!"

"Patricia!" she shrilled. "That is enough of that vulgar speech!"

"To Hell with propriety!" the girl shouted. Abruptly, she burst into tears and collapsed on the sofa.

Trembling, Sarah went to her, laying her hand on her daughter's heaving shoulders.

"Oh Mama, why does love have to hurt so much?" Patricia sobbed, reaching for her.

She sat down, taking her daughter in her arms. "I am so sorry that I had to forbid you to continue on in this path, but I was forced to use my better judgment. You will get over it."

"Will I?"

Sarah took a deep breath. Had *she* gotten over Lord Spenwick? "It takes determination. You will survive." She paused for a long moment. "And someday you will thank me."

Patricia sat up. Taking her mother's handkerchief, she dried her eyes and blew her nose. "I will endure, but I will never stop loving Lisle . . . just as you have never ceased loving Lord Spenwick. And Mama, I will never, *ever* thank you for keeping us apart. You are wrong, and someday you will realize it. Hopefully, it will be soon enough to rectify this awful situation."

Chapter Three

After Sarah's declaration, the house was blanketed with a disheartening pall. Patricia moped about, refusing to entertain callers, to go shopping, to Almack's, or even to a particularly fashionable ball. The servants, too, wore long faces and did not perform their duties quite so cheerfully. But no matter how depressing their homelife was, Sarah refused to back down in her decision. Lord Darlington was ineligible for her daughter's hand.

Patricia did see the young man once, during the mournful period. Obtaining Sarah's permission to bid him adieu, she exchanged a few whispered sentences with him in the hall. Afterwards, though he went away slumped and dejected, the young lady seemed to be slightly relieved. Her expression brightened, her step became lighter, and her appetite improved. Sarah prayed that the fancy was extinguished.

Having directing her life around her daughter, she now found that she had a great deal of time on her hands. At Bradbury Manor, she could have tended the garden, visited friends, or embarked on some homemaking project. In London, she did not feel like doing so. The house and garden belonged to someone else. Seeing friends meant explaining Patricia's absence. When Lord Spenwick came calling, she was tempted to receive him, but her better sense stopped her in time. Being with him would only overburden her heavily laden heart. So she did nothing and was bored. Therefore, nothing could have made her happier than the day Patricia, at last, came fluttering in to join her at lunch, a brilliant smile on her face.

"With your permission, Mama, I wish to go out."

"That is very good news," Sarah applauded. "What is the occasion?"

"I shall go for a drive in the park with Lord Spenwick. Hastings has agreed to act as chaperon," she announced, seating herself with a flourish.

Sarah's heart fell to her toes. "How did this come about?"

"I wrote him a note and asked him if he'd do it." Patricia casually began helping herself to the array of foods.

"What?" she cried. "How could you be so forward? He will think you are nothing but a shameless hussy!"

"Now, Mama, don't fly to the boughs." Plate filled, she dipped her fork into her fruit. "He replied that he would immensely enjoy the outing."

"I see." Compressing her lips, she tightly laid down her silverware.

"Isn't this what you wished? For me to make a match with Lord Spenwick?" her daughter asked sweetly.

"Well . . . yes." She lowered her eyes as a vision of Patricia dancing with the earl at the Chardon ball floated through her mind. She remembered how much she'd admired their appearance. Now, strangely, it didn't seem so wonderful.

Patricia chewed thoughtfully, eyeing her. "M-m-m, these peaches are delightful. You should try some."

Sarah shook her head. Her throat was so tightly constricted

that another bite would surely choke her. "My appetite is sated."

"Why, you've scarcely touched your meal! Mama, that worries me. I hope you are not ill."

"I . . . I ate a large breakfast," she croaked.

"Perhaps that explains it." The girl continued to relish each morsel, cleaning her plate and helping herself to another serving of fruit. "If you are feeling poorly, however, we must summon a physician at once. At your age, one cannot be too cautious."

She clenched her teeth. "I am a long way from my grave, young lady."

"I fervently pray that is so, but you must admit that those of your generation cannot be too vigilant in matters concerning their health," her daughter proclaimed.

A new thought assailed her. "Patricia, you cannot be thinking of marrying Lord Spenwick in hopes that he will soon die; whereupon, you will wed Darlington."

The girl laughed. "Now there's an idea!"

"Well, do not depend on such a ridiculous scheme," she snapped. "Lord Spenwick and I, for that matter, are in our prime. In fact, I have never in my life felt better! There will be no more talk of doctors and coffins. I resent it!"

"I do apologize, Mama." Patricia reduced her laughter to snickering. "On numerous occasions, you have stressed your age. Being concerned, I merely conformed to your lead."

"So there's an end to it!" Sarah tossed her napkin onto the table and rose. "And there's an end to this luncheon. I have many things to attend."

"What are they?" she inquired, rising to follow.

Sarah's mind raced. What important occupation could she claim? "I thought I might begin planning a party."

"Oh, how marvelous! May I help? Before we commence, however, I wonder if you would assist me in choosing what I should wear to the park today."

"The blue ensemble," she said spontaneously, leaving the room and turning down the hall to the salon.

Patricia tagged behind. "Yes, it is pretty, but is it dashing enough to catch Lord Spenwick's eye?"

"It expresses good taste."

"I was thinking of the red. It has those raffish epaulets. They are the very first stare of fashion."

"The blue is more feminine." She strode through the door and went straight to her desk.

"Yes, but the scarlet shows off my figure to greater advantage," the girl mused.

Sarah sat down and gathered pen, ink, and paper. "The rust dress and paisley shawl would also be attractive."

She groaned. "Too drab."

"The yellow is nice."

"Too ordinary." Her daughter yawned. "Goodness, but that meal has made me sleepy. Perhaps I should take a nap, so that I may be at my best when I accompany the earl."

"Indeed." Sarah dipped her quill and began with a list of refreshments. Her delicious receipt for punch would be excellent for the young ladies. She would serve champagne to the gentlemen and the elder women. She wished she had a glass of it now, to lift her spirits. She wanted her daughter to make a match with Lord Spenwick, but the thought of it definitely depressed her. Goodness! For the sake of them all, she must put him out of her mind.

Patricia yawned again. "Yes, I believe I shall doze for awhile. May I postpone my assisting you until later?"

"Please do," she readily agreed. She needed to be alone to digest this latest development. At last, the girl was doing as her mother wished. She was in pursuit of the prize catch. So why was it not pleasing?

"What will you wear this afternoon, Mama?"

Sarah startled. "I? I am going nowhere. You told me that Hastings would act as chaperon."

"But you will be greeting Lord Spenwick. Won't you wish to change?"

She swallowed with difficulty. "I perceive no necessity."

"Very well, Mama. I will see you later." She departed, leaving her mother to her list.

Sarah inscribed the names of several of her favorite delicacies, then found herself peering blankly at the page. Her mind was still a-twirl over Patricia's plot. What had Lord Spenwick thought when he received the girl's note? She didn't really believe that he'd label her daughter a hussy. Probably, he considered her to be merely naive. He had not been driven away by her forwardness. Indeed, he was interested enough in the girl to accept her proposition. In spite of Patricia's tendency toward outspokenness and this shocking audaciousness, Lord Spenwick knew that she was an innocent. He would behave towards her in a gentlemanly fashion. His intentions would be totally honorable.

Sarah sighed. This entire episode proved that the earl was attracted to Patricia. His unsettling conduct towards the mother was nothing but a combination of old memories and pure flattery. He knew he must marry someone young. He was seeking the one who was right for him.

She continued to ogle the paper, her mind now as void as her stare, until suddenly Patricia swirled into the room, clad in her dashing scarlet ensemble.

"Mama, you look half-asleep. Aren't you aware that it's almost time for Lord Spenwick to arrive?"

Sarah snapped from the hypnotic state. "How much time has passed?"

"Hours! How do I look?"

She blinked. "Quite stunning, my dear."

"I hope he likes red. Oh, it will be good to get out of the house." She smiled with anticipation, as a rap sounded on the door. "There he is!"

Blake escorted the earl to the salon and withdrew as the greetings began.

"We had best be on our way, my lord," Patricia chirped when the niceties were satisfied. She slipped her arm through his.

He seemed somewhat surprised. "You are not coming, too, Lady Bradbury?"

Sarah smilingly shook her head. "My maid will act as chaperon."

"Let us go." Without further ado, Patricia hastened him from the room.

Sarah hurried to the window to watch them leave, secretively plucking aside just enough of the underdrapery to allow her a view. My, but they did make a handsome couple! This was just what she wanted. But tears pricked her eyelids. Soon they were trickling down her cheeks. She quickly dabbed them with her handkerchief. She was crying with happiness for Patricia, of course. Then why did she feel so totally miserable?

I love him, she whispered aloud. *I love him and I cannot seem to cease.*

"My lord, I need your help," Patricia said without preamble, as soon as they were out of sight of the house. "If you are agreeable to listening to me, perhaps we should not go to the park where we would face constant interruption."

Ashby curiously glanced at her. This whole business smacked of intrigue, probably schemes against Sarah. He had been suspicious when he had received Patricia's note. He knew the young lady was not attracted to him, so he'd hoped that Sarah had changed her mind about him and was using this ploy to gain his company and demonstrate the fact to him. When she had remained behind, however, he'd begun to have misgivings. He was inquisitive enough, though, to continue to play the game.

"Hastings is aware of what's afoot," the girl went on, "and she is sworn to secrecy. We may speak frankly."

"All right." He ordered his coachman to tour through the city, avoiding the park. "Now, Miss Bradbury, how may I be of service?"

"My lord, you seem like a father to me," she said blatantly, "so I felt comfortable in begging your guidance. Moreover, you have been in the world much longer than I and, therefore, you must have gained wisdom in situations such as this."

He smiled ruefully. "Just what is your situation?"

"Being totally straightforward, Mama will not allow me to wed Lord Darlington."

"Has he asked for your hand?" Ashby quizzed with astonishment. The young man had told him no such thing. Surely Darlington would have begged his opinion before doing anything so rash.

"No. Let us say that Mama anticipated him. But *I* know that Lisle wants to marry me, and that is what I wish with all my heart," she wrenched out. "I love Lisle! And he loves me."

"And the problem is . . ."

"That Mama thinks him too young! She believes I should wed an older, established gentleman. She wants me to marry you!" In the throes of her emotional turmoil, Patricia tightly clasped his hand. "We know that would never do."

"You're right about that."

"Tell me what can be done," she tearfully pleaded. "Do you believe Lisle is too young to wed me?"

Once more, Ashby felt the error of his youth come crashing down upon him. He took a deep breath. "No. It would be a terrible mistake to separate you from your young gentleman."

Patricia exhaled with relief. "Thank God you believe as I do."

"It comes from experience. You see, I was very much in love with a certain young lady when I was Lisle's age," he slowly began. "People would call it a passing fancy, I suppose, but I know it was a great deal more. I've never stopped loving the lady. I've never married for that very reason. I couldn't offer my heart to another, because she owns it still.''

The girl nibbled her lip, gazing at him through damp lashes.

''I thought I was too young to press my suit,'' he ended, ''and so she was wed to an older gentleman. Dammit, I've cursed myself ever since, for I've reason to think that her father would have welcomed my suit.''

''Who was the lady?'' Patricia breathed.

Ashby leaned back his head and looked heavenward. ''I've bared my soul to you. I might as well tell you all. The lady is your mother, Patricia. I am in love with your mother.''

The Bradbury servant burst into loud, ragged sobs, startling them both.

''Hastings!'' Patricia cried. ''What is wrong?''

''It is all so sad!'' the maid wailed.

Ashby's coachman blew his nose, and the footman snuffled.

''Good God.'' The earl looked out at the teeming streets, wincing when they narrowly missed scraping the side of a halted vehicle. ''Pay heed to your business!''

''So sad!'' Hastings wept. ''What can be done?''

''We will find a solution.'' Patricia gripped Ashby's hand even harder. ''My lord, my mother suffered a disappointing crush in her younger days. On you! I believe that she still loves you very much. She refuses to admit it, because she considers herself too old for romance.''

''I would marry her in an instant,'' he vowed, heart leaping with happiness.

''She says you need heirs and must marry a young woman.''

''Sarah is young!'' he asserted.

''She doesn't think so.'' Patricia mischievously tossed her head. ''But I have been working on the obstacle.''

''Besides, I already have an heir. My cousin is eminently suitable for the role. I will explain that to Sarah. Surely then, she will drop her defenses." His heart was now turning handsprings. Sarah loved him! All would be well.

"Well, we have one match," the girl decided. "What about mine?"

"Darlington wishes to marry you. He confided in me. I will speak with Sarah and convince her to accept his suit."

She nodded, releasing his hand to nervously twist the fabric of her dress through her fingers. "There is one other way. If you wed my mother, you would become my father and the head of our family, wouldn't you?"

"Yes, I would hope to be looked upon as such," he acknowledged.

"And you would agree to my marriage to Lisle."

Ashby caught his breath. "Against Sarah's wishes?"

Patricia smiled coyly. "As her husband, couldn't you find a way to cajole her into changing her mind?"

All of his senses were stimulated by the implication. He grinned. "Yes, I would stand a good chance of doing that."

"I know I may rely on a favorable outcome." Spirits uplifted, she laughed. "Now, my lord, my soon-to-be papa, shall we return to the house and begin our campaign for our heart's desire?"

The coachman was turning before Ashby gave the order.

"Praise all Heavens," murmured Hastings. "Now both my ladies'll be happy!"

Wretchedly sipping champagne, Sarah was dumbfounded to hear Patricia and Lord Spenwick in the hall. They hadn't spent nearly enough time to complete the circuit in the park. What could have happened? Surely her obstinate daughter had not ruined her chances so speedily. She heard them laughing, however, so they must be in good humor. As the door opened, she rose uncertainly.

"You are back so soon?" She glanced inquiringly from one to the other.

"Yes, Mama," Patricia giggled. "Lord Spenwick wishes to speak with you."

So soon? She nearly gasped aloud. She wasn't quite accustomed to the idea, yet. But why not? She was the architect of the plan. What was there to become used to? Patricia would wed Lord Spenwick, and she would be alone. Her love and her daughter would . . .

Somehow she managed to walk woodenly to the sideboard and refill her glass. "I am drinking champagne, my lord. Would you care to join me?"

"I should like it above all things." He strode toward her.

"I'll leave you two alone!" Patricia called and shut the door.

"You wish to converse with me about my daughter?" she asked breathlessly.

"Yes, among other things."

She tremblingly filled his flute and handed it to him. "Well then, let us speak of Patricia."

He looked down at her, frowning. "My lady, are you ill? You appear ghastly pale."

"I am enjoying robust health!" she emphasized, her voice hideously shrill to her ears.

"Excellent. I was concerned."

"I am fine!" She tried to stroll casually to the sofa. "Do continue, sir . . . about Patricia."

He seated himself beside her. "She is a lovely young lady. I know you must be very proud, and that you wish the best for her."

Get on with it, Sarah silently implored. *I cannot bear this much longer.*

"Lord Darlington would make her the best husband I can imagine."

The glass slipped from her hand to the floor, saturating the carpet with the wine. Lord Spenwick quickly picked it up. "I'll fetch you another."

"I believe I need it," she mumbled. Darlington! Lord Spenwick was pleading Lord Darlington's case?

"I know you have reservations about the gentleman," he said as he crossed the room, "but I think I can change your mind."

"You do?"

"Yes, let us examine the young man's assets. He is handsome and well-behaved. He has no vices. His father provides him a substantial allowance." He walked back to the sofa and pressed a glass into her hand, sitting down even more closely beside her. "He's heir to an earldom. But more important than any of that, he cares a great deal for Patricia, and she, for him."

"He is too young to know how he feels for her!" she cried. "And I do not agree that she truly knows her own heart. They are too inexperienced!"

"My lady, do you honestly maintain that no one of Patricia's and Lisle's ages could ever form a lasting love?" he asked quietly.

Breast aching, she lifted her glass and drank. Guilt nearly overwhelmed her. At her daughter's age, she had wed Viscount Bradbury. She had never loved him. She had merely tolerated him and accepted her lot. Her heart had always belonged to the man beside her. Did Patricia love Lisle as much? Was she condemning her beloved child to such a heartbreaking future as hers?

"But she needs stability!" Sarah protested, as much to herself as to him.

"Lisle Darlington is constant. He is the most dependable young man I've seen. He would be loyal to her and conscientious in providing for her."

She sighed. "You certainly are in favor of this. I must say plainly, my lord, that I had hoped for a match between you and Patricia. It would have been for perfect. Each of you would have supplied the other's needs."

He laughed faintly, shaking his head. "Not mine. I have only one need. I crave you in my life, Sarah. I wish you to marry me."

Blood pounding through her veins, she stared at him.

"I have loved you from the moment I first saw you." He took the champagne from her hand and set it on the table. Gently tilting her chin with his finger, he lowered his mouth to hers.

Sarah melted at the sweet touch of his lips. This was true bliss. It was heaven on earth. And he wanted to marry her? She slipped her arm across his shoulders and fondled the thick dark hair at the nape of his neck. He responded by deepening the kiss and fully embracing her, holding her solidly yet as tenderly as if she were a piece of rare porcelain. Her mind reeled. He loved her! He had always loved her! And now . . . She stiffened. Now, it was too late.

She broke away, sliding away from him and holding her burning cheeks. "Lord Spenwick . . ."

"Ashby," he corrected.

"No!" she choked. "It cannot be."

"Sarah, look me in the eye and tell me you don't love me," he said raggedly.

"I cannot! It wouldn't be right!" She burst into tears. "It is too late! I cannot be the sort of wife you deserve."

"You are the only wife I want!" He reached for her.

Sarah leapt to her feet and backed up, raising her hands, palms outward, as if to push him away. She took a deep breath, hoping to calm herself. "My lord, you need a young woman. I cannot give you the heirs you require."

"I don't care about heirs!"

"But you must! It is your duty."

"Sarah, I have a cousin, an exemplary man. If you and I do

not have children . . ." He rose and eased toward her. "Our happiness is more important than any earldom."

"Stay where you are," she ordered. "I cannot bear you to come any closer!"

He halted. "You must listen to me."

"No! Listen to *me,* my lord." She bit her lip, breast heaving. "I do love you. I always have! I love you so much that I could not endure it if, one day, you came to resent me, which you would. No cousin can replace one's own child."

"My darling, we can have children."

"The odds are too great. No, it is impossible." She looked for the last time at his adored face. "You must do your duty, and I will do mine. All mothers wish to provide their child with their heart's desire. I shall not stand in the way of Patricia and Lisle. For them, it will not be too late. That is the only way I can mend when the past has done . . . by learning from it!"

Whirling, Sarah ran, heartbroken, from the room.

Sarah did not distinguish when day ended, night commenced, and daylight came again, until Hastings touched her shoulder.

"My lady, it is late in the morning, and Lord Sissonby and Lord Darlington have come to see you."

She rolled onto her back and pushed the covers away from her face. Sometime, someone, probably Hastings, had disrobed her and dressed her in her nightrail, but she was not comfortable. Her face was too puffy and her eyes, too raw. She miserably pushed herself into a sitting position. How could she receive these guests who were so important to her daughter's future?

"I've brought tea, my lady." The abigail sniffled as if she'd been crying, too.

"Oh, how can I see them?" Sarah moaned. "And yet, I must."

"This will help." Hastings placed a cool, damp cloth on her mistress's eyes.

"Ah, that's better." Blindly, she brought the cup of warm, fortifying brew to her lips. "Do they know I am not out of bed?"

"Yes, my lady, and they are willing to wait. Miss Patricia is with them."

"For her sake, I must hasten." She drained the cup and slipped from bed. "I'm sure I'll be as good as new very quickly."

"Perhaps so, my lady," the maid answered doubtfully.

"I imagine the household is rife with rumor." She performed her morning's ablutions and pulled a dress from the rack. "I'll wear this one."

"Yes, my lady. As to servants' gossip, we know that you'll accept Lord Darlington's suit for Miss Patricia's hand."

"Yes." Sarah nodded shortly. "They will make an admirable couple."

"And we know that you turned down Lord Spenwick." Hastings stuck out her lip.

She clenched her teeth. "It wouldn't have worked."

The abigail shook her head, helping her into the gown. "My lady, I came to you when you were a bride. I always guessed that you loved somebody else. The old lord wasn't right for you. Now's your chance to be happy."

Sarah sighed. "I am too old. Lord Spenwick needs children."

"That man needs you! And you need him. Children'll come. You're not too old for them."

"It's too great a chance." She sat down at the dressing table and dragged a brush through her tangled hair. "Let us speak no more of it. This is a happy day for Patricia, and we must be cheerful for her."

"She's not as happy as you think. She's worried about you."

"That is needless." She shrugged. "As soon as I formally

accept Lord Darlington, she will turn all her concentration on him and her upcoming nuptials.''

''I don't think so.''

Sarah refused to believe her mind. Patricia must be in high spirits. After all, she was obtaining the husband she wanted.

She relinquished the brush to the skilled Hastings and let her tackle the snarls of golden hair. Sitting idly, she couldn't help focusing on her face. The tiny crow's feet at her eyes and mouth seemed deeper today. Hadn't Lord Spenwick noticed those telltale signs of aging? If he had not, he must be dazzled by a vision from the past. No one could prefer a face like hers to the dewy, flawless countenance of a young woman.

Hastings twisted her hair into a chignon and applied a soothing powder around her eyes. ''There, my lady. I doubt anybody will guess what a horrible night you had.''

''It doesn't really matter. Patricia is the jewel.''

Hastings smiled mysteriously. ''We'll see about that.''

''I care nothing for my looks, anyway. This is my daughter's day.'' She stood, and without a backward glance, hurried to meet Lord Sissonby and his son.

She entered the salon, surprised to find the company rather quiet and not nearly so joyous she she expected. She greeted the guests and apologized for her tardiness, glad to see that Patricia had the foresight to order tea. Her daughter poured her a cup of the brew, kissed her cheek, and departed.

''Well, Lady Bradbury,'' the earl declared, ''shall we come right to the point?''

''Father,'' Lord Darlington murmured.

''Oh, bother!'' his sire professed. ''Do the pretty then, but it's a waste of my and my lady's time.''

The young man grimaced. ''Do pardon my father, Lady Bradbury. He's outspoken.''

She smiled. ''So is my daughter.''

''I like that quality,'' the earl defended. ''One always knows where one stands.''

Darlington flushed. "My lady, you may know that my affections toward Miss Bradbury have deepened day by day . . ." He launched into his elaborate marriage proposal.

"Whew!" cried his father when he had finished and Sarah had accepted. "How long have you been practicing, Lisle?"

"Father!"

"It was a very sweet proposal, Lord Darlington," Sarah complimented him to ease the young man's embarrassment.

"I suppose it was." His father chuckled. "Now, on to business! I don't mind saying that I balked at this idea, at first, Lady Bradbury. Nothing against your daughter, of course. I thought Lisle was too young for this step. Humph! When my son and Lord Spenwick finished talking to me, I was convinced that it was the right thing to do."

Sarah nodded, tears suddenly springing to her eyes. She lowered her head. "It would be a mistake for us to attempt to put a period to their love, my lord."

"Thought so myself, so here we are! With your permission, madam, we'll leave the settlements to our men-of-business."

"That is agreeable to me."

"Good! My wife will call a bit later. She's all excited about the arrangements." He cleared his throat. "Lady Bradbury, we've never had a gel in the family, so I hope you'll let her in on all the female wedding preparations."

"Of course." She smiled at Lisle. "I've never had a son."

He leapt to his feet and knelt before her, kissing her hand. "I'll do anything to please you, ma'am."

"Just be kind and loving to Patricia. That will delight me beyond everything," she advised. "Now, I do presume that there is a very anxious young lady waiting in the hall."

"Yes, my lady!" He dashed toward the door.

She laughed and poured another cup of tea for herself and his lordship. "They are very young."

"There is no age limit on love," stated a deep male voice.

Sarah jumped, nearly dropping her cup. With a great rattle

of china, she caught it and stared over her shoulder. "Lord Spenwick! Why are you here?"

"You did not expect me to give up so easily?" He casually strolled into the salon. "Sissonby, will you join me in explaining to Lady Bradbury how wrong she is in tossing me aside?"

"He's right, you know," the elder earl urged. "You should have heard what a fine case he presented me, last night, when I tried to thwart Lisle's suit."

Sarah winced. "Does all of London know about this?"

"Not at all, my dear." He grinned. "I did, however, recruit a few good minds to assist me in my dilemma."

She suddenly became aware of a din in the hall. There was a mayhem of voices, shufflings, and . . . of all things . . . babies' cries. "What is going on?" she demanded.

"In a moment, love. Is it not true that you refuse to marry me because you cannot give me heirs?"

"My goodness!" She cast a sheepish glance at Lord Sissonby. "Lord Spenwick, this is . . ."

"Please answer me, Sarah. Is it not true . . ."

"I know the question!" She blushed deeply. "The answer is yes. Must you make this a public event?"

"I fear you have forced me to such desperate measures." Lord Spenwick signaled to the group in the entrance.

Patricia and Lisle came in first, accompanied by Eloise Chardon and two dignified ladies whom Sarah recognized to be Lady Sissonby and, of all people, Lady Spenwick, Lord Spenwick's mother. They were followed by a throng of women and babies. Behind them walked Sarah's entire staff of servants from butler to kitchen boy.

"What is this?" Sarah cried.

Her daughter giggled. "Mama, while you were crying the night away, we were searching London for all the mothers and babes we could find."

"These women are your age or older, my love," Lord Spenwick explained, "and they all have newborn babies."

She gaped.

Lady Spenwick came forward and took her hand. "Please put my son out of his misery, my dear. Until you came into his life again, I had given up hope of his ever marrying. Yes, I would like to have grandchildren, but there will be no chance at all, unless you marry him."

"You can accomplish it, Sarah!" insisted Eloise Chardon.

Patricia hugged her. "Mama, how can Lisle and I be truly happy if you are left alone and mourning for the gentleman you love?"

"Lady Bradbury," Lisle said brokenly, "Patricia and I have decided not to wed, unless you do, too. Patricia refuses to leave you alone."

"Oh, no!" cried Lady Sissonby. "I cannot bear to see my son as heartbroken as Lord Spenwick!"

"The staff will quit," Hastings added direly.

"This is blackmail!" Sarah shrieked. Pulling away, she fled to the window.

Lord Spenwick followed, laying a hand on her shoulder. "I would not force you, darling. I love you too much for that. But we thought you needed a bit of a nudge."

"A bit!" She turned. He had made his point. Women her age *could* have children, and obviously many did. Whether she could was another story, but she knew, gazing into his marvelous face, that she could not resist him. She would marry him and take her chances on providing him with an heir. If she failed, she would, at least, endeavor to make him the happiest man in the world.

"A-Ashby?" She tentatively tried his name on her tongue. It sounded agreeable. More than pleasing! Her heart turned somersaults.

"Ashby," she said with confidence, "I have an irreplaceable staff. I cannot afford to lose them, so the answer must be yes."

He swept her into his arms. "You will never regret it!"

"I pray you will not."

"Never! No matter what the future brings!" Unmindful of the onlookers, he bent to kiss her.

The crowd cheered. Babies cried. The stirring kiss was interrupted by well-wishers.

"Mama," Patricia wept. "Somehow I knew we'd both end the Season as brides."

Heart overflowing with love, Sarah looked up at her lord. "In a sense, you will be a father upon our wedding day."

"Yes, and I am very proud of my daughter. But I am confident that you will give me a son, one day." He leaned over to whisper in her ear. "Even if you do not, we will have a magnificent time, trying to bring about this feat."

Cheeks flaming, Sarah giggled girlishly. "My wonderful lord," she murmured back. "I fear I possess a dreadful reputation for overly concerning myself with the years. In accordance, perhaps we should set an early wedding date. At our ages, we haven't a moment to lose!"

Epilogue

Ashby gave up any hope of maintaining sobriety in the tense situation. Directing his steps toward his liquor cabinet, he poured himself a full glass of brandy. His condition made no difference, anyway. He'd assembled the finest staff of physicians and midwives in England. If they couldn't help Sarah, no one could. Least of all, him. The matter was totally out of his hands. In addition to that, he was freezing cold. The spirits would surely warm him. Taking his drink, he paced to the hearth, laid another log on the fire, and sat down on the edge of a chair.

"Thank God," Darlington muttered.

Ashby sent a quick, frowning glance toward his son-in-law.

"I'm glad you sat down. You're making me nervous as Hell," the young man explained, pushing a lock of damp hair from his forehead. "I'm burning hot, too, but that's preferable to your marching."

"It's cold in here," he countered. "If you don't realize that, something's wrong with you."

Patricia's husband merely shook his head.

Ashby's teeth began to chatter. He took a sip of the brandy and felt the fiery fluid warm his veins. But it did little to aid his overall malady.

Lisle gaped at him. "You really are cold."

He shrugged impatiently. Not only was he chilling, but his stomach was wildly twisting itself in knots. He wouldn't tell the young man about that. Nor would he admit that he was utterly, shamefully *terrified*. The cool, sophisticated Lord Spenwick should be calm during the birth of his child, not brutally frightened at the thought of losing his wife.

"I know!" his son-in-law suddenly said. "You're afraid for Sarah!"

Don't be ridiculous," Ashby snarled. "She has the best doctors money can buy."

"But her age—"

"Shut up!" cried the earl. "For over a year, I have heard enough of *age* to last me for the rest of my life! Sarah is in the best of health."

"Yes, but—"

"I tell you I don't want to hear it!" Ashby began to pace again.

"Oh, I am certain that all will be well," Lisle said cheerfully. "Evidently, you are too, so shall we adjourn to the billiard room? I'm positive that I can defeat you this time."

"Lisle?" he demanded, pausing. "Don't you think you'll be somewhat concerned when Patricia's time comes in several months?"

"Well, of course, but—"

"I'll be keeping *you* company then. Perhaps we can take out your hounds for a bit of sport."

"Foxhunting? At a time like that? When my wife is . . ." Darlington blanched, rising. "Oh, my God. Sir, do you realize that women can die during childbirth?"

"So can men. I swear I am going to throttle you, Lisle."

He started toward the young lord, but was halted by his step-daughter's joyful entry.

"Dear Papa Ashby, it's all over now!"

Icy tendrils gripped his spine. "How is Sarah?"

"She is vastly excited. Naturally, she is weary, but she wishes to see you immediately. The baby—"

"Patricia!" her husband interrupted. "You must sit down and rest. Do you realize how dangerous these times can be? No, lie down. Oh Lord, I must get you home at once!"

"Lisle, what has gotten into you? I am feeling marvelous!"

Leaving the two to their chattering, Ashby dashed from the room and up the stairs, passing festive servants and nearly colliding with the team of medical specialists coming from Sarah's chamber. "Is she all right?"

The senior of the group bowed. "Lady Spenwick is fit as anyone could wish, and already looking forward to future youngsters. Your—"

"We won't go through this again!" He pushed past them. "Sarah?"

Comfortably propped on a mound of pillows, she smiled at him and extended her hand. "Hello, my darling. What were you saying to them?"

Warm relief chased away his fears. He advanced to the bedside. "I told them that this is the end of the nonsense."

"Oh? But just look at the reward." Catching his hand, she drew him down on the edge of the bed and gently laid back a sheet to reveal a small, red, wrinkled face. "Look at your son. Isn't he beautiful?"

Ashby peered at the wriggling infant encircled in her arm. He seemed rather ugly, but if Sarah thought he was handsome, he would agree. He nodded.

"He is a fine, healthy fellow." She giggled as their offspring tried to grasp her finger. "Would you like to hold him?"

"No, I'm not good at that."

"My lord, you should practice. It is not difficult." She sat up and gathered the babe in her arms. "You see? Try it. He will not break."

She looked so anxious that he complied, awkwardly holding his son. The baby's big eyes stared back at him. Suddenly the little mouth opened and expelled a loud wail. "You'd better take him back. He knows I'm an amateur."

"Fustian!" she laughed. "Rock him a bit."

"He'd rather be held by you, and I don't blame him," he protested, but did as she suggested. The child ceased his squalling and closed his eyes, apparently settling down for a nap. After a moment, Ashby cautiously returned him to Sarah's side.

"I am so happy." She tucked the covers around their progeny and gazed fondly at Ashby. "I can scarcely believe that I ever doubted that such an event could take place. Now, I am truly a good wife to you."

"You already were." He caressed her cheek. "This is mere icing on an exquisite cake."

Her eyes sparkled. "Perhaps, but now I am satisfied. I shall be even more so, when our son has a brother or sister."

"Sarah!"

"He will need someone to play with," she mused. "Now that I have proved I can do it, I don't mind providing."

"He can play with Patricia's future brood," he vowed. "You may have done all the work, my love, but I cannot bear another day like today."

She lifted an eyebrow. "You were worried?"

"I was frantic."

"Poor Ashby," she mischievously crooned. "Couldn't you become accustomed?"

"No!" he exclaimed.

"My, my." She caught his hand and brought it to her lips, kissing his fingers. "We shall see, won't we?"

Ashby sighed. Sarah would have her way. He could deny her nothing. Besides, he couldn't deny himself the ecstasy of making love to her. She had him entrapped.

"Very well, my lady," he acquiesced. "It shall be as you wish."

"Excellent! We will commence our next project as soon as the doctor permits." She chortled lightly. "After all, at *my* age . . ."

Groaning, he smothered her preposterous comment with a lingering kiss.

THE AUNT AND THE
ANCIENT MARINER

Carola Dunn

Dearest Aunt Chloe,

I am in the greatest *Despair*. Papa grows ever more determined to see me wed and off his hands by the end of June so that he need never endure the Trouble and Expense of another Season in Town. Now he vows to marry me to an *OLD MAN*. Sir Lionel Tiverton is the richest of my suitors and the only one with a title, though he is no more than a Baronet. Papa would have preferred a Marquis, or at least a Baron. But in spite of our grand Connexions, I am not pretty enough to catch a Nobleman, as did my sister, without a larger portion as bait than I possess. Dear Aunt, you know I care naught for wealth or title. I could be perfectly happy with a country Squire, or even a Clergyman, if he were but amiable and *young*. Indeed, I have written to you of the several agreeable, perfectly unexceptionable, young gentlemen I have met here. Though I am not madly in love with any of them, I should willingly wed Papa's choice among them if only

he will not force me into the arms of an Elderly Husband.
He will not hear me, but rants and raves and swears I
shall have Sir Lionel.

So you see, my dearest Aunt, I am in desperate straits.
Pray come to London at once and persuade Papa to listen
to reason.

Your affectionate, afflicted Niece,
                    Georgina.

Chloe dropped the tear-blotched letter in her lap. Persuade
Edgar to see reason? As well ask her to persuade the Emperor
of China to fly to the moon. The most she had ever managed
was to divert her brother's easily aroused wrath from his children's heads to her own.

Poor Georgie! She was suffering because of the beautiful
Dorothea's marriage to Lord Welch. Catching the heir to an
earl for a son-in-law had set up plain Edgar Bannister, Esquire,
in his own conceit. Now nothing would do for his younger
daughter but a title and a great fortune.

It was not as if the Bannisters were in urgent need of funds.
Whatever his failings as a father and brother, Squire Bannister
was a knowledgeable agriculturalist and a competent landlord.
His farms brought in excellent rents, though any stranger entering the room where Chloe sat might have been pardoned for
doubting it.

She glanced about the shabby parlor, dingier than ever in
the chill grey light of the rainy April day. Edgar saw no point
in lavishing the blunt on new furniture and carpets which his
muddy riding boots and breeches and his muddier dogs were
certain to besmirch in no time.

Dene Manor had more than enough rooms to set aside one
as dog-free. Chloe had never dared suggest such sacrilege.

As though aware of her thoughts, the setter slouched on the
hearthrug pricked up his ears, then rose and came to lay his

head on her lap. Hastily she moved her sewing out of his way. Georgina's letter fluttered to the floor.

"What am I to do, Fury?" she asked, scratching behind his silky ears. He closed his eyes in bliss.

Her eldest nephew strode into the room. "Aunt Chloe, Merrow says there's a letter from Georgie?" Seeing the paper on the floor, he stooped to pick it up.

"It's addressed to me, but you had best read it, John. I need your advice."

"Mine?" The sturdy young man positively glowed. Though proudly in charge of the estate during his father's absence, he was not accustomed to being consulted by the aunt who had been a mother to him for half his life.

He dropped into a chair. Fury changed allegiances, and John absently fondled his head as he read.

"Look at these spots, she's been crying!" he said indignantly. "Can Father really make her marry an ancient cradle-snatcher?"

"You know your father," Chloe said.

"He'll bully her into it. But nothing you can say will make him change his mind. Just going up to Town without his express command would be enough to make him kick up a fine dust. He'll foam at the mouth if you try to argue with him."

Chloe shuddered. "Yes, but how can I abandon Georgie without even trying?"

"Then you want to go?"

"I don't *want* to go." Nothing could be further from her wishes than to travel so far from her Lancashire home, to a terrifyingly unknown metropolis, to confront her choleric brother. "I feel I must. At least I should be there to support her spirits."

"I hate to think of poor Georgie alone. Doro will not be of the least use to her." He scanned the letter again. "Sir Lionel Tiverton—what business has he taking a bride of eighteen? I wish I could go with you and have it out with the old goat, but what with the planting and the lambing. . . .''

"No, you cannot leave Dene, John. Edgar would never trust you again. But you have given me an idea. If he proves adamant. . . .''

"*When* he proves adamant.''

"I shall try to see if Sir Lionel will not be more reasonable. Surely he cannot have considered the feelings of a young girl tied to an elderly gentleman, the natural repugnance. . . .'' Chloe could not continue. Her own father had proposed just such a match for her, and only the decrepit bridegroom's timely demise had saved her from the fate now threatening Georgina.

"Darling Aunt Chloe, I knew you would come to the rescue!''

Chloe turned from the superb Canaletto view of Venice hanging over the marble mantelpiece, just in time to catch her niece in her arms. Georgie hugged her fiercely.

"I am come, dearest, and I will do my utmost, but you must not count on your papa listening to me.''

"At least you are here. You cannot guess how I have missed you.''

"And I you, Georgie.'' Chloe had not meant to make that confession. It was in the nature of things that her charges must grow up and go their own ways.

Come autumn her youngest nephew, Paul, would be off to join Bernard, his middle brother, at school. Dorothea was Lady Welch. John was courting the vicar's daughter, a pleasant, sensible girl who would rightly expect to take over the reins of the Dene Manor household when they wed. And Georgina was bound to find a husband to her liking soon, if, by a miracle, Chloe contrived to preserve her from the aged Sir Lionel.

"Doro is sympathetic when she remembers,'' Georgie said, "but you know how she is. She cannot keep her mind on any subject for more than two minutes together. And my brother-in-law and Lord and Lady Chingford are all that is civil but quite distant. I cannot confide in them.''

''It was very obliging in Lord Welch's parents to invite you to stay for the Season.''

''I wish they had not!''

''Come now, dearest, you cannot tell me you have not enjoyed yourself at all.'' With a tired smile, Chloe looked her favorite niece up and down. She was a charming sight in a fashionable high-waisted gown of peach sarsnet, her light brown curls threaded with a matching ribbon. ''Gracious, such elegance. What is this nonsense about not being pretty enough to snare a peer?''

''I shall never be half so beautiful as Doro,'' Georgie said dispassionately, drawing Chloe down to sit beside her on a blue striped satin sofa. ''It takes that sort of beauty to be noticed if one has neither great family nor great fortune.''

''Dorothea is a beautiful widgeon. You have ten times her intelligence!''

''Most gentlemen do not wish for intelligence in a wife. Only look at how Lord Welch adores Dorothea.''

''Still? I own I have felt some concern as to whether he might grow disillusioned.''

''No need to fret, Aunt Chloe. He is not much cleverer, just enough to let him feel superior! But even if some clever men desire a clever wife, one must first attract notice or there is no opportunity for conversation. The balls in London are quite different from the assemblies at home, where one knows everybody except a few visitors—like Lord Welch when Doro caught his eye. Here the gentlemen see me as just one among dozens of hopeful young ladies.''

''But you do have admirers, Georgie,'' Chloe said, distressed.

''Oh yes, young men with insufficient prospects to please the blue-blooded heiresses, or Papa. And Sir Lionel.'' Georgina raised hopeful brown eyes to meet Chloe's. Her expression changed abruptly. "Oh, how selfish I am, dear Aunt. You are much too tired to think about my troubles this afternoon."

"I daresay I look positively hag-ridden," Chloe said wryly. "As Edgar's traveling carriage is here in London, I came overnight by the Mail rather than face the expense and complications of a post-chaise and having to stay alone at an inn. I am not certain what I ought to do tonight. Lady Chingford is not expecting me. She will think me horridly encroaching."

"I'll ask Doro," said Georgie, rising, but at that moment the drawing-room door flew open and her father strode in.

"Chloe!" he bellowed. Already, rich food and lack of exercise had increased his bulk, though city living had not noticeably paled the carmine complexion. "What the devil are you doing here?"

Chloe flinched. After a few weeks of blissful peace and quiet she found herself unprepared for Edgar's loud, perpetually angry voice. The thought of the storm she would raise when she explained her errand appalled her. Her head began to ache.

"Hello, Edgar," she said apprehensively.

"Hello? Is that all you have to say for yourself? You're supposed to be supervising the dairy and poultry yard at home, not gadding about like a damn spring chicken!"

"John promised to keep an eye on the maids, though they are all quite competent and honest."

Her brother snorted. "They'll steal me blind without constant watching."

"It is only for a few days, Edgar."

"And what about Paul?"

"He has gone to stay with the vicar while I am away, so he will not miss his lessons, nor run wild."

"It's you that's run wild, devil take it! What the deuce do you mean by chasing after—"

"How do you do, Miss Bannister," said a cool, calm voice. A tall woman advanced into the room, richly clad in a pomona-green gown of gros de Naples silk, trimmed with yards of the finest Valenciennes lace. Her cap was an elaborate froth of matching lace lavishly adorned with green satin bows and ribbons. She made Chloe feel drab and dowdy in her practical carriage dress of slate-grey merino, the one she often wore at home to drive the gig to the village or to visit tenants.

Edgar fell back, bowing. "You recall my sister, Lady Chingford?" he enquired in a much moderated tone.

"Naturally. I trust your journey was not too shockingly tiresome, ma'am?"

"A little, thank you, my lady." Chloe curtsied.

She was not surprised at Edgar's respectful demeanor. Quite apart from his esteem for a title, the Countess of Chingford was an imposing figure who would certainly not allow herself to be browbeaten by a mere country squire. Only habitual indulgence toward her son could explain why she had permitted him to marry a lovely nobody like Dorothea.

Meeting her at their wedding, Chloe had found her distinctly awe-inspiring. Now, travel-worn and uninvited, she felt altogether inadequate to deal with her ladyship.

To her relief, Lady Chingford did not ask her reason for coming but merely said, "Dorothea will be happy to see you. I expect you will like to take a dish of tea while a chamber is prepared for you. Pray ring the bell, Miss Georgina."

Over tea, Chloe meekly, if sincerely, agreed that she would be glad to lie down for an hour or two. Edgar took himself off with a disgruntled mutter about an appointment at his club. Dorothea came in and greeted Chloe with delight.

Blue-eyed and golden-haired, Doro was an amiable, sunny young lady, not at all vain. Her manners and conduct were above reproach, thanks to her compliant nature and her aunt's training. Chloe had early realized that to attempt to inculcate anything more profound into that featherhead would be labor lost. She was not at all surprised when her elder niece showed not the least curiosity about the reason for her unexpected visit.

Lady Chingford was taking both girls to pay some calls and

visit a modiste. Before leaving, Georgie escorted Chloe up to a small but elegantly appointed chamber, the bed and window hung with rose-pink damask.

"Go properly to bed and sleep," she urged. "We shall drive in the Park after the modiste, so we'll be out for several hours. When I come back you will be rested and we can discuss what to do about Sir Lionel. I know you will think of something. Bless you for coming, dearest Aunt."

"I only hope I can be of some use," Chloe said wearily.

Her clothes had already been unpacked for her. A maid brought hot water and took away her carriage dress to be cleaned. After washing off the worst of the travel dirt, Chloe unpinned and brushed her long, fair hair, then slipped between smooth sheets, lavender-scented just like at Dene.

The bed was as comfortable as it was elegant, yet slumber eluded her. Her stomach rumbled ominously, reminded by the cup of tea that dinner yesterday was two spoonfuls of lukewarm soup, breakfast a buttered roll hastily downed before the Mail dashed on. It was her own fault. Too timid to assert herself with a demand for fast service in the inns' coffee-rooms, she had been equally too shy to ask the countess for something to eat with her tea.

There was no getting away from it, she was a milk-and-water person, Chloe told herself sadly. By the age of six-and-thirty she ought to have learned to stand up for herself, or at least to stand up to Edgar rather than shaking in her shoes whenever he raised his voice. Instead here she lay, unable to find oblivion in sleep, filled with dread at the coming interview.

But Georgina relied upon her. She had to compose herself and prepare her arguments. Since she could not sleep, perhaps a walk would calm her spirits, as it always did at home.

When she recalled Lady Chingford's silk and lace, Chloe's best walking dress, a blue cambric muslin, seemed woefully provincial. For want of better she donned it, adding a darker blue spencer. She pinned up her hair, put on her chipstraw bonnet with the blue ribbons, found her gloves, and made her way down to the vestibule. A footman in grey livery and white wig stood there, a trifle intimidating in his stiff impassivity.

Lily-livered she might be, but Chloe refused to let herself be intimidated by a servant. "If anyone asks for me," she said, "tell them I shall be back shortly. I am going for a walk."

A flicker of surprise was instantly suppressed. "Alone, miss? You don't wish me to attend you?" he enquired stolidly.

"No, thank you." On a sudden impulse, she asked, "Do you happen to know where Sir Lionel Tiverton resides?"

"Yes, miss. Sir Lionel is staying with his sister, Lady Molesworth, on Albemarle Street. Number fourteen, I believe."

He gave her directions and opened the front door for her. Setting off along the pavement, Chloe thought she might as well go and take a look at the old gentleman's residence. It might inspire her with some idea of how to approach him when, inevitably, she failed with Edgar.

The traffic in the streets was fascinating. Carriages of every size and description rumbled past with jingling harnesses and hooves clopping on the cobbles; the pedestrians ranged from ladies and gentlemen clad in the height of fashion to a grimy sweep and his black-faced boys; pedlars hawked everything from clean sand for scouring pots to hot pies with a savory smell that made Chloe's mouth water. Her empty stomach squawked so loudly she was surprised no one turned to stare. Unfortunately she had left her purse behind, or she would have abandoned genteel manners and devoured a pie right there in the street.

Her mind on food, Chloe came to Number Fourteen, Albemarle Street. She stepped up to the green front door and rapped with the brass lion-head knocker before she recollected she had only been going to look.

Aghast, she was ready to turn and run, but the door swung open. "Yes, madam?" said the black-clad butler.

Chloe gazed at him in despair. It was no good asking for

Lady Molesworth: how would she explain her visit? Her only hope was that Sir Lionel was out or, more likely in view of his age, taking an afternoon nap.

"Is Sir Lionel Tiverton at home?" she asked, heart in mouth.

"If you will step in, madam, I shall enquire." Closing the door behind her, he proffered a silver salver.

She had no cards. At home, she never called on anyone who expected one. "Pray tell Sir Lionel, Miss Bannister requests a word with him," she said with dignity.

"Certainly, madam."

Ushered into a handsome drawing room, flooded with afternoon sunshine, Chloe sank weakly onto the nearest chair. What had she done? Sir Lionel was not out or the butler would have told her so right away. However aged and infirm, he would hardly refuse to see the aunt of the young lady he hoped to marry. What in heaven's name was she to say to him?

The door opened and a tall, broad-shouldered gentleman strode in. In a sun-browned face, tiny lines radiated from the corners of his dark eyes, as though he had often narrowed them against the sun. Creases about his mouth suggested he found the world amusing. His hair was raven-black sprinkled with grey, with pure white wings at the temples—but he could not possibly be much above forty.

"You are not elderly!" Chloe blurted out, starting to her feet in her agitation.

"And you are not Miss Bannister!" he retorted.

His frowning face swam before her eyes. Her limbs turned to water. "I believe I am going to faint," she faltered, and she did.

Sir Lionel leapt forward to catch the stranger as she crumpled. He laid her on a sofa and stood gazing down at her in dismay. What a damnable coil! Here he was alone with an unknown young woman who had fainted in his arms. Surely he was not so great a catch as to be persecuted by marriage-mad females determined to compromise him?

No, it was a genuine swoon, to judge by her pallor. She looked deuced uncomfortable, too, with her straw bonnet between her head and the cushion. He untied the blue ribbons and gently removed the offending hat. Her hair was escaping from its pins, which were more than likely sticking into her scalp, so he pulled out those he could see.

Fair tresses, soft and herb-scented, spilled over his hand. He hastily drew back.

She mumbled something, and her eyelids flickered. Thank heaven, she was coming round! Was there something else he could do for her? He'd heard of loosening the stays of a swooning female, but he drew the line there. Nor was he ready to call for servants with smelling-salts, to observe and spread word of this disgraceful incident.

He could provide a glass of wine, though, when she regained her senses. In the sideboard were decanters of his brother-in-law's best Madeira and Canary, ready to offer to favoured visitors. Lionel felt he could do with a glass himself. He drained one, and poured another for the girl.

As he set the glass on the small table by the sofa, he noted with relief that a little color was returning to her cheeks, and to a pair of delectably kissable lips. Studying her, he realized she was not after all a girl. Her face, even smoothed by unconsciousness, had a definite maturity, and her figure, though by no means plump, was pleasingly womanly. Who the devil was she, and what did she want?

And why had she announced herself as Miss Bannister?

Her eyelids flickered again. As though reading his mind, she flushed to the roots of her hair.

"Are you feeling better, ma'am?" Lionel asked. When she did not stir except to stiffen, he said severely, "I believe you are recovering, so quit shamming it."

Blue eyes flew open. "Oh no, I did not mean to. . . . I just could not think what to say. I feel such an utter ninnyhammer.'' She struggled to sit up. ''I have never fainted before in my life.''

He sprang forward to help her as the color again ebbed from her cheeks. ''Careful, now, or you will go off again. No, keep your feet up. I did not mean to suggest your swoon was not genuine. I am afraid I frightened you when I accused you of not being Miss Bannister.''

''I hope I am not quite so poor-spirited, though I was a little surprised.'' She gave him an uncertain smile. ''You see, I *am* Miss Bannister, but I realized at once that you expected to see my niece, Georgina, who is no doubt introduced thus here in Town.''

''You are Miss Georgina's Aunt Chloe?'' Lionel bowed. ''I am happy to make your acquaintance, ma'am. But if I did not overset you, then what on earth caused you to faint, for the first time in your life? Oh, I forgot.'' He reached for the glass of Madeira. ''Here, this wine will restore you.''

''Thank you, sir, but wine cannot be considered advisable on an empty stomach. I fear that must explain why I disgraced myself.''

''An empty stomach is no disgrace, unless you are on a reducing diet such as Byron is said to indulge in.'' He ran his eyes over her figure. ''You certainly have no need for such a ridiculous affectation as dining on potatoes and vinegar.''

''Heavens no. Is that what Lord Byron does?''

''So I hear. But if not that, then how came you to allow hunger to render you lightheaded?'' As he spoke, he crossed to the bell and rang to summon a servant. ''Lady Chingford has a famous chef—or do you not stay with the Chingfords?''

''Yes, for a few days, but I only arrived this afternoon and. . . .''

''Oh lord!'' Turning, he caught sight of her bare head and tumbled hair. ''Quick,'' he said, snatching up her bonnet from the floor, ''put this on and tuck your hair away.''

Miss Bannister obeyed with admirable promptness. At the same time she swung her legs down from the sofa, revealing a glimpse of a slender ankle. The butler arrived just too late to be shocked by the delightful sight.

"Tea for Miss Bannister, Doan," Lionel ordered, "with plenty of cakes and biscuits and such. And something more substantial for me, if you please. Cold meat and bread and butter will do very well. I am unaccountably sharp-set."

Unaccountable indeed, after his substantial luncheon, but the butler did not so much as blink. "Very good, sir," he said and departed.

Sitting down opposite his visitor, Lionel said with a smile, "The meat is for you, of course, ma'am, sweet stuff being not much better than wine in your state. My prevarication you may lay at your niece's door as she informed me the other day that ladies are supposed to be seen to eat like birds, whatever their appetites. But that was purely for Doan's benefit. I trust you will feel able to eat like a horse in my presence. If you have any qualms, tell me so and I shall close my eyes."

Her laugh was a trifle shaky. "I am a countrywoman, sir, and have not been used to consider a healthy appetite a disgrace."

"So I supposed, since Miss Georgina spoke with some scorn, and you had the upbringing of her, did you not? But that being so, why did you allow yourself to grow feeble with hunger?"

Miss Bannister blushed. "Because I am a fainthearted poltroon," she said in a constricted voice. "I traveled on the Mail coach and was too timid to press my claim to be served at the inns where we stopped. And then, when Lady Chingford offered me tea I was embarrassed to request food as well."

"Goosecap!" Her startled look gave him pause. "I beg your pardon, Miss Bannister, it is not for me to castigate your folly!"

Her lips twitched at this two-edged retraction. "Indeed it is not, Sir Lionel, especially when I have already acknowledged myself at fault. I fear you must think so weak-willed a creature sadly unfitted for the responsibility of raising children," she added wryly.

"How can I, when you have succeeded so admirably with Miss Georgina? She is charming, the only thoroughly unaffected young lady of my acquaintance."

For some reason his tribute dismayed her. Puzzled, he recalled that he still had no notion of what had brought Miss Chloe Bannister to call upon him, nor of the cause of her excessively odd greeting.

So shy as to starve rather than put herself forward, she had called, uninvited and unexpected, upon a stranger, and an unattached gentleman at that. To be sure she was beyond the age of missishness, but it must have taken some urgent errand to make her defy both propriety and her own nature.

Dying of curiosity, he was about to probe when the door opened and Doan appeared, followed by a footman bearing a large tray. Enquiries would have to wait.

Chloe was glad to postpone the questions she read in Sir Lionel's eyes. She owed him answers, and since she was here, though unintentionally, she might as well plead Georgina's case, but she still felt a trifle lightheaded.

He obviously admired Georgina immensely, she reflected as she munched her way through the plateful he set before her, contenting himself with tea and a biscuit. He had not chosen Georgie at random as one of many possible suitable brides. Of course Chloe was pleased and flattered that her niece was properly appreciated, but it was going to make her task much more difficult.

The difficulty was multiplied by the fact that he was by no means in his dotage, as Georgie had led her to expect. Studying him covertly over the rim of her teacup, she decided her first guess was right. Sir Lionel was about forty years of age— more than twice Georgie's eighteen, so she might be forgiven for thinking him ancient, especially in view of his prematurely greying hair. In the eyes of the world, however, it would be an eligible match, no food for scandal.

What a shame her niece allowed his years to outweigh his manifest qualities, Chloe thought. With every excuse for vexation, he had treated her with the utmost courtesy, kindness and good humor. And besides, the white at his temples made him look very distinguished.

"Do I pass inspection?"

"I beg your pardon? Oh, I beg your pardon! Did I stare?" Chloe felt her cheeks grow hot. Ridiculous! She had outgrown her tendency to blush years ago. "I was woolgathering, I fear." Stifling a yawn, she added apologetically, "I scarcely slept a wink on the Mail last night, and all of a sudden I am monstrous drowsy."

"Oh no you don't!" Sir Lionel's voice was stern, but he was smiling at her, the corners of his eyes crinkling in a most attractive fashion. "I want a round tale from you, Miss Chloe Bannister."

"How do you know my Christian name?"

"Your niece has spoken of you, generally wishing you were here to share her enjoyment of some sight or entertainment. She must be delighted that you have joined her at last."

"Only for a day or two," Chloe said wistfully, for the first time regretting the shortness of her stay. "Edgar—my brother—would not countenance my being away from Dene longer. Indeed, he did not like my coming at all, but. . . ." She hesitated.

"Ah, have we come at last to the meat of the matter? To what do I owe the pleasure of your company, ma'am?"

"Georgina wrote to me in great distress." Chloe poured herself another cup of tea so as to avoid looking at him. "She said her father meant to force her to marry a . . . an elderly gentleman."

"And Aunt Chloe bravely rushes to the rescue. But I don't

quite see . . . or do I? Aha! Am I correct in thinking *I* am the elderly gentleman in question?''

"Yes," she said miserably. She risked a peek at him. Unbelievably, he had a mischievous twinkle in his eyes.

"So Aunt Chloe, claiming to be unable to say boo to a goose, beards Sir Lion-el in his den!" He grinned. "I have been hoping for an opportunity to say that ever since I became Sir Lionel instead of plain Captain Tiverton."

"Captain?" she asked, diverted.

"I was in the Navy until a distant cousin died, quite recently, and I inherited the baronetcy. Miss Georgina failed to reveal my history? I am disappointed in her. Just think, she wasted the opportunity to inform you she was to wed the Ancient Mariner!"

"Oh dear," said Chloe helplessly, then their eyes met and they both burst out laughing.

"That's better," said Sir Lionel with satisfaction. "I was afraid you were going to cry, and how should I have explained it to Doan?"

"It's all very well, but I assure you my errand quite sinks my spirits, and I might have spared myself the worst if I had only stayed with my original plan."

"How so?"

"I ought to have talked to Georgie first, when doubtless I should have heard a more precise estimate of your age. Then I intended to tackle Edgar—a useless effort, I fear—before attempting to persuade you not to offer for her. You have not yet done so, have you?" she asked anxiously. "No, surely Georgie would have told me at once were she already betrothed."

"No, not yet," he assured her, with an enigmatical look. "How did your plan go astray?"

Rubbing heavy eyelids, she explained the course of events which had led her, quite inadvertently, to knock on his sister's front door. "So, you see, my mind was vulgarly fixed on food, though I daresay I was influenced also by an overwhelming hope of avoiding a scene with Edgar.''

"Ah, yes, the inimitable Edgar. And how, exactly, do you propose to persuade me not to propose to Miss Georgina?''

"I cannot quite recall,'' said Chloe, engaged in a struggle to keep her eyes from closing and her chin from sinking to her chest. "I don't suppose you would just tell me you have changed your mind? Then I could tell Edgar I shall go home tomorrow, and everyone will be satisfied.''

"I fear not. I am prepared to say I am open to persuasion, however. It is up to you to convince me.''

"Oh . . . yes . . . well. . . .'' Finding words, let alone reasoned arguments, was like wading through cotton-wool. "That is. . . .''

"Not now.'' There was an odd laugh in his voice. "You are three-quarters asleep. I shall drive you back to Chingford House, if you think you can stay awake long enough not to fall out of my curricle. Tomorrow I'll pick you up at two o'clock. We shall go for a drive and discuss Miss Georgie to your heart's content.''

"Thank you, sir.''

"But I want a promise from you: that you will not mention this matter to your brother as long as there is a chance I may make it unnecessary.''

"*Thank* you, sir,'' Chloe said fervently. "I mean, I promise, and thank you for listening to . . . for letting me . . . for. . . .''

"I'll send for the curricle,'' said Sir Lionel, laughing aloud.

" 'My dear Miss Bannister,' '' Georgina read aloud, perched on the end of her aunt's bed, " 'this is to remind you of your acceptance of my invitation to drive with me tomorrow. I shall pick you up at two.' ''

"I remember that very well,'' said Chloe crossly. Sleeping during the day always made her feel out of sorts. With her elbows she viciously prodded the pillow behind her into a more comfortable shape. "What I cannot recall is the drive back here from Albemarle Street, nor how I reached my bed."

"One of the footmen helped you upstairs, and Doro's abigail put you to bed."

"Oh." She had not exactly imagined that Sir Lionel might have performed that office, she assured herself.

"It's signed L. Tiverton," Georgie continued, "and then there is a postscript: 'Do not forget, you promised not to speak prematurely of a certain matter to a certain person.' How mysterious! I daresay he was afraid the person might read his note. What does he mean, Aunt Chloe?" She blenched. "You did not promise not to warn me he is going to offer?"

"Of course not, goose. He asked me to postpone any attempt to make your father listen to reason until he has made up his mind whether to ask for your hand."

"Then he is not set upon it?" Georgie asked joyfully. "Papa gave me to understand he is on the point of popping the question."

"Pray don't use such a vulgar phrase, you abominable girl."

"I was quoting Papa. Is Sir Lionel—or is he not—determined to marry me?"

"He says he is open to argument. That is why I am to drive with him, to present my arguments."

"How clever of you to think of approaching him, dearest Aunt. I was in the depths of despair when I wrote to you, ready to clutch at any straw, or I should never have imagined Papa might heed you. I must have been all about in my head. But Sir Lionel will not insist upon taking an unwilling bride. He is too good-natured by far."

"Good-natured!" Chloe exclaimed. "If you have such a high opinion of him, why are you so averse to marrying him?"

"I told you, he is *old.*"

"Not near so old as you led me to believe."

"I never said he was decrepit, or senile. But he is more than twice my age, more than old enough to be my father. Arabella Molesworth says he complained last winter of a twinge of rheumatism and her mama advised him to wear flannel next to the skin!''

''Disgraceful!''

''He is quite her favorite uncle, hers and her brothers', but only think how shocking to be married to a friend's *uncle!* Why, I should be Arabella's aunt, and she is a year older than me.''

''I do see what you mean, my dear. However, I doubt Sir Lionel can be counted upon to see things in quite the same light. He spoke very highly of you. I believe him to be deeply in love, or why did he not assure me immediately that he would not pursue his suit?''

''If he truly loves me,'' Georgie cried, ''he will not wish to make me unhappy. You must explain to him, Aunt Chloe. Tell him I like him very well as a friend, but . . . but my sentiments are not such as he must hope for in a wife.''

''Oh, Georgie, it is really very awkward. When I believed him a dotard of sixty or seventy, though I hesitated to confront a stranger at least I had arguments aplenty. Since you regard him as a friend, can you not inform him yourself of your sentiments?''

''Not before he makes me an offer. It would be shocking presumption.''

''I suppose so,'' Chloe agreed reluctantly.

''And if I wait until he proposes—he can hardly do so without Papa knowing about it, and if I refuse him Papa will never forgive me. He will shut me up at Dene forever, and not let me go even to the local assemblies, still less another London Season. He said so.''

''Oh dear!''

''He *never* changes his mind. You know he does not!'' Tears filled Georgie's eyes. ''I shall spend the rest of my life in disgrace, with Papa shouting at me, withering away into an old maid.''

''Like me,'' said Chloe through stiff lips.

''Dear Aunt, that's not what I meant!'' Georgie scrambled along the bed and put consoling arms around Chloe. ''You have not withered a bit, I swear it, and you have been a mother to us, to me and Doro and John and Bernard and Paul, so you don't count as an old maid. But you do see, don't you, that my only hope is for you to persuade Sir Lionel not to ask Papa for my hand?''

Chloe had brought with her only one evening gown, almost new, and her best, of course. When she wore it to a local assembly, she had been pleased with the simple pearl-grey crepe frock opening over a claret satin slip, attractive yet dignified. The pearl-grey toque made a statement, if only to herself, that her fair hair was as yet untouched by grey; its spray of dark red silk rosebuds seemed to reinforce the roses in her cheeks.

Not that anyone had noticed. She was just Georgina Bannister's chaperon, Squire Bannister's spinster sister, poor thing. Her role was to sit with the matrons and add her murmurs to their chatter of servants and receipts and childish ailments and their daughters' chances of making respectable marriages.

Lady Chingford noticed her dress. As Chloe entered the drawing room with Georgie and Dorothea, who had kindly collected her from her chamber, the countess turned from her conversation with her son, Lord Welch. A look of dismay crossed her face, quickly hidden.

She came forward to greet Chloe. ''My dear Miss Bannister, I trust you are quite recovered from your journey?''

''Yes, thank you, Lady Chingford,'' Chloe responded, hugely relieved that the countess had apparently not been informed of her afternoon's escapade. ''My room is most comfortable.''

"Excellent. I daresay, however, you will not wish to be gadding about this evening. We are bound for Lady Jersey's rout, always an exhausting experience."

Chloe obliged: "I shall be the better for an early night, I believe, ma'am."

"Very true. And tomorrow you will wish to visit a dressmaker, a tedious and tiring but unavoidable business." Her ladyship looked round as Edgar came in. "I have just been telling your sister, Mr. Bannister, that she will do well not to delay ordering the necessary gowns for her visit. The modistes are excessively busy at this time of year."

"New gowns?" Edgar stared. "Chloe don't need new gowns when she's off home in a day or two."

Lady Chingford fixed him with an incredulous eye. "A day or two, after traveling such a distance?" she said. "Perhaps I did not make myself clear. As Lady Welch's aunt, Miss Bannister is naturally welcome to stay at Chingford House as long as she chooses to remain in Town."

"By Jove, of course she is," Lord Welch put in, stepping forward. "Dorothea's always saying, ma'am, how she wishes you had come up with Miss Georgina instead of . . . er, hrumph . . . to enjoy the Season, that is."

Dorothea nodded, cast a nervous glance at her father, and scurried to the safety of her husband's side.

Edgar looked about to have an apoplectic fit. Before Chloe could soothe him with an assurance that she did not plan a long stay, Lord Chingford came in and dinner was announced.

Seated between the earl and his son, Chloe had to endure no worse than glares from Edgar during the meal. Afterwards, in the bustle of departure for Lady Jersey's rout, she was about to slip away when her brother cornered her.

"I don't know what sort of game you're—"

"Oh, Miss Bannister!" Lady Chingford interrupted. "Will ten o'clock be too early for you to accompany me to the modiste?"

"Why, no, ma'am, but—"

"One must be seen to appear at Lady Jersey's, but I have no intention of staying late, so ten o'clock in the morning will suit me very well. We shall avoid the rush."

"But indeed, there is no need!" said Chloe, flustered.

"There is every need," Lady Chingford proclaimed, her imperious gaze turned on Edgar, not Chloe.

"I daresay m'sister could do with a dress or two," he said grudgingly.

The countess gave him a pitying smile and said to Chloe, "Gentlemen have simply no notion of the demands of fashion. Ten o'clock it is. Good night, ma'am. Your arm, sir, if you please." And she whisked Edgar out to the carriage.

Chloe could not decide whether Lady Chingford's aim was to be kind to her, to put Edgar in his place, or just to alleviate the agony of seeing a relation-by-marriage badly dressed. Or all three. It hardly mattered. Edgar was bound to insist on her returning to Dene the day after tomorrow, and then he could cancel the order.

One or two gowns in the latest London mode to dazzle her neighbors with would have been nice, but she did not spend long in vain regrets. She fell asleep the moment her head touched the pillow.

Waking in the morning with a feeling of anticipation, Chloe at once recollected that she was to drive out with Sir Lionel that afternoon. She ought to be nervous. The drive was no pleasure excursion and baronet had every right to take exception to her meddling. Yet the prospect filled the day with sunshine.

In sudden alarm, she slipped out of bed, crossed to the window, and peeped out between the pink damask curtains. Yes, sunshine! For once the weather was cooperating.

As she opened the curtains, a maid came in.

"I'll do that, ma'am. Here's your tea, ma'am. Her ladyship's compliments and she'll send her dresser to help you dress. Was you wishful to take breakfast in bed, ma'am, or to go down?"

Breakfast in bed? What a treat! Chloe was very tempted, especially as it would enable her to avoid Edgar for a little longer. "What do the other ladies do?" she asked.

"They stays in bed after a party, ma'am, which is mostly, 'less Miss Georgina's meeting her friends for an early ride in Hyde Park."

So Chloe breakfasted in bed, lingering over a second cup of tea until the countess's tall, stately dresser arrived.

She suspected the woman had been sent at least partly to make sure she wore something which would not put Lady Chingford too much to the blush. A grim silence followed the opening of the wardrobe door. The contents offered very little choice. At last the abigail took out the blue cambric muslin walking dress, already miraculously washed, dried, and ironed.

Chloe could have told her it was the only possibility.

The visit to the dressmaker proved not half the ordeal she had expected. Lady Chingford, having complimented her on her sense of color, took the reins into her own hands as far as materials and modes were concerned.

"Living isolated in Lancashire, my dear Miss Bannister, you cannot be expected to know what is being worn this Season. I shall not take you to my own modiste, who is, I confess, a trifle expensive, but this woman has dressed Miss Georgina most adequately."

All Chloe had to do was stand still to be measured. She ventured a timid protest when she understood the vast quantity of gowns Lady Chingford considered indispensable. The countess assured her her brother was well able to stand the nonsense.

"I daresay you are unaware of the depths of Mr. Bannister's pockets," she said kindly. "Naturally Chingford enquired into his circumstances when first my son acquainted us with his desire to marry Dorothea. I was, of course, more concerned with her character. A pretty-behaved girl, and with sound principles, I believe, as is Miss Georgina. You are to be congratulated.''

Silenced, Chloe reminded herself that Edgar would be able to cancel the order long before more than two or three gowns were even cut out.

By the time they left the modiste, she was beginning to fret that she would be late for her appointment with Sir Lionel. She could not very well ask Lady Chingford to order her coachman to make haste, since she was not supposed to be acquainted with anyone in Town.

Then it dawned on her that Sir Lionel could not possibly pick her up at Chingford House without the whole household knowing—including Edgar. How on earth was she to explain?

All the way back in the comfortable barouche, she racked her brains in vain.

When they reached Chingford House, a smart landaulet with both hoods down stood before the door, a groom holding the horses. "Lady Molesworth's, I believe," said the countess, rather to Chloe's surprise, as she had expected Sir Lionel's curricle. At least he had not taken umbrage and left on finding her not at home, though it must be quite ten minutes past the hour. She hurried down from the barouche the moment the footman let down the step.

"I shall be happy to make you known to Lady Molesworth," said Lady Chingford, descending in a more leisurely manner. "A charming woman, and she is bringing out her youngest daughter this Season, so you will find common ground, no doubt."

Perhaps Sir Lionel had come, in his curricle as expected, and gone again. Chloe's heart sank. Her discourtesy in missing him must have offended his sister, and Chloe's dowdy appearance would confirm Lady Molesworth's disdain. Not that her opinion really mattered if Sir Lionel was equally offended.

On the other hand, if they both held Georgina's aunt in contempt, Sir Lionel might change his mind about wanting to marry Georgie. Somehow the notion did not cheer Chloe as it ought.

As she plodded up the steps and into the house after Lady Chingford, another horrid possibility struck her. Could Lady Molesworth have come to say her brother had belatedly recalled an earlier appointment—that is, had found something better to do with his afternoon than to drive out with a drab provincial spinster?

A distinctly peculiar spinster, Chloe thought, blushing as she remembered her freakish behavior of yesterday afternoon. She could not blame Sir Lionel if he wished never to set eyes on her again.

The butler murmured something to Lady Chingford and she nodded. As he moved towards the drawing-room door, her ladyship turned to Chloe and said with a significant look, "Not Lady Molesworth—her brother has called. Unless I am much mistaken, Sir Lionel is quite taken with Miss Georgina. An excellent match if she can catch him. Come, I shall make you known to him."

He had come! He had waited for her! Chloe's spirits soared.

But what would he say when they were introduced to each other as strangers? Between the butler, opening the door, and Lady Chingford, Chloe caught a glimpse of her brother. He looked smugly self-satisfied. His smugness would quickly turn to fury when he discovered she had already met Sir Lionel.

Altogether flustered, she turned a beseeching gaze on the baronet as he came forward to bow to Lady Chingford, though how he was to guess what she meant, she could not imagine.

Straightening from his bow, he smiled at her, and one eye flickered shut in a fleeting but unmistakable wink. Chloe scarcely heard a word of Lady Chingford's introduction.

Sir Lionel bowed again and said gravely, "How do you do, ma'am."

Curtsying, Chloe managed to stammer some sort of reply.

"Miss Georgina has often spoken of her aunt," he continued.

"I am happy to make your acquaintance. May I present my niece, Arabella Molesworth?"

A freckle-faced young lady with a friendly smile curtsied to Chloe. "Uncle Lionel has promised to take Georgie and me to Kensington Gardens to see the spring flowers," she said, then darted a quick glance at Sir Lionel. "Do say you will come too, ma'am."

"Yes, do come, Aunt Chloe." Georgina's eyes sparkled with mischief. "It is far too fine to be shut up indoors."

"Since you're here," said Edgar, "you might as well make yourself useful. Georgina ought to have a chaperon and I've better things to do with my time than looking at flowers."

Lady Chingford added her approval, which settled the matter. In no time, Chloe found herself seated beside Sir Lionel in the landaulet, facing the two girls. The groom mounted to the box and they set off.

Chloe hardly dared open her mouth for fear of saying the wrong thing. Obviously Sir Lionel had planned carefully to keep their prior acquaintance secret from Edgar and Lady Chingford—so very generous when Chloe was after all out to thwart him. He had enlisted Miss Molesworth in his plot, but did she know the reason for it, or even that her uncle was in love with her friend?

"I am so glad you arrived in time to come with us, ma'am," the girl said gaily. "When Georgie told me last night at Lady Jersey's that you had arrived in Town, Uncle Lionel suggested it would be just the thing. He had already offered to take us to Kensington Gardens, you see. Then you were not there when we reached Chingford House, and since Lady Welch was out, too, if you had not come back Mr. Bannister would have insisted on chaperoning Georgie."

"Cease, chatterbox," said Sir Lionel. "Must you put me to the blush?"

Miss Molesworth was mildly abashed. "I beg your pardon, ma'am, I quite forgot he is your brother. I did not mean. . . .

Only Mr. Bannister would have offered me his arm, and I have a great deal to say to Georgie. Besides, I don't see why she needs another chaperon when my uncle is escorting us, any more than if Papa took us somewhere.''

"Pray disregard my abominable niece, ma'am,'' Sir Lionel said ruefully to Chloe, "and consider yourself invited less to chaperon your niece than to shield me from their prattle!''

At this the girls went off into fits of giggles. Chloe was amazed at Georgie's cheerfulness in the presence of the gentleman she was determined to escape. She was so plainly on friendly terms with him, it seemed a great pity she could not bring herself to overlook the difference in age. She was not likely ever to find a more amiable husband.

Yet she did not want him, so her cheerfulness indicated she had great faith in her aunt's ability to extricate her from the threatened marriage. Chloe prayed she was up to the challenge.

Her companions soon distracted her from her worries, pointing out the sights as the landaulet drove down Piccadilly, past Devonshire House and Green Park. Just short of the toll gate they turned into Hyde Park, to roll along Rotten Row by the still, blue waters of the Serpentine, reflecting the azure sky. They came to the public part of the gardens of Kensington Palace. The carriage stopped in an avenue bordered with elms, their leaf-buds just breaking amidst clusters of winged seeds.

Not waiting for assistance, the girls bounced down to the gravel drive. Sir Lionel descended next, and turned to help Chloe. As he handed her down, he smiled at her and waved at their nieces, already several paces away, their heads together, chatting busily.

"You see, ma'am, with those two I have a choice of bombardment with babble or silent solitude. By combining our interview with their excursion, I have, I trust, pleased everyone.''

"I cannot tell you how grateful I am that you contrived to prevent my brother's finding out we had already met. I was dreading—''

"Oh ma'am!" Miss Molesworth turned back. "You will not mind if Georgie and I go ahead? We want to see everything, but pray do not trouble to follow us. If you grow fatigued, there are benches everywhere."

"You are a ninnyhammer, Bella!" Georgie said scornfully. "Looking at flowers will not tire Aunt Chloe. At home, at Dene, we walk for miles. I wager your uncle is more likely to grow tired."

"Wretches!" said Sir Lionel. "Go away, do, and leave us old folks in peace." As the laughing girls scampered off between two elms and down a walk, he continued, "I scarcely dare offer you my arm now, Miss Bannister, lest you should take it as a reflection upon your stamina."

"Thank you, sir, but I cannot think even my aged bones need support when the path appears perfectly smooth," Chloe said, trying not to sound regretful. She could not recall when last a gentleman had offered her his arm.

Side by side they strolled after Georgie and Miss Molesworth. "Not a single puddle to be seen," said Sir Lionel mournfully. "I shall not even be able to emulate the gallantry of that other Ancient Mariner, Sir Walter Raleigh."

"You have no cloak, and besides, I am no Queen Elizabeth." Chloe gazed down at the toes of her shoes as they appeared alternately from beneath the hem of her dress. "She would never have behaved as ill as I did yesterday. I must apologize for making such a cake of myself."

"You *were* ill, and besides, I am not one of those males who affect to despise sweet things."

For a moment she pondered this in silent perplexity. What did he mean? Could he possibly think she was sweet? No, "sweet" was a word for lovers, or children, not maiden aunts. He was just indulging a penchant for plays on words.

She peeked up at him, to find him looking down at her with an enigmatic light in his eyes. "Well, I assure you," she said hastily, "I am not usually so caperwitted nor so shockingly wanting in conduct. I am still mortified by the memory . . ." she hesitated. ". . . though I confess I have no very clear memory of exactly what I said to you."

"No wonder! By the time I took you home you were talking in your sleep."

"I did not . . . Surely I did not refer to you as the Ancient Mariner?"

"Good Lord no. I very much doubt whether even in your sleep you are capable of such a *want of conduct.*" He laughed. "No, that is an epithet I applied to myself. You merely informed me that Miss Georgina had described me to you as an elderly gentleman."

"Oh dear!" Chloe raised her hands to cover her hot cheeks. "It is true, I fear, but I might have put it more tactfully had I been more *compos mentis.* I did explain why I came to Town? Why I came to see you?"

"You did," he said dryly, "but do you know, I find I don't want to waste a fine afternoon in a beautiful garden with a charming companion discussing such a painful matter. Let us postpone it till a dull day."

"I cannot. My brother expects me to return to Dene tomorrow."

"Disappoint your brother's expectations for once."

"I dare not." She could not help the waver in her voice. "You cannot imagine what he is like when he is angry."

Sir Lionel's face hardened. For the first time, Chloe could picture him as a resolute, authoritative sea-captain, in command of his crew and responsible for his ship through calm and storm, peace and war.

Yet he spoke mildly, coaxing not commanding. "You have already braved Mr. Bannister's anger by coming to Town," he pointed out, "and I have freed you, at least for the present, from the confrontation over his daughter. Take the courage you had stored for that battle and use it instead to defy him as to the date of your departure."

"Courage! I only wish I possessed any."

"On that subject, you may recall, we have agreed to disagree. Well, will you do it?"

"I wish I could."

"Look at it this way," he said persuasively. "If you choose to avoid conflict over your wish to stay a few more days, you condemn yourself to an immediate fight over Miss Georgina's marital prospects, since you have not yet dissuaded me from offering."

"You will not let me try?"

Sir Lionel was adamant. "Not today."

Nonetheless, Chloe ventured to set before him the most formidable side of her predicament. "If it were only a question of when I am to leave London, I might nerve myself—as my nephews say—to face Edgar's wrath, though I would not encourage anyone to wager on my victory. But if I stay, what am I to do about the gowns?"

"Gowns?" he asked blankly.

"Georgie did not tell you that Lady Chingford took me to the dressmaker this morning? She has ordered *dozens* of new dresses for me, I cannot guess how many. I am sure they must be horridly expensive. If I go home to Dene, Edgar will be able to cancel the order and save a great deal of money."

"And if you stay?"

"I daresay I could cancel it anyway," Chloe said hesitantly, "but Lady Chingford was most insistent that I must have a new wardrobe for London. I should not wish to offend her when she has been so kind, and I doubt Edgar is willing to cross her."

Sir Lionel smiled. "Then your course is clear. Don't inform him in advance, but when the gowns and the bills begin to arrive, refer him to her ladyship. Now enough of that. You have not yet spared a glance for the flowers. I rely upon you to tell me what I am admiring, for we mariners are ignorant fellows when it comes to gardens."

Chloe had indeed been totally oblivious of her surroundings. She looked around now and exclaimed in delight. The extensive gardens were laid out in lawns, walks, and avenues, with statues and bowers here and there, and flowerbeds everywhere.

As they walked on, Chloe named the flowers they passed. Narcissus, hyacinths and stocks scented the air; violets and forget-me-nots clustered in shady nooks; marigolds blazed in the sun; pansies raised their funny faces; the pure white of candytuft offset clumps of vivid purple honesty.

"Honesty? Why so?"

"The seedcases look like silver coins. It is sometimes called penny-flower."

"Have you all these in your garden?"

"Many of them. The old-fashioned ones which grow easily. New varieties can be quite expensive and . . . and I have little time to cosset delicate plants."

"And your brother has no interest in flowers." Sir Lionel sounded angry.

"Edgar is more interested in the kitchen garden," Chloe admitted. "I thought all men were."

"A kitchen garden has its merits," he mused.

"I do not want to bore you with looking at flowers," she said anxiously.

"My dear Miss Bannister, I am enjoying myself no end. Look, those are tulips, are they not? What a splendid array."

The tulips stood stiffly ranked like soldiers of a score of regiments in multicolored uniforms, pink, scarlet, yellow, and white, glowing flame and a crimson so dark it was almost black. Beyond their orderly bed, daffodils sprawled in careless drifts across the lawns beneath the trees.

" 'I wandered lonely as a cloud,' " Sir Lionel quoted, " 'That floats on high o'er vales and hills.' "

Surprised, Chloe continued the verse. " 'When all at once I saw a crowd, A host, of golden daffodils.' "

With a smile, he jumped to the end: " 'And then my heart

with pleasure fills, And dances with the daffodils.' There is little to beat Mr. Wordsworth's poetry when one is far from home.''

"Coleridge's Ancient Mariner, and now Wordsworth! I should not have supposed sailors to be great readers.''

"It is not uncommon. I claim no particular merit. We have long hours at sea with little choice of occupation.''

"Like the long winter evenings at home in the North. Georgie and I read a great deal together." Chloe recalled her niece's conviction that gentlemen do not like intelligence in a wife. "Georgina is *very* clever," she said. "Indeed, in my opinion she would have profited more from proper schooling than my nephews.''

Sir Lionel confounded her. "It is a pity that society as presently constituted fails to utilize the talents of women. You taught your nieces yourself?''

"Yes, to the best of my poor ability. Though my father sent me to school when my mother died, we were taught little beyond housewifery and a few genteel accomplishments. What else I know I learned from my own reading, and I flatter myself I have passed on a love of books to Georgie, if not to Dorothea.''

"A love of books is the best gift any teacher can give. What do you like to read?''

They talked of books as they wandered on, until they came to the bank of the Long Water, the continuation of the Serpentine, where they found the girls.

Georgina and Miss Molesworth had made the acquaintance of a nursemaid and her two charges who were feeding the ducks and gulls. The young ladies had joined in and were having a wonderful time, grown-up decorum forgotten, tossing crusts to the voracious flock. They were a charming sight in their colored muslins beside the sparkling waters, surrounded by the mallard drakes with their glossy blue-green heads.

Charming also in their childlike delight, Chloe thought, hoping Sir Lionel would take note of Georgie's youthful behavior and decide he was too old for her.

He sighed. "I would not deprive them of their pleasure by begging a few crumbs," he said, "but we shall have to come again bringing our own supplies. So much for birdlike appetites—look at that seagull! Did you see? It caught the bread in midair. When I was a midshipman I used to throw scraps to the gulls. Beneath the dignity of a captain, alas."

"But not beneath the dignity of a baronet?" Chloe teasingly enquired.

"Good Lord, I'd forgotten. I suppose I ought not?" he said with a wistful air.

"Why not? As captain you had to uphold your authority, but if a baronet cannot please himself in so small a matter, what is the use of being one?"

"Well said, Miss Bannister!" Which was all very well, but did not in the least advance Georgie's cause. "When shall we come? Tomorrow morning? Do you ride?"

"Yes, but I don't think. . . ."

"Come now, ma'am," said Sir Lionel sternly, "if we don't meet, how are you to plead Miss Georgina's case?"

Georgie followed Chloe into her chamber and closed the door. "Thank you, dearest Aunt," she cried. "Was it horridly embarrassing?"

"Don't thank me too soon." Untying her bonnet ribbons, Chloe turned away to set it on the dressing table and tidy her hair.

In the looking-glass, she saw Georgie's face fall. "Why? What did Sir Lionel say? Oh, *don't* tell me he insists on marrying me?"

"No, no, my dear, nothing so definite. He said the day was too fine and the gardens too beautiful to address so painful a subject."

"Painful? Then he truly loves me?"

"So it appears. Does that change your mind?"

"Not a bit. It is very flattering, of course, but it does not cut a single day from his age." Tears filled Georgie's eyes. "Aunt Chloe, what shall I do?" she wailed. "A husband with grey hair and rheumatism!"

"Hush, love." Chloe put her arms around her sobbing niece. "Sir Lionel has not refused to listen to me, only postponed it. I am to ride with him tomorrow in Hyde Park. His brother-in-law has a mare he thinks will suit me. I only hope it is not a dreadful slug! Is it not fortunate that I brought my riding habit?"

Georgie's tears dried like magic. She went to the clothes-press, saying in a voice full of foreboding, "Let me see it." Taking out the plain, dark brown cloth habit, she spread it on the bed and shook her head. "Oh dear, it is even shabbier than I remembered. You cannot wear that to the park, Aunt Chloe. All the Fashionables ride and drive in Hyde Park."

"We shall go early in the morning," Chloe argued. "Sir Lionel said few people are about then. Besides, it is not as if I am an eligible young lady trying to fix his interest. Rather the reverse—if he should take me in dislike, perhaps he will change his mind about marrying you."

"No one could possibly take you in dislike," Georgie said absently. "I have some gold braid . . . yes, and Doro has a bonnet with gold ostrich plumes." Seizing the habit, she dashed from the room, calling, "Dorothea!"

With the aid of Dorothea's abigail and the sacrifice of Dorothea's bonnet, Chloe's well-worn riding dress and hat were rapidly refurbished. Chloe thought they looked quite smart, but Georgie was still dissatisfied as she hung it in the wardrobe.

"Did Lady Chingford bespeak a new habit for you?" she asked.

"I cannot recall. I was quite bewildered by the whole business, and that reminds me, what am I going to say to your papa?"

"Never mind Papa, you need a new riding dress. You will have far more use for it when you go home than any number of ball dresses."

"Ball dresses!" said Chloe, aghast. "Surely her ladyship did not order a ball dress for me!"

"I expect so. I have three, and she thinks it not half enough, but Papa put his foot down."

"You came to London to go to balls and dance. I do not need a ball dress! What *will* Edgar say?"

"Just tell him you dared not gainsay Lady Chingford. I am sure she expects you to relieve her by chaperoning me to balls while you are here. She says Doro is too young and far too scatterbrained to be a proper chaperon."

"I meant to go home tomorrow," Chloe moaned.

"You cannot," Georgina pointed out. "You are to ride with Sir Lionel and convince him I should make him a terrible wife."

"I told him you are clever, Georgie, but it did not deter him, I fear. He thinks women's brains are wasted for lack of proper education."

"Truly? What a shame he is so old!"

"If you married him, I daresay he would buy you any books you wished for. Are you beginning to change your mind?"

Georgie merely shook her head. "It is time to change for dinner," she said. "Maybe by tomorrow evening you will have one of your new gowns."

"Unless Edgar packs me off on the Lancashire stage," Chloe said pessimistically. She had not wanted to come to London, yet now she was here, she found she had no desire to leave.

"The dressmaker promised to deliver an evening gown for you tomorrow, Miss Bannister," said Lady Chingford at dinner. "We are engaged to attend a musicale, I believe. It will be the perfect occasion to make you known to a few people."

Edgar opened his mouth—and closed it again. His glare, however, promised Chloe a reckoning at no distant date.

To her relief, he went off to a ball with the rest after dinner. Georgie said he always watched her like a hawk, to make sure she did not encourage any gentleman he considered ineligible.

Chloe read for a while, a book about Brazil Georgie had borrowed from Hookham's Subscription Library, but she retired to bed long before the others came home. Snuffing her candle, she lay in the dark trying to plan what she was going to say to her brother.

With Edgar already in a state of simmering fury, he was going to boil over as soon as he got her alone, whatever she did, she thought with a shudder. No argument would save her from a tongue-lashing, though his awe of Lady Chingford might stop him actually ordering his sister to leave. But Chloe suspected she herself might depart in defiance of the countess's wishes rather than stay in defiance of her brother's.

Where was the courage Sir Lionel was so sure she possessed? He did not understand how intimidating Edgar could be. Boys were taught to be bold and fearless as surely as they were taught Latin and Greek. Girls learned needlework and to be meek and compliant. At an age when Chloe had barely set the last stitch in her first sampler, Sir Lionel had been a midshipman sailing around the world.

Drowsily she wondered whether he had ever been to Brazil. She must ask him. She would like to hear about his adventures.

"I don't know how adventurous a rider you are, Miss Bannister," said Sir Lionel, gesturing to the street where a groom held three horses, "but Molesworth assures me the mare is possessed of both a docile nature and a fair turn of speed. I hope you will be satisfied."

"She sounds ideal." Chloe approached the pretty dapple-grey mare with a white blaze on her nose. Offering her a lump of sugar, she asked the groom, "What is her name?"

"Opal, ma'am."

"She has superb shoulders and quarters."

The man nodded approving agreement. "But a tad long in the back, ma'am."

"A trifle, perhaps." She rubbed Opal's nose in apology for this criticism.

"Will she do?" Sir Lionel asked. "We sailors are notorious for our ignorance of horses."

"A pretty mount with a pretty name," said Chloe, laughing as she took Opal's reins from the groom. "What more can a lady demand?"

"I can see your expectations are higher! She was purchased for my niece, but Arabella is nervous of horses and only rides when not to do so would mean missing an outdoor party."

The groom grinned. "That's right, sir."

"What a shame! Well, Opal, shall we try your paces?"

Sir Lionel lifted Chloe into the sidesaddle. The firm clasp of his hands at her waist flustered her, and of course Opal picked up her perturbation. The mare sidestepped and tossed her head, but Chloe quickly curbed and soothed her.

She smiled down at Sir Lionel, who looked anxious. "She is a dear. We shall do very well."

"Sure?"

"Quite sure."

He mounted his roan gelding and they set off for Hyde Park through the busy streets. After his remark about sailors and horses, Chloe watched him with some concern at first. However, he seemed perfectly at home in the saddle, though he sat rather more slouched than a purist might approve.

"Do I pass muster?" he enquired with a grin.

"I should have to see you in the hunting field before I pronounce an opinion." She glanced back at the groom, following a few paces to the rear. "However, I doubt you need him to pick you up when you fall, and I do not."

"My sister assures me a groom in attendance is *de rigueur* when a gentleman rides out with a lady otherwise unaccompanied."

"With a young lady, certainly, but I am of an age to *be* not to *need* a chaperon."

"You will have to take that up with Elizabeth," he said, a disturbing glint in his eye. "I am her younger brother, you see. She finds it impossible to accept that I am now elderly, so to her you appear scarcely mature."

"Humbug! I have not even had the pleasure of meeting Lady Molesworth."

"A deficiency I hope to remedy soon. Do you ride a great deal at home?"

"Yes, quite often. Two of Edgar's farms are up on the moors and they are frequently snow-bound for a month or two in the winter, accessible only on horseback. And at all seasons our lanes are liable to be hock-deep in mud. I had rather ride than get stuck in the gig and have to wait for someone to come along and push it out."

"You drive too?"

"Oh yes. For many errands the gig is more convenient than going on horseback."

Under his interested questioning, Chloe found herself telling him about her life in Lancashire: visiting the tenants and taking care of their needs; overseeing her brother's household and his poultry-yard and dairy; shopping in the village with occasional trips to Lancaster or even Manchester.

"I am amazed you ever found time to mother your nieces and nephews," said Sir Lionel, "still less to grow flowers and to read."

"From what little I have seen of London, life moves more slowly in the countryside."

"I confess I have not yet quite found my sea-legs in the

tidal flow of country life. London is amusing for a month or two, though I suspect the constant round of entertainment will pall after a while. Both are distinctly different from life on a warship, which tends to be long periods almost 'As idle as a painted ship upon a painted ocean,' rudely interrupted now and then by tempests and battles.''

''And calls at foreign ports,'' Chloe said eagerly. ''You must have seen a great many interesting places.''

''What, you don't want to hear about the battles? Everyone demands to hear about the battles.''

''Do you wish to talk about them?''

''Not in the least,'' he said, sobering. ''They are best forgotten.''

''I had much rather hear about your travels. Have you ever been to Brazil? I have been reading about it.''

Sir Lionel's ship had been one of those transporting the Portuguese royal family and their entourage to Brazil when they fled from Napoleon's invasion of Portugal. Chloe was fascinated by his stories of the people and places. Suspended only for a brief, exhilarating gallop in the nearly empty park, the subject lasted until they returned to Chingford House.''

''We never fed the ducks,'' Chloe exclaimed as he helped her dismount.

''To tell the truth,'' Sir Lionel admitted, ''I forgot to bring bread. I've been hoping you would not ask.''

''Oh dear,'' gasped Chloe, a much worse omission dawning on her. ''I have not said a single word about Georgie!''

''We shall simply have to ride again tomorrow.''

''Yes, I suppose so,'' she said doubtfully, stroking Opal's nose.

''Then you *are* staying?'' he asked with a smile.

''At least until tomorrow. Lady Chingford wishes me to go to a musicale with them tonight.''

''Miss Georgina mentioned the musicale when I danced with

her last night. I shall be there. Your brother raised no objection to your attending?''

"He will not go against Lady Chingford's express wishes." She bit her lip. "But I am certain he is waiting for me inside right now, to rake me over the coals.''

"You can handle him," said Sir Lionel confidently.

"Where the devil have you been?" roared Edgar. "You knew damn well I wanted to see you.''

"Good morning, Edgar," Chloe said with an outward composure she was far from feeling. Refusing to stand before him like a naughty child, she crossed to a chair and sat down. "I did not know you especially wished to speak to me this morning, and if I had, I did not know at what time you would come down. Is there something particular you wish to say?''

He stalked across the room and stood towering over her, his ruddy face distorted in a fearsome scowl. She forced herself not to quail visibly. Sir Lionel trusted her to stand up to him.

"First tell me where you disappeared to at an ungodly hour of the morning.''

"It was much later than we rise at home at this time of year," Chloe pointed out, hastily adding, as his cheeks purpled, "Sir Lionel Tiverton invited me to ride with him.''

Edgar looked flabbergasted. "You went riding with Tiverton?" he asked incredulously.

"I thought you would not wish me to offend him by refusing, since, I gather, you expect him to make an offer.''

"For Georgina, not you! Why the deuce would he want to ride with an ape-leader?''

What would he do if she told him her real reason? The mind boggled. He might literally explode! Chloe felt a smile forming on her face and quickly wiped it away.

A smile? When Edgar loomed over her, swollen with rage? Her mind boggled again. "I *am* Georgie's aunt," she reminded him. "No doubt Sir Lionel wishes to become better acquainted with her family, and perhaps to ingratiate himself."

"Can't see why he'd want to turn *you* up sweet," Edgar grunted. "You've got no say in the matter."

"How should he be aware of my lack of influence?" Chloe prevaricated.

"Daresay he's not," her brother grudgingly conceded. "Be damned if he knew of your existence before you turned up. And you still haven't explained that!"

"Georgie mentioned in her last letter that you were wearying of the trouble of escorting her to the Season's entertainments. It is a task I am very well able to take off your hands."

"True enough, though you'd no business quitting Dene without asking leave."

"Letters do go astray." True enough—if irrelevant since she had not written for permission. Permission! She was his sister, not his servant, and an old maid, not a young maiden. Chloe was surprised to find herself quite indignant.

"What's more, you don't need fancy gowns to chaperon Georgie," Edgar went on, his ire reviving. "Spending my hard-earned blunt on fal-lals and fripperies as if I hadn't already got the expense of catching Georgie a husband to match her sister's. Not that she can expect a lord! She'll never match Dorothea's looks, so she'll just have to take what she can get. But as for springing for new dresses for you, Chloe, you're too old for anyone to care what you're wearing."

"The new dresses were Lady Chingford's notion, not mine," said Chloe, trying to hide her hurt. She knew Edgar was right, but need he put it so bluntly? "Her ladyship, at least, cares what I wear, if only so I do not disgrace her and Doro. I fear I had not the courage to argue with her, but doubtless you will know how to explain that you intend to revoke her order."

"Well . . . er. . . ." Edgar blenched and tugged on his neck-cloth as if suddenly aware it was tied too tight around his bull neck. "I didn't mean you're to countermand her, you looby," he blustered. "A fine return that would be for her ladyship's condescension in inviting Georgie for the Season. Sometimes I wonder if you haven't got more hair than wit. If anything makes Lady Chingford take snuff, I'll know who's to blame!"

He flung from the room, leaving Chloe limp but triumphant.

The evening gown ordered by Lady Chingford arrived just in time for Chloe to change into it for dinner. An overdress of dark blue British net fell from the high, brief bodice to reveal several inches of the pale blue satin slip, set all around with white silk roses. Posies of tiny white rosebuds adorned the short, puffed sleeves, and a matching wreath ringed the small turban of blue crape.

Her ladyship's dresser condescended to arrange Chloe's fair hair in a topknot, with curls over her forehead and ears. Pinning on the turban, the woman looked Chloe up and down.

"Gloves, madam?" she said. "Slippers?"

Georgina had foreseen the need and consulted her sister. Dorothea, whose pin-money—excluding modiste's bills—for a month exceeded her aunt's dress allowance for an entire year, was only too delighted to oblige. The girls had dragged Chloe out to the shops that afternoon.

White kid slippers and elbow-length gloves, even half a dozen pair of silk stockings, Chloe gratefully accepted. Doro was sadly disappointed when she was not permitted to purchase for her aunt a charming fan painted with cherry-blossoms in the Chinese fashion, and a shawl of the softest cashmere.

"I shall buy them for myself," she had said, "and you shall borrow them, Aunt Chloe."

With the addition of her gold chain and cameo pendant, Chloe wanted for nothing.

"I believe her ladyship will be satisfied," the dresser deigned to admit.

Chloe stared at herself in the looking-glass. She was really quite smart, fine enough not to be discomfited by the fashionable matrons to whom Lady Chingford proposed to present her. Lady Molesworth would not be able to disdain her as a provincial dowd.

Presumably Lady Molesworth was going to attend the musicale, since Georgie expected to meet her daughter, and her brother had told Chloe he would be there. She could not wait to tell Sir Lionel about her passage at arms with Edgar.

Edgar cornered her in the drawing room before dinner. After a brief animadversion on the extravagance of her dress, he apprised her of the names of the ineligible young gentlemen she was to prevent Georgina from encouraging.

"I suppose I must trust you to judge any new acquaintances," he said discontentedly. "If she should contrive to attract some greater prize than Tiverton, I'll have to decide whether a bird in the hand is worth two in the bush."

"You are so certain of Sir Lionel?" Chloe asked.

"Of course I am, devil take it! Everyone says he's looking for a wife—stands to reason, he needs an heir now he's inherited the baronetcy—and he don't spend half as much time with any other female. And why else should he bother to do the pretty to you?"

"Yes, of course," she murmured sadly.

"So keep what wits you have about you and tell me if any better prospect looks set to bite. But don't be taken in by a title. There's many a lord living on the edge of the River Tick. Understand?"

"Yes, Edgar."

Satisfied, he went off to give Georgina her instructions. Chloe promptly resolved to report to him at once any young, amiable lord who so much as exchanged a word with her niece—and to suppress any eligible who was disagreeable or over the age of thirty.

After dinner, Edgar went off to his club. Lord Welch and Dorothea had dined out with friends, so the carriage had plenty of room for the Chingfords and Chloe and Georgina. The musicale was held at a house just around the corner, but Georgie had explained to her aunt that one simply did not walk to an evening engagement.

They were shown into a large saloon, formed by two apartments thrown into one. At one end was a dais with a pianoforte; sofas and easy-chairs stood around the walls and the centre was filled with rows of straight chairs, many already occupied.

The first person Chloe noticed was Sir Lionel. He must have been watching for Georgina, for he came towards them at once, before they had even greeted their hostess. His face was alight with pleasure.

Chloe's breath caught in her throat. How could Georgie fail to succumb to such a devastatingly attractive gentleman? And one so obviously delighted to see her!

Gathering her scattered wits as Lady Chingford presented her to the hostess, Chloe curtsied and received a nod and a smile in return. Then Sir Lionel was beside them, bowing to the Chingfords, greeting Georgina, and turning to Chloe as her niece whisked off to join Arabella and another girl.

"Are you fond of music, Miss Bannister?" he asked.

"Yes, sir, though I have had no opportunity to hear any but the band at our local assemblies and the amateur performances of neighbors' daughters."

He grimaced, his dark eyes twinkling down at her. "That is what I expected this evening. A horrid penance! But it seems we are in for a treat. Our gracious hostess has secured the services of Muzio Clementi."

"Clementi? The name is familiar," said Chloe, feeling sadly ignorant.

"No doubt you have seen it on printed music. Signor Clementi is a publisher, as well as a composer, piano-builder, teacher, and a very fine pianist. I believe you will be impressed. But come, we have a little time to spare. May I make you known to my sister, Lady Molesworth?"

"I shall be happy to make her acquaintance." Chloe laid her hand on his proffered arm. Another proof of his devotion to Georgina—he wanted his family to meet hers. Not to mention that her presence must be the reason he came to a musicale he had originally regarded as "a horrid penance."

He was saying something in a low voice.

"I beg your pardon?" she said in confusion.

"This is your first *ton* party, is it not? I daresay you find it as overwhelming as I did my first. I was just begging you to excuse Elizabeth if she does not rise to meet you. She is not in the most robust of health."

"I am sorry to hear it, sir."

Elizabeth Molesworth was on one of the sofas at the side, sitting very upright with a cushion at her back. Approaching on Sir Lionel's arm, Chloe picked her out at once, for Lady Molesworth had her brother's prematurely greying hair. In contrast, despite lines of pain, her face was youthful, her expression lively and interested.

She patted the sofa beside her. "I expect Lionel has told you about my wretched back, Miss Bannister," she said. "Do pray sit down so I need not crane my neck. I have been looking forward to meeting you. Go away, Lion, and see what Arabella is up to. Miss Bannister and I mean to have a comfortable cose."

"Only until the music starts," he warned with a smile, accepting his dismissal in good part.

Or rather, accepting his sister's permission to join Georgina, Chloe realized.

"Lionel is very fond of music," said Lady Molesworth. "He has become the chief prop and stay of the Philharmonic Society, I vow."

"Sir Lionel seemed very pleased that Mr. Clementi is to play tonight."

"Quite enraptured!" she agreed, laughing. "It is delightful to see how he blooms since leaving the sea, now he has the opportunity to enjoy the many activities for so long unavailable to him. But I would not have you suppose he has no time for his family. He has been an indispensable help to me in escorting Arabella about, for her father is much occupied with government business, and I find it necessary to limit myself, I fear."

"How very distressing for you, ma'am, and for your daughter."

"She goes on well enough, having a fortunate disposition to be contented. But please, do call me Elizabeth, for I am sure we are going to be the greatest friends, like Arabella and your Georgina. I must tell you how glad I am that they are so often together. Arabella is a sad scatterbrain and much in need of a leavening of Georgina's common sense. What, Lion, back already?"

"They are opening the pianoforte." Sir Lionel waved towards the dais. "I don't want to miss a note."

Chloe rose.

"Will you not sit with me?" exclaimed Elizabeth.

"I ought to find Georgina."

"The girls will come to no harm. It is not a public concert, after all, and dashing young blades avoid musical evenings like the plague," Elizabeth assured her with a smile.

So Chloe found herself seated between her new friend and Sir Lionel as their hostess led an elderly gentleman onto the dais.

"We are honored tonight by the presence of Signor Muzio Clementi," she announced to a burst of clapping. "Signor Clementi will begin his recital with one of his own compositions."

Chloe was convinced nothing could distract her from the presence of Sir Lionel so close beside her, his sleeve brushing her arm. Yet after the first few notes she was conscious only of music. The flood of glorious sound filled her head, driving out all else.

She emerged from her daze too late to join in the applause. Sir Lionel was regarding her with a slight smile.

"There is a concert of the Philharmonic Society next week," he said. "Will you go with me?"

"Oh, I. . . ."

"And Miss Georgina, of course. You are going to stay in Town?"

"I think so. I want to tell you about Edgar—"

But Arabella Molesworth came over with Georgie to say hello, and as she turned away to ask after her mama's comfort, Lady Chingford arrived. The countess bore Chloe off to be introduced as "my daughter-in-law's aunt" to a bewildering number of ladies and gentlemen.

"Excellent," said Lady Chingford as people began to drift back to their seats. "Now you may take Miss Georgina about with no need for me or Dorothea to accompany you. I am glad you came to Town, Miss Bannister, and I cannot imagine why your brother did not send you in the first place. So much more suitable!"

Chloe wondered whether she ought to go and sit with Lady Chingford or return to her former seat. She did not want to force herself upon Elizabeth Molesworth, who, for all her professions of friendship, was a very new acquaintance. Nor did she want to offend her by deserting her if she was expected. As she dithered, feeling rather lost, Sir Lionel appeared at her side.

"Come, Miss Bannister, you know I shall never forgive you if you are not settled before Signor Clementi reappears."

"I should never forgive myself, sir," she retorted with a grateful smile, and returned with him to the sofa.

The second half of the concert was if anything better than the first. Clementi played a sonata by Mozart, and then, as an encore, two nocturnes written by his own pupil, John Field.

Afterwards there was supper, with no chance of private conversation. Chloe listened with interest to the talk of the new, romantic style of composition represented by Field's work. Several people spoke of the Philharmonic Society concert next week, where a new symphony by Beethoven was to be played as well as an old one of Haydn's.

"I should very much like to attend the concert," she said shyly to Sir Lionel when he took his leave.

"Splendid. I shall get half a dozen tickets and we'll make up a party. May I still hope to see you tomorrow morning, or is an early ride too much to expect after a late night?"

"Oh no, not at all. I believe fresh air and exercise will help me to put the impressions of tonight in perspective."

"Opal will be delighted, and I look forward to hearing about your skirmish with your brother. Until tomorrow, Miss Bannister."

His sister and Arabella came up then, Elizabeth leaning heavily on her daughter's arm. "We have had no chance for a proper talk," she said. "Will you and Georgina take tea with us tomorrow afternoon, Chloe, if you are not otherwise engaged?"

"Gladly, if you are sure we shall not disrupt your rest?"

"Nothing suits me better than to have a few friends favor me with a call. We shall expect you tomorrow at four."

She took her brother's arm and he supported her effortful steps from the room. Chloe watched, thinking how wonderful it would be to have a brother like Sir Lionel instead of the tyrannical Edgar.

Not until she snuffed her candle and settled for sleep did she realize that once again she had failed to say so much as a word on Georgie's behalf. There had been no opportunity, she excused herself. But tomorrow she simply must address the subject before she told Sir Lionel about the ousting of Edgar.

Opal recognized Chloe and greeted her with a happy whicker.

"Did I not say she would be delighted to see you?" said Sir Lionel.

"She recalls the sugar," Chloe said, laughing as she gave the mare another lump.

Again Sir Lionel lifted her into the saddle, but this time she was prepared for the curious shiver that shot through her. She controlled her reaction, and Opal stood firm.

As he passed on his way to his roan, the mare turned her head to nuzzle at the bulging pocket of his riding coat.

"That's for the ducks," he told her severely. "I remembered to bring bread today," he said to Chloe. "I only hope it will not rain and cut short our ride."

Surprised, she looked up at the sky, hung with a pall of grey. For some reason she had had a vague impression that the sun was shining. "It is quite warm," she said quickly, afraid he might decide not to go at all. "I don't mind a wetting, and surely a sailor must be inured to being soaked through."

" 'Water, water, everywhere,' " he intoned, mounting. As they set off for the park, followed by the groom, he went on, " 'Nor any drop to drink.' Probably Coleridge's best known lines, yet elsewhere in the same poem he writes charmingly of 'merry minstrelsy' and music like an angel's song."

His quoting from *The Rime of the Ancient Mariner* gave Chloe the perfect opening to speak of Georgina, but instead she found herself saying passionately, "How I wish we had music at home like last night's! I shall go to as many concerts as possible while I am here, for I shall never have another chance."

"If you succeed in persuading me not to marry Miss Georgina, you will have to come to London next year to find her a husband."

She shook her head. "No, Edgar will not permit her another Season if she wastes this one by refusing your offer. He wants her wed by the end of June, or, he swears, she shall never attend even our local assemblies again. He threatens her with dwindling into spinsterhood, like her aunt." Chloe wanted to smile, to show she did not care, but she was afraid it would be a pitiful effort. She stared straight ahead, between Opal's ears.

"Like her aunt!" Sir Lionel's voice was oddly constricted, as if he were suppressing some violent emotion. "And are you so content with your lot that you consider spinsterhood a better fate for your niece than marriage to me? Or am I so objectionable as a husband that any fate would be better?"

"No! Oh no!" she cried, turning to him, aghast. "I . . . She likes you very well, and I am convinced you would be a wonderful husband, if it were not. . . ."

"That I am so old?" he said wryly.

"That Georgie is so much younger than you."

"Then you do not consider me past all hope of finding an acquiescent bride?"

"Of course not," Chloe assured him, though her heart sank at the idea of his looking elsewhere for a wife should he decide to relinquish Georgina. "There are sure to be many young ladies perfectly willing to overlook the difference in age in view of your . . . your. . . ."

"My title and my fortune?"

"I was going to say, your manifest qualities and virtues," she replied, blushing.

Sir Lionel smiled. "But you hesitated to utter such a sweeping encomium after so short an acquaintance."

"No, it just sounded so horridly fulsome. I feel as if I have known you forever. Heavens, here we are at the park already. Opal and I are dying for a run." She urged the mare forward, glad of an excuse to flee her embarrassment.

His roan soon matched Opal's stride. Side by side they galloped across the grass, slowed to a canter, then a trot, and stopped beside the Serpentine. Chloe slipped down from the saddle before Sir Lionel had time to dismount and come to help her.

The groom held the horses while they fed the ducks and screeching seagulls. Laughing over the birds' antics, Chloe had time to recover her composure, and she accepted with equanimity Sir Lionel's aid in remounting. She had a sudden horror of becoming one of those old maids who take the slightest attention from an attractive man as a sign of fond interest.

Her only business with Sir Lionel, she reminded herself firmly, was Georgie's business. She had made a start already; perhaps she could finish it off on the way home. Maybe she should stress Georgina's fear of her father?

"Edgar is always pigheaded and often intimidating," she began.

"Ah yes, you were going to tell me how you prevailed upon him to agree to your staying."

"I offered to take over the tiresome duty of chaperoning Georgina and making sure she does not encourage the wrong beaux. He could not deny that he wearied of the sort of parties young ladies must attend to meet eligible *partis.*"

Sir Lionel laughed. "So you won by undermining his position. Excellent strategy."

"Perhaps, but it was a most unpleasant skirmish, and he is still angry with me for coming. I cannot be comfortable. If you will just tell me you don't mean to offer for Georgie, I can go home and escape his resentment."

"You have not yet explained why you think the difference in age is an insuperable obstacle to our happiness together." He looked up at the sky, then held out his hand, palm up. At once dark spots appeared on his York tan glove. "And this is no time for discussion! If I'm not mistaken we are in for a cloudburst."

"I felt a few drops on my face," Chloe admitted.

They cantered out of Hyde Park and trotted through the streets as the spitting rain became a downpour. By the time they reached Chingford House, Chloe was soaked to the skin.

"Promise me you will change your clothes at once," said Sir Lionel, lifting her down and escorting her to the front door.

"I promise, but I also promise you need not fear, I shall take no ill."

"No, I don't suppose you will," he said lightly. "You are a remarkable woman, Miss Chloe Bannister."

Remarkable? Chloe pondered the word as she dripped up the stairs. It was two-edged, she decided. Sir Lionel might conceivably mean that she was admirable, or—far more likely—that she was simply eccentric. Eccentricity was one of the labels people hung on old maids.

Sadly, she turned her mind to how she was to explain to Georgie why she still had no final answer.

Days passed, weeks slipped by, and still Sir Lionel proved elusive. That is, he evaded the issue of his proposal to Georgina, not her presence, nor Chloe's.

He invited them to the theater, and whenever they went with a different party, he came to their box in the interval. He procured tickets for every concert, accompanying Chloe even when Georgina chose not to attend.

Escorted by Sir Lionel, Chloe with Georgina and Arabella saw all the sights of the city, from wild beasts at the Tower to steam boats on the Thames, from Lord Elgin's marbles to a balloon ascension.

He took them to Astley's Amphitheatre. "The girls will enjoy the show," he told Chloe tolerantly. But as she marveled at the amazing feats of the bareback riders and laughed at the tricks of the clowns, she noticed that he was enjoying himself just as much as the girls were, and as she was.

Sir Lionel was young in spirit, she thought, recalling his pleasure in tossing crusts to the gulls. How could Georgie resist him?

Besides these particular occasions, the baronet rarely failed to turn up at whatever evening entertainment they graced with their presence. At first Chloe was nervous of attending balls and routs without Lady Chingford. The toplofty ladies of the countess's circle graciously acknowledged her presence but remained aloof. Georgina's friends and admirers, though polite and sometimes even attentive, were too young to be a support to Chloe. To them she was a chaperon, there to sustain Georgie, too old to be in need of succor herself.

The Welches' friends were somewhat closer in age. Doro and her husband were a popular couple with a large acquaintance, but their set, however courteous, had little in common with Dorothea's aunt.

It was through Elizabeth Molesworth that Chloe met the ladies she came to look for on arriving at an assembly, those who looked out for her, who invited her to sit with them. Elizabeth rarely attended evening parties, but her invitation to tea and a private cose was followed by many more, to small, intimate gatherings of unpretentious people.

Elizabeth's friends were her brother's friends, so it was hardly surprising that Chloe saw as much of Sir Lionel at balls as did Georgie. Or more. Etiquette dictated that he must not stand up with Georgie or even with his niece more than twice in an evening, and he asked no other young ladies to partner him.

He did, however, ask Chloe.

At her third ball, already she felt quite at home sitting among a group of matrons with marriageable daughters. Sir Lionel came up to her, bowed, and begged for the pleasure of the next dance.

"I cannot!" she said, disconcerted. "You know I am a chaperon, a double chaperon since I promised your sister to look out for Arabella."

"Ladies," he appealed to her neighbors, "is there any rule to say that chaperons may not take to the floor?"

"If I could only winkle my husband out of the cardroom!" sighed one, laughing.

"Provided one's charge is safe," said another.

"Miss Georgina can scarce be safer than standing up with her brother-in-law, as she is at this moment, and Arabella is with her cousin. Come, Miss Bannister, I promise not to step on your toes. We sailors have our faults but we are a sure-footed breed."

"Georgie has never complained of your stepping on her toes," Chloe admitted.

"She would have if I had." He held out a commanding hand.

"Go along, Miss Bannister," urged one of the others. "If the girls return before you, we shall keep an eye on them."

Chloe gave in to her own inclination. She took Sir Lionel's arm and they joined a set for a country dance.

"Do you not dance at home, at the assemblies there?" he asked.

"Yes, occasionally, but there I am among friends."

"I had hoped you might regard me as a friend by now."

"Oh, I do. I meant, among people I have known all my life."

"There must be advantages to being so well acquainted with all one's neighbors."

"And disadvantages, I assure you!" Chloe said with a smile. "Everyone expects to know everyone else's business. But on the whole we rub on very well."

"Since I inherited my country estate, I have failed abysmally to fathom the rural temperament," said Sir Lionel ruefully.

"You have only owned the place a short time, have you not? Country people, gentry and tenantry alike, are slow to accept newcomers, especially those unfamiliar with the country way of life. Where is your house?"

"In Warwickshire."

As the movements of the dance allowed, they talked of his new home. It sounded like a comfortable, well-kept manor, not very different from Dene. Reading between his words Chloe suspected Sir Lionel, used to the companionship of his fellow-officers, had found his few months there a lonely time. No wonder he was looking for a wife to keep him company and had fixed upon a country girl who would know how to go on with his neighbors.

But Georgina remained adamant: Sir Lionel was amiable, obliging, even charming, but he was too old.

Georgie continued to stand up with the baronet twice at every ball so that she could tell her father she had. After the first time, he also requested a dance with Chloe at every ball, no doubt because a third with Georgie was not permitted. However, they seldom spoke of Georgina, and he always turned the subject if Chloe tried to explain her niece's feelings.

Georgie was quite satisfied, sure that his silence meant he would not press his suit where it was not wanted. Chloe began to despair, and to wonder why he had not yet declared himself. Edgar grew impatient.

April turned into May. The days grew longer and warmer. Arabella and Georgina between them teased Sir Lionel into planning a picnic at Richmond.

The sun shone, the birds sang in the nearby woods, the grass was bright with buttercups and daisies. Equally bright, Lionel's guests, seated on rugs and cushions, were making deep inroads into the feast provided by Gunter's. Moving from group to group, he observed with pleasure the disappearance of hams and pies, cold chicken and thin-sliced sirloin, salads and confections. Lemonade and ale vanished by the gallon.

The fresh air sparked the hunger of even those ladies who generally claimed to eat like birds, he noted. Perhaps the sight of blackbirds and thrushes dashing about to feed their families had its effect.

On all but Chloe. With concern he saw that her plate was almost as full as when he had handed it to her. He had not been able to stay beside her, both because he was host and because her brother was one of his guests. He did not want to draw down Bannister's wrath upon her head.

She had been subdued lately, retreating somewhat into the shell from which Lionel thought he had coaxed her. Was she unwell? Or had Bannister found out that she spent so much time with him to thwart, not to forward the match with Georgina?

That situation could not be drawn out much longer. Perhaps the moment had come for a *dénouement,* but Lionel found himself still very much unsure of the outcome.

He ought not to agitate Chloe if she was not in plump currant. Before he decided whether to chance his luck today, he had best consult Georgina about her aunt's health.

His guests were beginning to rise. In pairs and small groups they roamed about the pasture or made for the Terrace Gardens to admire the view. Georgina, in pink with a beflowered straw bonnet, with Arabella and several friends strolled towards a group of browsing deer. Lionel hurried after them.

"May I have a word with you, Miss Georgina?"

She turned back, calling to the others, "Go ahead, I shall catch up with you. Don't frighten the deer away!" Smiling up at Lionel, she said with enthusiasm, "It is a simply splendid picnic, sir."

"I'm glad you are enjoying yourself. I fear your aunt seems a trifle out of sorts."

Georgina frowned. "Yes, I have noticed, the last few days. I don't believe she is ill. I wonder if she is fretting about Paul— my little brother, you know. He is only eleven, and he's staying with the vicar at home while Aunt Chloe is here. She has been gone much longer than she intended."

"She takes her duties as substitute mother very seriously," Lionel said ruefully.

"She does not regard it as a duty," said Georgie, indignant. "Aunt Chloe loves us like a mother, all of us."

"I know, my dear, I know. Why else would she have taken

on the awkward task of talking me out of asking for your hand?''

Before the abashed girl could answer, Bannister came up to them and clapped Lionel on the shoulder.

''Doing the thing up right and tight at last, are you?'' he enquired heartily.

''I have your approval, sir?''

''Of course, devil take it! I want her off my hands, and the sooner the better. A June wedding, that's what I'm looking for.''

''I shall see what I can do,'' Lionel said sardonically, ''but do you, pray, grant me a little privacy.''

''That's right! Go do your billing and cooing in the woods where there's none but the birds to see.'' He strode off, mighty pleased with himself.

Lionel glanced around and saw Chloe about to disappear among the trees, alone. ''For once your father is right,'' he said. ''Let us proceed to the woods with all due haste.'' He looked down at Georgina, who gazed up at him in horror.

''You would not!'' she gasped.

''Don't look so terrified, my dear. I'm not about to snatch you from the cradle, but I need your help. If I go without you, your papa will be after me in no time.''

The woods were carpeted with bluebells. Now and then, through the trees, Chloe caught a glimpse of the winding Thames at the foot of the hill and mile after mile of woodland beyond, a hundred shades of green fading into the blue distance. The view failed to raise her spirits.

The dreaded moment had come. She had watched Sir Lionel follow Georgina and call her aside, watched Edgar approach them and clap his future son-in-law on the back. Even now the proposal was doubtless being uttered. Chloe ought to be there, trying to the last to protect her niece, but she simply could not face it.

She had failed Georgie. Yet she could no longer deny that her heartache was not caused by fear of Georgie's future unhappiness with Sir Lionel. The truth was, she wanted him for herself.

Why, oh why, had she come to London? Safe at Dene, she had been well on the way to convincing herself she would not mind going to her grave a spinster. But since meeting Sir Lionel. . . .

"Sir Lionel!" Startled, she stepped back.

He smiled at her. Georgie, at his side, looked remarkably merry. "Aunt Chloe . . ." she started.

"Run along, there's a good girl," interrupted Sir Lionel, "and don't let your papa see you until everything is settled."

Georgina scampered off, giggling.

Chloe found her voice. "Everything is not settled yet?" Perhaps he was allowing her a last chance to plead for Georgie.

"Nothing is settled." He took both her hands in his strong clasp. "Miss Bannister, will you do me the honor of becoming my wife?"

Chloe's head whirled. "But you love Georgie!"

"I like Georgie. I cannot imagine a more delightful daughter."

"You wanted to marry her."

"Ah, now there you are wrong. My desire to wed your niece never existed outside your brother's head."

"Truly?" she said, perplexed. "But even with Edgar, something must have put the notion there. You must have paid her a great deal of attention."

"She is Arabella's dearest friend, and I have frequently taken Arabella about, to relieve Elizabeth's burden. Besides, as I told you at our first encounter, Georgina is the most unaffected young lady I have met in Town. I like her—but I never did love her."

"Are you sure?"

Sir Lionel grinned, "Quite sure."

"But you came up to London to find a bride, and Georgie would have suited you admirably but for her stupid prejudice against your age."

"What a number of misconceptions you labor under, my love! I had no intention of seeking a bride before I felt myself thoroughly settled in my new life on shore. Now I see that I shall never settle properly until I am hitched."

"Not to Georgie? Why did you not tell me sooner? You could have spared me so much worry if you had told me at our first meeting!"

"I was afraid you would disappear back into the country."

"I would have," Chloe admitted.

"I could not risk never seeing you again," he said softly, "because, you see, I fell in love at first sight."

"Oh, Lionel! At first sight?"

"Well, perhaps at second." He considered. "Yes, I cannot claim I was entranced by your greeting, however complimentary—you told me I was not elderly, you recall? I believe it was when you described yourself as a fainthearted poltroon. . . ."

"Lionel!"

He drew her into his arms and kissed her thoroughly, and Miss Chloe Bannister discovered she did not at all want to go to her grave still a spinster. Her limbs turned to water, just as if she was going to swoon, yet she had never felt so alive in her life. Every nerve tingled and her heart thudded in her breast, matching Lionel's beat for beat.

"But I cannot marry you until Georgina is wed," she said reluctantly, straightening her bonnet as he led her, an arm about her waist, to a nearby rustic bench, "and what about the boys in the school holidays?"

"The boys may come to us for the holidays if they choose. Georgie shall make her home with us and may go to as many assemblies as she pleases."

"And have another Season next year if she does not find a husband to her liking in Warwickshire?"

"Of course, my love. We shall come up for the concerts, in any case."

"I fear she will be very hard to please," Chloe sighed. "Anyone who can resist you must be practically impossible to satisfy."

His finger beneath her chin, Lionel raised her face to his. "Do you mean that?" he demanded, gazing deep into her eyes.

"Why yes, Lionel."

"Say it."

"I love you. I believe it was when you first described yourself as the Ancient Mariner. . . ."

"Chloe!" Lifting her onto his lap, he silenced her with another kiss. When at last they emerged, he said, "Georgina may wait as long as she wishes before she marries, but our banns will be read next Sunday without fail."

"So soon?" she said, snuggling against him.

Lionel laughed, the sound booming in Chloe's ear, pressed to his chest. "I don't care to disappoint my brother-in-law-to-be," he said jubilantly, "and I promised him he should see a June wedding!"

ARABELLA TO THE RESCUE

Mona Gedney

A cheerful fire crackled in the old nursery of Boxwood Hall, now claimed by the Standish sisters as their private sitting room. Arabella Standish, perched precariously on a toy chest, tossed down a well-worn copy of *La Belle Assemblée* and turned to her older sister, who was busily sketching Gingersnap, a golden lump of catly contentment on the hearthrug.

"Why doesn't anything ever happen here, Elinor?" she demanded. "Nothing ever happens to us! We might as well be living in a convent!"

Elinor chuckled, but thirteen-year-old Julia, always inclined to be literal, looked up from her reading and said matter-of-factly, "I don't think so, Bella. Then we'd have to wear habits, wouldn't we? Unless we weren't nuns and were just going to school there, of course. Besides, Papa couldn't live with us if we were in a convent." Having dealt with Bella's comment to her own satisfaction, she crunched loudly into an apple and returned to her volume of Marco Polo's adventures in the mysterious East.

Bella sighed in exasperation and pressed her flower-like face to the icy window. Her father had always joked that she was deceptively fragile in appearance. She was delicate in face and figure, her dark hair and eyes emphasizing the paleness of her skin, but her spirit and her health had the strength and resilience of whipcord.

"Papa doesn't really live here any more," she responded gloomily, drawing tiny stars on the frosted window glass and clearing a patch so that she could look out across the park. "He's away too much with his business affairs. He's been gone six weeks this time and soon he'll be going off to the West Indies for heaven knows how long. If we didn't have Flossie, we'd be orphans."

Elinor shook her head reprovingly. "Don't make it worse than it is, Bella. Papa needed to have something to spend his time on after Mama died—that's why he decided to look after his own investments. You know that he cares about us."

"Things would be different if Mama were still alive," Arabella continued, ignoring her sister's comment as she idly decorated the window pane, adding angels to her pattern of stars. "At least we would have company more often. There were always dinner parties and balls and guests coming to stay. With Mama gone, we should call this place World's End instead of Boxwood Hall. We should—"

A sudden movement in the gathering twilight attracted her attention and she hurriedly cleaned a portion of the window pane with her shawl so that she could see clearly. "I can't believe it! There's actually a carriage coming up the drive— but it's not ours, so it can't be Papa!" she exclaimed. "I don't recognize the carriage or the horses."

Julia joined her at the window, but Elinor drew them both away after a quick glance at the carriage below. "Don't stare, girls. It isn't well-bred."

Bella sniffed. "As though I care a fig for that! I just want to see who's come. Don't be such a stick, Elinor."

Slipping past her sister's outstretched arm, Arabella pressed back against the window and watched Bruton, their elderly butler, hurry down the steps to the carriage. Before he could reach it, however, the door had opened and a tall, square-shouldered man sprang nimbly to the drive.

"It *is* Papa!" shrieked Julia, who was peering over her shoulder. She tossed down her apple and Marco Polo and prepared to race downstairs.

"But whoever is that with him?" asked Bella breathlessly. Both her sisters looked at her with wide eyes and then hurried to her side. Their father never traveled in company, and they hadn't had overnight guests at the Hall in more than three years. Not even Elinor could resist the temptation to peek down at the newcomers, and together the sisters stared down at the scene below them. A sudden gust of autumn wind rattled the window panes and tossed back the hood of the lady's cloak, revealing guinea-gold hair that gleamed in the light of the lantern held by the coachman.

"I don't know who she is," Elinor said softly, "but she's lovely."

"And she must be wealthy," observed Arabella practically. "That carriage must have cost the earth and I know those horses did. I'll wager that she's dressed as though she just stepped out of one of the fashion plates in *La Belle Assemblée*."

She looked at Elinor with lifted brows. "Whatever is someone like that doing here at Boxwood Hall? And why did she come with Papa?"

Before they could recover from their shock, the door opened and Miss Floss, tiny and white-haired, bustled in. "Come along, girls. You must hurry and get yourselves dressed for dinner. Your father has come home with a guest."

Disregarding her order, the girls surrounded her. "Tell us who she is, Flossie," Bella demanded. "We saw the carriage and we've *got* to know what she's doing here."

Miss Floss had spent six years with her young charges, and

she knew that she might as well tell them the truth or they would never leave her in peace. "I don't know, girls," she responded, lowering her voice to a conspiratorial whisper, "but the sooner you're dressed, the sooner you'll know. He is waiting for you in the library."

The girls stared at one another as the door closed behind her. "Do you think Papa's getting married?" whispered Julia, her eyes wide.

"Of course not!" replied Bella sharply. "He would have told us."

Julia looked at her doubtfully. "When Colonel Twickenham got married again last spring, he never told Amanda and Susan about it beforehand."

"Well, Papa has got his faults, but he at least he isn't like the colonel. I daresay the old gentleman forgot to tell his girls about the wedding just as he forgets everything else. Susan says he would go to town in his dressing gown if it weren't for his valet."

Julia laughed reluctantly, still looking doubtful.

"Papa *has* been gone longer than he had planned," Elinor observed, her expression grave. Seeing Julia's eyes widen in dismay, she added quickly, "But doubtless we're making a great fuss over nothing. Let's do as Flossie advised—dress quickly and go down to see Papa in the library. His guest will probably be resting after their journey."

To their surprise, however, when the three young ladies arrived in the library, they discovered that John Standish was not alone. Beside him stood the woman that they had glimpsed from the window, elegantly arrayed in a gown of cerulean blue, her bright curls dressed *á la Grecque,* her china blue eyes surveying them coolly. Under normal circumstances they would have run to their father and hugged him, but the presence of the newcomer standing so close to him made them feel too awkward to do anything other than murmur their greetings.

Even Julia, always heedless of decorum and eager to see her father, kept her distance.

Mr. Standish took the stranger's arm and led her forward proudly, saying, "Rebecca, these are my girls—Elinor, Arabella, and Julia."

As the girls curtsied, they inspected their guest, their gaze veiled by their lowered lashes. She turned to their father and smiled.

"Shouldn't you say, John, that they are *our* girls?" she asked archly.

The sisters exchanged startled glances and rose to stare at their father, who had turned a little pink. "Well, of course they are our girls now, Rebecca," he responded uncomfortably. "I was going to tell them tomorrow, but this will do just as well, I suppose."

He turned to his daughters, his voice becoming suddenly jovial—quite unlike his usual manner. "Girls, Rebecca has done me the honor of becoming my wife. We were married some three days ago and have hurried home to share the good news with you."

"Married!" exclaimed Julia, her tone sounding like one just informed of the death of a loved one. "But you said nothing about getting married when you left us, Papa! Why did you not tell—"

Julia broke off abruptly as gentle Elinor, seeing their father's troubled expression, stepped suddenly upon her foot as she went forward to kiss him and take the hand of their new stepmother. "How wonderful for you both," she said with composure, pressing her lips first to her father's cheek and then to the smooth, cool cheek that Rebecca offered her. "I am sure that we all wish you very happy. It is just that it comes as such a surprise to us, you know."

"Well, to be sure it's a surprise to you!" exclaimed Mr. Standish in relief. Then he added laughingly, "Why, it's almost as much a surprise to both of us!"

"Was your marriage so sudden, then?" asked Arabella curiously as she stepped forward to do her duty, pulling Julia along behind her.

The new Mrs. Standish looked a trifle annoyed by the question, but their father answered cheerfully. "It happened just as things do in one of those novels you are so fond of, Bella. There I was at a dinner party in London—one of those deadly boring affairs old Jefferson gives—and I was wondering when I would be able to slip away from the prosy old bore next to me. Then I looked down the table and I saw Rebecca." He paused for a moment, seeming to remember the scene. "She was seated behind a bouquet of hothouse roses—and she put them to shame!"

He smiled fondly at his bride. "That was just two weeks ago. It was all over for me then and there. Marriage held no terrors for me after I saw her."

The sisters stared at him in astonishment. Their father was normally a rather quiet, reserved man, very fond of his children but very preoccupied with his business investments. Such an outburst from him seemed most extraordinary—and a little embarrassing. Also, for a man who prided himself upon his good business sense and practical judgment, marrying so quickly seemed shockingly out of character.

"John is fond of exaggerating," the new Mrs. Standish said smoothly, patting his arm. "I cannot imagine that he was ever afraid of marriage—or of anything else."

Mr. Standish seemed to grow a little taller as she spoke, and he straightened his shoulders under her admiring glance, looking rather like a pigeon who had fluffed his feathers and puffed up his chest, remarked Arabella later.

"I have looked forward to seeing Boxwood Hall—and to meeting the three of you, of course," said Rebecca, including them all with a graceful gesture and quick smile. "Your father has talked of you so much that I feel I quite know you already.

I must say, though, that he hadn't told me how beautiful his daughters are.''

She slipped an arm around Elinor's waist. "I do so want to spend time with all of you, and especially to help you prepare for your coming-out, Elinor.''

Mr. Standish nodded in agreement, pleased by their surprised expressions. "I have been worrying, you see. I don't like to sail for the Indies so soon and leave you girls alone again, but Rebecca will be just the one to see to it that you have a good time during the holidays.''

He turned to his eldest daughter and patted her on the cheek. "And she'll help you have your gowns made, Elinor, and show you just how you should go on in London. We hadn't talked of your coming-out, and I'm sure you haven't been certain whether or not I realized that you will soon be eighteen, my dear—but I do know. When I come home again, we'll take you to London together, but until then Rebecca will help you prepare for your entry into society by having some soirées at home.''

"Soirées?" repeated Arabella in astonishment, seeing that Elinor was too stunned to reply. "Do you mean that we shall be having *parties* here at Boxwood?''

Her father nodded. "I haven't had the heart for it since your mother died, but Rebecca has changed that. She met some of my friends in London and I will be introducing her to all of the neighboring families before I leave for the Indies, so I shall expect all of you to be cheerful and busy and to have a good time while I am gone.''

He leaned over and patted Elinor's cheek affectionately. "And we want you to have as many chances as possible to practice your dancing, my dear.''

Elinor had blushed in pleasure and dinner had passed in a flurry of excited questions and plans for the future. Only Julia had seemed withdrawn, picking at her food and refusing to be drawn into the conversation.

Elinor and Arabella lay awake late that night, talking of the astonishing change in their father and the many pleasures that lay ahead for them. Julia, being less interested in balls and gowns and still distressed by the unexpected turn of events, retired to her own bed at her accustomed time, taking Ginger-snap and Marco Polo to keep her company.

"Do you think we should go sit with her?" asked Elinor anxiously as the door closed behind her.

Arabella shook her head. "You know that she doesn't take change very well and she likes to be alone to sort things out. If we go in, she'll only pull the covers up over her head. Reading will take her mind off of things."

Elinor nodded and they climbed into their huge bed of carved walnut and nestled under the covers to protect themselves from the autumn chill. "It is difficult to believe that Papa has married again—and done it so suddenly. But he does look happy."

"He looks besotted," observed Arabella a little tartly. "That's what I find most difficult to believe. He never looked like that with Mama."

"Well, of course they had been married a long time, Bella," Elinor demurred, always eager to keep family relations pleasant. "And you must admit that our new stepmother is beautiful—and very kind to be thinking of me."

"I agree that she's beautiful," conceded Arabella, who had not yet placed her stamp of approval upon the stranger. "It's not at all difficult to see why Papa lost his head."

"I would never have imagined such a thing, Bella," Elinor sighed in contentment, settling comfortably among her nest of pillows. "I had no idea that Papa had even thought of my having a coming-out party, let alone holding it in London."

"Nor I," agreed Arabella. "There seemed nothing to be having a coming-out *for.* I mean, after all, we would probably attend two balls in an entire year if things went on here as they have been. I daresay you're right and that this is our stepmother's doing."

For a few moments she lay staring silently at the dancing patterns on the wall cast by the flickering firelight. "Do you suppose I might be able to dance, too, Elinor—even though I am supposed to be still in the schoolroom?"

"I don't see why you can't if we have an evening party here at home, Bella—after all, this is the country, not London."

Bella smiled wickedly. "I shall see to it that Will Russell is invited. I have been longing to dance with him since I saw him at church last summer. I still remember seeing him dance at the last ball Mama and Papa gave here."

Elinor sat up in bed and stared at her sister. "Why, Arabella Standish! Are you planning to set up a flirt when you're not even sixteen yet?"

Bella grinned wickedly. "Don't fly into a pelter, Elinor. He hasn't noticed me yet." She plumped up her pillow and settled herself more comfortably, then added confidently, "But he will! You may depend upon it."

She had first seen Will Russell six years ago at the last ball before their mother's death. He had been down from Oxford, visiting his cousins at Longview Manor for the holidays. With his dark hair and dancing eyes, he had been quite the handsomest young man Arabella had ever seen, and she had watched him eagerly from the top of the stairs, finally venturing down so that she could watch the dancing more closely. He had come upon her there and had looked down at her with the same charming smile he had been using to such effect on his partners.

"And where is *your* partner, lovely lady?" he had inquired. "Are you all alone?"

She had shaken her head silently and pointed to the landing above them, where Elinor and Julia were perched. Will had seen them and bowed and smiled, which had set them to laughing, then he had turned back to Arabella.

"I believe that I know precisely what you ladies are lacking. If you will excuse me for just a moment, I will take care of the oversight."

Puzzled, the girls had stared at one another, and Arabella had maintained her position at the foot of the stairs. Will was as good as his word, returning in a very brief time with a tray laden with ices and pastries, tiny sandwiches, and cups of lemonade. He and Arabella had carried them up to the other girls and the four of them had sat there, the girls listening and laughing as he told them about his adventurous trip from Oxford on the stagecoach. Another young blood, a friend of his from school, had paid the driver to let him take the reins and had overturned them, frightening one of the ladies into spasms.

"And I must say," he had told them gravely as he concluded his tale, "I felt that she was quite in the right of it. I found myself head over heels in a snowbank, and we had a long and icy walk to the fireside of the nearest inn. I strongly considered going into spasms myself."

"*You* wouldn't have overset the stage," Arabella had observed confidently. "The coachman should have given the ribbons to you."

His dark eyes had lighted with mirth at this pledge of faith and he had kissed her hand. "My thanks for your good opinion, my lady."

One of his friends had appeared at the foot of the steps and called to him impatiently. "Will! Are you coming? We need you to complete the set."

He had stood up and sighed as he straightened his white waistcoat, then bowed to them and winked. "Forgive me for leaving you, ladies, but duty calls." And he had been gone as suddenly as he had appeared.

Arabella had seen him at a distance twice more during that Christmas holiday, then he had returned to Oxford and she had not seen him again until a few months ago. One June Sunday he had appeared at services with his aunt and uncle and their daughters.

"Did you see him?" she had demanded of Elinor as they

emerged from the cool darkness of the sanctuary into the sunshine.

"Who?" her sister had asked, glancing at the clusters of people along the path.

"Will Russell," Arabella had said in a low voice. "He was here with the Gibsons. Libbie sat right next to him."

"Will Russell?" It was clear from Elinor's tone that she did not remember the name.

"Yes, Elinor. You remember him," said Arabella impatiently. "He was the one at our last Christmas ball—the one who brought us refreshments and sat with us all those years ago."

Elinor smiled. "I remember how distressed you were when you discovered that he left for France a few months later. You were so afraid that something would happen to him."

Arabella grimaced. "And instead, something happened to poor Charlie." Charles Gibson, the cousin that Will had come to visit and the only son at Longview Manor, had been killed in a hunting accident the previous spring, making Will the heir to Longview. Libbie, the eldest daughter, was a year younger than Arabella, but she had always been a good friend.

Together they had watched as the Gibsons' carriage had pulled away. That had been their only glimpse of Will, and they heard that he had returned to London the following week.

"We will most certainly be inviting the Gibsons to our ball— and he, of course, will come with them," observed Arabella.

"What makes you think he will be here at Christmas, Bella— or that we will have a ball?"

"He is the heir and this is their first Christmas without Charlie—surely he will be nowhere else," Arabella had returned confidently. "He will be here and naturally we will have a ball again. After all, Papa has said we're to dance and have a good time. And Will Russell will come to the ball."

"But you must remember, Bella, that you are only a schoolroom miss," Elinor cautioned her gravely, her gravity belied by the twinkle in her eyes, "and that you must hold the line. *I*, on the other hand, am about to become a member of the *ton*."

"But of course I will," Bella had answered with equal gravity. "When have you known me *not* to behave with propriety?"

When her sister's response was too long in coming, Arabella had thumped her with a pillow and the sisters had finally settled down to sleep, dreaming of balls and dark-eyed, laughing young men.

The next few days were a whirl of activity. The girls accompanied their father and Rebecca on some of their calls on neighbors, and they were astonished to see their quiet father talking easily with people he had avoided for years.

"It's all Rebecca's doing," commented Elinor in wonder, after they had returned from a call upon Squire Norton and his wife. "Just imagine his going out and seeing dozens of people and actually talking to all of them. Papa wouldn't have dreamed of doing such a thing if it weren't for her."

"It seems very strange to call her Rebecca," observed Julia disapprovingly, not particularly pleased by the sudden flurry of social activity.

"Well, we can't very well call her Mama," returned Arabella briskly, examining her complexion carefully in the glass and then pulling her curls into a knot on the top of her head and examining the effect judiciously. "We wouldn't wish to do so, and she certainly doesn't wish for us to."

"She's quite right, though," said Elinor. "She is far too young to have children as old as we are—and it does seem rather pleasant and cozy—like having another sister."

She examined her new kid gloves with pride. "And it was so kind of her to bring each of us a gift, especially when she had so little time to shop for us."

"Yes, I suppose I have to like her," said Bella thoughtfully, "although I dislike the idea of someone taking Mama's place. And Papa does quite dote upon her."

Julia, having no patience with her father's loverlike behavior, snorted in response. "It's embarrassing to see how he behaves. He sits and watches her all the time with that ridiculous little smile. He doesn't even know the rest of us are here." She looked at her sisters defiantly. "I'm almost glad that he'll be leaving soon. Perhaps his affection for her will die down a little bit while he is away and he'll come home acting like Papa again."

"Julia!" exclaimed Elinor, shocked. "How could you speak that way about Papa? And how could you be glad that he is to leave us?"

"Well, I'll miss him, of course," conceded Julia, "but I miss him right now and he's still here. Only he might as well not be. He has no time for any of us—only for Rebecca."

"It won't always be like this," responded Elinor encouragingly. "After all, they've only been married a few days."

"And he's only known her for two weeks," returned Arabella dryly. "I still can't believe Papa was capable of doing such a henwitted thing." She stared at her reflection for a moment, tapping her chin thoughtfully. "I'd like to believe that he married her for us—just as he told us—so that we wouldn't be left alone here during all the months he's away in the Indies. But all I have to do is watch him with Rebecca and I know that's not the only reason he married her."

"We wouldn't have been alone! We've got Flossie!" protested Julia. "We didn't need Rebecca!"

She buried her head on Elinor's shoulder and Elinor patted her head soothingly, raising her eyebrows at Arabella. "We'll just have to make the best of it, Julie dear. Rebecca has been very kind to us—and perhaps we *will* have a good time even though Papa is gone. Just think what it will be like to have guests for Christmas this year!"

But Julia was not to be comforted by the thought of Christmas pleasures. "That's over two months from now anyway," she said crossly. "By that time Papa will already be in the Indies. I'd rather be going with him. At least he'd talk to me if Rebecca weren't there!"

There was no getting round Julia's adamant dislike of their new stepmother, but Elinor and Arabella managed to conceal it from their father during the few days he had left to spend with them. He was so caught up in his own happiness that it clearly seemed impossible to him that everyone else might not be quite as pleased with the world.

They held an evening party the night before his departure, and Elinor and Arabella looked forward to it with an intensity that far exceeded its importance. It was, after all, the first party in their home in six years, and their first grown-up party. They could scarcely sleep for talking about it.

"I'm sorry we haven't had a chance to get you a new gown for tonight," Mr. Standish told Elinor, watching fondly as she arranged some flowers that Colonel Twickenham had sent from his hothouse. "I had intended to begin outfitting you before I left England. I hope you're not too disappointed."

Elinor hugged her father, smiling. "I'm not disappointed at all, Papa. I have a perfectly lovely white gown that I haven't had an opportunity to wear, and Bella has added some trim to it. It will do wonderfully well. I will be too busy looking at everyone else and trying to remember the steps to the dances to worry over my own appearance."

"I'll get your mother's pearls out for you," he responded, patting her cheek. "I had intended to wait to give them to you until you go to London, but you can wear them tonight and have the pleasure of them now."

"Oh, thank you so much, Papa!" she exclaimed. "How very kind you are!"

He smiled down at her and then looked across at Arabella. "And you needn't think that I'm playing favorites, Bella. You and Julia each have a set of your mother's jewelry coming.

You have the diamonds and Julia is to have the sapphires. Your mother decided which would best suit each of you.''

"Thank you, Papa," said Bella, with a small smile. "I shan't be needing mine for a while, though. Rebecca just told me that I'm too young to be downstairs for the dancing tomorrow night."

"Oh, Bella!" Elinor regarded her with distress. "How can I enjoy myself if you're not there, too?"

"Now, now," replied their father soothingly. "I know you're disappointed, Bella, and I've got to admit I'm a little disappointed, too, but Rebecca reminded me that you're far too young to be mixing at a party. I've been out of touch for quite a while, and we wouldn't want our old friends to think that I've raised you to be fast."

"Fast!" exclaimed Bella indignantly. "I should like to hear anyone say such a thing about me!"

Elinor's gentle eyes darkened as she put her arms about her sister. "I shan't go either," she announced. "I couldn't take pleasure in the evening knowing Bella is unhappy."

"You'll do no such thing!" announced her sister firmly. "If you didn't go, I certainly *would* be unhappy!" Determined not to ruin Elinor's pleasure in her first party, she forced herself to smile. "Julia and I shall watch from the stairs just as we used to do in the old days, and you and Papa shall bring us ices and lemonade when supper is served. We shall go on famously."

Elinor reluctantly allowed herself to be persuaded and Arabella sighed in relief, promising herself that she would say nothing else to stand in the way of Elinor having a good time tomorrow night at her first grown-up party. She also promised herself, however, that she would have a good time, too. Humming lightly, she adjourned to her chamber to examine a charming gold gown that she had stitched herself, modeling it as closely as she could upon one featured in an issue of *La Belle Assemblée*. Papa and Rebecca couldn't be everywhere at once tomorrow night, and one dance was all she asked. One dance with Will Russell.

When they had called upon the Gibsons, Arabella had been delighted to learn that he would be arriving later that day and planned to spend a fortnight with them. The invitation to the party had immediately been extended to him, and Arabella was looking forward to the night with great anticipation. She had not the slightest intention of allowing him to slip through her fingers without having at least one dance with him—Rebecca or no Rebecca.

She did not confide her plan to Elinor, however, fearful that it would make her sister more nervous than she already was. She helped Elinor dress that evening, admiring the string of pearls and the dainty earrings that had belonged to their mother.

"You look beautiful, Elinor," she said sincerely. "Mama was right when she thought that the pearls would be just the thing for you." And she spoke no more than the truth, for Elinor's soft skin and golden brown hair seemed to catch the luster of the pearls.

Elinor's eyes brightened at her sister's praise, but she leaned toward the glass to pinch her cheeks and study her face worriedly. "You don't think that I look too pale, Bella?"

Arabella shook her head firmly. "You have a lovely rose color in your cheeks, just as you always do. *I* am the one that will need a rabbit's foot and a pot of rouge."

Before Elinor could respond to this shocking indication that Arabella might do such a thing, Julia, who had been watching quietly from a low rocking chair, said suddenly, "Then you can borrow Rebecca's. When Sarah was tidying her chamber, she saw all sorts of pots of cream and color."

"Sarah shouldn't be spying on her mistress and carrying tales," said Elinor firmly. "You are not to be gossiping with the servants about Rebecca, Julia. It isn't at all proper."

Julia hunched one shoulder in reply and turned her face back to the fire.

"I'm just surprised that Sarah was allowed in at all," responded Arabella, disregarding Elinor's ban on gossip. "Hudlow guards Rebecca's bedchamber and dressing room like a dragon."

Hudlow was Rebecca's abigail, a spare, angular woman who seemed never to smile and who considered herself above the other servants.

"You mean *Mama's* bedchamber and dressing room," said Julia gloomily.

Neither of her sisters said anything to this, but Arabella stepped over and hugged her younger sister fiercely. "Perhaps you'll be able to sneak in and borrow the rabbit's foot for me in a little while," she whispered. "I'm going to make a grand entrance later on and I wouldn't want to look like a ghost."

Her joke had its intended effect, and Julia's eyes brightened immediately. Elinor missed this byplay, for she had moved to the cheval mirror and was smoothing her skirt nervously. "Do I look all right?" she asked anxiously. "I'm shaking like a leaf and I daresay I shall step all over my partner."

"You look radiant, and you'll do no such thing," Arabella assured her, hurrying to her side. "The young men will throw themselves at your feet."

Elinor chuckled. "I can just see it. Bodies strewn all about the drawing room, clutching at my slippers. It's a pity we don't have an abundance of eligible young men hereabouts. Tommy Norton and Andrew Barrisford will be the only ones—unless of course you were thinking of the Squire or Colonel Twickenham."

"Don't forget Will Russell," Arabella reminded her. "Although naturally you must leave him for me. And do be careful of the colonel. He is very likely to forget he is dancing and wander off in the middle of the set."

This sally at the colonel's expense improved their spirits, and Arabella and Julia accompanied their sister to the top of the stairs cheering her on as she made her way gracefully down to the entrance hall, where she joined their father and Rebecca to receive the guests who had just begun to arrive. They watched for a few moments, then Bella beckoned to Julia and they hurried back to the bedchamber that she and Elinor shared.

"Are you really going to do it?" demanded Julia when the door closed behind them. "Are you going to go down to the party? Flossie will never let you do it."

"Ah, but you are going to take care of that, dear sister," said Arabella, drawing her dress from the wardrobe and holding it up to her in front of the mirror. "Flossie will have no time to spare for me."

"Why not?" asked Julia apprehensively. She had been involved in some of Arabella's schemes before, and not all of them had proved painless. "I'm not going to have to have an accident, am I?"

Once before Arabella had been quite determined to go riding when Flossie had told her she must stay home and do her lessons, so she had arranged for Julia to pretend to fall on the steps and hurt herself. While Flossie was caring for her young charge, Arabella quietly made her way to the stable and had her ride. Unfortunately, Julia actually did fall down the front staircase and broke her leg. There had been no question of Flossie being fully occupied; it had been four months before things had returned to normal at the Hall, and Julia thereafter had little faith in her sister's schemes.

"You wouldn't have had a real accident then if you had been paying attention, goose. All you had to do was to make a great thump and arrange yourself at the foot of the stairs— just as I told you to do."

"Well, I *intended* to do that, Bella, only I got nervous and I didn't notice that Gingersnap had come from the nursery with me. We sort of got tangled up together and we fell all the way down." She leaned toward the cat, who had rushed over to greet them and was twining herself around Julia's ankles. "Poor kitty,'' she murmured, stroking Gingersnap's arched back, as the cat vibrated with satisfied purrs.

"Poor kitty, my eye,'' murmured Arabella, as she pulled her hair atop her head and secured it into a becoming tumble of dark curls. "That cat can take care of herself, Julia. You're the one that ended up with the broken leg, not Gingersnap.''

Her sister had gathered Gingersnap into her arms and was rocking in front of the crackling fire. It was difficult to tell which of them was the more contented. "Well, I'm glad that it happened that way!'' responded Julia. "Dr. Green could mend my leg, but I don't think that he could have done so for Gingersnap.''

"You needn't worry about Gingersnap; she won't get herself hurt—cats never do. They're cleverer than we are and far faster on their feet.'' She studied her face in the mirror, pinching her cheeks to redden them as Elinor had.

"Do you want the rabbit's foot now?'' inquired Julia with interest. After hearing from Sarah about Rebecca's vast number of pots of cream and color and perfume, she had been longing for an opportunity to see them for herself. "Shall I go to Rebecca's chamber and get it for you? And a pot of rouge?''

Arabella paused for a moment, then shook her head. "No. That would land us both in the briars if Papa found out about it.''

Julia's face fell, but she looked more cheerful when Arabella drew a piece of marchpane from a box in the drawer of her dressing table and handed it to her.

"You need to practice having the toothache, for that's what you must do to occupy Flossie tonight. You can tell her that it suddenly started to ache while you were eating the marchpane.''

Julia, in the midst of happily biting into it, stopped suddenly and stared at her sister in dismay. "You don't think that she'll try to make me go to the surgeon tomorrow to have it drawn, do you, Bella? I remember when Sarah had to do that last year—she told me how horribly it hurt!''

"Of course she won't," replied her sister briskly. "Tonight all she can do is to sit with you and drown you in chamomile tea and kindness. All you need do is toss about and look miserable and beg her to read to you to take your mind off of your suffering. Haven't you a volume about Sir Francis Drake you've been reading?"

Julia, comforted by the thought that she might at least finish her book tonight, adjourned to the nursery to gather up Sir Francis Drake and Gingersnap and to practice moaning gently. The ruse was successful, for only a few minutes later Arabella heard Flossie in the corridor, ordering Sarah to go down to Cook immediately and ask for a pot of chamomile tea for Miss Julia's toothache.

Certain that she was perfectly safe from Flossie's eagle eye for the next few hours, Arabella retired to her chamber and carefully arrayed herself in her gold gown and knotted ribbons the same shade in her dusky curls. She had no real jewelry of her own, except for a simple gold locket with her mother's picture. That she fastened carefully about her neck before giving herself a final inspection and making her way slowly down the stairs.

There was no Will Russell in the hall tonight, but as she stood behind a screen just inside the drawing room, she saw him dancing. Boxwood Hall possessed a real ballroom, but it was not used for a small gathering like this one. The servants had cleared the north drawing room of most of its furniture and opened the doors to the adjoining music room, where the two musicians for the evening, one at the pianoforte, the other with his violin, were playing gaily. It was a small affair, to be sure, but to Bella it seemed festive beyond belief.

She watched admiringly as Will made his way gracefully through the figures of the quadrille, bowing to the new Mrs. Twickenham, a plump, cherry-cheeked woman, as the dance ended and he squired her back to her chair. Elinor, she noted, had been dancing with Tommie Norton, and was evidently about to stand up with the colonel, judging by the way he was hovering close by. Arabella knew that they were to have some waltzes tonight, for she had heard Rebecca discussing the matter with her father. He had protested at first that it seemed a little fast to have such a daring dance in this country place, but Rebecca had laughed at him, saying Londoners had been waltzing for some three years. Not surprisingly, he had given way to her, saying that if she favored it, it could not be in poor taste.

Remaining in her hiding place, she watched with pleasure as the others began to waltz. To her surprise, Colonel Twickenham, despite his absentmindedness, proved to be quite adept at this fashionable new step, moving with a nimble grace she had not thought him capable of. She and Elinor had practiced the waltz time and time again in the empty ballroom with Flossie at the pianoforte, and Elinor now performed flawlessly. Arabella found herself swaying to the music, but she didn't wish to draw attention to her presence. Quietly she stepped out into the hall where she would have more room and began to dance in time to the lilting melody, closing her eyes and imagining herself in a lighted ballroom filled with elegantly arrayed dancers.

So lost in her fantasy world was she that at first she didn't realize that she was no longer alone.

"I hope that I am not intruding, ma'am," said a merry voice that she knew by heart.

Her eyes flew open and Will Russell was gazing down at her, and she realized with a sudden shock that she was in his arms, no longer dancing alone.

"Will!" she exclaimed, too startled to observe the proprieties. "How long have you been here?"

His eyebrows shot up at this use of his first name, but he responded smoothly, "We have been dancing together a minute or so—I wasn't sure that you realized I had joined you, so I thought I had best make myself known."

He studied her face as they swept gracefully past the staircase.

"Have we met, ma'am?" he inquired, puzzled. "I swear that I'd not forget you, had we done so."

She dimpled and raised one eyebrow provocatively. "Ah, yes, Mr. Russell, indeed we have met. How very humbling it is for me that you don't remember."

He frowned, searching his memory. "Was it in London?" he asked, trying to place her. "Did we meet at Almack's?"

Arabella shook her head, enjoying his discomfiture—and his belief that she could have been at such a fashionable place.

"It couldn't have been here," he said slowly, coming to a halt as the music ended and he bowed to her, still studying her face as though he would find the answer there. "I know that we didn't meet this summer and I hadn't been to Longview for years before that."

She curtsied gracefully. "I fear that the last time we met, sir, you deserted me to dance with another lady."

He shook his head emphatically. "I may occasionally be rag-mannered, ma'am, but I would never be such a slow-top as to leave you for another lady."

"A very pretty speech, sir." Smiling at his compliment, she decided to take pity upon him. "It was indeed all those years ago that we met, Mr. Russell."

She gestured to the stairs. "You have bowed to me before, sir, and kissed my hand and brought me lemonade and pastries—but I was much younger then."

His eyes lighted with sudden amusement. "The charming little girl on the stairs! How much I enjoyed the picnic on the landing with you and your sisters." He lowered his voice. "I would have greatly preferred to stay with you on the stairs instead of dancing that night."

She shook her head in amazement. "Your words are still as honeyed as they were then, Mr. Russell."

"But you have the advantage of me, ma'am. I beg you to tell me your name so that I may humbly apologize for not recognizing you."

"I am Arabella Standish," she replied. "You met my sister Elinor as you came in tonight."

"Indeed I did," he responded, "and I fear that I didn't recognize her either."

"Well, it is possible of course that we have changed slightly over the years," Arabella conceded gracefully.

"You were charming then and you are even more charming today, Miss Standish," he replied, reclaiming her hand and bending over it. "I did myself the honor of kissing your hand then. How can I do less now?"

Before she could reply, she heard a sharp exclamation from the entry to the drawing room, and Arabella looked up to see her father and Rebecca standing there. One glance was enough to tell her that the angry gasp had been Rebecca's. Her father merely looked dismayed.

"Mr. and Mrs. Standish," Will began easily, smiling at them as he released her hand, "I have just renewed an old acquaintance with your daughter. I was deprived of a dance with her six years ago, and we have made it up tonight."

"You have been dancing, Arabella? And doing so out here, without a chaperone?" inquired Rebecca sharply, disregarding Will's startled expression at her tone. She looked Arabella over from top to toe, taking in every detail of her outfit, and her expression grew grimmer. "I see that you did not take me seriously when I said you were not to come down tonight."

"I beg your pardon, Mrs. Standish," interrupted Will, looking troubled, "but I'm afraid that I caused the problem. In a manner of speaking, I forced her to dance with me."

Rebecca regarded him with a faint smile. "How very gallant of you, Mr. Russell—but I'm afraid that the problem lies with Arabella's behavior, not your own."

Mr. Standish had been watching all of this uncomfortably. He had never been strict with his daughters, but he felt distinctly out of his element now that they were older and needed to adhere to certain standards of behavior. Still, he said a little hesitantly, "Surely we are creating a tempest in a teapot, my dear. I'm sure no harm was intended and no harm was done. No one else has even seen Arabella except Mr. Russell—and I'm certain that he'll not be gossiping about it."

Will looked blank. "Why would I be gossiping about seeing her?" he asked.

Rebecca spoke abruptly before Mr. Standish could reply. "Because she is only a schoolroom miss, far too young to be wearing a gown like that and standing up with a young man she doesn't even know—and *waltzing* with him at that! Her behavior is quite shocking."

This was entirely too much for Arabella. "What nonsense, Rebecca!" she exclaimed impatiently. "Papa said that there was no harm done, and there wasn't! The others are all dancing now, so they're too busy to notice me."

Certain that Rebecca was about to order her back to the nursery and determined not to allow her that satisfaction, she turned to Will and smiled. "Thank you for the dance, Mr. Russell. It was delightful to see you again after all these years."

Bowing, he smiled into her eyes. "I assure you that the pleasure was mine, Miss Standish. I am sorry to have caused you any distress by my actions."

"*You* caused me no distress, sir," she assured him. "I'm going upstairs now, Papa," she added. "I don't want anything to spoil Elinor's party." Without a word or a glance for Rebecca, she turned and walked up the stairs, her head held high, aware that the others were watching her.

Once in her own bedchamber, she stood in front of the mirror once more, studying her gown—not out of vanity, but to compare her creation to some of those she had seen the other ladies wearing. Analyzing the gowns in the fashion plates was one of her favorite pasttimes and she was a clever needlewoman. She had added some beadwork and ribbon ruching to Elinor's simple white gown that had made it look quite elegant.

She nodded at her reflection. All in all, tonight had been

quite successful, despite the scene that Rebecca had created. She *had* danced with Will Russell, and she had no doubt that he would now remember who she was. He had clearly been distressed to have caused her a problem with Rebecca, and she had confidence in his ability to apologize again. She had made a beginning with him.

Thinking of Rebecca's behavior, she frowned. She had been extraordinarily high-handed for someone new to her position as a stepmother, but possibly she really thought that Arabella had been damaging her reputation by her behavior. Doubtless Rebecca would be more reasonable once she became accustomed to life here in the country. Although Arabella had had few opportunities to mix socially with their neighbors in recent years, she knew that other young girls like Colonel Twickenham's daughters were allowed to attend informal parties like the one tonight even though they were not yet out.

Arabella carefully put away her gown and made herself comfortable beside the fire to wait for Elinor and hear her account of the evening. Gingersnap, who had apparently made her escape from the sickroom, fluffed herself into a ball of fur and settled like a rug across Arabella's slippers.

Much sooner than she had expected, the door opened softly and Elinor hurried into the room with a glass of lemonade and a plate of dainties from the supper table below.

"I was going to take something to Julia, too," said Elinor, handing the glass to her sister and putting the plate on the butler's tray, but Flossie says that she is in terrible pain from a toothache."

Arabella's eyes glinted merrily. "I think it would be wise to save Julia some of this feast for later—perhaps after Flossie goes to bed."

Elinor stared at her for a moment, then laughed. "What have you been up to, Bella?"

It took no more than a minute or two to apprise Elinor of

the situation. Wide-eyed, she asked in astonishment, "You *waltzed* with him, Bella? Out in the hall?"

Arabella nodded. "And Rebecca was as cross as crabs when she saw us. And poor Papa," she chuckled remorsefully. "He didn't know what to say or do because Rebecca was so angry. I don't know who looked more startled by her bad temper— Papa or Will."

"You didn't call him Will, did you, Bella?" asked Elinor, anxiously.

"Only once," she reassured her sister. "After that I was perfectly proper and called him Mr. Russell. Have you danced with him yet, Elinor?"

Elinor shook her head. "I haven't said more than two words to him yet, but I am to stand up with him for the quadrille."

"Do tell him I am sorry for any discomfort I caused him," said Arabella, pleased to be able to send a message. "He didn't know which way to look when Rebecca began to rail at me."

"I will," Elinor reassured her, turning to go. "I must get back before they wonder what has happened to me, Bella."

She paused at the door and hurried back to hug her sister. "I'm so sorry that you couldn't come, Bel, and that Rebecca was so horrid to you."

Arabella smiled mischievously. "Don't be sorry, Elinor. It could have been quite a good thing. Will won't be able to forget me quite as easily as he might had he danced with me in the ordinary way."

Elinor hurried away, relieved to have found her sister in such a cheerful frame of mind, and Arabella waited by the fire, stitching carefully on an embroidered bandeau she was making for Elinor and watching the clock. When the hour grew late, she laid her work aside and went to the window in the darkened nursery to watch the guests leaving, the footmen lighting their way to the waiting carriages on the gravel drive.

Finally she saw the figure she sought. Tall and erect, Will Russell swung himself lightly into the saddle and took his place to ride next to the Gibsons' carriage on their homeward journey. Sighing, she let the curtain fall back across the icy window glass. At last she had truly met him—and danced with him. And she knew he would remember her.

She was even more certain of her success when Elinor came up to bed.

"I have a message for you, Bella," she whispered, looking over her shoulder as though she expected to see Rebecca listening, "although I'm not at all certain I should be delivering it to you."

Arabella shook Elinor's wrist lightly. "What is it, you goose? What did he say?"

Looking cautiously at the door again, Elinor whispered, "Mr. Russell asked me to convey his regret for any embarrassment he caused you tonight, and he said to tell you that he frequently rides in the early morning."

Arabella's heart leaped. This was more than she had hoped for. "Did he say where he rides, Elinor?" she asked, shaking her arm again.

Elinor nodded, her eyes large. "He said that he particularly admires the view from the bridge." A tiny stream trickled along the boundary between Boxwood Hall and Longview. After a heavy rain it could be quite difficult to cross, however, and many years ago a footbridge had been built across it.

"Will you go, Bella?" she asked, already certain of the answer. "Should I go with you?"

"Of course, I will go, goose—and no, you won't come with me. No one will notice if I go out early, for I do it often—but you never do."

And at last, quite overcome by the excitement of the day, the sisters slept.

Morning dawned cold and clear, and Arabella slipped from the house unnoticed. Although this was unusually early, even for her, she had spoken no more than the truth when she said that she often went out early, either to ride or to walk. This morning, not wishing to alert anyone in the stables, she chose to walk. The footbridge was almost a mile from the house, but she walked briskly, secure in the knowledge that no one would be spying upon her. The exercise was a pleasure to her, and she had the satisfaction of knowing that the faint flush that stained her cheeks because of it was becoming, quite offsetting her sturdy little boots and dark woolen cloak. A knot of scarlet ribbons in her hair was her only other hint of color.

She saw him waiting at the bridge as she came to the top of the rise overlooking it. She stood for a moment, reveling in the knowledge that he was waiting for her, after all these years of dreaming of him. He had tethered his mount on the Longview side and was leaning against the bridge, hat in hand, watching for her. Seeing her at last, he started eagerly up the hill toward her, offering his arm when he reached her side.

"You are out early, sir," she observed lightly, placing a small gloved hand on his arm. "Have you enjoyed your ride?"

"I always enjoy an early morning ride," he responded, his tone equally light, "but this one was particularly delightful since I had the hope of seeing you, Miss Standish. I'm grateful that you were willing to come."

Her dimples deepened as she glanced up at him. "I fear, Mr. Russell, that you learned last night that it is my sister Elinor whom you should address as Miss Standish. Since I am younger, I must yield that right to her."

He bowed. "Very well, then—Miss Arabella. I confess that it was a great surprise to me to learn that you are—" Here he paused, considering the most tactful way to phrase his thought.

"To learn that I am, to quote Rebecca, 'only a schoolroom miss'?" she inquired.

He nodded ruefully. "Your manner and dress led me to believe otherwise—and I'm afraid that I caused you embarrassment because I acted upon that belief."

She shook her head. "Not at all. I enjoyed our dance—and I will, after all, be out soon enough myself. My new stepmother appears to be taking her role quite seriously, however."

He nodded. "I could see that was so, and I wanted to be certain that I had not brought any trouble upon you. I wouldn't wish to leave with that upon my conscience."

"Leave?" she cried. "Are you leaving Longview so soon?"

"I intended to stay only a few days on this visit—just long enough to complete some business arrangements. I'll come again at Christmas, however, and I hope I shall have the honor of calling upon you then."

She mustered a smile, determined not to allow her distress to show. It would never do to have him guess how she had counted upon seeing him now that she had finally made his acquaintance.

"But of course, Mr. Russell. We will look forward to seeing you then." She extended her hand. "And it was most kind of you to worry about my well being, but I assure you that there will be no problem because of our dance last night." Arabella was more than confident of her ability to deal with Rebecca, and she had no wish for Will to leave with any uneasiness over his own conduct in the matter.

He held her hand for a moment longer than was necessary, then bowed. "I am glad to hear it, Miss Arabella. I shall look forward to Christmas."

She made him a brief curtsey and turned back toward home, trying to ignore the magnetism that urged her to return to him. It was so strong that she was certain he felt it, too.

Smiling over her shoulder, she said lightly, "I too shall forward to it, sir. Forgive me for leaving you now, but I will be needed at home. My father leaves today for the West Indies, and there is much to be done before his departure."

Will stood at the footbridge, watching her climb the rocky path to the rise. When she reached the top and turned to wave to him, he raised his hat in a parting salute, and she had the satisfaction of knowing that he watched her until she disappeared from sight before he departed.

When she arrived home, her father's baggage was being loaded into the new carriage, and the rest of the family was already sitting down to breakfast, an unusually early gathering that marked the importance of the occasion.

"Ah, Bella, you're back from your walk," said her father in relief as she took her place at the table. "I was afraid that I might miss seeing you, my dear."

"Of course not, Papa. I made certain of the time and did not linger."

Rebecca eyed her sharply. "Is going out this early—and alone—something you make a habit of, Arabella?" She was not an early riser herself, so her stepdaughter's activities had thus far escaped her notice.

Arabella nodded. "I have always enjoyed being out in the early morning."

Julia nodded in bitter agreement. "She does. She has made me go with her too many times." It was clear that her night of simulating a toothache had done nothing to sweeten her disposition.

"You shouldn't go out alone, Arabella," said Rebecca.

"But I don't, ma'am. You have just heard Julia say that she often goes with me," she responded lightly.

"Julia alone is not a suitable companion," replied Rebecca. "It would be best, of course, if you did not go out at all at such an ungodly hour, but you must have a groom with you if you do go out."

Arabella felt herself flushing, and she stared at her father, trying to catch his eye. "I don't wish to have a groom with me, Rebecca. I am only walking or riding on our own property, after all. It's not as though I were going several miles away."

"That isn't the point, Arabella. You may not walk out alone. You must be accompanied by a suitable servant or by a member of the family. I must insist upon it."

Everyone sat in uneasy silence, looking at Arabella, who stared at her stepmother with undisguised fury. When she spoke, however, her voice was soft.

Rising from the table, she said, "I'm afraid that you must excuse me, ma'am—from the breakfast table and from your rules. What you require is foolish—and with what authority you require it, I am uncertain. *There* sits my father, the only one present who has authority over me."

Mr. Standish looked miserably uncomfortable. "Now, now, Bella," he temporized. "Let's talk about this for a minute and be reasonable."

Arabella's back was rigid as she stood behind her chair. "I will be in the nursery, Papa, when you wish to speak with me. I suppose that is quite a suitable place for our meeting, considering the restrictions that are being placed upon me. I can only be surprised that you think I can find my way there alone."

The fire in the nursery had been laid but not yet lighted, but Arabella felt no chill, her anger heating her thoroughly. When her father appeared beside her, she was still seething.

He pulled a low chair next to her and seated himself uncomfortably. "Now, Bel," he said, "will you not say goodbye to your father before he sails so far away?"

Tears suddenly misted her vision. Even though he had been away often enough in the years since her mother died, this was the farthest he had ever gone, and the West Indies sounded like the ends of the earth.

Throwing her arms around him, she sobbed into his shoulder. "I don't want you to go, Papa! It's not too late to change your mind—stay with us!"

He smoothed her hair consolingly. "Now, now, Bel," he murmured awkwardly, "I'll be home before you know it. And even though you're angry with Rebecca now, remember that she's just trying to take care of you, and all that she knows is the way she was reared. Can you understand that?"

Arabella looked up at him, her eyes red from weeping, and nodded. "I can understand that, Papa," she said, "but I don't think that Rebecca can understand that things are different here. I can't be made a prisoner on our own land, with a servant tagging after me everywhere."

"Of course not." Her father nodded. "I'll speak to her about that before I go. I like your early habits—they're like your mother's."

He looked into her eyes gravely for a moment. "Rebecca will do her best for you, Bella. Do I have your word that you'll help her here?"

There was a barely perceptible pause and then Arabella nodded, wiping her eyes and pressing her lips together firmly. "As long as she doesn't try to rule our every move, Papa, I will do my best."

He hugged her again. "That's all I ask, Bella. You're the strongest of my children, so I trust you to take care of everyone until I'm home again next year."

It was a forlorn little group that stood on the gravel drive and waved to Mr. Standish for as long as he was in sight. He leaned from the window, waving his pocket handkerchief like a flag until the carriage disappeared around a bend. He was in the new barouche, and he had promised Rebecca that John Coachman would bring it back from Liverpool as soon as he arrived so that they would have it for their own use at home.

The girls discovered in short order that life at Boxwood Hall would not remain the same. When Arabella went out for her walk the next morning after her father's departure, she discovered James, one of the footmen, waiting for her at the bottom of the stairs. He had been apologetic but determined, and it was clear that Rebecca had meant that she would not walk unchaperoned, no matter what her father had said. It was disconcerting to know that he was following along behind her, and equally disconcerting to have Henry, one of the grooms, riding with her. Reluctantly she gave up her early morning rambles—except on the mornings when she could convince one of her sisters to accompany her.

Mr. Standish had been gone no more than a week when the next great change occurred. As Arabella was passing Flossie's room, she heard the sounds of an unusual amount of activity. Their governess was packing her trunk, weeping into her handkerchief all the while.

"Where are you going, Flossie?" asked Arabella in concern. Flossie had never had her trunk out in the six years she had been with them. "Has something happened to your sister?"

The only relative Miss Floss had in the world was her sister in Yorkshire, who wrote to her faithfully on birthdays and Christmas. At this mention of her sister, Flossie sobbed more loudly and shook her head.

"Well then, what's wrong? Where are you going?" demanded Arabella, taking Flossie's shoulders and turning her around.

"I've been let go," she sobbed. "I don't know what I'm to do now. Mr. Standish always said that I wouldn't have to worry, but now—"

At that point, Flossie was speaking to a vacant room, for Arabella had left abruptly, marching purposefully toward her stepmother's boudoir.

She found Rebecca there with Hudlow, carefully preparing herself for the callers she was expecting.

"May I speak with you alone, ma'am?" she asked, leaving the door open for Hudlow.

Rebecca stopped in her careful scrutiny of her complexion in a small hand mirror and regarded her for a moment with curiosity. "I don't think that we need have any secrets from Hudlow," she said carelessly. "What is it that is so urgent that you must interrupt me, Arabella?"

"Why have you let Flossie go?" Arabella demanded abruptly. "I'm sure that Papa never told you to do so."

Rebecca shrugged carelessly. "You and Elinor have no need of a governess, Arabella. How many times have you told me yourself that you are quite grown up?"

"And what of Julia?" she asked.

"I have decided that Julia will either go to Miss Brennan's school in Overton, or I will hire someone locally to give her her lessons. It will be better for her. Miss Floss is far too indulgent with you girls."

"But my father has promised Flossie that we'll take care of her! We can't just turn her out like this with nowhere to go!"

"Your father is far too kind for his own good," observed Rebecca. brushing a length of golden hair and arranging it carefully on her shoulder, admiring its brightness against the blue of her dressing gown. "He can't afford to be taking care of someone just because she cannot earn her way elsewhere."

"Of course Flossie can earn her way elsewhere, but she wasn't expecting to have to leave us!" protested Arabella. "Julia still needs her—she won't wish to go away to school!"

"Simply because she doesn't want to do something doesn't mean that it won't be the best thing for her, Arabella. As you are aware, your father left me in charge of his household affairs, and this is the decision I have made. It is in your father's best interests."

"In *your* best interests, you mean!" fumed Arabella. She paused a moment in her tirade and stared at her stepmother. "I wonder why you *really* wish to be ride of Flossie," she said slowly. "What would you not wish her to know?"

Rebecca laughed gaily. "What a very vivid imagination you have, Arabella. One would think that you did nothing but read novels. I could see that when you attempted to flirt with Will Russell—how embarrassed I was for you that night! And poor Mr. Russell scarcely knew where to look while you were behaving so boldly. I think that you need something a little more serious to occupy your time.''

Arabella stared at her. ''Whatever are you talking about, Rebecca?''

''You will see very soon,'' her stepmother responded. ''Now do leave us so that I won't keep my guests waiting.''

Arabella left the room seething in indignation. Rebecca's patronizing remarks about Will infuriated her, but she forced herself to put that aside and to concentrate on their present dilemma. Try as she would, however, she could think of no way to help Flossie. When she returned to her governess's chamber, she found Elinor and Julia there, all of them dissolved in tears at the prospect of parting.

''Is there nothing we can do, Bella?'' asked Elinor. ''Can't we reason with Rebecca? She surely wouldn't do this if she understood about Flossie. Why, she's like a member of the family.''

Arabella shook her head grimly. ''She knows, but she doesn't care. There's nothing we can do to change her mind.''

Too angry for tears now, and determined to be practical enough to help Flossie, she took her governess by the arm and led her, still sobbing, to a chair.

''Julia, ring for some tea. We need to make some arrangements before Flossie has to leave.''

A cup of tea helped a little in calming Miss Floss's nerves, and Arabella sat patting her hand and talking to her. ''Have you any money put aside, Flossie?'' she asked.

Miss Floss nodded, still dabbing at her eyes with her handkerchief.

''Is it enough to keep you until Papa comes home again? Do you have that much?''

Again Miss Floss nodded and Arabella sighed in relief. ''That's all right then, Flossie. When Papa comes home, you know that he will take care of everything, just as he always promised to do for you.''

"But where will she go now?" Elinor asked in concern. "We can't just let her go without knowing where she'll be."

Miss Floss straightened her small, plump shoulders. "I'll go to my sister in Yorkshire," she said. "She has a spare room and I can help with her expenses so that I won't be a burden. If it's just for a few months, I can do that."

Arabella hugged her. "Of course you can, Flossie. Now, write down her name and direction for us so that we'll be able to write to you and send for you as soon as possible."

While Miss Floss was doing so, Arabella wrote down the direction of her father's man of business in the West Indies and gave it to her. "Now, Flossie, as soon as you get to your sister's, write to our father and tell him just what has happened here."

Flossie nodded firmly, folding the slip of paper carefully and placing it in her reticule.

"And tell him, Flossie," Bella added, trying to think of the best way to say it so that no one would be more worried, "tell him that Rebecca has a plan of some sort for us here at the Hall. She is rearranging things more than I think he had planned for her to do."

"What sort of plan, Bella?" demanded Julia. "And how am I to have my lessons if Flossie is leaving?"

Not wishing to upset her by mentioning the boarding school, Arabella merely shrugged. "I'm not certain just what Rebecca has in mind, Julia, but you know that we are more than equal to her—so try not to worry."

The three of them stood again on the drive, waving this time to Flossie, who was seated in the dogcart for her ride to town. There she would take the stage to Yorkshire and her sister Betty to await the arrival of Mr. Standish in England.

As they turned back toward the house, Arabella caught a glimpse of movement and glanced up. The curtain had been drawn back at the window of Rebecca's private sitting room, and had just been allowed to fall again. Arabella had no doubt that her stepmother was watching everything.

"I wonder what she has in mind for us now," she mused in a low voice to Elinor.

They had not long to wait to find out. Hudlow arrived at their bedroom door before dinner was served that evening, announcing that they were to join their stepmother in her boudoir.

Rebecca sat at her dressing table, seeming not to notice the presence of the girls as Hudlow carefully curled her hair. An elegant gown of green moiré and matching slippers were laid out close by, and Arabella noted that Rebecca seemed to be taking remarkable pains for a quiet dinner at home, but she soon understood the situation.

"I will be dining with Squire Norton tonight," said Rebecca casually, taking notice of them at last. "And I have given Bruton orders that Sarah is to bring your dinner to the nursery tonight."

"To the nursery?" responded Arabella blankly . "Why are we to dine there? Has something happened in the dining room?"

"No, of course not, Arabella." Rebecca paused to dust her cheeks with powder, using the fabled rabbit's foot. Julia and Elinor, despite their interest in what their stepmother was saying, could scarcely take their eyes from it.

"It's simply more practical to arrange things this way," she explained catching Arabella's eye in the glass and looking at her coldly. "You will all take your meals there from now on, unless I inform you otherwise. It will be so much easier for the servants and so much less fuss."

"And you will be served in the dining room?" asked Arabella.

"Naturally. And of course I will be having guests quite regularly. As your father said, it's important to have people here more often."

"But he was talking about Elinor!" exclaimed Julia.

"Yes, of course he was," responded Arabella quickly. "What about Elinor, Rebecca? Papa said that the company was to help her prepare to come out next spring."

"Your father simply doesn't understand that it's not appropriate for a young girl to be seen in company until she is actually out," explained Rebecca. "He will trust me to do what is best for Elinor."

"What is best for you, you mean," said Arabella in a low, tight voice, glancing at Elinor's stricken expression.

"What did you say, Arabella?" demanded Rebecca, staring at her with eyes like blue marbles.

"Was Elinor included in the invitation to Squire Norton's dinner?" asked Arabella, ignoring the question.

"Yes." Rebecca laughed briefly. "How very rustic things are down here. I would have supposed they would know better than to do such a thing."

"They invited her because such things *are* acceptable here, Rebecca, and because you and Papa held a party here and she was a guest and danced. They understand that Elinor is to come out in the spring and they are helping her become accustomed to the way things will be, just as Papa had planned. It will just be a small party of friends."

Rebecca shrugged one shoulder. It was clear that she had no interest in talking any more about it, and Hudlow opened the door and motioned for them to leave.

"By the way, young ladies," said their stepmother before Hudlow had closed the door behind them.

"Yes, Rebecca?" asked Elinor, knowing that neither of the others would say a word.

"I had mentioned to Arabella earlier today that I think you all need some serious occupations to keep you busy, and so I have spoken with Cook."

"Spoken with Cook?" responded Arabella blankly. "What has that to say to anything?"

"I have told her that she is to undertake teaching the three

of you how to cook and keep house. It is an important thing
for a woman to know. I have instructed her that you are to do
some of Sarah's work, too."

"You're making us maids?" demanded Arabella angrily.

Rebecca shook her head. "Merely providing you with a
practical education," she responded. "It is not likely that you
will marry men of substance, and you must know how to keep
house."

"She is a witch!" Arabella fumed when they were back
within the confines of the nursery walls. "Imagine doing this
to us! Imagine saying that we would marry men of little fortune!
She isn't doing this to be kind or to teach us to be practical;
she's doing it because she knows it will make us unhappy!"

"But, Bella, dear, it's not so very terrible after all. All she
is asking us to do is to learn how to keep a large household—
and that *is* important."

Arabella shook her head in vexation. "Don't be such an
innocent, Elinor! She'd doing this simply to make us unhappy.
She wants us to feel that we are less important than she is. She
wants to break our spirits and humble us."

She looked around the nursery. "And she is going to begin
it by confining us to the nursery—except when we're doing
the work for Cook or the maids, of course."

"Well, who would want to be with her?" asked Julia bluntly.
"I would *rather* eat here with you and Elinor than in the dining
room with her."

"But she has no right to do such a thing!" Arabella, unable
to sit still, paced up and down the length of the nursery.

"She has every right," Elinor reminded her mildly, sitting
down in the low rocker by the fire and picking up Gingersnap.
"She is our stepmother and she is in charge of us in Papa's
absence."

Arabella never allowed herself to be deterred by facts. "You
know very well, Elinor, that Papa never intended for things to
be like this. Why, he was planning for you to have an especially

busy, happy time! He certainly never dreamed that you'd be consigned to the nursery!''

Elinor smiled gently. ''There's no need to work yourself into a passion, Bella. I won't really mind waiting until Papa comes home. We have quite enough to do if we are to give Julia her lessons—and now, of course, to take our lessons from Cook.''

Rebecca had said nothing more about Julia's education, and, fearing that she might be sent away to boarding school if they brought the matter up, Arabella and Elinor had decided to teach her themselves. They still had a good many of Flossie's books and her globe, and they planned Julia's lessons carefully so that she wouldn't be deprived after Flossie's departure.

Despite their banishment to the nursery, the late autumn days seemed to pass swiftly by. Rebecca was as good as her word. Cook took over their education and from her they learned how to make apple tart and to fillet a sole, from Sarah they learned how to dust and to lay a fire, from the little laundry maid they learned how to remove stains from their gowns and how to starch their linens.

In the nursery schoolroom, Julia studied geography and French with Elinor, the pianoforte and watercoloring with Arabella, and they took long walks together in the chilly afternoons. In the evenings they read aloud from Sir Walter Scott, and discussed what life would be like when their father came home again. And always, Arabella thought of Will Russell. She had hoped that she might hear from him, if only a message through Libbie at Longview.

The only times they really had a chance to see other people now were on the Sunday mornings when they walked to church. Rebecca did not attend services herself, and she informed the girls that there was no need to order the carriage for them—walking would be healthy. And they did not mind the walking except when the weather was inclement, but as winter drew closer, they were sometimes obliged to give up their walk to Sunday services.

"Cut off from the world!" said Arabella dramatically, staring out the nursery windows at the steadily falling snow. "Why did it feel obliged to do this on a Sunday? Couldn't it have held off until tomorrow? What if they've heard from Will at Longview and know when he'll be coming for the holidays?"

She dropped onto the sofa and pulled her feet up under her, staring at the fire.

"If they've heard from him, Libbie Gibson will let you know, Bella," responded Elinor soothingly.

Arabella was forced to smile. "That was a good idea of mine, wasn't it?"

Elinor nodded in agreement. "After we were restricted to the grounds, putting in a little postbox down by the footbridge is the only way you could have stayed in touch with Longview."

She smiled at her sister. "And so you have the satisfaction of knowing that Mr. Russell has asked about you, and that he has sent you his regards and his hope that he will be allowed to see you at Christmas."

"And we've heard from Tommie Norton, too," Arabella pointed out quickly, "sending his regards to you."

"You needn't be trying to make that into something, Bella," said Elinor mildly. "Tommie and I are friends, nothing more."

"Well, *I* don't especially mind not wading to church in the snow this morning," said Julia cheerfully, who was at an age to be readily comforted by cinnamon toast and a cup of chocolate. "At least we didn't get caught in the storm. It would have been worse had it started while we were at services and we'd had to trudge home in it."

"We wouldn't have had to walk home," retorted Arabella. "Someone would have taken us up in their carriage and brought us back—since Rebecca thinks that we're not important enough to have use of our own carriage."

Elinor shook her head. "You know that she has forbidden us to accept rides, Bella. She'd be very angry if she found out we had done so. Remember Tommie."

Tommie Norton and Andrew Barrisford had called upon Elinor soon after her party, only to be turned away by Rebecca, who had informed them that she and Mr. Standish had decided that Elinor was a little young as yet to have gentleman callers. Later, after one of their long walks, Tommie had come upon them on their way home just as it was starting to rain. He had taken them up in his gig and they had crowded merrily in, Julia sitting on her sisters' laps and trying to hold the umbrella to shelter all of them.

It was from Tommie that they learned of his call and Rebecca's response. Elinor grew quiet, but Bella gave full vent to her fury.

"Do you mean to say that your father didn't agree to that?" asked Tommie, wide-eyed.

"Of course not!" replied Arabella angrily. "He intended quite the opposite—that's why he had the party!"

"The party was also for Rebecca," Elinor reminded her calmly. She smiled at Tommie. "Thank you for coming to call, Tommie. Perhaps you and Andrew will come again when Papa returns."

"We will most certainly come then, Elinor," he responded with a smile, "but we'd rather not wait so long. Do you think that we should try again?"

They had known Tommie since childhood, but they had not seen much of him since their mother's death, which had occurred at about the same time he had gone away to school. He had always been a pleasant-mannered boy, and it was clear that he hadn't changed in that respect.

Elinor shook her head and tried to smile. "I don't think that would do anything more than make Rebecca angry with us," she replied. "It's very kind of you to offer, though."

"Well, we'll surely see you at the Christmas ball, won't we?" he asked.

The girls looked at him blankly.

"What Christmas ball?" inquired Arabella. "Is your father giving one?"

"We're giving a small evening party, of course," he replied. "We never let the season go by without that. And we have invited you—all of you—but my mother said that Rebecca wrote in her note that she was the only one of the family who could accept."

He looked at Elinor regretfully. "But the ball is to be at Boxwood. Didn't you know about it?"

All three of the girls regarded him with astonishment. *"We're* to have a ball?" demanded Julia. She turned quickly to Arabella. "I shan't have the toothache this time, Bella, I warn you— and I shall have my share of the refreshments instead of lying in bed, pretending to be sick."

Tommie looked a little startled at this outburst, but Arabella merely laughed. She had been thinking hard, trying to overcome her frustration with the situation well enough to be able to come up with a plan of some sort, and her expression had brightened with Tommie's news. They had known that Rebecca was having house guests during the holidays, but they had heard nothing yet of her other plans.

"A Christmas ball!" she exclaimed. "Wonderful! Nothing could be better!"

As they drew up in front of Boxwood and Tommie had hurried around to help them down, she had given him a radiant smile despite the rain. "We shall most certainly see you at the Christmas ball, Tommie, and I assure you that you will be able to call after that."

They had thanked him for the ride and hurried inside to change from their wet things. Before they could do so, however, Sarah had appeared and told them with a nervous look that they were to see their stepmother immediately.

They hurried to Rebecca's dressing room immediately—or, more precisely, Elinor and Julia hurried and pulled Arabella along between them. Rebecca's expression was ominous as she turned to face them.

"I saw you arrive with Tommie Norton," she began, and Elinor, eager to avoid more trouble, had interceded quickly, hoping to keep Arabella from saying something to make Rebecca angrier than she clearly already was.

"Yes, it was kind of him to try to save us from the rain and mud."

"I see that he was not particularly successful," replied Rebecca, eyeing their muddy skirts and boots with annoyance. Fortunately they had already removed their dripping bonnets.

"The reason I have summoned you," she continued, "is to tell you that I don't expect you to accepts rides in anyone else's equipage—not Tommie Norton's, not Colonel Twickenham's, not anyone's. Do I make myself clear?"

"More than clear," responded Arabella tartly. "You wish for us to have to trudge through the mud and be exposed to the elements so that you can show us how very insignificant we are, while you make use of our father's carriage and horses. I wonder what he would think of your treating us in such a shabby manner."

Rebecca flushed. "Your father has complete confidence in my judgment, young lady!" she snapped. "Walking in the fresh air is healthy for young, growing girls, while accepting rides with others—particularly young, unescorted men—is simply not acceptable behavior. If I cannot trust you to keep the line in your behavior, I shall simply forbid you to leave the grounds of Boxwood."

"Oh, I assure you we will be more cautious, Rebecca," Elinor hastened to assure her, alarmed at the thought of losing their opportunities to walk abroad together and fearful that Arabella might say something that would cause their stepmother to become still more unreasonable. "And I'm certain that we should remove ourselves from the carpet. I'm afraid we've made a fearful mess of your dressing room."

"You mean of *Mama's* dressing room," said Julia, ignoring her stepmother's angry glance. "And those were Mama's jewels," she added accusingly, pointing to an open velvet case.

Arabella moved closer to see what Julia was pointing to and gasped when she saw them. The diamonds that lay there, a delicate necklace and bracelet, two graceful pairs of earrings and a dinner ring, comprised the set that her father had told her would be hers.

"What are you planning to do with those, Rebecca?" she asked angrily, pointing to the jewels.

"Why, wear them, of course," responded her stepmother, picking up the necklace and holding it up to her throat, admiring the effect in the mirror of her dressing table. "They are just what I will need for the ball."

"Who gave you permission to wear them?" she demanded.

Rebecca raised her eyebrows. "Gave me permission?" she inquired. "Allow me to remind you, Arabella, that I am mistress here. I may wear them if I please to do so."

"Papa never gave those to you," she responded. "He had intended them for me."

"Well, they aren't for you any longer, Arabella. It would be such a waste, at any rate. At least I wear my jewels—there is no need for you girls having such things just now."

Rebecca casually opened another case, and to Arabella's horror, she saw that it contained Elinor's string of pearls, as well as the other pieces of that set. She heard the sharp intake of Elinor's breath as she saw them, too. Even Julia's eyes grew larger.

"And what are you doing with Elinor's pearls?" Arabella asked in a deliberately even voice. "You know very well that Papa gave those to her just before he left."

Rebecca shrugged carelessly. "That was a foolish thing for John to do. He simply hadn't considered the possibility that I might need them, nor that Elinor is really too young for such expensive jewelry."

"You know that isn't true, Rebecca," said Arabella in a low voice. "She will need them for the Christmas ball."

Rebecca threw back her head and laughed, her golden hair rippling in cascades down her back. "No, she won't, Arabella, I assure you. Elinor won't be going to the Christmas ball, so there will be no inconvenience at all."

"Why wouldn't she be going to the ball?" asked Julia, puzzled. She could see the distress in Elinor's eyes and the anger in Arabella's.

"As I have been telling you," said Rebecca with an air of exaggerated patience, "all of you are too young for that kind of thing. The schoolroom is where you belong."

She rose from her dressing table and tossed the diamond necklace back into its case. "And I am quite weary of having to explain the proper rules of behavior to the three of you. I have a guest downstairs, and when I come back up in a little while, I will expect to find the mess in this room straightened up."

After she had swept from the room, the three girls stood staring at one another. Suddenly Arabella walked to the dressing table and began closing the velvet cases.

"What are you doing, Bella?" asked Elinor in a horrified whisper.

"I'm taking our things," Arabella responded. "These are not hers, whatever she might say." And she opened a dark blue box that lay to one side. There sparkled the blue sapphires that John Standish had said would one day belong to Julia. She added that to the other two boxes and started toward the door.

"Bella, you can't do that! She'll be furious and she'll take them back anyway. We'll just be making her angry for nothing."

"I'm not taking anything else, Elinor—only the three sets that I know belong to us. And she *won't* find them, I promise you—no matter how angry she becomes!"

Elinor began hurriedly trying to remove some of the mud

from the carpet, using a handkerchief to pick up some of the larger pieces, but Arabella took her arm and pulled her from the room.

"And never mind doing that, Elinor. She can call one of the maids to take care of it. She just wanted to show that she could order us about and force us to be her servants."

Under Arabella's instructions, Elinor and Julia returned immediately to their chambers and changed their gowns and slippers.

"But where are you going, Bella?" asked Julia.

Arabella shook her head and put her finger to her lips. "I'll tell you later," she whispered.

When she reappeared almost an hour later, Julia and Elinor were waiting anxiously by the nursery fire. She had changed from her muddy things, and her eyes were bright with triumph.

"Well, Lady Rebecca won't find them now," she said in a satisfied voice.

"Where did you put them, Bella?" demanded Julia. "Are you certain she can't find them?"

Arabella nodded. "Remember the trunk filled with Mama's things that Papa had the footmen haul up to the attic?"

The others nodded. "They are inside that trunk, under some of her gowns and a packet of letters bound in blue ribbon."

Julia clapped her hands together. "What an excellent place, Bella! No one ever goes to the attic. She'll never think of looking there."

Only Elinor looked grave. "You know that Rebecca won't let it go at this," she said. "She wants to show us that she's in charge, and every time we go against her, she does something to punish us."

"Let her," replied Arabella. "She is already punishing us. What else can she do to us? If she tries to force me to tell her where the jewelry is, I shall announce that I am going to report her to Colonel Twickenham." The colonel was the local magistrate.

"I shall write to Flossie, too, and tell her," she added. "Even though it seems odd that we haven't heard from her yet, we do have her sister's direction. I shall give the letter to Libbie to send for me."

Rebecca must have believed that Arabella was fully capable of carrying her complaint to the colonel, for she satisfied herself with a lesser punishment than they had expected. She forbade them to leave the grounds of Boxwood on their daily rambles. They had shown an appropriate amount of distress at her announcement, enough to give her some satisfaction, but in reality, the weather had grown so unpleasant that there was little temptation to walk very far abroad. Arabella very quickly set up the postbox arrangement with Libbie, much to everyone's satisfaction, for even Julia got notes through it. And, in the meantime, there was the ball to look forward to. The house guests for the holiday would be arriving in less than a week.

"The house looks wonderful, doesn't it?" sighed Elinor. The servants had been hanging greenery everywhere, and the whole house had begun to acquire a festive look. The wooden floors had been polished until they shone and Julia, who had sneaked down to the ballroom to slide across it in her stocking feet, announced that it was better than skating on the frozen pond at Longview.

Only Arabella, who had been down to check the postbox a dozen times each day, seemed unmoved.

"Don't worry, Bel. You know that he's coming," Elinor comforted her.

"Yes, but what if something has happened to him?" she asked. "The roads have been dreadful, and—"

She was interrupted by the arrival of some of Rebecca's house guests. Bruton ushered in a dark, imposing gentleman accompanied by a slender young man with chestnut hair. Rebecca had not confided in them the identities of her guests, but since she was not present to greet them, Elinor felt that someone from the family should do so.

"I'm Elinor Standish," she said gently, extending her hand to the older gentleman. "We are so pleased that you could join us for the holidays."

He bowed over her hand. "It is a great pleasure to meet you, Miss Standish. I am—"

"Lord Wraxton!" exclaimed Rebecca, hurrying down the stairs. "I am delighted to see you here at Boxwood Hall!" She surged toward them and presented her hand to him.

"Mrs. Standish, Miss Standish, allow me to present my nephew, Robert Halliday," said Lord Wraxton, indicating the young man at his side. "Robert is the clever one in the family, the one who writes all my speeches for the House of Lords."

Mr. Halliday bowed and smiled as Lord Wraxton glanced over at Arabella and Julia, who had kept their distance from the group at the door. "And who are these lovely young ladies?" he inquired, raising his glass to look at them.

Before Rebecca had a chance to reply, Elinor responded, "These are my sisters Arabella and Julia," whereupon those two young ladies dropped a curtsey to the others.

Lord Wraxton turned to Rebecca, smiling, "You had not told me how lovely your stepdaughters are, Mrs. Standish."

Rebecca's smile was so brief as to be almost nonexistent. "They are just on their way to the schoolroom," she returned, directing a speaking glance at the girls. "They still have their lessons to finish."

She had no way of knowing whether they did or didn't have lessons to finish, of course, Arabella reflected. She simply wanted them out of the way—and, of course, she wished to emphasize their position.

"I shall look forward to seeing you at dinner this evening, ladies," Lord Wraxton responded, bowing to them as they started toward the stairs.

Rebecca looked unhappy. "They won't be joining us for dinner, Lord Wraxton. We have other guests coming, too, and the girls are rather young for company."

Lord Wraxton stared at her intently. "Too young? Nonsense! Miss Julia might be a trifle young, but it will do her good—and it *is* the holidays."

He paused a moment, still looking at Rebecca. "Come now, Mrs. Standish, surely you won't deprive us of the pleasure of their company." It was clear that Lord Wraxton was a man accustomed to having his way.

"Of course I would not do anything to make your stay less pleasant, Lord Wraxton," she responded, defeated. Turning to the girls, she added in a sterner tone, "Be certain that you have taken care of everything you need to before coming down to dinner."

The young ladies nodded, bowing to their guests and smiling at Lord Wraxton, and departed demurely.

Dinner that evening was a pleasant event for everyone except Rebecca. She was arrayed in a breathtaking gown of her favorite cerulean blue, and even Arabella was forced to admire her.

"It is a thousand pities, though, that her behavior is not in keeping with her appearance," she murmured to Elinor.

Four other couples had been invited, including the Nortons and the Twickenhams, so the numbers were uneven. Elinor was escorted in to dinner by Mr. Halliday, while Arabella gave Julia her arm and they went in smiling. Julia was not particularly charmed to be a part of such an event, but she was pleased to see that Rebecca had been forced to invite them. That would have been quite enough to guarantee her pleasure in the evening. Colonel Twickenham and Squire Norton were particularly attentive to the young ladies, even insisting upon leaving the table to join the ladies early so that they could play at jackstraws with the young ladies. It was, Arabella was certain, scarcely the sophisticated evening that Rebecca had hoped for. She and Lord Wraxton had played cards with some of the other guests, but there was a substantial amount of noise and laughter from the group playing jackstraws.

"It was a much better evening than I had thought it would

be,'' announced Julia as they went upstairs by the nursery fire at the end of the evening. "I had expected to be bored, but it was really great fun playing jackstraws. I didn't know that Squire Norton and Colonel Twickenham played at games like that."

"Well, they do have families of their own," Arabella pointed out. "And I think that they were trying to be particularly kind to us. Libbie said that some of the neighbors are worried about us now that Papa has gone."

"Mr. Halliday was very nice—and very good at jackstraws," observed Julia. "I believe he could have won the game if he hadn't spent so much time talking to Elinor."

"Ah, Elinor—a conquest!" murmured Arabella wickedly, turning to look at her sister. To her surprise, Elinor was flushing a fiery red.

"How can you talk so, Arabella?" she asked sharply. "I wasn't flirting, nor was Mr. Halliday. He was a perfect gentleman."

Both of her sisters stared at her in amazement. Sweet-natured Elinor never snapped at anyone.

"You know I was only teasing, Elinor," said Arabella, patting her sister's hand. "Don't be angry with me."

Elinor's high color subsided and she gave a little laugh. "Of course I'm not angry, Bella. It's just—well, don't make sport of Mr. Halliday as you do of everyone else. He is too kind to be treated so."

"Of course I won't if you don't wish me to," Arabella reassured her, amazed at this reaction from gentle Elinor. "Tell us about him, Elinor. What did you two talk about?"

"He told me about his family," she responded, turning her face to the fire and studying the flames. "He has three sisters and a mother to provide for, and his father was Lord Wraxton's younger brother, so there isn't a great deal of money. Lord Wraxton is helping him and Mr. Halliday is so very grateful to him—and very serious about his work. I believe Lord Wraxton was correct when he said that Mr. Halliday is very bright.''

Elinor stopped talking, but continued to rock and look into the flames, a little smile curving the corners of her lips.

Arabella watched her, astounded by her sister's behavior. Mr. Halliday would bear watching.

The next two days were quiet, pleasant ones. Three other house guests arrived, a Mr. and Mrs. Justin Coates and a tall, spare gentleman named Eustace Blair, who appeared to be of a philosophical turn of mind and spent his time in the library. There were lavish late breakfasts, long country walks, occasional games of cards and billiards, and quiet conversation.

Arabella had some trouble determining just who the guests were and why they had been invited, but she began to fit together her bits of information. All of them, except Mr. and Mrs. Coates, knew her father in some way or another. Lord Wraxton had business investments with him, so Rebecca had taken advantage of this connection to invite a peer of the realm. She appeared to be interested in furthering her social aspirations, Lord Wraxton, his financial ones. Mr. Blair had been invited at her father's request, for Mr. Blair had helped him after Mama's death and he had recently lost his own wife. Mr. and Mrs. Coates were more of a mystery. They appeared well-bred enough, but precisely where they made their permanent home and precisely who they were seemed impossible to discover. Fortunately, however, everyone appeared to get on well together, and life at Boxwood Hall was busier and happier than it had been in a long while.

On the second morning after Lord Wraxton's arrival, Arabella found a note from Libbie, written in a hurried scrawl. Will would be at Longview the following day and would assuredly attend their ball that night. Bella flew back to her chamber, scarcely seeming to touch the ground, and began a careful inspection of the green velvet gown she would wear the next night. Rebecca had not mentioned the ball to them, neither inviting nor forbidding their attendance. Arabella suspected that she was rather nervous of Lord Wraxton's reaction should they be forbidden. It did not matter to Arabella whether she forbade it or not. She had every intention of attending and of dragging Elinor along with her.

"Should we be doing this?" Elinor asked her nervously on the evening of the ball. Arabella had just tied a silver sash under the bodice of Elinor's white gown, and was studying the effect. Julia, who planned to slip down and sit behind one of the screens to watch the whole event, sat in the rocker, Gingersnap in her lap.

"Of course we should, dear," returned Arabella absently, still absorbed in the proper arrangement of the sash. "It is, after all, our home and we should be in attendance. You know that it's what Papa wanted."

"How could he have married someone who would treat us like this?" demanded Julia.

"Well, of course he had no way of knowing that Rebecca would change after he went away," said Elinor pacifically. "He wanted us to be happy."

Julia snorted, her face in the cat's furry back, causing Gingersnap to turn and stare at her reproachfully. "Then he should have stayed home!"

"Here you are, Elinor, the final touch, my dear. Your pearl necklace and earrings." Arabella brought forth the box from a box of painting supplies in the corner cupboard, where she had carefully hidden them after bringing them down from the attic.

"Do you think I should wear them, Bella?" asked Elinor hesitantly. "Rebecca will be furious when she sees them."

Arabella shrugged. "What can she do? She can't take them away from you there, nor say that they aren't yours, for half the people there will have seen you wearing them at the evening party with Papa. Besides, Papa would want you to wear them."

Elinor regained a little of her color and nodded, slipping on the earrings carefully.

"You look beautiful, Elinor," said Arabella sincerely. "Mr. Halliday will be mesmerized."

"You promised you wouldn't tease, Bella," Elinor reminded her, her color increasing.

Elinor had talked with Mr. Halliday in the drawing room each evening after dinner, and had played a request from him on the pianoforte. It was difficult for someone of Bella's temperament to gauge the amount of interest there, but, knowing her quiet sister as well as she did, she suspected that it was increasing daily—and she had begged Arabella not to tease her about Mr. Halliday, saying that they were merely friends.

"What about your diamonds, Bella?" asked Julia. "Will you wear them?"

Arabella shook her head. "They're still safely put away in the attic. I'm too young for diamonds, and besides, Papa hasn't presented them to me yet."

The girls waited until the ballroom was quite full, knowing that Rebecca would not wish them to be in a receiving line with her and fearing that she might find a way to send them back if she saw them then. Almost everyone was dancing when they entered the room. Julia slipped immediately behind a screen, in front of which had been arranged several palms.

Arabella and Elinor started to place themselves discreetly behind a small clutch of elderly ladies who were deep in discussion of someone's outrageous gown when Bella heard her name. Turning, she saw Will Russell striding toward her, his smile warm.

"I was hoping that you would be coming in soon," he said warmly, taking her hand and bowing to Elinor. "I had been lingering in the hall, ducking in and out the door into the cold to keep from being called in to take a partner for the opening set."

He smiled down at her. "I'm afraid that my hostess will not

be pleased with my ungentlemanly behavior, but I was hoping to dance with you."

"Go ahead, Bella," said Elinor as Arabella glanced at her sister. "I'll talk to the ladies or check on Julia. Don't worry about me."

"I don't think that's what you'll be doing," returned Arabella in amusement, for she had caught a glimpse of Mr. Halliday making his way around the room toward them.

And so they joined the others on the dance floor, none of them noticing Rebecca's expression when she saw them. She was dancing with Lord Wraxton and was not at all pleased when he noted with pleasure that his nephew was dancing with Elinor.

"She is a lovely young woman," he said, watching them. "Robert is very taken with her. I have never seen him this attentive. He even accompanied her to the conservatory this afternoon, and I know that being around so much greenery causes him to have sneezing fits, but he went like a lamb to the slaughter."

"How touching," murmured Rebecca, promising herself that she would put an end to any further outings.

"I haven't been here in years," he remarked, looking around the ballroom, the glow of candlelight reflected from the polished floors and the pier glasses along the wall. "Not since Caro died has there been a party in this room. It is a great pity that John isn't here to see his girls look so well—and you, of course, Rebecca," he hastened to add, seeing her eyebrows snap together.

"They really shouldn't be here tonight, Lord Wraxton, for, as I told you, they really are too young, and—" She broke off abruptly, a look of sudden confusion upon her face.

"And what?" probed her partner, frowning.

"Well, I hate to say anything, even to you, Lord Wraxton, although you are such a great friend of John's."

"Say anything about what?"

"Elinor seems to be such a quiet, lovely girl, but I'm afraid—" Here she paused and bit her lip, not meeting Lord Wraxton's eyes.

"You're afraid of what?" he demanded, growing impatient. "What is it that you're saying about Elinor?"

The movements of the dance separated them then, but not before his words had caught the attention of some of the nearby dancers, who looked at one another questioningly.

Once Rebecca had rejoined her partner, she knew that she had his full attention—and was quite certain that she had the full attention of several others.

She lowered her voice, but not enough to make it impossible to hear her words. "I fear that she is inclined to take things that don't belong to her," she said, watching his face.

Lord Wraxton stared at her in disbelief. "You're saying that little Elinor is a *thief?*" he demanded, lowering his voice only at the last minute. "What are you talking about?"

"John gave her Caro's pearls before he left for the Indies, thinking that they would be a comfort to her while he was gone, and I'm afraid that she likes jewels a little too well, for she wasn't content merely to have those."

Lord Wraxton merely stared at her, waiting for her to continue, while those dancing nearest attempted to look as though they hadn't heard a thing while straining to hear the rest.

"I found her in my dressing room several weeks ago, and after she had left, I discovered that I was missing a number of my own pieces of jewelry—pieces that I can't possibly replace."

"How do you know they weren't taken by one of the servants?" he demanded.

"Because I had had them out admiring them just before she came in to talk to me. I was called out for just a few minutes and when I came back, they were gone. Besides," she added, "even Arabella admits that they're gone. I think that she helped her sister to hide them—trying to protect her, I should imagine.

And, of course, I haven't wished to make an issue of it. I'm afraid that she has a very serious problem, and I shall wait until John is home to deal with it."

Lord Wraxton looked grave. "I'm sorry to hear of such a happening, Rebecca. It speaks well for you that your interest is in the girl's welfare, not in your own jewels."

Rebecca smiled, looking celestial. "You are too kind, Lord Wraxton. It is difficult, of course, trying to be a mother to three young girls. I'm afraid that they resent me."

"That's natural enough," he told her. "You're taking their mother's place, and you are young enough and beautiful enough to compete with them."

He paused a moment, looking down at her. "You know, I was afraid that John had made a dreadful mistake in marrying someone he had known for so short a time, but now I am strongly inclined to think that he was a wiser man than I had given him credit for being."

Rebecca blushed prettily. "Why, thank you, sir," she said, lowering her eyes modestly. "I am glad to know that I have someone like you to rely upon in John's absence."

"Of course you may depend upon me," he said sincerely. She noted with pleasure that his eyes were following Elinor and Robert, and had the satisfaction of knowing that *that* relationship would be short-lived.

Unaware of the trouble brewing about them, Elinor and Arabella spent a happy evening, dancing with their young men the three dances allowed with one partner, eating supper with them, and carrying dainties to Julia and Gingersnap, who were secreted behind the screen. Gingersnap was not pleased by so much movement and music, but she had come in search of Julia and had taken up residence upon her lap, appropriating her share of the delicacies.

"Are you having a good time?" she asked Will, who had just brought her a glass of lemonade.

"A delightful time," he assured her. "It could only be improved if you were free to dance with me."

She giggled. "What would we do with Gingersnap?" she asked. "I don't believe she dances."

Will regarded the cat seriously for a moment. "Are you certain?" he asked, and with one strong arm he scooped both Julia and Gingersnap from their chair and out into the hall.

Laughing, they joined hands and moved lightly to the music, Gingersnap riding in outraged dignity on Julia's shoulders. Once around the hall was quite enough for her, and she leaped to the floor and marched majestically up the steps, tail held high.

"You appear to do most of your dancing away from the ballroom, Mr. Russell," said Rebecca, appearing in the doorway with Lord Wraxton. "And always with females who are unsuitably young."

Julia's face fell and Will, noting it and thinking of the unhappiness that Libbie had hinted at, replied lightly, "And always with lovely young ladies of impeccable taste."

And he bowed formally to Julia, saying "May I escort you back to your place, Miss Julia?"

She bobbed a curtsey and smiled, pleased to see her stepmother bested. "Thank you, sir," she replied, taking his arm.

"Just a moment, Julia," Rebecca snapped. She had intended to announce that Julia could take herself to bed instead of back to the ballroom, but seeing Lord Wraxton's expression at her tone of voice, she caught herself in time.

Walking over to Julia, she straightened her sash, then patted the astonished girl on the cheek. "Enjoy yourself, my dear," she said sweetly.

Julia stared at her in disbelief, then quietly left the room with Will, looking back only once to be certain that Rebecca wasn't about to change her mind.

When it was time for the guests to leave, Will lingered beside

Arabella. "Do you still take your early morning rambles, even in the winter, Miss Arabella?" he asked in a low voice.

She smiled. "I used to, but I'm not allowed to walk unattended any longer."

"I assure you, ma'am, that you will not be unattended, should you walk tomorrow morning," he replied. "And I would like it beyond all things if you would dress as you did before, with those scarlet ribbons in your hair."

And so it was that Arabella set out early the next frosty morning, dressed in her dark cloak and boots, the scarlet ribbons knotted in the darkness of her hair. She did not leave the house alone, however, for Elinor, fearful of what Rebecca might do if she should hear from the servants that Arabella had left alone, insisted upon accompanying her most of the way and waiting for her at a distance while she talked to Will.

"Are you half-frozen?" he asked teasingly, catching her arm as she slid on the frosted grass coming down the hill.

"No, it feels wonderful to be out walking again," she said sincerely. Giving up her early morning rambles had been a real hardship for Arabella, and so this morning had offered double pleasure—Will and the walk.

"Yes, Libbie told me your stepmother wouldn't allow you to walk without a servant any longer—and that she had let your governess go." He frowned a little as he looked down at her. "Is everything really quite all right?"

"It will be all right when Papa comes home again," she responded, unwilling to air the family's dirty laundry, even to Will or Libbie. She had kept from Libbie most of the things that had happened with Rebecca, sharing only the things that would be publicly known. Even though she disliked her stepmother heartily, she was still her father's wife and, remembering him, she couldn't bring herself to discredit Rebecca.

"We have missed you here," she said lightly, looking up at him.

"Then I know that you have had very little to occupy your time," he responded with a smile.

She said nothing, but stared down at her small gloved hands, clasped together on the railing of the bridge.

After a brief pause, he put a finger beneath her chin, causing her to look up at him. "And what you were supposed to say," he said, "was 'I've been very busy, sir, but I've thought of you every day.'"

"And why would I say such a thing as that, Mr. Russell?" she inquired sweetly, smiling into his dark eyes.

"Because I've been very busy, Miss Arabella, but I've thought of *you* every day."

She studied him for a moment. "Yes, I can see that you have been pining away," she commented lightly. "Your family must fear for your health."

He threw back his head and laughed. "You occasionally make it very difficult to be lover-like, Miss Arabella. Are you this difficult with all the young men?"

"Always," she responded, acting as though there had been dozens. "And is this what you say with all of the young ladies?"

"Never." His laughter stopped abruptly and he bent toward her, taking her hand. "I have never—"

"Bella!" Elinor's voice rang out frantically from the top of the hill. "Someone's coming, Bella!"

"Goodbye, sir," said Arabella, reclaiming her hand and hurrying away. "Perhaps I shall see you before you leave again for London."

"I must leave this afternoon . . . Bella. That's what I intended to tell you this morning. I'll be abroad on business until May— I'll write to you," he called. "Don't forget me!"

And turning, he disappeared swiftly into the copse on the Longview side of the bridge, well aware that being seen with him could only do her more harm with her stepmother.

The disappointment of knowing he was leaving so soon was keen, but she had no time to dwell upon it for a while. When she reached the top of the hill and Elinor, they realized that it was Julia who was racing across the meadow toward them.

"They're leaving!" Julia gasped as she reached them.

"Who is leaving?" demanded Arabella.

"Lord Wraxton and Mr. Halliday. Their baggage was being brought down a few minutes ago."

Elinor had turned pale. "Do you know why they're leaving, Julia?" she asked. "Mr. Halliday had supposed they would be here for another week."

Julia shook her head. "I didn't hear a thing except for Rebecca telling them how sorry she was that they had to leave so soon and that she hoped they would come again."

They walked home at a rapid pace, but by the time they had reached Boxwood, Lord Wraxton's carriage was almost out of sight. They stood there a moment, dazed by the suddenness of their departure, and Arabella put her arms around Elinor's shoulders.

"There must have been an emergency of some sort," she told her sister soothingly. "I'm certain that Mr. Halliday left a note for you."

Rebecca was waiting for them just inside the door. "It is a shame that they had to leave without seeing you," she said sweetly, her voice indicating that it was anything but a shame. "Poor Lord Wraxton was called away and of course Mr. Halliday was eager to accompany him."

"Eager to accompany him?" echoed Elinor. "Is that what he said?"

Rebecca nodded. "Lord Wraxton told him that he needn't cut short his own holiday, but the dear boy insisted that he attend his uncle. I suppose he had become bored with our quiet company in the country."

"Yes, I should imagine so," responded Elinor tonelessly, turning toward the staircase.

"If you had not taken one of those early morning strolls, you would have been here to say goodbye," Rebecca called up the stairs after them. "Of course, I don't suppose it was a matter of any great consequence that you missed them."

"No, of course it was not," responded Arabella, looking down at her stepmother with intense dislike.

Smiling, Rebecca went into the drawing room to enjoy her victory. Lord Wraxton had obviously been alarmed by her story about Elinor and by his nephew's clear partiality for her. It had taken only a little push more to have him remove his nephew from danger. Rebecca had been more than happy to supply that push.

Late last night after the ball, she had gone to his room, looking troubled.

"Do you know to whom this belongs, Lord Wraxton?" she asked, holding out a heavy jeweled paperweight on the palm of her hand.

"Yes, of course I do. It's mine," he responded. "How do you come to have it, Mrs. Standish?"

She sighed and stared down at the floor. "I'm afraid that I found it in Elinor's room, on her dressing table. I knew that it wasn't hers, and I feared that it must belong to one of the guests."

She looked up at him with large, melting eyes. "I am so dreadfully sorry that this happened, Lord Wraxton, but I am grateful that it was you. You have been so very understanding about poor Elinor."

"I'm afraid that her problem is a grievous one," said Lord Wraxton seriously. "I have known one or two other people who suffer from this same kind of illness—not needing things but not being able to keep from taking what doesn't belong to them—and their families have had to take very strict measures to keep them from such behavior."

"I fear you're right," she said in a low voice. "This will break John's heart."

He patted her hand. "You'll help him all you can, I know." He frowned a moment, thinking things over. "What I must do is to remove my nephew before any real harm is done there. I can see that he's very interested in Elinor, and I wouldn't want him to break his heart over this.''

"Of course not," murmured Rebecca. "You must think of your duty to your family."

"Just so," he agreed. "I think that the best thing would be to remove ourselves to London tomorrow morning, if you'll forgive me for leaving you so abruptly, Mrs. Standish— Rebecca."

She looked up at him with admiration. "How could I be critical of someone trying to protect a member of his family, sir? I only hope that you'll return to us again."

"Of course I will, ma'am." And he had bowed to her as she left the room. All in all, she thought, it had been a most satisfactory experience.

Arabella had thought the day could grow no more unpleasant. Elinor refused to admit either that she had a reason to grieve or that she was grieving. Instead, she went quietly about her business, shedding not a single tear. The gloom in the nursery was intense, however, as both young ladies thought of the young men who had departed.

Suddenly the nursery door flew open and Julia rushed in, sobbing.

"I won't do it!" she cried, burying her face in Elinor's lap as she sat in the low rocker by the fire, sewing. "She can't make me do it?"

"Do what?" demanded Arabella. "What's happened, Julia?"

Her little sister raised a tear-stained face. "Rebecca has told me I'm to go to school in Overton. She's going to take me there next week!"

Elinor and Arabella stared at one another, dismayed. "Let

me go and talk to her," said Arabella grimly. "Perhaps I can change her mind."

She tried to marshall her arguments as she went downstairs to see her stepmother, but she was quite certain in her heart that Rebecca had already made up her mind.

"Surely, ma'am, it would be better for her to be home with us than sent to live among strangers," she said to Rebecca, as she stood before her in the drawing room.

Rebecca looked disinterested. "I think not. In fact, Arabella, I feel that you and your sister have had an unfortunate effect upon her. A little girl like Julia had no business being at a ball behaving as she was with Will Russell last night."

"She was only having a little fun!" responded Arabella hotly. "You know full well, Rebecca, that they were doing nothing wrong!" She paused a moment and looked at her stepmother. "I think perhaps you were simply a little jealous that all of the attention wasn't for you."

She was immediately aware that her remark was not a judicious one, for Rebecca's eyes grew malicious.

"You can't be distressed with Julia merely for being a little girl," she said, trying to redirect Rebecca's attention.

"Julia needs more careful attention and a better education than you and your sister can provide," replied Rebecca.

"Then why not send for Flossie?" asked Arabella desperately. "She would come back immediately."

"We have no need for Miss Floss," said Rebecca firmly. "It will be much better for Julia to be among others of her own age. I have quite made up my mind, Arabella, so there is no point in prolonging this interview."

As Arabella turned to go, her stepmother called to her. "Oh, Arabella, by the way—I've heard from your father." She held up a paper that had been lying beside her on the sofa.

Arabella started toward her eagerly, her hand outstretched for the letter, but her stepmother folded it and put it down beside her. "It is addressed to me and is quite private, but he does send his best to his daughters and begs me to tell you that he is well and that he expects you to obey me in all things." She paused a moment and smiled sweetly at Arabella. "Do I make myself quite clear?" she asked.

"Oh, yes ma'am, you do indeed," replied Arabella dully, turning to take the bad news upstairs.

And so Julia departed for Miss Brennan's school. The only point upon which Rebecca yielded was that Elinor and Arabella were permitted to escort Julia to her new residence, thus sparing Rebecca the trouble of taking the journey. It was only a twenty-mile drive, but it seemed as though they were taking Julia to the ends of the earth.

"I'm going to write to Papa," sniffed Julia in the carriage, "and tell him just what Rebecca has done."

"I wonder why we didn't receive any letter from him ourselves," said Elinor. "It seems most unlike Papa to go so long without sending us word."

"Remember that he sent us a message through Elinor," said Arabella. "Perhaps he considers that sufficient."

Elinor and Arabella were horrified by what they found at Miss Brennan's school, but they tried their best not to show their distress to Julia. The accommodations were stark and the rooms cold, the dormitory presenting a severe line of narrow beds with thin blankets.

"This is terrible, Bella," murmured Elinor as they unpacked Julia's things. "She'll catch her death of cold here." It was immediately clear that she had brought too much, for there was simply not enough space. They chose the warmest clothes and put them away, along with two or three of her favorite books, her drawing pencils, and a sketch of Gingersnap.

"I would say that we should take her home with us, but it wouldn't do a bit of good. Rebecca would bring her right back," responded Arabella. "There must be something we can do about this, but I can't think what it would be."

Their parting was distressing, with Julia crying bitterly and asking them to look after Gingersnap.

"We'll write, Julia, and come again as soon as we can. Perhaps you can come home for a holiday," said Elinor comfortingly as they left, trying to keep from crying herself.

Home seemed most unnatural without Julia, and January and February melted away into a gray and forbidding March. Rebecca continued to invite a variety of house guests to enliven her winter days in the country, but Lord Wraxton was never among them, and the girls resumed their habit of dining in the nursery, having no interest in becoming better acquainted with their stepmother's friends.

Arabella received several cheerful, unloverlike messages from Will, brought faithfully by Libbie to the postbox, but Elinor had had no word at all from Robert. It was late one afternoon when Libbie herself appeared, rushing up the steps to the nursery without any formal announcement of her presence.

"Libbie!" exclaimed Elinor as she flew through the door and collapsed on the sofa, gasping for breath. "Whatever is the matter?"

"It's the school," Libby wheezed, struggling to regain her voice. "Julia's school."

"What about the school?" asked Arabella. "Is there something wrong with Julia?"

"I don't know that there is," replied Libby, "but a friend of my mother's from Overton stopped by and told her that they have the putrid sore throat at Mrs. Brennan's school and that one girl has already died of it. My mother exclaimed, 'O my dear goodness, isn't that where little Julia Standish is? Libbie, run and tell her family right away!' "

"Thank you, Libbie," said Elinor, rising from the rocking chair with an unaccustomed briskness. And thank your mother for us." She looked at Arabella. "We must go and see Rebecca directly. She will have to bring Julia home now."

Arabella nodded, rising, but Libbie said, "One more thing before you go, Elinor! I heard another thing before that when I was listening to them talk." She stopped and looked suddenly embarrassed.

"Well, what is it, Libbie?" asked Arabella impatiently. "We have to go quickly."

"I don't know that I should tell you because it isn't true, and my mama said it wasn't, but—"

"What isn't true, Libbie? What was said? Tell us directly, please!" snapped Arabella.

Fearful that Arabella might decide to shake it from her, Libbie said hurriedly, "Mrs. Steerforth said that she had heard that Elinor had a sort of sickness."

"A sickness?" asked Elinor, puzzled. "I haven't been ill. What sort of sickness?"

Libbie blushed. "A sickness that makes you take things that aren't yours."

They stared at her in astonishment. "Take things that aren't hers? What things?" demanded Arabella.

"I heard them say some of Mrs. Standish's jewelry—and something belonging to a lord who stayed here at Christmas."

"Lord Wraxton!" exclaimed Elinor, her eyes wide. "No wonder they went away so suddenly!" She put her hands to her face. "What must he think of me!"

Arabella's face was scarlet. "If Robert Halliday believed such fustian, it's because Rebecca told him it was so! This is all her doing! I can't wait to tell her what I think of her!"

Elinor caught her sister's arm before she could storm from the room. "You can't say anything now, Bella, or we won't persuade her to bring Julia home."

Arabella drew a deep breath, knowing that Elinor spoke the truth, but it required all of her strength to keep from descending upon her stepmother and giving her the tongue-lashing that she longed to deliver.

"I am going to write a letter to our father, Libbie, and leave it in the postbox. Will you be certain that your parents send it for me?"

Libbie nodded. "I heard Mama say that she's going to write to him, too. She said that things have gotten out of hand over here and he needs to come home."

She stopped on her way out of the nursery and hugged Elinor. "I knew that you hadn't done anything wrong and so do did my mother and father. Only people who don't know you would believe something like that."

"Thank you, Libbie dear," said Elinor with composure. After the door had closed behind their guest, she turned to Arabella and said with unaccustomed sharpness, "And if only the people who don't know me believe it, Bella, that means that ten people don't believe it and everyone else does—including Mr. Halliday."

Arabella hugged her tightly. "As soon as we get Julia safely home, we'll straighten this out, Elinor."

The interview with Rebecca had been brief. They presented the news that they had heard, and when she tried to dismiss it as gossip, Elinor asked abruptly how she would explain his daughter's death to their father when he arrived home. "For we'll tell him, Rebecca, that we pleaded with you to bring her home and you coldly refused to do so." Startled by this display from the mild-mannered Elinor—and fully aware that she spoke the truth—Rebecca allowed them to go, saying that she was too exhausted to go and expose herself to illness.

In a carriage filled with blankets, hot bricks, and foods suitable for an invalid, they departed at dawn the next morning and arrived late that afternoon. Julia had indeed been ill, and they were all—even Rebecca—shocked by how thin and pale she had become. There was no question now of how they would spend their time: the sisters devoted themselves to caring for her. They set up a trundle bed in front of the nursery fire, and Gingersnap, nestled on a quilt at the foot of the bed, slept there night and day.

Despite Arabella's ardent desire to confront their stepmother with her lies about Elinor, she gave way to Elinor's plea that they concentrate their attention on Julia and do nothing that might make Rebecca wish to do them further harm. Arabella did, however, pen a detailed letter to their father, laying out the horrors that had taken place and ending with Julia's brush with death. This she gave to the faithful Libbie to have posted by her parents.

When the afternoons grew warm in May, they took Julia out to sit in the sun, fully ascribing to Flossie's belief in its healthful benefits. It was there they sat one still afternoon, listening to Arabella read aloud from a volume of Lord Byron's poetry, when they saw a gentleman in riding clothes striding toward them across the lawn.

Arabella paused in her reading when she heard Elinor gasp. "It's Mr. Russell!" she exclaimed, looking at her sister.

Arabella dropped her book and rose. Her first impulse was to rush toward him, but she remembered that his notes had been friendly and gentlemanly—but scarcely the words of a lover. So she remained where she was and smilingly held out her hand to him.

"How delightful to see you again, Miss Arabella," he said politely, holding her hand tightly. He held his hat and a bright nosegay in his other hand and, bowing to Elinor, he presented them to Julia. "For our invalid," he said, smiling. "I hope that you are well enough to dance with me soon."

Julia held them up to her nose and breathed deeply. "Gingersnap and I will be ready very soon," she promised. "Perhaps even in time for Rebecca's masquerade ball a fortnight from now."

"A masquerade?" inquired Will. "How exciting! Have you thought what your costume might be?"

Julia nodded, her eyes bright. "I shall be a pirate! Bella has just finished reading me the story of Blackbeard."

"A very commendable choice of costume. And what of you, Miss Arabella?" he asked, shifting his attention to her. "What will you be at the masquerade?"

"I don't know that I care to go, sir," she responded. "I can think of no particular reason I should desire to attend a masquerade."

"I see," he murmured, looking at Arabella with lifted brows. "Could I ask you, ma'am, to take a turn around the garden with me?" he inquired, extending his arm.

She took it silently, offering him no smile. As they strolled away, Julia called after them, "Will, if you don't marry Bella, will you marry me?"

He heard a small choke from Arabella's direction, and he turned back to Julia and waved, calling, "If she won't have me, Julia, I am yours."

Julia grinned with satisfaction and handed Elinor the book that Arabella had dropped so that they could continue their reading.

"I am afraid that Julia has stolen a march on me, Bella," said Will regretfully.

"You are very free with my name, sir," she responded coolly. "I noted that when we last met at the footbridge."

"That's because I call you Bella when I talk to you in my daydreams," he responded, smiling down at her.

"Indeed? And do you talk to me often, sir?" she inquired, still not smiling.

"All the time, ma'am."

"And what do I say?" she asked.

"Well, first of all, I say 'Bella, I have loved you since I first met you all those years ago at the Christmas ball and picnicked with you on the stairs of Boxwood Hall. In view of this long-standing attachment, will you do me the honor of becoming my bride'?"

Arabella still did not smile. "And what do I say to that, sir?' "

"You reply, 'I know that I could find men who are more handsome, more clever, more wealthy, Mr. Russell—but I know too that I couldn't find one who loved me better.' "

Arabella did not reply, but appeared to be studying the toes of her sandals carefully. Once more he lifted her chin so that she would look into his eyes. "Can you say that to me, Bella?" he asked softly.

Slowly she shook her head. "No, Will, I'm sorry, but I simply cannot."

The light in his eyes appeared to go out, and his hand dropped from under her chin. Bowing to her briefly, he said, "Please forgive me, Miss Arabella. I had hoped, despite the fact you are so very young, that if I stayed away a little longer, gave you a little more time to think, that you would decide that you could love me. I am sorry to trespass upon your good nature like this."

Before he could turn away, she caught his arm and smiled up at him. "Aren't you going to ask me what I *can* say to you, Will Russell?"

He nodded silently, waiting.

"I might find a wealthier man, Mr. Russell, but I could never find one more handsome or clever or one that I could love more."

He stared down at her for a moment, then swept her into his arms, cheerfully disregarding the frank stares of a passing gardener and his attendant and waving to Julia when she cheered.

Having agreed that he would wait and ask her father's permission when he returned and not trouble Rebecca with the news of their engagement, Bella told him of Elinor's great trouble and of how difficult her situation had been. She watched in satisfaction as his face grew dark and his fist clutched involuntarily.

"I hadn't wished to expose Rebecca to any public ridicule, but since she has done this to Elinor, I don't see that I have any choice. Do you think that you can get Mr. Halliday to come down for the masquerade?" she asked. "Perhaps Lord Wraxton, too, except he will be so against it because of what he believes about Elinor. He must have truly thought Mr. Halliday was serious about her to sweep him away so quickly."

Will nodded. "I think we might be able to get him here. Do you have a plan for restoring Elinor's reputation?"

Arabella nodded enthusiastically, and he groaned. "Why does that not surprise me?" he asked of no one in particular. "Tell me, my dear, what you would have me do?"

They laid their plans very carefully, telling Julia but sharing nothing about Lord Wraxton or Mr. Halliday with Elinor for fear of upsetting her. Rebecca did not look kindly upon having Will visit so often, but she was busy with the house guests who had begun to arrive for the masquerade, and with her customary round of calls and dinners.

Not until the morning of the masquerade did Elinor learn of Mr. Halliday's arrival with Lord Wraxton. It was only with some difficulty that Arabella and Julia had persuaded her to attend the ball as a princess, but when she heard of the new arrivals, she announced that she had no intention of setting foot out of the nursery while they were at Boxwood.

"Don't be such a goosecap, Elinor," scolded Arabella. "You know that Rebecca lied to them."

"And I know that they believed her," retorted Elinor. "I don't need to see that in their faces and the faces of all the other strangers at the ball tonight."

"But you *must* do this, Elinor—you must prove that they're wrong!" she pleaded.

"How will going to the masquerade prove that they're wrong?" Elinor asked suspiciously. "What are you going to do, Bella?"

"Elinor, you know that I love you, don't you?" Arabella

demanded, and Elinor nodded reluctantly, knowing what would be coming next. "And you know that I wouldn't do anything to harm you, don't you?"

"Oh, yes, I know that, Bella, but *you're* not the one everyone will be staring at."

"Nor will you be," returned her sister confidently. "Just trust me and go, Elinor. Remember that Julia needs you there, too, for her first big outing after her sickness."

And so it was that on that night, a tender, soft night when May had just melted into June, that the three sisters attended the masquerade. Everyone wore a costume and at least a half-mask; no identities were to be revealed until supper was served. The ballroom opened onto the terrace and the gardens below, where paper lanterns glowed softly.

"I feel ridiculous," Arabella murmured, trying to hold her shepherd's crook gracefully without knocking anyone over with it. "I'm just grateful that Julia gave up her idea of having me bring a real sheep."

"It was a good idea!" said Julia defensively. "I still know where there's a lamb if you change your mind."

She made a quite impressive Blackbeard, for her sisters and Will had carefully padded her jacket and she wore old-fashioned high-heeled shoes with gold buckles on the toes. Her beard and wig and eyebrows were thick and as black as the pirate's reputation. A patch covered one eye, a sword swung at her side, and a tall, cockaded hat set off the outfit. Julia had even stained her hands and face with walnut juice before Elinor could prevent it.

They scattered among the others and set their plan in motion. Elinor, dressed as a princess in a conspicuous dress of vivid pink silk and a matching domino, topped with a crown of paste diamonds, danced with Will, a tall, lithe Harlequin, who surveyed the room carefully.

"Wraxton is wearing a black cloak and domino," he said

in a low voice. "We wait until we see him dancing with your stepmother."

Elinor nodded. It wouldn't be hard at all to find Rebecca in the crowd, for she wore a towering wig and a crown in her guise as Marie Antoinette.

They had not long to wait. Almost as soon as the dance began, they started making their way toward their victim. When they arrived, the shepherdess and pirate were already in place, Julia having cut in between Rebecca and her partner.

"Forgive me, madam," said Julia in a gruff voice, bowing even as she slipped the sword from its sheath, "but I'm afraid that I must relieve you of your necklace—I'm Blackbeard the Pirate, you now, and I'm a dangerous, dangerous man."

Rebecca laughed a little nervously and said, "That's very clever, sir—but I don't believe I want to give you my necklace."

Blackbeard laughed heartily. "No one wishes to give their worldly goods to Blackbeard, but I takes them just the same! Give them now, ma'am! And you, too!" he exclaimed, turning on his own partner. "Don't think you're safe just because you dance with me."

"Yessir, of course, sir—please just don't hurt me sir," pleaded Arabella, shaking like a blancmange. Those closest to her, who had been a little nervous at Julia's speech, began to chuckle. Her fear and Julia's ferocity were so exaggerated that it was clear they were playacting.

Arabella, who was wearing her mother's diamonds, pretended to be having tremendous difficulty unfastening it because of her shaking hands. Growling at her, Julia moved behind her so that Rebecca had a clear view of the jewels Bella was wearing.

"Look!" Rebecca exclaimed, clutching Lord Wraxton's arm and pointing at Arabella's throat. "Those are my diamonds! The ones that Elinor stole from me!"

There was a gasp from the gathered dancers, and all eyes

were fixed upon Elinor, who had removed her domino and was looking steadily at her stepmother.

Before Arabella could continue the drama, however, the man in the black cape and domino spoke. "Those aren't your diamonds, Rebecca. They belonged to my first wife Caro, and now they belong to our daughter Arabella. Why would you say such a thing about Elinor?"

"Papa!" shrieked Blackbeard, and threw himself into the arms of the speaker.

Rebecca appeared to be trembling as greatly as Arabella had in jest. Removing his domino, John Standish gravely kissed his other daughters and then turned to his wife. "I think, madam, that it would be better if we were to continue this conversation in private."

Lord Wraxton, who had lent his cape and domino to his friend, made his way to Elinor's side. "Miss Standish," he said, "I must beg your pardon, but I'll understand if you can't find it in your heart to forgive me. I shouldn't have allowed your stepmother to mislead me—and so your father told me when he arrived at my home in London before coming here."

"Did he come because of my letter, Lord Wraxton?" asked Arabella eagerly.

"He already intended to come, for he had heard from your governess and several of your neighbors that things were not as they should be here. I would have known as much myself if I had been in the habit of coming here often as I did in the old days."

"You can't blame yourself, sir," said Elinor, laying her hand upon his arm. "You didn't truly know me, so why shouldn't you have believed my stepmother?"

Lord Wraxton looked at her ruefully. "Because I should have listened to my nephew," he said. "Robert was outspoken in his defense of you, but I wouldn't listen—I thought he was blinded by love."

Elinor blushed at the word, but her expression did not soften.

"Then why didn't Mr. Halliday tell me this himself?" she asked coolly.

Lord Wraxton looked more shamefaced still. "I'm afraid that I told him he could expect no help from me or his mother and sisters, that I would sack him immediately, should he come back here. I was afraid for him—but I see that I should not have been. His judgment is quite as sound as I had previously thought it."

"Will you forgive me, Miss Standish?" asked a slender grenadier standing beside her.

Elinor smiled slowly. "It is possible, Mr. Halliday, in view of the circumstances," she said softly, taking his arm. "Perhaps Lord Wraxton will not mind if we walk in the garden."

Mr. Halliday straightened his shoulders and spoke before his uncle could. "We'll walk in the garden even if he *does* mind, Miss Standish." And together they strolled out the French window and onto the terrace.

"As soon as your father is free, Bella, I will speak to him," murmured Will, drawing her close to him. "Come and kiss me while the lights are low and everyone is still masked."

Arabella allowed herself to be drawn into the little stand of palms by the terrace door and kissed resoundingly. The warm pressure of his lips with their lingering hint of mint was intoxicating—quite addictive, in fact. It's possible that Arabella might indeed have found herself labeled as a fast young woman had she not been rescued.

"What is that?" demanded Will, straightening up suddenly.

Arabella, trying to regain her composure, straightened her mask and her saucy little hat, then looked to see what the source of the problem was.

"I believe that the lamb has found me," she chuckled, as it bumped against Will's leg and nibbled at his stockings. "I should have known that Julia wouldn't let me get away without it." And they looked up to see Julia laughing in the open window.

"Ignore them," said Will firmly, turning her back toward the pair. "Shall I ask your father for a June wedding, Bella?"

She nodded, smiling. "And we will keep sheep and live in the country."

"Not at all," he said firmly. "There will be no sheep and we will visit the country only occasionally. I'm afraid that you'll have me walking all over the countryside if I give you the opportunity."

"Bella!" called Julia. "I think that you had better not ask Papa for a June wedding."

Arabella and Will looked up, surprised. "Why, Julia, I thought you were pleased we're to be married," said Bella.

"Oh, I am," she returned blithely, "but I think you had best ask Papa for *two* June weddings." And she swung the door open a little wider, revealing a grenadier locked in an embrace with a princess in pink.

"Well!" exclaimed Bella, laughing and looking up to see the answering light in Will's eyes. "To think that it was only last October when I said that nothing ever happens to us and that we might as well live in a convent."

Smiling, Will pulled her close. "There'll be no convent for you, dear heart. June is the time for lovers."

And so it is, she thought, lifting her lips to his . . . the time for lovers.

UNDERNEATH THE LEMON TREE

Jenna Jones

Chapter One

Juliana Dalton's hands were cold.

The awareness reanimated her, triggering the first sign of movement in her stiffly aligned shoulders since she had completed the carefully metered processional down the long center aisle of St. George's and arrived at the foot of the altar. Reflexively, she loosened her blue, kid-covered grip upon the small Bible and fragrant primrose nosegay she had been squeezing into pulp against her slim waist. Determined, this time at least, not to make yet another cake of herself, she next captured the wobble of her lower lip between her teeth and sent a deeply drawn breath into battle against a second rising tremble, at the same time concealing the warfare beneath a discreet downward glance and the masses of blue silk asters adorning her wide bonnet brim's nearly transparent gauze. Quite a clever maneuver, she thought with a satisfied wisp of a smile.

Until she spied the linden leaf caught upon her gown's blue flounced hem. The sight again unnerved her; quite without thinking, therefore, she shifted her weight so that she might

prod the malingerer from the underside of its silken perch with
her slippered toe. Just to her left, Alissa, ever the hoyden,
giggled her censure; spreading outward from behind her like
the soft clatter of the wooden tiles called dominoes which had
recently been brought into England by French prisoners, fans
snapped open and waved to mask an assortment of smiles.

And Juliana stumbled over her words. Horrified, her gaze
leapt toward the splendidly-robed man standing before her.

He smiled benignly; the guests strained forward. Soon a soft,
patient prompting echoed about the sanctuary's vaulting. She
began again.

And still her hands were cold.

Yet there was no help for it, she supposed, though the bright
June morning had delivered a warm and cloudless benediction
upon the day's perfection mere hours before. She was, after
all, standing in the most fashionable of houses of worship just
at the southwest corner of St. George and Maddox Streets in
the very heart of the *haute monde;* more, her every *faux pas*
was at that very moment under the intent scrutiny of at least
a hundred of the *crème de la crème* of the London *ton.* And,
as if that were not enough, it was her wedding day, she allowed
with a soft smile, at last daring to peer from beneath her bonnet's
brim to meet Stephen's avid gaze, gray as a storm-shrouded
lake. And she, at three-and-twenty, the dowager Countess of
Granville, widow of one of her father's closest acquaintances
and never expecting to know anything of what it meant to be
truly loved, was marrying him. And he was smiling down on
her as if the world did not exist beyond her sapphire eyes. And
he was taking her hand.

And Juliana marveled . . . at how his very nearness stirred
her, at how his warmth drew her like a babe to its mother's
arms . . . at how it had all begun . . .

* * *

It had been early in the Season when Juliana had received the letter from her mother at her most recent residence, the dower house adjacent to Granville Manor, a half-timbered Elizabethan relic guarding several acres of the Test riverbank not far from the village of Stockbridge in the county of Hampshire. It had been a year since she had gone about in Society, and the letter pleading—whining, Juliana had thought with a chiding purse of her shapely mouth—for her to come up to Town with all haste had come as a surprise; she still wore only shades of muted lavender and gray.

Yet Juliana had, after all, the viscountess argued in her meandering scroll, dutifully and most properly completed her year of mourning for her husband, the earl; therefore, there remained no reason at all why she might not come immediately up to Enniston House to enjoy the pleasures of the remainder of the Season. And, of course, as she would be in Town anyway, there also seemed to be no reason why Juliana could not assume the role of sponsor for her younger sister, did there? It was Alissa's come-out Season, after all, and the poor darling had been blue-deviled for weeks absent someone closer in age in which to confide . . . and, too, by coincidence, the viscountess *had* happily received an invitation to join a party of her friends for the next several months in the far more sedate Society of Bath . . .

. . . And had she mentioned, by the by, that a most perverse dyspepsia, certain to gain benefit from the curative powers of the Pump Room's mineral waters, of late had been all but ruining her appetite?

Juliana, drawing in a very deep breath, had summoned her maid, notified John Coachman, and had left with dutiful haste.

Her reception at her late father's town house in South Street several days later had been equally disquieting.

"Oh, Juliana, you have arrived at last!" Alissa cried when the curiosity of luggage being transported up the wide, mahogany staircase of Enniston House had drawn her from the first floor drawing room.

"Hello, darling," Juliana smiled up from the town house's small ante-room, her fingers busily freeing several of her traveling cloak's frogs.

Gathering handfuls of yellow sprigged muslin, fueled by delight, Alissa all but bounced into her sister's warm embrace. "Oh, Juliana, Mama shall be ever so pleased," she pronounced ebulliently, planting a quick kiss upon Juliana's smooth, softly curved cheek. "She was hoping to be away yesterday. Lady Chamworth and Mrs. Hodges already await her at the Pelican."

"Dear, I was afraid of that," Juliana replied, at last allowing her maid to remove her cloak of charcoal Cheviot. "No sooner had we left Granville Manor than a sudden storm west of Basingstoke rendered the road impassable," she explained, yielding up her gloves, reticule and the subdued rust-gray MacPherson hunting tam that had been artfully concealing a neatly-coiled, honey-colored chignon. "Unhappily, we were delayed two days before the ruts drained."

"Were you? Well, no matter, I suppose. You are here now," Alissa responded dismissively, taking her sister's elbow and piloting her toward the stairs, her remaining hand absently fluffing her lighter blond curls. "Mama shall forgive anything as long as she is at last able to quit her constant escort of me."

"You have the right of that," Juliana observed, shifting the skirt of her gray sarcenet traveling gown out from under her half-boots' path. "She does not relish the duty."

"No, she does not, does she?" Alissa grinned. "As I recall, she was at sixes and sevens the entire Season when you made your come-out."

"Rather at nines and tens," Juliana laughed, gaining the first floor landing and preceding her sister into the drawing room. "Where is she, by the way?"

"Making calls before attending the Lawtons' card party this afternoon," Alissa informed her, tugging upon the bell cord, then gesturing toward a Mona marble fireplace radiating a welcome heat beneath a gilded Adams mirror. "Oh, Juliana, it is so good of you to come!" she exclaimed, again drawing her sister into an exuberant embrace.

"Yes, it is, as a matter of fact," Juliana agreed with a teasing grin. "See that you remember that several weeks from now when you fall top over tail for some incredibly handsome nonpareil and visions of eloping to Gretna Green begin to swim about inside your brain. I warn you now, Alissa, I vow to be as sharp-eyed a matron as the worst of them, so you'd best mind your p's and q's."

Sudden surprise widened Alissa's answering smile. "A matron, is it?" she laughed, turning to settle herself stiff-spined before the fire upon a gold and green striped settee from Shera-ton. "Juliana, have you never looked into a mirror since your marriage to Granville? You are every bit as lovely as you were five years ago in your own come-out Season, you know. Why, I misdoubt but what your attendance at a single ball, even as my chaperone, shall have dozens of cards delivered to our doorstep. And each with its corner turned down, I'll wager."

"I certainly hope not," Juliana quickly replied, glancing toward the unobtrusive entrance of a tall, well-built young man dressed in Enniston livery carefully balancing a laden silver tray upon his arm. "It has, after all, only been a few weeks since my mourning for Granville ended," she continued, seating herself, too, upon the Sheraton, then relegating the footman to invisibility while he placed the refreshments upon a nearby table and began to pour them each a cup of oolong. "I cannot think it seemly . . ."

"Pish tosh!" Alissa inserted, her gaze all the while boldly scrutinizing the young man's graceful movements as he poured, then placed a slate blue Wedgwood cup into her hands. "Granville was of an age with our father, Juliana . . . an old man even five years ago at your wedding!" she continued, next raising an altogether brazen regard toward the footman's diverted face. "Why you ever turned down your other offers and agreed to marry him is quite beyond my comprehension."

"Alissa, you know why. Because it was Father's greatest wish," Juliana quietly explained as she took the second cup offered by the footman. "We all knew that there was little time left before his consumption took him, dearest," she continued, her mind already preparing the words of correction she would recite to Alissa concerning a proper lady's comportment with a servant living together with her under the same roof. "It was all that I could do to ease him at the end."

"Oh, Juliana, what nonsense! You were no more than a trophy. It was the outside of enough to expect your consent!"

"With family comes duty, Alissa," Juliana countered, rejecting the slice of lemon offered by the young man, "and marriage to Granville was mine. And kindly keep in mind that he was always very generous with me. I never wanted for anything as his wife."

"Except excitement!" Alissa argued, bursting to her feet and throwing her arms wide, "Except passion, Juliana! . . . love! . . . life!"

On a muted sigh, Juliana brought her cup to slow, deliberate port upon an adjacent table, then met her sister's enlivened gaze. "Those things are not for everyone, dearest," she softly replied.

"I wholeheartedly disagree, milady," the footman suddenly, and quite firmly, offered along with the pitcher of milk, his avowal most uncomfortably rending a rather large hole in the protective envelope of her martyrdom.

Instantly, Juliana's gaze slewed to his face. "I-I beg your

pardon?'' she breathed, her sapphire scrutiny twisting into a frown.

"Shall I repeat it, milady? Very well, then . . . without question, I definitely disagree," the young man restated, afterward politely adding milk to Juliana's cup.

"You do?''

"I do indeed. It is only logical, after all. We are all of us equally human, are we not? Why, then, should those things which give human life savor exist for only a select few to enjoy?''

"Well, I . . .'' Juliana began, altogether unsure as to how to respond.

"Exactly,'' the footman proclaimed. "You do see my point, do you not? I would be remiss, however, if I did not admit that there are problems with the concept; the worst being, of course, that finding those things is indeed rare. More, when found, more often than not some arcane societal convention requires that we reject them out of hand. Yet I am persuaded that life is meant to be relished, milady. Indeed,'' he nodded, "in my opinion, at all cost life's passions must be seized.'' Disconcertingly, then, and for far longer than was proper, the young servant began to peer unwaveringly into Juliana's eyes. "Prepare yourself,'' he at last intoned, his gaze surely piercing all the way within and without again to the farthest twist of Juliana's chignon. "What before was quiescent shall soon sweep *you* before its tide. Be ready.''

Suddenly, a warm smile broke out across the breadth of the footman's mouth.

"This time trust in your feelings, milady,'' he completed. Straightening to his full height, he afterward politely bowed.

Moments later the two sisters were once again alone.

"Alissa, who *was* that?'' Juliana asked when she had again regained her voice.

"Thompson,'' Alissa replied with a delighted giggle. "Well,

actually his name is Gavin Thompson. Oh, Juliana, is he not fascinating?''

"Fascinating? He is without a doubt the most insolent retainer I have ever encountered,'' Juliana complained.

"That is because he isn't really,'' Alissa explained. "Well, at the moment he is, of course, but he is not by birth. Oh, pish tosh, Juliana, Thompson is Welford's younger brother.''

"Welford? The one who recently lost his entire fortune to a game of hazard at Crockford's?''

"The same,'' Alissa responded. "As a consequence, of course, Thompson, too, is punting on tick. However, he swears that shall not be the case for long. Indeed, he is quite determined to make his own fortune, don't you know. This time, though, he intends that not a farthing shall find itself under Welford's control.''

"But how did he come to be here?''

"Mama was an old school chum of Lady Welford's. As a favor to her, she has agreed to provide for Thompson while he prepares to read for the bar. And he, of course, has refused to take charity of any kind, so Mama has taken him into service. It is quite sad, is it not? He is such a bold, entertaining man,'' she sighed, beginning to intertwine the ribbons hanging down onto her sprigged muslin skirt from the bow just beneath her bodice, "but insisting upon *that* direction, of course, has put him quite beyond the pale.''

"Yes, well . . . as we are on the subject, Alissa—''

"Oh, do say you will not scold him for stepping above his place, Juliana,'' her sister suddenly pleaded. "It *is* my fault, after all. I admit that I am the one who has encouraged his familiarity. Yet it did not seem unreasonable given his noble birth, and he has been so very interesting to talk to, you see . . .

"But, Juliana, only think of it! He has given you a foretelling!'' Alissa then whispered in quite the most head-spinning change of subject. "It is bruited about that he has a touch of Romany blood in his ancestry. Is that not beyond anything?"

"Rather the outside of enough," Juliana countered calmly, "and this is exactly the sort of behavior I only moments ago warned you against, darling. Alissa, you must promise me to be more circumspect in your comportment," she commanded. "No gentleman will drop the handkerchief before a woman he shall be ashamed to take about in Society."

"Shall he not?" Alissa grinned mischievously, seating herself again. "He shall have nothing but a pattern card, then? Is that what you are telling me?"

"Just so," Juliana replied with an emphatic nod.

"Ah, me . . . then I suppose he also would never have a woman who would drop her fan at his feet in order to gain his attention. And certainly not one who would do so in . . . oh, for example, the lobby of the Drury Theater," Alissa sighed, a pronounced glitter now beginning to animate her soft blue irises.

"No, he would not," Juliana tentatively agreed, beginning to grow aware of the all-to-familiar gleam and her own delicate brow's responsive furrowing.

"Without question, then, I should think he would likewise never consider a woman who would regard him so intently throughout the entirety of one of Lady Cowper's musicales that he would afterward seek her out to inquire after her well-being."

"Certainly, he would not," Juliana vowed with alarm, her eyes rounding even more, her heart beginning to pound. "Such behavior would be beyond anything. Alissa . . ."

". . . As would that of a woman who would rearrange the place cards on the whist tables in order to assure that she might partner a certain gentleman, I suppose."

Suddenly Juliana's saucer rattled back down upon the table's inlaid surface. "Alissa," she breathed, "to what, exactly, are you alluding by these examples? What under heaven have you done?''

Setting down her own cup, Alissa laughed softly. "I am alluding to my efforts, of course," she informed her with a secretive smile. "I have not been idle during the first few weeks of the Season, Juliana. Indeed, I have been very busy going about what I came to Town to do."

"And that is?"

"Why, to select the man I intend to marry, of course. And then, too, as might be expected, to secure his attentions and his declaration."

"And you have done so already?" Juliana breathed, astonishment growing even more evident in her voice, "and with these tactics?"

"Found him? . . . Yes. Secured him? . . . No, not exactly," Alissa confessed without the slightest sag in her confidence. "But I *am* persuaded he has noticed me," she breathlessly exclaimed, her blond curls bobbing animatedly. "Why, do you know, Juliana, only yesterday he retrieved my parasol as we passed each other in Green Park! He even delaying for a few moments afterward to again make sure I fared well! And more!" Alissa continued, placing one small fist between her breasts, with the other seizing her sister's wrist. "I am certain it was no accident his fingers brushed against mine when he returned my parasol to me. It could not possibly have been. Oh, yes, I have gained his attention," she declared with a nod, her smile stretching wide. "Indeed, only one thing remains now . . . and that I shall accomplish presently."

"Good heavens, Alissa, what can you be referring to? What remains?"

"A meeting between the two of us."

"A meeting!" Juliana gasped. "Alissa Crandall! Never say—!"

"Oh, Juliana, do cease ripping up at me," her sister pouted. "He shall be my husband, after all."

Employing all the self-control she possessed, Juliana bit back her threatening retort and, finger by finger, relaxed her hands.

"Who shall be?" she finally managed to ask more mildly, slipping fingertips up to her temples to slow her head's spinning.

"Stephen Bradford," Alissa sighed long and lingeringly, letting her blue gaze sink deeply into her musings' nebulous mist. "Earl of Ardmore. Rich as Croesus, of course . . . and the most handsome man I have ever seen. Oh, Juliana, every debutante in Town is over the boughs for him!" she suddenly added, slewing her eager focus back toward her sister's appalled stare.

"Alissa, you know I cannot approve!"

"Not now, perhaps, but I promise that you shall, Juliana," Alissa stated firmly, the tightness of her grasp willing it to be so, "once you have met him, of course. And you shall have the very opportunity in but two days."

"I shall?" Juliana all but stated by the flatness of her tone.

"Yes, indeed," Alissa responded, again brightly beaming. "Mama procured invitations weeks ago for the two of us to attend Lady Pettigrew's ball two days hence. Of course, now that you are here, you shall attend in her place. You shall meet Ardmore then, as he shall be there as well. Oh, Juliana," she cried, rising to pull her sister into her embrace, "I can hardly wait! In but two days, I am certain that I shall be his *fiancée!*"

With her heart giving her ribs a thorough drubbing beneath her bodice's pleated sarsenet, Juliana next attempted reason. "Alissa, you must be sensible, darling," she contended, gripping her sister's forearms. "In order to properly converse with the earl, you must have received a proper introduction to him. Who can give you that *entrée?* Certainly not I. And what assurance have you that he shall even attend the Pettigrew soiree?"

"The best of all assurances," Alissa laughingly replied.

"Which is?"

"Juliana, Lady Pettigrew is Ardmore's mistress," Alissa informed her.

"Good heavens!" Juliana gasped in response, clapping her palms to her cheeks.

"He dare not miss it, I should think!" Alissa added, again giggling at her sister's obvious *näiveté*.

"Alissa, this whole scandal broth is beyond anything!" Juliana finally insisted, throwing up her hands. "Surely you must be sensible of the impossibility of your aspirations! You are suggesting that you can actually gain a declaration from a man . . . an earl! . . . you barely know under the very roof of his mistress! What, under heaven, can you be thinking?"

"Actually, that it is time you once again visited a modiste," Alissa declared disconcertingly, allowing her gaze to skate disapprovingly over Juliana's soft gray half-mourning as she tapped her chin. "I have it! We shall go directly after breaking our fast on the morrow," she then pronounced. "We shall order you several new gowns, shall we? And something appropriate for the Pettigrews' occasion as well. It shall have to be wonderful, of course . . . no less than the *dernier cri,*" she added, gaily clasping her palms. "Something blue and flounced, perhaps. Or pink."

"Pink?" Juliana repeated helplessly. "Good heavens. Anything else?" she questioned, one brow arching.

"Of course," Alissa responded blithely, again seating herself before the fire's sluggish flame. "You must have accessories. For those, we shall pay a visit to the Pantheon Bazaar, I think. One can find the most wonderful bargains at the booths."

Taking up her cup again, Juliana softly sighed. "Very well," she conceded, "But, Alissa, your hopes for the earl—"

"Shall be accomplished splendidly," the young woman interrupted impatiently, "now that I am certain he has noticed me. Oh, do not look so Friday-faced, Juliana! In two days, I tell you I shall belong to Ardmore."

With her other brow rising helplessly to join its companion, Juliana took a sip of tea.

"If you had told me you wished another bauble, Annabelle, we could just as easily have driven to Rundell and Bridge," Ardmore chided the following afternoon as he handed his mistress down onto the polished cobblestones of Oxford Street.

"Not a bit of it," Lady Pettigrew laughed, reaching up to stroke the vexation from the earl's chiseled cheek. "Today I wish a bit of gypsy gold," she told him, allowing a reckless glitter to invade her gaze just before turning to precede him beneath the Pantheon Bazaar's colonnaded portico. "I saw just the locket I wanted at one of the Romany booths not far from the Crystal Conservatory."

"Then why did we not enter from Great Marlborough Street?" Ardmore grumped, nodding to a uniformed beadle as the two entered the Bazaar's huge arena and began to meander among the colorfully decorated tents and shopping stalls.

"Because then I would not be able to stroll the Bazaar's length to see what new goods had been put on display since yesterday," her ladyship informed him, reaching out to hook her gloved hand through Ardmore's bottle green superfine sleeve. "Now tell me what has put you in such a bad skin since I saw you last."

Caught off guard, the earl glanced down toward the woman walking sedately beside him, the dark curls feathered across her pale forehead all but hidden by her jaunty French bonnet of tulle and yellow satin. "You know very well, Annabelle," he replied, afterward occupying his metallic gaze with a passing perusal of several Colonial beaver pelts. "I dislike these public appearances of ours."

"And I have already told you, Stephen, that Algernon has had to return to Yorkshire to deal with problems at the mill," she returned quietly, stopping to finger a bolt of Honiton lace. "I also mentioned that he has suffered a recurrence of his gout. He shall be from Town indefinitely, darling . . . most likely for the entire Season. There is no reason for you to worry and you are well aware of that fact," she gently chided, moving away toward a display of delicately painted chicken-skin fans. "So what is really blue-deviling you?"

Faced with that assessment, Ardmore had been given only one choice. He took it. He ruefully smiled.

"It is truly frightening how well you have come to know me, Annabelle," he chuckled after a moment.

"Yes, I have, have I not?" the lady agreed. "Now answer the question, Stephen."

"Very well, perhaps what is gnawing at me is jealousy," Ardmore conceded reluctantly.

"Jealousy?" Lady Pettigrew questioned, turning toward him, her eyes sparkling with amusement. "Of whom?"

"Of Pettigrew," the earl replied, a soft sigh woven into his tone.

Her brows rising, Lady Pettigrew broke into light, descending laughter. "Algernon? Never say so! I shall never believe that you wish to be my husband!"

At the thought, Ardmore, too, began to grin. "And ruin our friendship? I should say not. What I am jealous of is Pettigrew's excuse to be from Town."

"Stephen, this is the Season!" Lady Pettigrew exclaimed, again taking his arm as she tapped it with her fan.

"Which, this year at least, I would be happy to avoid if I could," he completed, beginning to lead the lady toward a towering construction of sparkling glass not too far in the distance.

"Well, that you shall have to explain," Lady Pettigrew required, stepping out of the way of a speeding perambulator.

"I have come under siege, it seems. Is that the booth you are looking for, my dear?" he questioned, pointing with his cane toward a scattering of gleaming objects displayed under a limp canvas of brightly painted gold and red.

"Yes, that is it exactly," the lady responded, quickening her step. "But, Stephen, what did you mean by being under siege?"

"I mean that I have been been singled out," he told her, coming to a halt before the sun-sparkled items.

"How very odd," Lady Pettigrew observed, releasing a brief chortle. "And you such an antidote, darling. Who is this tasteless creature?"

"One of the Season's crop of new debs," Ardmore replied, giving her fingers a quick squeeze. "A Miss Alissa Crandall . . . daughter of the late Right Honorable Viscount Enniston, I believe. I will allow that she is a rather lovely chit, but quite beyond the pale."

"Ah, she has formed a *tendre* for you," Lady Pettigrew easily assessed, selecting two lockets from the counter for her closer scrutiny.

"And has become a distinct annoyance in trying to force an acquaintance as a result," the earl completed in a grouse. "She is everywhere, I tell you. She has even taken to exchanging place cards."

"Then I suppose it only fair to warn you, darling," his companion stated, holding the lockets up to the light, "that she and Lady Enniston shall be attending my ball."

After a glance in her direction, the earl turned away, his mouth stretching into a very thin line.

He looked, then, off across the crowded walkway toward an adjacent booth displaying folded rows of Norwich shawls. Deeply filling his lungs, he sank back against the gypsies' counter.

"Stephen?" Lady Pettigrew asked, peering up at him while she placed several fingers upon his sleeve. "Darling, what are you thinking?"

"I am thinking, Annabelle, that when a man really needs it, he damn well ought to be able to muster an attack of the gout."

That was the last thing Ardmore remembered saying before
the loveliest woman he had ever set eyes on suddenly rounded
the corner of the booth of shawls across from him and strolled
straight into his heart.

Chapter Two

She had golden hair; plaited, he discerned from the bit of braid that had been left unguarded by her simple chip-straw bonnet just at the nape of her pale, slender neck. Several wisps of it framed almond-shaped eyes of clear blue brilliance, upon occasion clouded with the indecisions of shopping choices, at other times charmingly sun-flecked. Her figure was slender; yet not that of a girl new to her womanhood, he realized, but fully formed; enticing. Trim gray-stockinged ankles peeked from beneath an unadorned hem. She had not been many months distant from loss, then. The questions mounted . . . who? . . . why? . . . how much longer would her mourning last?

"Stephen? Stephen, darling!" Lady Pettigrew's voice broke into his mind's meandering.

"What? Oh . . . I beg your pardon, Annabelle. What is it?" he rather impatiently queried.

Across from him, the woman took a piece of sea-green silk from her reticule, then held it up to the stacked rows of shawls, assessing, comparing, her complete attention given over to finding the perfect complement.

"I asked you which locket you liked best, darling," the lady replied, holding his two choices up before him.

Hastily, the earl glanced in her direction. "I hardly think my opinion matters, my dear," he responded, twisting slightly to toss several silver crowns upon the counter, then quickly returning his attention to the adjacent booth. "After all, you shall be the one wearing it."

Across the walk, the proprietor separated the woman's choice from the others, then spread its glorious softness across the counter. The woman, however, wanted none of it. Gathering the thick expanse of wool into her hands, she quickly buried her entire face within the shawl's crumpled folds. When she at last looked up again, to his inordinate pleasure, Ardmore saw her smile.

"Yes, but you shall be the one paying for it," Lady Pettigrew countered. "Oh, Stephen, never say you are still vexed over the Crandall chit's attendance at my ball!" she then scolded, giving the swarthy proprietor her choice, then carefully watching to see that he did not substitute what she had given him for something of little value. "It doesn't signify, you know. You need not even see her if you do not wish it," she told him, glancing toward his face's firm profile. "After all, there *are* other diversions available to you," she continued *sotto voce,* leaning slightly toward him as she again concentrated upon the gypsy's hands. "In my chamber, for instance . . . once I have opened the dancing with the first quadrille."

But the earl was watching the woman take up the wrapped shawl, tuck it beneath one arm, then begin to work open the strings of her reticule. Next, balancing both, she tried to draw forth a handful of coins and count them one by one onto the booth's counter. The parcel, however, suddenly slipped a bit from her elbow's grasp. In response, on a soft cry, she whirled

about. In the next moment, everything—coins, shawl, and reticule—scattered about upon the ground.

"Stephen?" Lady Pettigrew asked again, tucking her boxed
locket into her own lace-trimmed bag. "You will still attend,
will you not?"

Yet when she turned toward him once more for a response,
she discovered that she was standing alone.

Juliana was able to do nothing more than stare. It was perverse. A gentleman was kneeling before her, collecting her
parcel, gathering her scattered coins from the ground, carefully
cleaning each one with his handkerchief of finely woven lawn,
then, with meticulous precision, stacking them one by one onto
the palm of her hand, and she was able to do nothing more
about it than to feel her jaw drop.

And, goodness, he was altogether beautiful, she thought,
surges of delicate color washing over her at that most indelicate
perception. As he worked, intermittently he gazed up at her
with eyes of polished pewter; dark waves of hair beneath his
curly beaver's brim licked at the wide wrap of his impeccably
tied cravat.

At last he slowly rose, his eyes all the while observing
her, seeming to probe, to touch deeply, physically, into each
distinctly feminine part of her. Disconcerted, still Juliana raptly
stared.

It occurred to her as the man settled into his stance that she
liked his height—not so tall as to tower over her, but of the
exact stature which would allow the tip of her nose, if she but
moved one step forward, to fit itself precisely into the small,
clean-shaven cleft bisecting his chin. The perfect height for
her. In fascination, her gaze frolicked over his features, pausing
to duel with his steady perusal, then, reeling with mortification,
skittering away again.

* * *

It *had* been perverse, Juliana remembered, yielding up her primrose nosegay to Alissa with another soft smile, then kneeling beside Stephen's steadying presence. Reacting in such a fashion to a perfect stranger; thinking such things . . . feeling what no lady should feel. And yet she had; incomprehensibly, she had. And now the vicar of St. George's was laying a hand atop her head.

"I . . . th-thank you, sir," she recalled stammering, folding her fingers over the neat stack of coins, feeling herself the veriest clodpole to have lost even the most basic facility for polite discourse.

"My pleasure, madam," the man's rich baritone softly replied as he replaced her wrapped shawl upon the counter. Quite suddenly, then, he seized the hand she still clenched around the coins, turned it, and raised it to within a hair's breadth of his lips—far too close for propriety, far too distant for the tingling anticipation curling just beneath her skin.

And he knew it, it seemed, Juliana realized as her cheeks caught fire again, for his eyes grew liquid and sparkled with amusement when he finished, "Till we meet again."

One brief bow later, he crossed to the gypsies' booth just across from where she stood, took the arm of the stylish woman waiting rather impatiently before it, and disappeared with her into the milling commotion.

Her face radiating enough heat to melt the ice at Gunter's all the way over in Berkeley Square, Juliana whirled around.

Alissa appeared, then, just rounding a dangling display of puddings two booths distant. "Oh, there you are," she gaily called, quickly gaining her sister's side. "Did I chat too long with Miss Drayton?" she breathlessly asked. "How rag-mannered of me. Oh, but you have bought something, Juliana! What is it? Let me see!''

''Only a shawl,'' Juliana replied, her senses still buzzing strangely in the aftermath of her encounter with the unknown gentleman, her thoughts oddly adrift. Giving up her parcel to Alissa's inspection, she began wandering along the path of her musings. When at last she again looked up, she found that she had come to a halt before the gypsies' tent. Somewhat startled, she smiled slightly at the proprietor, then absently fingered a hammered gold, Celtic-style brooch.

''But it is perfect!'' she heard her sister pronounce from across the walk as she held both the parcel and her own sample of Juliana's sea-green silk up to the bright sunlight. ''The color is only slightly darker. We shall have Fern do your hair *à la Tite,* shall we? . . . with an assortment of green ribbons! And with Mama's emeralds and . . .

''Ohhh!''

''Alissa?''

''Oh, Juliana!'' her sister breathed, her movements stilling completely, her intent gaze focusing somewhere off into the swarm of distant shoppers. ''Look!''

Worriedly, Juliana hurried back across the walk. ''Alissa, what is it?'' she asked, taking her sister's elbow.

''It was him!'' she breathed, still staring ahead.

''Who?'' Juliana asked, searching, too, in the direction of Alissa's gaze.

''Ardmore! He was here! Did you not see him?''

''No, of course not, dear,'' Juliana gently responded. ''How could I? I do not even know the man.''

''He was here with Lady Pettigrew,'' Alissa continued, one hand rising to still the tremble of her bodice's pleats.

''Oh?'' Juliana stated, a protective impulse beginning to gather within the column of her spine.

''Oh, yes, Juliana! He was here with her . . . yet still he noticed me!'' Alissa exclaimed proudly, reaching over to seize her sister's waist. "He turned back just as I was speaking," she elaborated, three fingertips rising to support her bottom lip. "We each saw the other quite plainly. Oh, Juliana, everything is going just as I had hoped it might. Ardmore's mistress was on his arm, yet he turned back to look at me. At *me!*"

"Did he indeed?"

Her jaw clenching in quite the most unladylike fashion, Juliana immediately seized her sister's arm and all but dragged her toward the Crystal Conservatory. Seconds later, they exited the Pantheon Bazaar and stepped into the teeming traffic of Great Marlborough Street.

The day of the Pettigrew ball arrived protesting such insipid human entertainments with bluster and low scudding clouds. For the Town birds, it had not signified, however. They had known that nothing existed which could have brought the proper progress of the London Season to a halt. Therefore, the day proceeded as usual at Enniston House. For Juliana, it meant that she was awakened by Fern, her lady's maid, at precisely ten o'clock with a soothing cup of chocolate.

"Mmm, thank you, Fern," she murmured in a sleep-warmed voice after the efficient woman had placed pillows behind her back and given her the delicate porcelain cup. "Is my mother about?"

"Already anxious to be off," the maid replied, pouring warm water into a basin of Sèvres porcelain. "Best drink up, milady. Her ladyship'll not wish to be delayed."

"No, she'll not, will she?" Juliana knowingly laughed. "Very well, then," she continued agreeably, swinging her legs over the side of the bed, "take out the blue-striped Nainsook, will you, Fern? Today is as good a day as any to set aside my half-mourning, I suppose. And do take what you wish of it for your own use, of course."

"Thank you, milady. And 'bout time you carried on with

things, if you ask me,'' Fern judged, opening up the huge rosewood clothes press.

''Me, too,'' Juliana replied, smiling over the disk of chocolate tipping toward her lips.

Only a short time later, she was ready for the day, having been washed and dressed in one of the new morning gowns which Madame Fanchon had rushed to complete and deliver the previous evening, and having patiently endured Fern's dressing of her hair. Then, remembering that the viscountess had of late become more and more prone to the taking of odd notions into her head, she abandoned her usual half-hour in which she dealt with her correspondence before breaking her fast, and instead hurried down the stairs to discover her mother's plans.

It had been a wise decision. Alissa and the viscountess had already been awaiting her in the anteroom.

''Mama, will you leave so soon?'' Juliana asked as she drew the commanding woman into her embrace.

''Yes, yes, I wish to be at least to Knightsbridge before it begins to rain,'' the viscountess stated. ''It is that demmed river, don't you know, just past the Hyde Park toll gate. Positively everyone gets stuck there, even the Flys. Highwaymen abound.''

''Then, of course, you must be on your way, Mama,'' Alissa soothed, smoothing her mother's traveling cloak over her wool-clad arm.

''Indeed. Well, do not think that I am not aware of why you wish me so soon away, Alissa,'' the viscountess warned, enfolding her youngest, too, in a brusque embrace before starting for the carriage door being patiently held open by Thompson. ''You think that because I have left Town you may do as you please. You may not, however. Juliana is here now, authorized to stand in my stead and noting every word I say. And I am saying, daughter, that you are not to ride out with young Bentley today if it rains, and that is the end of it.''

"Of course, Mama," Alissa contritely conceded. "It shall be just as you wish. Do have a pleasant visit with your friends."

"Yes, do, Mama," Juliana added with a far more sincere smile.

"I shall," the viscountess stated, taking Thompson's hand to climb aboard. "Well, John, shall you wait all day to chop the bloods?" she next called up to the coachman.

On the driver's seat, the old retainer shook his head slightly, then cracked his whip with a subdued smile. Only moments later, and without a backward glance, Juliana noted, her parent had rounded the corner into South Audley Street and was on her way toward the Great Western Road. Still standing upon the steps of the mansion's portico, both daughters dutifully waved one last goodbye.

"Well, shall we go inside?" Juliana suggested after a gust of wind had tugged rather indecently at their skirts.

Alissa nodded.

"What shall you do today before the ball?" she asked after they had been blown quite unceremoniously into the anteroom and had begun to follow the odors of coffee and ham into the deeper recesses of the house.

"Entertain our guests, of course," Alissa responded every bit as breezily as the gusts beyond the mansion's stuccoed walls.

"Guests?" Juliana replied as the two entered the dining room to again find Thompson in service.

With great solicitation, the footman immediately turned from the sideboard at their entrance and quickly assisted them into their chairs. Alissa smiled her appreciation—an altogether proper thing to do, Juliana allowed as she watched the sweet formation steal across her sister's lips; not, however, when done with quite that degree of coquettishness, she next assessed with chagrin. She really must speak to Alissa about her conduct with the staff, she immediately decided, and at the first opportunity, too, she thought, judging by the boldness of her sister's glance.

"Yes . . . just the usual callers, however," Alissa answered, glancing toward the sideboard as the footman placed her serviette onto her lap. "You shall have to hurry at the table, though, Juliana. They shall begin arriving shortly," she told her, perfecting the Attitude, 'Venus Rising,' in the large mirror hanging over the sideboard. "They always do.

"But Thompson, are there no deviled kidneys today?" she suddenly inquired, a pout of innocent dismay pursing her appealingly bowed lips.

"No, milady," the footman stated, beginning to fill their plates.

"But I do so have a taste for them," she informed him, her voice a sweet plaint. "Do ask Cook to prepare some, will you? I shall not mind the wait."

"Cook, however, shall," the young man replied.

"What?"

"I said that Cook *shall* mind, milady," he countered most astonishingly, facing Alissa with a half-filled plate in his hand. "Are you the least bit sensible of what you ask, I wonder? Do you comprehend at all that Cook shall have to send someone to the butcher's because of your ill-considered request? Perhaps to several if the closest shop has run out? Not to mention the fact that she shall have to prepare them during the hours she should have at her disposal to prepare the refreshments you will also no doubt require later to sustain your legions of admiring Tulips."

"Thompson!" Juliana interjected. "I really must insist—"

"Will you, or will you not, ask Cook to prepare them?" Alissa interrupted, her gaze beginning to blaze blue heat.

"I shall not."

"Then you, sir, are—"

"To go immediately to the kitchen for a bit of blackberry jam," Juliana quickly ordered, a bit appalled at her defense of the brazen footman. "I fear I have grown weary of lemon curd."

"Very well, milady," the footman said, his manner still quite properly cool and detached. Bowing, he quietly complied.

"Oooh!" Alissa cried after he had gone. "Sometimes that man makes me so furious!"

"Then by all means, let us change the subject while you compose yourself," Juliana wisely suggested, noting how very pretty her sister's complexion had grown during the exchange. "What were you saying about our callers?"

After taking in a huffily drawn breath, Alissa subsided.

"I was telling you that they shall begin arriving soon. And you look altogether lovely to receive them, Juliana," she added as Thompson unobtrusively returned to the room. "We really do look quite alike, do we not?" she continued, sniffing dismissively as the footman placed a dish of dark jam close to their rack of toast, "with our blond hair and blue eyes? You shall turn every one of our callers' heads. I believe I shall change into my yellow Mull, though. I do so like it, and it shall put me in a much better frame of mind to simper and smile while I tread the delicate line between giving each of the gentlemen too much hope and too little rejection. Such a pity, is it not? In the end, of course, I shall wed someone else."

A plate of kippers, ham, eggs, and poached fruits suddenly clattered down before Juliana's disconcerted glance.

"Ardmore," Thompson muttered, moving back toward the sideboard again.

"Yes, Ardmore," Alissa affirmed, looking squarely up at the footman, her eyes glistening with defiance. "And I required a plate of deviled kidneys, Thompson, if you recall."

"So you did," the footman remarked, boldly meeting her defiant stare as he placed her plate, too, beside her knife and spoon.

"Well get them!" Alissa commanded.

"Let Ardmore get them for you," the footman grinned,

afterward strolling toward the door to the rhythm of the jaunty tune he had begun to whistle.

"Good heavens," Juliana murmured when he had gone.

"Oooh! He makes me so mad!" Alissa hissed, stirring a large dollop of blackberry jam into the tea cooling in her dish.

Soft rain began to fall not a quarter-hour before Alissa departed Enniston House that afternoon for the ride Viscount Bentley had promised her two days earlier to show off her new spotted satin pelisse and matching muslin poke bonnet. Not long after, two deliveries arrived upon the town house's curved, porticoed steps—the first, a large box containing the sea-green ball gown Juliana had ordered from Madame Fanchon; and the second, two letters which were placed into Thompson's hand by one of London's scarlet-liveried postmen, one addressed to each of the two sisters. Surprisingly, for Juliana could not imagine how she had contrived it, the letters had been sent by their mother. Smiling, Juliana carried both letters to her chamber on the second floor; then, sitting at her rosewood *escritoire,* the spring shower already a steady patter against her window, she opened the one addressed to her.

It was a list of instructions, of course—do's and don't's for the substitute chaperone along with yet another sharp admonition against allowing Alissa to suffer the slightest dampness to her hair at the risk of that horrid brain fever, yet with no clues whatsoever as to how Juliana was to stop her. And when her mother concluded by directing her to look kindly upon Lady Welford's dear boy, Gavin, encouraging him and congratulating him on how easily he was learning to subjugate himself in his new circumstances, and in so doing, to become the pattern card of the humble servant, most improperly leaning back against her chair, Juliana did not even try to suppress her burbling chuckles.

Folding up her letter, she next fingered the letter for Alissa still resting against her wax jack, wondering what, under heaven, the viscountess might have instructed her. She did not satisfy her curiosity, however, as that would have been most improper. Instead, still amused by the workings of her mother's mind, she arose and took Alissa's letter across the hall to her room, then propped it up against the red lacquered box on her writing desk containing her writing implements—extra nibs, a bottle of India ink, and a dozen or so fresh quills.

Yet, as she turned to leave, a piece of paper laying adjacent to the box fluttered in the slight current created by her body's passing. Her gaze caught upon it; she paused. Through its half-opened folds peeked several dark, precise slashes of neatly worked calligraphy; a private communication to Alissa, obviously. Odd . . .

Immediately, however, she took herself in hand and again turned toward the door.

Still, calligraphy? On Alissa's desk? she wondered, again slowing her steps.

Yet it was clearly none of her affair, she decided, chiding herself and starting forward once more.

And yet . . .

She almost made it all the way into the corridor before the bold black slashes suddenly coalesced within her mind's eye to form, ''. . . meet in the rose bedroom.'' Abruptly, Juliana stilled. Only the twentieth part of a moment later, the note's signature floated into sight. And on the heels of that image, all ten fingers flew to her lips.

Good heavens, he certainly *had* noticed Alissa, she thought, spinning back into her sister's chamber again. The scoundrel! The jackanapes! Had he thought no one would know? she exclaimed, seizing, then jamming the missive into her bodice. The note was signed with a single letter—''A.'' Ardmore, of course.

The *roué!* The libertine! The varlet!

* * *

Moments later in her own room, Juliana bent toward the dim, rain-streaked light of her window and quickly began to read, all the while hoping that she was mistaken in what she had seen earlier, that the implication of the invitation was not what it seemed.

Her hopes quickly died. The note was explicit. Alissa—"Darling 'A,'" the slashes named her—was to come to the rose bedroom after the second waltz on the night of the Pettigrews' ball where she was to meet with this . . . this *gentleman* who had obviously been all too open to succumbing to her flirtations, a man who could only have been Ardmore, of course. Feeling suddenly weak-kneed in the aftermath of her anger and her growing realization of the immensity of the scandal broth Alissa had been brewing since the first of the Season, Juliana slowly lowered herself into her writing desk's chair.

What was she to do? she wondered as she sent her gaze skipping over the appalling message once again. Her duty was clear. She must protect Alissa at all cost, but how? Forbidding her to attend the ball seemed the logical solution, but Juliana did not think that such a tactic would work. Knowing her sister as she did, Juliana was persuaded that Alissa would simply find another way to accomplish her goal. No, she decided, if the assignation were to be thwarted, it would have to be through Ardmore's choice. Somehow, she considered, *he* would have to be the one convinced to withdraw. But how to accomplish it? She did not even know what the scoundrel looked like.

And then, suddenly, the solution unfolded.

Instantly straightening, brightening considerably, Juliana's heart began to thrum. She was her mother's surrogate, was she not? Therefore, why not discourage Ardmore's attentions in the same way that the viscountess would have done? With boldness, with finesse, and most importantly, with consummate underhandedness. And she had just the plan. On the evening

of the ball, she would have delivered into the earl's hands a
note of her own concocting, one which would lead him to think
that it had been sent by Alissa changing the place of his proposed
assignation with her, but which would instead divert him into
Juliana's grasp.

But where could she hold her meeting? She had no knowledge
of the Pettigrew town house, after all. And yet, did that really
signify? she questioned as she returned the note to Alissa's
room. She could ferret out a location for their meeting as quickly
as she could after her arrival, could she not? Then add its
direction to her note in the ladies' withdrawing room early on
after the commencement the ball? True, it was rather unusual
to carry a bottle of ink and a quill in one's reticule, especially
to one of the premiere events of the Season, but the chances
were small that anyone would see it, and it was, after all, no
more odd than the chicken bone and dried *petit-fours* she had
been carrying around somewhere in there since her little cousin
Edward's visit to Granville Manor the previous All Hallows.

And so, she assessed, a finger aside her chin . . .

Alissa would be safely waiting in the rose bedroom . . .

Lady Pettigrew would be occupied with her guests . . .

Ah, but *there,* Juliana concluded with satisfaction, wherever
it was that she found suitable to lure him, exactly as the viscountess would have done, and just as he deserved, *she* would
be happily occupied with cutting the *roué* to ribbons with the
best of her jaw-me-deads.

Chapter Three

It was after eleven that evening when the town carriages, fresh from retrieving their owners from their earlier entertainments at the opera and the theater, began to queue for position in front of the Pettigrew mansion in Duke Street, taking care to debouch their passengers upon sections of cobblestones as yet unslicked by gas-lit puddles of questionable character. Lady Pettigrew was alone, of course, to receive her guests at the head of the stairs leading to the first floor ballroom, as her husband continued to rusticate, still suffering his disabling ailment. Yet daringly dressed as she was in ostrich feathers and dampened yellow silk, judging from the volume of throat-clearing that was necessary on the part of the gentlemen, it was doubtful his lordship's absence was even once remarked.

One by one her ladyship's guests paraded before her, assessing and, in turn, being assessed; quizzing glasses raised before arrogant squints. At the proper time, the orchestra, consisting of two violins, a harp, and a cello, began to tune; Lady

Pettigrew turned at the dissonant sound, preparing to signal her major domo to announce the formation of the first quadrille.

Yet, suddenly, the door again opened. Returning her attention to the anteroom, Lady Pettigrew watched the Honorable Miss Alissa Crandall, followed breathlessly by a woman she did not recognize, spill into the mansion, capes billowing before an intrusive gust, several ostrich feathers performing a *pas de deux* atop their heads.

"Alissa, it is almost midnight," Juliana softly hissed, glancing up in time to note the pause in her hostess's retreat to the ball room with embarrassment while one of a battalion of hovering footmen approached to divest her of her green satin cloak. "Being fashionably late might be all that is proper for the Beau, certainly for the Prince, but hardly for us."

"Gammon," Alissa dismissively judged, gathering her skirt of flounced, pale blue muslin into her gloved hands, righting her feathers, and beginning her ascent. "I have timed our arrival perfectly. Do you see how our entrance has forced Lady Pettigrew to return to her place in order to greet us?" she whispered excitedly, leaving Juliana to hastily snatch at a portion of her own green embroidered hem and hurry after so as not to be summarily left. "Already I have her jumping to my tune.

"Lady Pettigrew," she then intoned much more coldly when she had gained the landing. Barely bending her knee in her brief curtsey, she afterward quite pointedly continued on into the ballroom.

Lady Pettigrew's face flamed at the appalling cut.

Juliana, reaching the top of the stairs just in time to witness her sister's unconscionable slight, gasped with embarrassment; her eyes growing huge, she, too, felt her cheeks scorch.

Altogether mortified, slowly the two women's gazes swung together, skittered away, then, after dual swallows, probed again and met.

"Lud!" Juliana uttered into the rustling silence.

"Oh, no, my dear," Lady Pettigrew corrected with one brow raised. " 'The deuce!' serves better, I think."

Then, of course, unable to help themselves, the two began to laugh.

"We must look like two jam tarts," Lady Pettigrew at last ventured, taking a delicate lace-edged handkerchief from her pocket to dab away the remnants of her mirth.

"Two of my watercolors," Juliana countered with a chuckle, giving her head a shake. "Lady Pettigrew, please allow me to apologize for my sister's behavior," she continued, self-consciously fingering the loops of her shawl.

"Your sister?" Lady Pettigrew repeated. "But, of course. You must be Lady Granville."

"Yes, I am," Juliana replied, her smile genuine but slight.

"But, my dear, I hope that your presence here tonight does not mean that the viscountess has taken ill!"

"Oh, no!" Juliana quickly told her. "Mama has taken herself off to Bath at the invitation of friends. I, unfortunately, was ordered out of my mourning in order to take her place as Alissa's chaperone. And it seems that already I have not acquitted myself very well. I greatly regret Alissa's rudeness, Lady Pettigrew."

"Think no more of the matter, my dear," Annabelle reassured. "Your sister is so young yet, is she not? Mistakes in comportment are to be expected until one has acquired the proper Town bronze."

"I suppose so," Juliana smiled. "Yet still, you are being most kind."

"Probably because I sense that you are destined to become one of the Season's more delightful diversions," her ladyship replied, taking Juliana's hand. "I believe I am rather fond of you, Lady Granville."

"And so you should be," Juliana laughed, squeezing Annabelle's fingers. "After all, it is not often one finds a matching set of watercolor cheeks."

And as easily as that, a friendship was made.

As easily as that, too, Alissa slipped her sister's censuring scrutiny, gave the note she had written in careful calligraphy to a footman for immediate delivery, and, as she had intended all along, managed to enter the ball room unescorted to begin her pursuit of her "Darling 'A' ' ".

The earl saw her enter, her blue gown accentuating her fashionable endowments to perfection, her blond tresses twisted into a comely *à la Tite*. Standing somewhat apart in the company of one of his bows from his days at Oxford, Lord Frederick Eaton, he snagged a glass of champagne from the pristine tray of a passing footman and, raising it, gestured with its stem.

"See there, Freddie?" he asked, taking a sip as he nodded toward the young beauty framed within the ball room's entrance. "There lies trouble."

"The deuce you say!" Lord Eaton exclaimed, his attention focusing, his whole stance becoming eager. "Well, you always were a bit of a stick, old fellow. That kind of trouble *I* wouldn't at all mind baring, if you take my meaning!"

Dutifully, Ardmore chuckled at the pun, yet still cast his friend a chiding glance. "You would if you but knew her," he afterward informed him, watching her begin a slow promenade. "She's a schemer, my friend. Take my advice and avoid her like Seven Dials."

"Not a chance, old lad. My arbor vitae is already jumping about in my unmentionables with enough vigor to direct a string quartet. Enjoy your evening, my tulip," he replied, tugging order into his white silk waistcoat before setting off in a direction that would quickly intersect Alissa's path. "I believe I shall engage the lady in the dinner dance."

In reaction, taking another sip of champagne, Ardmore ruefully shook his head.

Again his gaze began a slow perusal of the room, his next thoughts a consideration of whether or not to sign his name, too, to one of the newly fashionable waltzes on the card of an equally fashionable lady, or whether to make his way toward the card room on the chance that he might win a pony or two at piquet. Already he was growing bored. He drained his glass, returned it to another passing tray and took another; inhaling wearily, he shifted his weight.

Then, suddenly, he stiffened like a hunter at point.

She was there . . . the woman from the Pantheon Bazaar! . . . standing in the ball room doorway in a flowing gown of green . . . ah, no, *sea* green, the earl smiled in correction, watching as her expressive sapphire eyes began rapidly scanning the milling guests, probing, delving betwixt and between, searching for something.

Hmm . . . likely some*one*, the earl immediately amended, a fist of vexation squeezing at his chest.

As he regarded her, she hesitantly began to step forward, her manner growing anxious, her honey-colored hair catching, then mirroring, the soft spangles of the room's faceted light.

Ardmore's blood warmed quite pleasantly. Smiling slightly, he drew in more of his drink.

''The Countess of Granville,'' he heard announced, the syllables bouncing around rather muzzily inside his head.

Granville? he quickly recollected, his fingertips beginning to tingle the tiniest bit, his heart picking up its pace. Yes, he had heard that the recluse earl had died not long ago. So, her half-mourning was for a husband older by at least a score of years! he thought, letting the remainder in his fluted champagne glass midwife a widening grin.

Across the room, the lady apparently located the object of her search among the dancers then assembling for the opening quadrille. A look of relief erased the anxiousness from her wide-eyed gaze; slight shoulders beneath her gown's tiny puff sleeves suddenly relaxed, easing somewhat the gathers of soft green being tautly pulled across her bodice. As Ardmore watched, slowly her lips pursed, then reformed their lovely natural shape. She shook her head bemusedly, then drew in a deep breath.

And then, quite suddenly, she headed like a cricket pitch straight for the French windows leading out onto the Pettigrews' terrace.

Thoroughly charmed, Ardmore began to laugh.

Quite by accident, she saw it through a sentinel cluster of newly-budded lilac branches, which, just as she had chanced to glance toward the French windows, had suddenly stuttered in the soot-laden wind. It caught her eye immediately, when light from the house pouring out into the thick night flickered over several of its panes of wavy crown glass. She would not have seen it otherwise—she had been intently searching for Alissa—and on this night, there was no abetting moon. Yet there it stood: a greenhouse, ghostly and remote in the mansion's large garden, a hub radiant with spokes of orderly paths; a fragile anchor restraining the garden from scattering over the length and breadth of the west end in the bluff, blustery wind.

Slowly, almost reverently, Juliana's fingertips came to rest upon one of the French window's sparkling glass panes. Leaning forward, her nose almost touching upon another, she narrowed her intent gaze. Overhead, clouds tacked in the wind, dulling the night into matte with their passing, washing the garden with silver in between. And, suddenly, as Juliana watched, within the greenhouse globes of yellow gleamed in the brief starshine.

A lemon tree! she realized with surprise . . . in the seclusion of a greenhouse. Hmm.

Snapping her fan closed, Juliana instantly decided that if she had ordered it from Fortnum and Mason, she could not have found a more perfect place. All that remained, then, was to excuse herself to the ladies' withdrawing room which had been set aside by her hostess at the end of the gallery, and name the greenhouse in the calligraphy note she had already penned. Quickly, she checked her dance card. There was little time remaining; the second waltz loomed. Another brief search of the dance floor assured her that Alissa was, for the moment anyway, safely occupied. So it was to be now, it seemed, she concluded; there would be no better time.

Immediately she spun about and stepped forward . . . only to collide quite abruptly with a familiar cleft-curved chin.

"Oh! I do beg your pardon, sir!" she quickly rebounded, using the gentleman's forearms to regain her balance, then glancing up at him. Suddenly she stiffened; stilled. "You!" she breathed, staring up into the earl's amused expression as a lovely rush of raspberry arose to deeply stain her skin.

Bowing, Ardmore chuckled softly. "Well, I suppose I have been called worse things. Do you fare well, madam?" he asked, his pewter eyes gleaming with flecks of polished brass, "after your mishap of yesterday morning, I mean?"

Unable to help herself, Juliana warmly laughed. "It seems not, sir," she responded, again snapping her fan open to cool her mortification. "Only regard the evidence!"

"Indeed, madam," the earl replied with a bow, "I find it quite impossible to tear my eyes away."

Juliana's eyes rounded; her fan picked up its pace.

"I-I cannot think that such a comment is proper, sir," she finally stated in spite of a rather bothersome difficulty in getting air to flow to and fro from her lungs.

"How so?" the earl asked, a smile claiming one corner of his lips. "It is, after all, the truth. Would you rather I lie?"

"Oh, yes," Juliana immediately replied.

"Yes?"

"Yes," Juliana again affirmed, the glitter of amusement beginning to edge back into her cloudless gaze.

"Whyever would you rather that?" Ardmore asked, his words interspersed between the escape of several soft chuckles.

"Why, because then I shall be able to cease this disagreeable blushing, sir."

"Ah, but I like your disagreeable blushing," the earl countered, completely enchanted by the naturalness of her manner.

"Ah, but you shan't," Juliana warned, "when we gain everyone's notice because smoke shall have begun rising about my neck."

"Perish the thought!" Ardmore replied after a bark of laughter, waving both white-gloved hands. "By all means, then, let us lie like Newgate solicitors!"

"Just so."

"Then tell me, madam," the earl inquired, "what shall you lie about concerning me?"

"Your nose, I think," Juliana responded, staring at the appendage assessingly.

"My nose?" the earl repeated, seizing the protrusion in his gloved grip.

"Yes, indeed," Juliana grinned, thoroughly amused by the earl's action. "I shall tell all who will listen that it is quite prodigious . . . all lumpy and red-veined . . . and with that lovely mole right at its end—"

"Enough!" Ardmore laughed.

"Well, you did insist that we lie," Juliana justified.

"On the contrary, madam, you did," the earl countered with a smug grin.

"Oh . . . so I did," Juliana acknowledged, her lips slightly pursing. "How kind in you, sir, to call that to my attention."

"A man must do what a man must do, my dear," Ardmore intoned, his features cherubic. "No, lying was most definitely your idea. *I* would much prefer to have spent this conversation rhapsodizing over hair that is the sunset beyond Land's End," he continued, his voice softening, his gaze following his words' command, ". . . over eyes that are the autumn sky over the sarsens of Stonehenge . . . over . . .

Suddenly, quite beyond his notice, it seemed, the earl's words drifted. Slowly his gaze began to feather across Juliana's features; forehead . . . cheeks . . . chin.

"I wonder . . ." he murmured after a time, his perusal snagging upon her mouth . . . her lips, "is your new shawl even half so soft?"

"S-so soft as what, sir?" Juliana stammered under this new round of scrutiny, her breath snagging slightly on the little bulb of flesh hanging just at the base of her palate.

"As your skin," the earl replied, slowly stroking a knuckle back and forth beneath his lower lip. Moments later, as if just coming back to himself, he drew in a deep breath. "I must make a point of finding out someday."

Juliana's breath lodged just behind her heartbeat. And held.

"A-and I . . ."

But she was rescued from responding, for just then the orchestra began the introduction to the evening's first waltz, the *Kaiserwalzer* from Strauss. Alarmed, Juliana blinked herself free from the earl's spell and glanced about.

"And I must be about my duties, sir!" she finally gasped on a long-retained breath. "Besides, it is most improper for us to be speaking together when we have not been properly introduced."

"An oversight easily remedied," the earl pronounced, turning toward the assembling dancers for a mutual acquaintance. "I am aware that you arrived unescorted, Lady Granville. Who here is known to you?" he continued, his alert gaze scanning the crowd. "I am persuaded that somewhere in this sad crush we have a mutual friend. Come now, madam, speak up."

Yet when he turned back to teasingly chide her, he discovered to his vexation that the lady was nowhere to be found.

To her great relief, when Juliana entered the room customarily provided for the female guests' personal needs, only one matron had been within, and she presenting her back to the room while her maid deftly repaired the rip she had recently sustained in her stocking beneath her previous partner's exuberant gallop. After nodding a brief greeting, Juliana made straight for the room's tiny *escritoire*.

The penning of the location of her meeting took slightly longer. Juliana worked carefully, steadying her quill and the slant of her nib as she matched, "in the greenhouse beneath the lemon tree," to the strokes she had previously written. When that was accomplished, she drew forth a chicken bone . . .

Lud, Juliana groaned, tossing the crisply shriveled article back into her reticule's depths.

She drew forth a packet of sand she had brought along for the purpose, then sprinkled it over the ink's wetness; tapping it, too, back into the packet when the ink was dry, as it was not at all the thing, after all, to waste what one possessed. Next, after melting a bit of wax over a nearby candle, she sealed the note. Only moments later, she rang for a footman and gave him the instruction to place the note in none but Ardmore's hands.

His lordship, Earl of Ardmore, up to the present moment at any rate, was not best pleased with his evening's entertainment. The woman whom more than any other he wished to impress with his person, his consequence, his smoothly-styled repartee, had all but vanished off the face of the planet; even more vexing, the mistress he had no need to impress seemed not to be able to fix on the place she had offered to soothe his growing pique.

And he had had far too much champagne.

Not that he minded, he supposed, fingering the two parchment notes in his hand . . . Annabelle's indecisiveness, that is. From the moment Lady Granville had entered the ball room, he had lost interest in any but her. But where had she gone? . . . And why? he wondered as his brows migrated across his forehead into a single dark slash. More, when the deuce was he ever to see her again?

"Whatever is the matter, darling?" Lady Pettigrew asked, materializing beside him, her dance card held in her hand.

"I am persuaded that *you* shall have to straighten it out," Ardmore growled after a brief glance in her direction. "Deuce take it, Annabelle, I have little patience for games. Which is it to be? The rose bedroom, or the greenhouse?"

"Whatever are you talking about?"

"These, as well you know," the earl informed her, giving her the notes. "Two missives from you . . . two directions. Which is it to be, then? Or have you changed your mind yet again and now wish to meet me under the scullery sink?"

"Neither, I'm afraid," Lady Pettigrew chuckled, handing the parchments back to him, "as neither note is by my hand."

"No?" Ardmore questioned, cocking his head. "Then who?"

Suddenly Alissa swept by in the arms of Viscount Merton, her conversation obviously captivating the young Pink of the *ton;* her attention, however, most definitely centered on him. Eyeing the earl brazenly, she coyly smiled, then wiggled the fingers of the hand she had rested upon the viscount's shoulder before disappearing with him once again into the dance's flowing rhythm.

At her passing, suddenly Ardmore's eyes widened in comprehension.

"Alissa!" he sharply spat, crumpling the parchments in his hand.

"I beg your pardon?" Annabelle queried, studying his frown.

"The signer of the note," Ardmore again ground out, raiding

another passing tray of champagne. "This 'A' mentioned here. I thought it referred you. But it could be none other than Alissa Crandall. It has to be."

"Oh, surely not!" Lady Pettigrew quickly exclaimed. "Stephen, the gel's untried!"

"Nevertheless," he countered, throwing down a mouthful of the sparkling wine, then tossing the ball of paper out a nearby window into the garden, "the scheme is all of a piece with her other ploys."

"She is young and very foolish, Stephen. Obviously she has no comprehension of the dangers to her reputation in this game she plays," Annabelle argued with a shake of her dark head.

"She will."

"What do you mean?"

"I mean that this time she shall get her wish. This time I intend to yield to the lady's invitation," Ardmore replied. "She wishes to meet me in the greenhouse? So be it."

"Ardmore, you shall ruin her!" Lady Pettigrew softly asserted, glancing about to assess her guests' interest.

"On the contrary, I shall merely teach her the lesson she so richly deserves," he countered, draining his glass, his words carefully pronounced.

"Anymore champagne, darling, and you shan't have the facility to teach any woman anything," Annabelle commented wryly. "And give me that," she next commanded, rescuing her flute of costly Baccarat from his rather tentative grasp.

"Good point," the earl conceded, starting for the supper room. "A cup of coffee is called for, I think."

"Stephen!"

"Perhaps two," the earl reiterated, not hesitating a whit at her plaint. "After all, there isn't much time before the second waltz begins, and right at the moment, Annabelle, I am not altogether certain I am stepping on my own feet."

* * *

By the time that Juliana at last freed herself from the belated, but assuredly heartfelt, condolences of Mrs. Alfred Blythe-Lytleton, with whom she had collided during a skulk between two potted parlor palms lining the gallery, and managed to slip back unnoticed into the ball room, Alissa was nowhere to be found. The intelligence alarmed her. Having not seen her sister leave, she had no idea whether Alissa had merely taken it into her head to view the cloud ceiling in the library or had actually acceded to the earl's dastardly plans. Worse, the second waltz had long since begun, leaving her no time at all in which to discover the truth. She had no other choice, therefore, other than to simply choose.

The rose bedroom, then, she quickly decided, starting toward the iron-framed French windows. Alissa would be there. Of course she would.

After all, there was no reason to think otherwise, she allowed with a moue of chagrin, knowing Alissa as she did. She would keep her assignation, and she misdoubted so would the earl. Yet if only she had had the time to procure an introduction to the scoundrel! she thought as she slipped out through the window onto the terrace. It was much more the thing, she was persuaded, if one had at least a passing acquaintance with the gentleman over whom one rang this sort of peal.

Ardmore saw the chit slip through one of the floor-length windows leading out onto the flagstone terrace; he had been watching for her to make her appearance since his arrival in the greenhouse several minutes earlier, of course. Odd, but in silhouette she seemed more slender somehow than he had perceived her to be before. Perhaps it was the light, he considered, watching as the wind took possession of the colorless gown hanging loose below her breasts, animating it into a lively dance about her slim legs once she had gained the terrace, then molding it to her surprisingly appealing form as she had then crossed the distance to the path with light, springing steps.

But no, he must not entertain such thoughts, he quickly recanted, immediately banishing all comparisons from his mind with a shake of his head. It would not do to forget his purpose, he reminded himself, watching as the young woman next clutched her shawl about her shoulders and stepped lightly down the terrace steps onto the garden path. After all, he was only there to teach the innocent a much needed lesson, he reaffirmed above his jaw's clench. It mattered not a whit that halos of brushed silver starlight crowned her blond hair, the softly rounded contours of her shoulders, or the delicate arch of her neck.

Not yet wishing to reveal his presence, upon her arrival at the greenhouse's entrance, the earl blended himself into the lemon tree's mass, then held himself in readiness within its shadowed branches. He peered at her through the leaves, watching; and she entered, pausing for a moment while her eyes adjusted to the deeper level of darkness. Her faculties restored, next she began to look about. Spying the lemon tree, she afterward approached, her shawl drawn tightly about her body, her features masked by the darkness. Yet at the passing of the scudding clouds, her wide, wary eyes were star-kissed.

Clenching his jaw even tighter with determination, Ardmore suddenly stepped out from his concealment.

''So you have finally come,'' his voice rumbled in the darkness.

Juliana's whole being jerked convulsively at the statement. Spinning about, she saw the man just long enough to glimpse his face in the starlight, for the shock of recognition to stun her speechless, before she was pulled tightly against his length and pressed against the trunk of the lemon tree, and her mouth was buried beneath his.

God help him, she was returning his every touch. The surprise of it astonished him completely, weakening him; he had not anticipated the warm, willing yielding that followed her first soft struggle, or the strength of his reaction to the tentative sweep of her hands across his back beneath his cutaway, the sweet dueling of her tongue, the restless arch of her body within his body's curve. He fought against it, for a time, desperately he tried. But she was magic, an irresistible union of abandon and innocence unlike anything he had ever encountered before.

Easily, she became the teacher; easily the lesson to be learned that night suddenly became his. And with that realization, no power on the face of the earth could have prevented what then took place.

On a low groan, Ardmore felt himself yield. Slowly, his gentle touch grew more purposeful; again she responded in kind. And he fell deeper, deeper still, at last leaving behind whatever particle of regret for Miss Crandall's innocence remained before his passion's rising tide.

His hands found her hips; pulled them against his need.

And she moaned in response.

And pressed herself closer still.

And he was lost in her warmth, in her lips, in the depths of her star-kissed eyes.

Beyond reason, driven as he had never been before, he pressed her even more firmly against the trunk of the lemon tree.

On a soft sigh, she gave him her weight, slipping her slim legs about his waist. He entered; moved within her once . . . twice.

And, clinging to him, she gasped her release.

And he followed, afterward pouring out the remnants of his

pleasure on a warm, moist exhalation against the blond curls clinging to her soft, damp cheek.

Slowly, then, awareness returned; and with suddenness, reality. Still linked, together they stiffened; an instant later they had broken free.

Quickly adjusting his clothing, Ardmore faced her. Unsure for the first time in his life, he stared tautly down into her shadowed face.

Yet it was Juliana who first broke the palpable silence.

"Dear God in heaven!" she softly cried, her eyes huge with disbelief, her fingertips slowly rising to cover her nose and mouth.

The earl's body grew rigid at the gentle plaint. He swallowed deeply; his expression grew pained.

"I swear to you," he stiffly began, grabbing for a branch of the lemon tree to subvert a sudden wash of dizziness, "it was never my intention for things to go this far between us."

"Nor mine," Juliana whispered in return. "And yet they have, have they not?" she asked, sudden tears pooling in eyes grown diamond-faceted in the negligible light filtering through the greenhouse's crown glass.

"Nevertheless, you are not to be concerned," Ardmore reassured her. "I will be at Enniston House at eleven o'clock tomorrow morning. I give you my word as a gentleman that I shall not allow your reputation to suffer, Miss Crandall."

Miss Crandall! Juliana blinked in surprise.

Then he thought she was . . .

He had not realized . . .

On a thunderclap of understanding, Juliana's conscience reeled.

Gasping from the enormity of what she had done, pushing away from the lemon tree, stumbling past Ardmore's solid form, she began to run.

"Miss Crandall!" Ardmore called after her in alarm. "Miss Crandall!"

Yet in moments, only his heartsick sigh and a strand of sea-green wool which had snagged unnoticed upon the trunk of the lemon tree remained to give evidence that Juliana had ever been in the garden.

Chapter Four

Juliana affixed her seal to the letter she had just written to the viscountess requesting her immediate return to London just as Fern entered her chamber the following morning balancing several empty hat boxes. Glancing up at the maid's entrance, she smiled softly, then stood and walked toward her.

"Thank you, Fern. See that this goes in today's post, will you?" she asked, waiting until the woman had put the boxes down upon her bed beside her two open valises before handing her the letter.

"Of course, milady. Now what shall I do about this?" the woman wondered, holding up her mistress's new sea-green shawl.

Slowly, pensively, Juliana took the soft construction into her hands, fingering the small unraveling Fern had discovered earlier when she had begun their packing. Images came to her; thoughts with texture, like the slight abrasiveness that had rimmed warm, insistent lips, the slick silkiness of a waistcoat, the knotted roughness of lemon tree bark against her back. And remembrances . . . of feelings that had arisen with a suddenness that had stunned her, of unaccountably daring to embrace them, and then, just as suddenly, of being unable to help herself.

In the arms of Ardmore, Juliana painfully admitted, turning away to squeeze her eyes shut. Stephen Bradford. The man her own sister had chosen.

What had she been thinking of? How was it that she had so completely forgotten herself?

More importantly, what was she to do now with the knowledge she had gained of the earl's character? Obviously, he harbored little in the way of feelings for Alissa, she reasoned. He had, after all, arranged an assignation between the two of them with the intention of behaving in a thoroughly improper fashion . . . though, to his credit, he had admitted that things had gone farther than he had planned, she was forced to allow. Yet, at the same time, had he not been engaging in a flirtation with her? There could be no doubt of it, both at the Pantheon Bazaar and at the ball, Juliana assessed, again fingering the soft loops of green wool.

And that was not at all the thing, of course, she decided with a nod, the mist that had been blurring her eyes drying somewhat in the face of that nudge of self-righteousness.

So what was she to do? Confess all to Alissa and warn her that her chosen *parti* was a man of less than admirable character? No, she quickly concluded, not with her sister's success so close at hand. After all, no one save her—not even Ardmore evidently—knew that *she* was the one he had encountered in the greenhouse. And owing to that, even now he was more than likely on his way to offer Alissa his hand. Therefore, no real harm had been done, had it? she questioned, a small crease burrowing a path between her brows.

No, it had not! she assured herself, taking her doubts in hand with a renewed jut of her chin.

Of course, there were points of tenderness still lingering here and there about her body . . .

But they would soon heal, she immediately insisted.

Yet the memory . . . what was she to do about that? she wondered, tightly clenching the green wool.

Leave, that was what . . . as she had known she must from the moment, there beneath the lemon tree, when she had first comprehended what she had done. She would return to her dower house just as soon as her mother returned from Bath . . . so that she would not have to live in close proximity with them, watching her sister as wife to the man to whom *she* had recklessly yielded her body . . . to whom *she,* for the first time, had inexplicably, incomprehensibly, lost every shred of her carefully maintained control.

But she would keep her memories, of his touch, of his whisper-gray glance. That much at least was her right, was it not? Yes, she would keep her memories, she vowed. She would not lose a one.

"Can you mend it, do you think?" she asked at last, returning the shawl to Fern.

"Hard to say, milady," the maid replied, assessing the tear. "Lost a bit of wool by the looks of it. Well, never you fear. I shall make the rounds of the drapers before we leave. If I cannot find a match in London, it's not to be found."

"Thank you, Fern," Juliana replied. "It is important to me."

" 'Course it is, only worn once an' all."

"Yes," Juliana commented, starting for the door. "Well, I must go and inform Alissa of my plans."

"Hmph! Best take a weapon with you on that errand," Fern warned. "You shall need it, pother *that* one woke up in this morning!"

"Oh?" Juliana gently smiled, turning the door's brass knob. "Well, I suppose she has justification. Matters did not go last night exactly as she had planned. But what awaits her this morning should make up for all that. Is she below?"

"In the morning room, milady," Fern replied, already busily removing several gowns from the clothes press, "having a go at poor Thompson."

"Dear! Well, keep your ears open, then," Juliana ordered, stepping into the corridor. "If you hear the crash of crockery, fetch the basillicum."

Juliana was grateful for the company of Fern's chuckles as her feet reluctantly carried her toward the ordeal that even then was bearing down upon the Enniston mansion.

"I have never been so insulted in my life!" Juliana heard Alissa insist as she joined her in the bright yellow morning room.

"And with good reason, if you ask me," Thompson evenly agreed, bending to refill her cup of chocolate. "Imagine. The scoundrel did not even have the decency to show up for your deflowering. How utterly contemptible of him."

In the face of the footman's calm riposte, Alissa shot to her feet. "Oh, why do I bother discussing things with you? Of course I could not count upon you to understand, could I?"

"On the contrary, I understand perfectly," Thompson replied, glancing up and, seeing Juliana, pouring a second cup.

"Oh?" Alissa queried, her fists planted solidly upon her hips. "And what is it that you think you understand?"

"I understand that you have set your feet upon a course that will only bring you unhappiness," he told her.

"And?" Alissa urged, her eyes sparkling with chips of blue ice.

"And that you are a twit," the footman concluded, placing a spoon on the saucer beneath Juliana's cup.

"A twit!"

"A twit," Thompson reiterated.

"Oooh!" Alissa expelled after a deep inhalation. "Oooh!"

she said again, stamping her foot. "Gavin Thompson, you make me so furious!"

"Better than making you *enceinte,*" the servant replied with a grin.

"Oooh!" Alissa boldly parried. Afterward, seeing herself once again bested, she stalked away toward her day's round of social engagements.

"Dear!" Juliana remarked, staring after her sister until the room had grown quiet again. "Thompson," she then said, turning toward him, "perhaps this is might be a good time to speak to you about the proper distance a member of the staff ordinarily maintains between himself and his employers."

"Perhaps," he quickly returned. "Then again, perhaps it might be a good time to speak to you, milady," he countered, his sudden glance easily capturing her startled one with its uncanny depth, "about what has happened."

"What do you mean?" Juliana asked, turning away and clasping her hands.

"It has been as I foresaw, has it not?" the footman explained, following her, staring deeply into her, his thoughts seeming to touch within her very mind. "The tide has come; I can see it in your eyes."

"N-nothing of the sort," Juliana replied, tearing her gaze away and picking up her cup of chocolate.

"You may deny it all you wish, milady," Thompson replied with a shrug, "but it is there for me to see quite plainly. Yet you are fighting it. Why, I wonder?"

"I am fighting nothing," Juliana replied, her voice taut.

"Except your feelings. Why are you not trusting in them as I said you ought?"

Suddenly, Juliana's cup rattled in her hand. "I did," she whispered, putting the chocolate away from her as if she had been burned. "I did trust!"

"Trust again," Thompson murmured, his eyes luminous in

the firelit room as he bowed low before her. "Life never runs smoothly, milady. Trust again."

The sudden appearance of the butler spared Juliana from any further discomfiture.

"His lordship, Earl of Ardmore is without, milady," the man intoned, drawing her attention away from the footman. "He asks to speak with Miss Alissa's nearest male relative, or failing that, her mother."

Slowly, Juliana straightened and nodded, using the deliberate actions to mask the banishment of every sign of emotion from her countenance and bearing. At the effort's completion, she affixed a pleasant smile.

"Please show his lordship into the library, Paulson," she requested, her calm manner muffling the resounding fracturing going on in and around her heart. "I shall join him presently."

"Very good, milady," Paulson replied. Efficiently, then, he bowed his unobtrusive exit.

"So he has come," Thompson stated when the two were again alone. "What shall you do?"

"What I must do," Juliana responded.

"Ah, of course," the footman returned. "It *is* eleven o'clock, is it not?"

"What is that supposed to mean?"

"Only that you had best hurry, milady," he replied, bowing himself toward the door.

"Hurry to do what?" Juliana again asked, her tone beginning to hint at her vexation.

"Why, to offer up your noble sacrifice, of course," Thompson replied, hesitating to look back toward her within the door frame. "Most improper, you know. The day *is* wasting, after all, and you have yet to manage a single one."

Juliana's jaw remained agape until well after the footman had gone.

And then she snapped it shut.

"That is the most insolent retainer I have ever encountered," she finally muttered into the silence surrounding her. And then she sank back down upon the settee and began to fidget with the tassel sewn to the end of its rolled velvet cushion.

Ardmore chose not to take the seat offered by the Ennistons' butler, Paulson, upon his entrance into the library. Instead he wandered about the room's perimeter, touching idle fingers to the corner of a large claw-footed writing desk, the edge of the gilded mantel, the slow spin of a tilted globe; all the while wondering what the devil he was to say to Miss Crandall's representative when he finally deigned to join him. How the deuce was he to explain what had happened? he wondered, pausing for a moment to rub at the piercing headache thrumming between his temples. Lud, how could he explain when he did not even know what had happened himself?

He had completely lost control. That much alone was clear; that, and the overwhelming nature of his reaction to the girl. It had hit him like a thunderclap, like nothing he had experienced since he had taken his first mistress. At least then he had had an understandable reason, however: he had been a green boy of fifteen at the time.

But what could possibly be his excuse now? Damned champagne, no doubt. Why the deuce had he drunk so much when he wanted so much to remember? Had to remember. Because there was something there ... some nagging something ... something that did not ring true in the whole scandal broth. He knew it. Yet he was damned if he could put his finger on what it was.

And damned, too, if he knew how he was going to make a life with the Crandall girl, he worried, removing his beaver to rake fingers through his thick dark curls. How could he when his hopes were already bound by sweet sapphire shackles?

When his heart was even now wrapped so tenderly within the folds of a sea-green shawl? What the deuce was he to do? Biting his lower lip, the earl spun away, not even sensible of the fine, gilt-framed study by Hogarth hanging nearby, begging to engage his intellect.

Then, suddenly, the door latch softly clicked. The earl turned toward the sound.

And started with disbelief.

As if his own thoughts had conjured her, *she* was once again standing in the doorway, quietly regarding him ... the last person in the world he had ever expected to see; the last person he wanted to.

Devil a bit! Lady Granville. Muscle rolled at the edge of Ardmore's cheek.

"Lord Ardmore," Juliana greeted with a taut smile, her spine altogether inflexible.

"Lady Granville," the earl responded, almost forgetting in his astonishment to take her extended fingers for a kiss. "Forgive me. I had not expected ..." he stumbled, "that is, I had thought—"

"That you would be received by Alissa's nearest male relative, I misdoubt," Juliana completed softly, gesturing toward a saber-legged armchair adjacent to the desk. "I am sorry to disappoint you. Please, do be seated, Lord Ardmore."

"Thank you, no," the earl responded, his respiration slowing with wariness, "and I am anything but disappointed, Lady Granville. It is true, however, that I had expected to speak with the head of your household," he added, his gaze intent upon the slight tremble worrying her bottom lip, "... that is, Miss Crandall's."

Sensible of the direction of his stare, Juliana moved closer to the protective shadows of the fire. "And so you are, sir," she stated. "Absent my mother, the viscountess, I stand in her stead."

"Your mother?" Ardmore repeated in surprise. "Then Miss Crandall . . ."

"Alissa is my sister, yes. May I take it that you have come to offer for her?"

At the question, the earl's breath clotted. "I . . . I had no idea. That is . . ."

"I can see that, sir," Juliana softly helped, staring intently at the glowing coals.

His desperation building, Ardmore scrubbed a hand across his mouth.

"My lady, please tell me that you are not the one to whom I must speak of this," he finally whispered, closing the distance between them, his gaze an agonized outpouring against her fire-warmed skin.

Slowly, Juliana turned to face him, her eyes emotionless, red-rimmed. "There is no one else," she said.

Deflated, Ardmore turned, too, toward the fire's soothing flicker. "Then it seems I have no choice but to confess to the one person in all the world from whom I would wish to hide the fact that I am here to offer an *amende honorable.*"

"I know."

"You know?" Ardmore repeated, his gaze slewing toward hers. "Then Miss Crandall has spoken to you of what passed between us last night?"

"I . . . know what happened," Juliana evaded.

"Then you know that it was all a mistake."

"I know that Alissa shall welcome your declaration, Lord Ardmore," Juliana told him, clasping her fingers together until they had grown white. "However, I would know, sir, do you care anything at all for her?"

"No," Ardmore admitted. "Ah, forgive me for being so blunt, Lady Granville," he sighed, tunneling more fingers through his hair. "But, deuce take it, how can I be expected to feel anything for her?" he asked, pounding upon the mantel with his fist. "I do not even know your sister. All I do know of her is that from the moment she arrived for the Season she has beset me."

"Indeed! And yet you were the one to arrange your assignation!" Juliana quickly retorted.

At the accusation, the earl stiffened. "She told you this?"

"Yes."

"Then she has lied, Lady Granville," Ardmore responded, a bulge rounding the corner of his jaw. "I arranged nothing!" he asserted, staring hard into Juliana's eyes. "In fact, I have done everything in my power to avoid your sister since her arrival in Town. But when the notes were delivered to me at the ball—"

"Notes!" Juliana interrupted in surprise.

"Yes, notes," Ardmore affirmed. "There were two of them."

"Two?" Juliana again questioned, her eyes growing huge.

"Yes, two," Ardmore reiterated. "The first I received invited me to the rose bedroom, and the second changed the place to the greenhouse. When I got them, it seemed too good an opportunity to let pass." Suddenly the earl's shoulders sagged. "I confess to champagne-befuddled judgment, Lady Granville," he then admitted before stiffening again, "but only that. My sole intention in meeting with her was to teach her a lesson . . . to frighten her a bit. I had no other agenda, I swear it!"

Gasping, biting her lip, Juliana spun away.

"And then, God help me, for reasons even now I cannot explain," Ardmore continued, slumping against the fireplace's green Mona marble, "things . . . happened between us."

A long pause then hyphenated the passage of time.

"And was it so terrible?" Juliana at long last whispered, her back still toward him, her fingertips rising to press propriety into the tremble of her lips.

"No," the earl responded, his gaze bleeding against the shapely contour of her spine. "To my everlasting shame, it was not.'' Suddenly he propped his elbows upon the mantel and buried his face in his hands. ''Damme! How can I speak of this to you? To *you*? Ask me to say no more of it!''

Slowly, Juliana turned, too, toward the fire. Inhaling deeply, she joined him in staring into its depths.

''Many good marriages have begun with less,'' she whispered.

''Yes,'' Ardmore softly replied, ''when both parties are free to build upon such as that. I am not.''

''Because of Lady Pettigrew?'' Juliana breathed.

''No. Because of you, my lady.''

Dear God! Juliana sobbed within her mind.

''And you know it,'' Ardmore continued, daring to place his warm palm against her cheek, giving his fingers free rein among the tresses curving about her delicate ear. ''Say that you do.''

''Yes,'' Juliana nodded. Suddenly, at the edge of her composure, she quickly crossed to the desk. ''I-I shall be leaving for Stockbridge as soon as Mama returns from Bath,'' she told him, her eyes filling with tears.

''But why?'' he instantly asked, his voice a pleading.

''Because . . . how could I ever stay?''

Yet another soft silence settled over the room. Nearby, the fire rustled within its charred oak host; the slow ticking of an ormolu clock paced the steady thump of heartbeats.

At last the earl nodded.

''You could not,'' he tautly admitted, closing his eyes against his pain.

''You will be kind to her, will you not?'' Juliana asked.

''Yes, always. She is part of you.''

''Then there is nothing more to say. Paulson will show you to the drawing room, Lord Ardmore,'' Juliana told him, catching a tear with two fingertips after she began a slow glide toward the door. ''I shall have Alissa come to you presently,'' she finished, waiting while the earl opened it, then preceding him into the corridor.

With every polite phrase he had ever learned clumping stag-
nantly about his tongue, Ardmore instead bowed his resignation.
When he straightened again, the only one present to acknowl-
edge the courtesy was Paulson.

Chapter Five

"Will you be wanting me to press this for dinner, milady?" Fern asked shortly after their arrival back at the Granville dower house a fortnight later.

"Yes, thank you, Fern," Juliana replied, rising from her dressing table. "His lordship has invited me to join the family this evening. The *moiré* should do nicely."

"As would this had I been able to mend it," Fern remarked next, removing the sea-green shawl from one of Juliana's valises and holding it up to the light. "Pity I had so little time to look for wool of the proper color. Quite took m'breath away, however, with the haste of our departure."

"It was necessary, Fern," Juliana interrupted. "Shan't you need to begin heating the iron on the fire?"

"Yes, milady."

"Then you may be excused to do so," Juliana stated.

Chastened, dropping a brief curtsey, the maid quickly left her mistress to her solitude.

Alone, Juliana took up the shawl and carefully folded it,

taking pains not to widen the unraveling further as she then crossed to her clothes press and fitted the garment into one of its large drawers. Unwanted thoughts pressed upon her consciousness, the same nagging conclusions she had finally drawn over the endless hours of her sennight's solitary travel back to her home. She had tried to shunt them aside, but again and again they had returned. She had fallen in love, she had realized several days' distance down the Great Western Road. For the first time, helplessly; and like a cork-brained cocklehead she had simply turned her back on all that it might have meant.

Without a care for Ardmore's feelings in the matter.

Without the twentieth part of a moment's consideration for her own feelings as that rag-mannered footman Thompson had insisted she should.

Foolishly.

And with that realization had come the complete comprehension of the full measure of her folly.

For Ardmore had not been the scoundrel in the whole scandal broth, it seemed; Alissa had. It had been she who had written the note Juliana had found on her *escritoire,* she who had arranged the meeting at the ball and set Juliana's own response into motion, she who had used an insult toward Lady Pettigrew as a way to escape her guardianship. She who had manipulated them all. And Juliana had not seen it until it had been too late . . . until the earl had come to believe that he had ruined an innocent . . . until she had been caught between her duty to Alissa as her sister, her guilt over her own wanton response, and her belief that she had very nearly stolen what Alissa had claimed.

But how to undo it? Juliana again wondered for the hundredth time since her departure from Town, closing the drawer and sprawling in a most unladylike fashion across her cluttered bed. Quite simply, there was no way.

By now, the engagement notice must already have been

published in the *Post,* she assessed, and Ardmore shall have become betrothed to Alissa.

A woman he does not care for, she next added in her thoughts; a duty he has accepted because he thinks that he must.

And why is that, Juliana? she almost chided aloud, feeling a fresh spurt of hot tears boil about between her eyes' red rims.

Because I did not tell him the truth, that is why, she admitted, willing away a small sob ... because I could not. Because I rejected my own feelings and instead took Alissa's part. I behaved in an unconscionable manner with a man I barely knew; and, faced with it all, I believed that there had been no choice in the matter. Never once. For any of us.

But they could make a good marriage, could they not? Juliana then countered, swiping at her eyes with her sleeves. Alissa was so lovely, after all, and the earl *had* promised to be kind. It could come about.

Yes, if you never again see him in your life, she responded from another portion of her consciousness ...

And if the memory dies, which it never will ...

And, of a certainty, if England sinks into the sea ... which has a better chance of happening, Juliana assessed, than of her ever ending what she had come to feel for the man who was now her sister's betrothed.

And none of it had been necessary ... and all of it had.

How was she to bear it?

What have you done? Juliana then cried, rolling over to bury her face in the white cotton of her coverlet. Oh, Juliana, you idiot! What have you done?

The grey, misted drizzle that sifted through the plane trees to pearl upon the wool of Ardmore's great coat all the way to Lady Pettigrew's the following morning matched his mood. His hands were curled into fists; had been, in fact, for days, he realized as his brougham came to a halt before the Pettigrew's

Georgian mansion and he unhurriedly stepped down onto the glistening cobblestones. Starting down the short walk to the town house's wide porticoed entrance, he purposefully unclenched them and stretched his fingers within his York tan gloves. It would do no good to fight against his fate, he knew, so why was he even contemplating the attempt? He had brought it all down upon himself, after all.

Upon his footman's announcement of his presence, he was ushered by the Pettigrew's black-clad butler into the mansion's first floor drawing room.

"Stephen!" Lady Pettigrew greeted, rising from an armchair to accept his kiss upon her cheek. "I had just been wondering when you might appear."

"Oh?" Ardmore replied, sagging against the scrolled arm of the Grecian sofa directly opposite her.

"I saw the announcement in the *Post,* darling," she continued. "Naturally I have been expecting my *congé.*" Suddenly her gaze sharpened. "Or should I have been, considering your choice? Stephen, never say you have been entertaining the idea of continuing our arrangement!" she exclaimed, her lips playing with a mischievous smile.

"You know better than that," the earl chided, glowering in her direction as he slipped a macaroon into his mouth.

"Just as well, I suppose," Annabelle shrugged before pouring him a cup of chocolate. "I shall be leaving in two days for Yorkshire anyway."

"Shall you?"

"Yes. Pettigrew is complaining that he misses me. Poor old darling," her ladyship smiled, setting her own cup of chocolate aside. "I shall likely have to dance attendance for weeks. I only hope I have accumulated a suitably entertaining number of *on dits* in so short a time here in Town. Algernon does love to have an ear to everyone's lips, you know. I shall probably have to miss your wedding, too, darling."

"Alissa complains that she has been left by her mother

to handle the arrangements herself,'' Ardmore responded. ''I expect the affair to be quiet and small.''

''Mmm,'' Annabelle thoughtfully replied, ''as if there were secrets to quell. Are there, Stephen?''

''I have no idea what you mean,'' the earl responded, leaning forward to join his palms between his knees.

''Oh, yes you do indeed!'' Annabelle gleefully cried, tugging upon his sleeve. ''I can see the truth of it in your expression. Oh, Stephen, what's toward? I confess that, considering what you had told me of your feelings concerning the Crandall chit's behavior toward you these past weeks, the announcement of your betrothal to her was astonishing.''

''To me as well,'' Ardmore confessed. ''But it was requisite, I am afraid. Unfortunately, when I met with her in your greenhouse on the night of the ball to educate her in the dangers of her course of action, things . . . got out of hand.''

''Not surprising, if you ask me,'' the lady assessed.

''I am not attracted to her, Annabelle,'' Ardmore insisted. ''Not now . . . not then.''

''I am not speaking of attraction, Stephen,'' Lady Pettigrew argued. ''I am speaking of the fact that you have never been a man given to excessive drinking, yet upon the occasion of my ball, you were four sheets to the wind.''

''It was not that bad,'' Ardmore stiffly insisted. And then he sagged. ''Oh, very well, it was. And I know there was no excuse for it. But, deuce take it, Annabelle, I knew Alissa would be in attendance that evening and she had been driving me daft!''

''Under the circumstances, any man would have been weakened, darling,'' Annabelle soothingly replied.

''Perhaps,'' Ardmore allowed, a slight flush staining his cheeks. ''But it was more than that.''

''More?''

''Yes,'' Ardmore asserted. ''Something about the whole bumblebroth was different than it ought to have been.''

"How so?"

"I cannot put my finger on it," Ardmore replied. "I have been trying, believe me. But all I can truly recall is the darkness . . . the sensations . . . and not being able to hold two thoughts together. I can remember nothing else."

"Then you must try again," Annabelle firmly pronounced.

"To what end?" Ardmore asked, splaying his hands. "The deed is done."

"If so, then describe it to me."

At her insistence, the earl began to chuckle. "It *is* just the slightest bit personal, Annabelle," he chided with a shake of his head.

"As have we been," the lady immediately replied. "Now, close your eyes and recall the greenhouse. Tell me what you see."

Still chuckling, Ardmore did as he had been bid. "Very well . . . I see her approaching on the path," he began, reaching up to rub memory into his forehead.

"What do you think of her?"

"She is more slender than I imagined . . . her gown is blowing against her form. I feel . . . desire."

"Go on," Lady Pettigrew prompted dispassionately.

"She enters the greenhouse. Her eyes are sparkling . . . it is all that I can see of her face."

"And then?"

"And then she is in my arms, and I cannot stop what is happening," Ardmore shakily breathed. "She is soft and warm, and our mouths are joined. She is clinging to me. Afterward . . . she runs away."

"Stephen, forgive me, but are you certain the act was completed?" Lady Pettigrew asked, an odd flicker illuminating her clear gaze.

The earl colored again. "That is the one thing in this whole scandal broth, Annabelle, of which I have no doubt."

At his response, the lady nodded. "Very well, then," she

said, her eyes sharpening. "But what did Miss Crandall say as a result?"

"I cannot remem . . . wait! She did say something. She expressed regret that things had gone far beyond what either of us intended."

"I see," Lady Pettigrew replied, her eyes now narrowing almost into slits. "And that is all that she said?" she then asked. "You are certain of it?"

"Yes," the earl softly replied. "I am certain. There was a 'Dear God in heaven,' I believe, but that was after we had . . . set ourselves to rights again."

"And you are absolutely certain of this?"

"Yes!" Ardmore responded, beginning to grow a bit vexed by the repetition.

"Then, in my opinion, Stephen," Annabelle stated, gusting out an affronted breath, "you would do well to hasten to Enniston House this very moment and break your engagement to that disreputable chit!

Ardmore's jaw swiftly dropped. "What! Whyever?"

"Because, my darling," her ladyship explained, "quite simply, if Miss Crandall is the innocent party all have led you to believe she is, where were her maiden's tears at the act's beginning, tell me that! Where was her cry of pain or distress?"

For several seconds, Ardmore merely stared at his mistress. Then, resembling quite closely the launching of one of Mr. Whinyate's rockets, he was grabbing for his beaver, calling for his rain-speckled great coat, and bolting back out into the mist.

"More tea, my lady?" Thompson inquired of the viscountess just as Ardmore's carriage turned into South Street and began its approach toward Enniston House's stuccoed portico.

"Yes, please, dear boy," Lady Enniston cooed, reaching up to stroke the footman's chin. "And you, Alissa, have done with your dawdling, if you please. Shall it be our own English Honiton for your wedding gown, or the Valenciennes?''

''I do not care,'' Alissa replied, refusing to turn her attention away from her absorption in the fashion plates contained in the family's current issue of *La Belle Assemblie.*

''Well, you had best begin,'' the viscountess scolded. ''And while you are about it, try to muster up at least a little enthusiasm for your betrothed when he comes to visit. I vow, Alissa, before I left for The Bath you could speak of nothing else but your desire for Ardmore. Now, when he is yours, you barely converse with the man.''

''And with good reason!'' Alissa suddenly exclaimed, afterward motioning for Thompson to refresh her cup. ''He has hurt me, mama,'' she pouted, ''grievously.''

''Indeed. How?'' the viscountess asked, her tone laced with traces of skepticism.

''It is nothing I can ever speak of,'' Alissa replied, pressing the back of her wrist to her forehead. ''Only know that I shall never be able to forgive him.''

''Twit,'' Thompson murmured, bending low beside her ear, tipping tea into her cup from his silver pot. ''If you cannot forgive the man, then why did you accept his hand?''

''Because he is the one I chose, of course,'' Alissa hissed, ''and because he finally gave in.''

''His lordship, Earl of Ardmore,'' Paulson suddenly intoned from the doorway.

Swallowing his retort, Thompson subsided into the background.

Moments later, Ardmore entered the drawing room. Fastening his iron-grey gaze upon Alissa, for long seconds he slowly drained a good deal of the disgruntlement from her with his penetrating stare, then began to advance with the stalking stride of a predator; he suddenly the mongoose, she the vulnerable reptile.

Uneasily, Alissa once more burrowed back into the world of fashion.

"Lady Enniston," Ardmore greeted upon his arrival in their midst, removing his glove to draw her hand to his lips.

"Dearest Ardmore," her ladyship replied, motioning toward the empty spot on the settee beside her. "We were just having tea. Shall you join us?"

"Thank you, no," the earl responded, indicating with his eyes for the footman to leave them. "I fear I have come to discuss a rather unpleasant matter."

"Unpleasant! Never say so," the lady insisted.

"Regrettably, it is true," Ardmore replied, again glancing pointedly at the footman and, for his trouble, receiving a bright, cheeky smile. Vexed, still he continued. "What I have to say is quite personal, Lady Enniston. Perhaps I might have your permission to speak with Alissa alone."

"Why, of course, dear boy," the viscountess readily replied, rising from her portion of the yellow upholstery. "You are, after all, betrothed to one another. However, I shall return in five minutes, not a second more. Come, Thompson, dear," she commanded, signalling the footman that she was to be followed. "I have eaten all the jam tarts. Do be a dear and fetch more for his lordship."

After an elegant bow, the retainer, too, departed and Alissa and Ardmore found themselves alone.

Instantly, the earl whirled about to face her. "You lied to me," he accused, impaling her shock with a pewter spear.

"What?"

"Do not bother to deny it," he dismissed. "I remember everything now."

"Everything of what?" Alissa cried, finding her spirit again in her ire.

"Of the evening of the ball," Ardmore informed her. "Of everything that happened that night between us in the greenhouse under the lemon tree . . . of the fact that you, my innocent Miss Crandall, experienced no pain!''

''What greenhouse?'' Alissa stormed. ''What pain?''

''I assure you, Miss Crandall,'' Ardmore returned coldly, ''there is no need for you to continue this charade. I know the truth.''

''What truth?'' Alissa cried, exasperated.

''That you entered into this betrothal under false pretenses,'' Ardmore stated. ''That you, Miss Crandall, are no maid.''

''How dare you!'' she cried, the twentieth part of a moment later scoring a stinging imprint across the length of Ardmore's face.

''Oh, I dare,'' he spat back in reply, rubbing at his cheek, ''just as I dare to break off this misbegotten misalliance.''

''Indeed? Is that what you intend? Well, you are sadly mistaken then!'' she responded, plopping her fists upon her hips just as Thompson sailed back into the room sporting a tray laden with tarts. ''As it happens, I am the one breaking this engagement! And I have no idea what you are referring to. I have never met you beneath a tree of any kind, nor have I ever done whatever it is one has to do to . . . well, what it is that you implied! And you are not the man I thought you, sir!'' she then exclaimed, huge tears popping into her eyes.

''Is that so?''

''It is,'' Alissa cried. ''Indeed, if there is a villain in this piece, sir, it is you. *You* are the one who led me on, to my way of thinking. It was *you* who retrieved my parasol—not once, but twice—*you* who asked after my health, and *you,* who afterward spurned me utterly!''

''Spurned you!'' Ardmore argued, raking his fingers through his hair. ''Miss Crandall, I asked for your hand.''

''Yes, but you never met me in the rose bedroom!'' Alissa accused, sinking down onto the yellow settee with a sob.

''The rose bedroom . . .'' Ardmore far more softly repeated. ''You awaited me there?''

"Of course, I did," Alissa wailed, "just as my note said I would."

"But you met me in the greenhouse," Ardmore insisted. "You diverted me there in your second note."

"I did not write you a second note!" Alissa screeched.

"Then who met me under the lemon tree?" Ardmore asked, throwing up his hands.

"I haven't the least idea, nor do I care," Alissa huffed, rising to stare out the window while dabbing at her tears with her handkerchief. "All I know is that I do not wish for the two of us to have any further congress. I cannot imagine why I ever wanted you for my husband. I shall have my betrothal necklace returned to you this afternoon. Good day, sir."

"Miss Crandall, are you certain?"

"Jam tart, sir?" Thompson offered.

Almost vexed beyond bearing, the earl glowered at the footman, then, assessing that any further attempts at discovering the truth were a lost cause, spun about on his heel and stalked off into the soot-streaked afternoon.

Still standing by the window, Alissa once more began to leak tears. "Oh, Thompson, I thought he would be the perfect husband for me."

"Yes, I know. Because you have no idea what is good for you," the footman stated, settling down his tray of tarts and crossing to her side.

"And you do, I suppose," Alissa half-smiled.

"As a matter of fact, I do," he told her, staring, too, out the window at a blurred plane tree. "You need a man who will not put up with your nonsense . . . who will tell you plainly when you are being a twit. And, you need a man who will love you in spite of it."

"And is there such a person somewhere in the world?" Alissa breathed, her lips trembling upon each word.

"There is . . . standing beside you, Alissa. Always standing by your side."

"And will you?" she asked, reaching over to take hold of the little finger of his nearest hand.

"I will," the servant replied, turning toward her and taking her cold hands into the warmth of his.

"But you are a footman, Gavin," Alissa softly reminded the both of them, her eyes huge beneath his own. "What will we do?"

"Find a Gretna blacksmith, of course," he replied, his smile cockily askew. "Are you for it?"

Staring at him wonderingly, Alissa blinked once and then again.

"Why, yes I am," she politely replied, beginning to grin.

"Then come here, love," the footman murmured, quite happily opening his arms wide, then enfolding her within.

"She swears that it was not her," Ardmore stated, striding back into the Pettigrew drawing room before the butler had even gotten to his title.

"Would you expect her to say anything else?" Annabelle laughed, looking up to see who had barged into her presence, then setting aside her copy of the newest offering from Mr. Lane's Minerva Press.

"No," he responded, dropping into an adjacent settee, "however, on this occasion I am inclined to believe she was telling the truth."

"Oh?"

"She swears that she was waiting for me in the rose bedroom that evening," Ardmore explained, "not in the greenhouse. In fact, she broke our engagement because I did not keep the assignation."

"Oh, Stephen, never say so! And the note directing you to the lemon tree?"

"She says she knows nothing about it, Annabelle," the earl replied, taking a bite out of a diamond-shaped watercress sandwich he had selected from a nearby tray, "therefore it can only have been written by the woman who came to the greenhouse that evening."

"But, darling, the two notes looked virtually the same," the lady argued.

"To me as well," he responded, finishing the morsel and wiping a few crumbs from his fingers with his napkin. "But obviously they must not have been, and what the second woman's purpose in inviting me to the greenhouse might have been I cannot comprehend."

"Perhaps the same purpose as Miss Crandall's in directing you to the rose bedroom," Annabelle suggested.

"Possibly. But quite possibly, too, her motive was altogether different. I confess that I gave her no chance to speak before I . . . began my lesson. Ah, Annabelle," the earl sighed, leaning back against the settee's velvet, "who was she? And why did she come to me beneath the lemon tree? What the deuce have I done?"

"That I cannot tell you, my darling," Annabelle told him. "But I do remember you throwing the notes out the window on the night of my ball. Come," she said, rising to her feet, "perhaps we might still find them in the garden and they'll give us at least a starting point from which you might begin an investigation."

Nodding, Ardmore arose, too, then escorted the lady from the room.

"It's no use, Stephen," Annabelle stated several minutes later from the midst of masses of fragrant perennials. "We have looked everywhere that the notes might be. My gardener must have found them and disposed of them."

"So it seems," Ardmore agreed, glancing about one last time before centering a black umbrella more accurately over Lady Pettigrew's simple chip straw bonnet. "They certainly are nowhere to be found,'' he observed, taking her arm and assisting her withdrawal from the garden's rain-beaded abundance and rich, spongy earth.

"Stephen, I am so sorry,'' Annabelle told him upon gaining the more stable surface of the flagstone path, shaking droplets of rain from her half-boots and hem. "I had so hoped . . .''

"I know . . . and thank you for it,'' he replied, threading her hand through his arm.

"But what will you do?'' she asked as the two of them slowly began to wander, neither one having a direction, only knowing that they must do so.

"There is little I can do, it seems,'' the earl observed. "I cannot leave Town, of course. Somewhere, more than likely not far from here, is a woman I have—''

"No, you cannot leave,'' Annabelle interjected protectively, the heavy scent of the rose-drenched arch framing the greenhouse entrance finding its way to her nostrils in spite of the damp, chilly wind. "If she finds herself with child . . .''

"Yes. But, deuce take it, Annabelle, I would give anything if it were not so!'' he ground out, watching runnels of drizzle snake down the building's small panes of crown glass, "if I could quit Town and return to Eastbrook! My betrothal has ended, after all. There is nothing here for me now.''

"Perhaps not,'' Lady Pettigrew replied, pausing while the earl opened the door to the greenhouse, then stepped aside for her to enter so that she might enjoy a respite from the sky's incessant drip. "Or perhaps, not the twentieth part of a moment after you leave here this afternoon you shall come upon the very woman you are destined to make your countess.''

"I am afraid it is too late for that, my dear,'' the earl ruefully smiled, collapsing the umbrella and shaking a shower of droplets off onto a foxtail fern. "We have already made one another's acquaintance.''

"Stephen, never say so!'' Lady Pettigrew exclaimed, pausing

in her stroll along a row of fledgling camellias to reach over and take his arm. "Who, pray tell?"

"The one woman in all the world I cannot have, of course," Ardmore told her with a quirk of his lips. "Alissa's sister, Lady Granville."

"Juliana?"

"Juliana . . ." the earl repeated, his gaze softening to silver. "Is that her given name?"

"You mean you didn't know?" Annabelle laughed, shaking her head over the odd sense of priority men sometimes exhibited.

"The subject never came up, I am afraid . . . and when I was in Alissa's company, hardly anyone spoke at all," he responded with a return of her grin. "Beautiful, though, is it not?"

"What, Juliana's name, or Juliana?" she asked, again taking his arm.

"Both," Ardmore answered after a more subdued smile. "But it does not signify, does it?" he added, for the first time turning to face the building's core. "I no sooner found her than I threw her away. Exactly there," he completed, his gaze fixed upon the dark green, leather-leafed canopy of the lemon tree. "Such a stupid . . . stupid mistake," he condemned, beginning to stroll toward it, his vision filled with staccato bursts of dark, night-shrouded memory; and of Juliana . . . the dance of laughter in her eyes . . . the soft, richness of her voice . . . the sunshine at the Bazaar setting fire to a wayward golden strand of hair.

"Life is full of such, Stephen," Lady Pettigrew reasoned, following him into the tree's cool, dark interior and settling herself against a thick, low-spreading branch where it joined the trunk. "Yet still people do overcome. Why can you not hold on to the hope that somehow matters will resolve themselves to the good? After all, you said yourself that Juliana's sister is no longer a concern. You *are* no longer betrothed to Miss Crandall.''

''Nor was there ever any need for me to be, it seems,'' Ardmore responded, cupping a dangling lemon in his palm and inhaling its tart essence, ''but for Alissa's youthful arrogance. Yet still I am bound by what occurred here, Annabelle, and to the woman I have compromised. I can do none other than to wait for her to come forward with her demands. There is no choice for me except that. For that reason, I cannot allow myself the luxury of hoping for a future with Juliana.''

No longer able to bear the bleakness tugging deep furrows across Ardmore's forehead, Lady Pettigrew looked away. Suddenly, her gaze fixed on a twig adjacent to her cheek, on a soft fluttering something snagged just at the corner of her eye. Leaning back a bit, she studied it; only the twentieth part of a moment later, her face brightened with delightful surprise.

''On the contrary, darling, I think that you can,'' she quickly countered, clapping her hands together beneath her chin.

''What do you mean?'' Ardmore asked, turning in her direction.

''Only look, Stephen!'' Annabelle commanded with a laugh, still looking at the twig.

The earl did. There, snagged just beside Lady Pettigrew's grin was a length of wool . . . no, *sea-green* wool, he corrected. And then a sudden huff of astonishment escaped him, the cockcrow that sounded the dawning of his comprehension.

''Juliana,'' he breathed. ''All this time, it was Juliana,'' he repeated, with the utmost tenderness, taking the piece of soft wool into his fingers, then staring at it as if it were the Holy Grail.

''Exactly so,'' Annabelle confirmed with a triumphant giggle.

''Then . . . she had to have known,'' the earl said suddenly. ''Deuce take it, she had to have known all along!''

''A logical conclusion, I should think.''

"Then why . . .?"

"Because she knew Miss Crandall wanted you, of course," Annabelle quickly answered with an unquenchable smile still firmly in place.

"So she just turned her over to me?" the earl exclaimed.

"Oh, Stephen," Annabelle laughed, reaching out to touch his arm, "only imagine how a woman like Juliana must have felt knowing that she had trysted with the man her sister had claimed!"

Halted in his tracks, the earl subsided against the lemon tree's trunk. "She would have been appalled."

"And torn with guilt."

"And quite certain that she must step aside in order to do the proper thing," Ardmore completed, his jaw bulging above his Mathematical's stiff confinement. "But why did she ask to meet me in the first place?" he then asked, rubbing at his forehead.

"I can only guess, of course," Lady Pettigrew offered, "but it seems likely that Juliana was merely acting the part of her sister's chaperone. Perhaps she discovered the note Miss Crandall had prepared and assumed it had come from you. You must admit, darling, that there are a great many 'A's' to deal with in this triangle. Perhaps her plan was to spare her sister a scandal broth by diverting you from your arranged assignation."

"Annabelle, if that were so, why did she not just confront me with my underhandedness when we spoke earlier near the French windows?" Ardmore exclaimed, pushing away from the lemon tree trunk.

"You were not aware that she was Alissa's sister, Stephen," the lady reminded him. "Perhaps she was not aware that you were Ardmore."

"Damme, Annabelle, you may have the right of it," the earl realized. "She might very possibly not have known who I was. We were never introduced."

"And so, without knowing you were Ardmore, she sent you off to the greenhouse," Lady Pettigrew concluded.

"Where we met," Ardmore murmured. "Where she, it is now quite obvious, must have recognized me. Annabelle, she alone of any of us knew the truth. And yet . . . she yielded."

"And what does *that* tell you, darling?" Annabelle grinned, watching the earl's face grow soft with emotion, with wonder.

"That she loves me," the earl breathed, a gentle smile curving the corners of his lips.

"And what shall you do about it, my dear?" the lady next inquired.

"Tell *her,* Annabelle," he replied, carefully giving the length of sea-green wool over into Lady Pettigrew's protection. "I am going to tell *her,*" he repeated, reaching out and beginning to stuff every lemon he could get his hands on into his pockets, his curly-brimmed beaver, and even the startled lady's reticule.

Juliana had ridden like the wind, spurring her mare on relentlessly over the Granville Manor parkland, concentrating on the even surges of muscle, the rhythmic drumming of the animal's hooves, desperately willing the pounding pulses to exorcise the demons of memory, but it had been no use. Nothing helped. For almost a week it had been so; nothing had eased a sense of loss a hundredfold greater than she had ever experienced for Granville.

Slowly, therefore, she drew on the ribbons and brought her mount to a walk, letting the mare rest awhile before urging her toward the dower house once again at a respectable trot, unmindful of the cool late May morning, the buzz of a mayfly about her mare's flank, the heat of a building sun soaking into the dark blue velvet of her riding habit. For nearly an hour she continued on until the chimneys of the dower house came into sight. Still discouraged, she slowed the mare to a walk and brought her to a halt in the stable yard. Then, after giving her into the keeping of one of the awaiting boys, she paced measured steps across the courtyard and up to the rear entrance of the house.

"Why, there you are, milady!" Cook smiled brightly as she passed the kitchen. "Welcome back!"

Startled by the normally brusque woman's greeting, Juliana paused. "Thank you," she replied, briefly studying the cook before slowly continuing on.

"Mornin', milady!" her footman called out to her from the scullery where he was washing the coins.

"And to you, Dougal," Juliana returned, her eyes widening at the taciturn Scot's enthusiasm.

"Glad you're home, mistress," the scullery maid giggled, casting Juliana a mischievous glance as she swept past with an armload of newly-washed dishes bound for the closet.

"Thank you, Tilly," Juliana replied, spinning about to follow her progress, then shaking her head.

What under heaven was going on? she wondered, passing through the green baize door almost backward before stepping into the large hall beyond. She turned then, so as not to trip upon the fringed edge of the room's thick Aubusson.

And then she saw it, centered upon the table: a basket filled to overflowing with lemons, garnished with clusters of glossy green citrus leaves and baby's breath, crowned with a huge bow of deep emerald satin.

"Oh!" Juliana gasped with surprise, immediately afterward clamping both hands over the sound and glancing about to reassure herself that her outburst had not gained the notice of the servants. Satisfied that it had not, her gaze returned to the basket again.

"Ohh!" she then breathed, cautiously moving forward, drawn to it like water into a parched sponge.

Arriving at the edge of the table, she looked down. Nestled

atop the lemons, pillowed by more of the leaves and delicate, spider-stemmed flowers, was a yellow velvet covered box. Attached to the box was a note that had been sealed with wax marked by two lions rampant above a horizontally striped field.

Ardmore's crest! Juliana quickly recognized, her heart careening down into her lower abdomen. Clenching her fingers into fists, still Juliana stared, vainly trying to force her lungs to draw in their next breath.

At last, unable to stand not doing so a moment longer, she slowly stretched out her hand and removed the box's lid. There, on white satin, lay a lemon tree, its bark fashioned of gold, its leaves of emeralds, its fruit a scattering of yellow diamonds, flawless and perfectly matched.

Awestruck, Juliana touched it, then drew in her lower lip; vexingly, the brooch blurred beyond feelings turned liquid within her wide open lids.

A quick swipe banished them; and then, finally, she took the note into her hands.

Breaking the seal and unfolding it, she gasped again. It had been neatly penned in calligraphy! Of course, it would be, she thought, drat the devious man! After a tiny smile of admiration, quickly she scanned the note's precisely slanted lines.

My dear Lady Granville,

This letter is to inform you that all is known.

It is also to accuse you of deceit, trickery, and blatant manipulation for the sole purpose of placing me in a position of compromise. More, it is to charge you with afterward callously casting me aside, only to then maneuver me into the possession of your sister who in turn misused me most foully by running off with a most deucedly insolent footman, a Mr. Gavin Thompson, who is now, much to the *ton*'s enjoyment, her lawful husband.

(Is this some sort of Enniston family weakness, Juliana? I shall hate for such behavior to show up in our future generations!)

Finally, this letter is to inform you that unless you accept the challenge I am hereby demanding and meet me at the dueling place of my choosing, I shall publish the facts of your spurious perfidy in every paper in London. I am sure you can see from the above charges that my honor demands nothing less than complete satisfaction. Understand, my lady, there is no escape for an alienator of affections such as yourself. You *shall* give satisfaction to me, and you shall do it before witnesses in St. George's, Hanover Square, at 10:00 A.M. on the first day of June this year. Required dress: wedding finery; *my* choice of weapons as I am not giving you any: marriage vows. My second and I shall await you on the day. Bring yours.

I remain your obedient servant, Stephen Bradford, Earl of Ardmore.

By the way, I love you to distraction, Juliana. Please come and marry me.

Ardmore.

There in the dower house entry, in full sight of a houseful of happily spying servants, the Countess of Granville promptly burst into tears.

"And do you, Juliana, take this man to be your lawfully wedded husband?" asked the vicar, startling Juliana back into the present again.

"I do," Juliana stated firmly, knuckling away the moisture of memory from the corners of her eyes.

"Damned right you do," the earl murmured out of the corner of his mouth, "and thus ends the duel. *Touché,* Juliana."

Not daring to look up at him, Juliana vigorously quenched a threatening smile.

"Am I to take it that you have now received your satisfaction, my lord?" she whispered, trying very hard to maintain the proper solemnity in her voice.

"Only once, I am afraid," he responded *sotto voce,* barely moving his lips, "to my everlasting regret. But just give it the wedding breakfast, my dear. Alienator of affections that you are, I have no doubt you shall give me cause to demand satisfaction from you yet again only a short while later."

Juliana gasped; Alissa giggled.

The vicar chided with a warbled, "Ahem! And have you a token, milord?"

"I do," Ardmore replied, reaching toward his new brother-in-law, Thompson—surely the cheekiest best man he had ever encountered, and absolutely the most insolent second he had ever employed.

Grinning widely, the footman placed something very small into the earl's hand. Immediately after, Ardmore turned toward Juliana again.

In the next moment, the earl removed her glove and slipped the object he had taken from Thompson over the fourth finger of her hand.

Curious, Juliana looked closer; seconds later could barely contain her startled cry. There on her finger was a tiny plaited circle she instinctively knew Ardmore had braided himself from a lock of his own dark hair, a plundered bit of her own golden tresses, and the missing length of sea-green wool.

"Oh, Stephen." Juliana whispered as the circle on her finger warped and blurred, remembering it all and cherishing the memory, looking up to smile happily now into Stephen's warm regard.

"I love you, Juliana," Ardmore breathed, enclosing her fingers within his own.

"As I love you," she pledged.

Nearby, Alissa giggled again.

The footman murmured, "Twit!"

And, in a voice warm with blessing, the patient vicar of St. George's finally managed to pronounce into the resultant choosing up of sides that the earl and his lady were now and forevermore joined.